# SHADOWS OF THE PAST

# AMNIE ♦ YOUNG

# THE STARCHASER CHRONICLES

### Volume 2

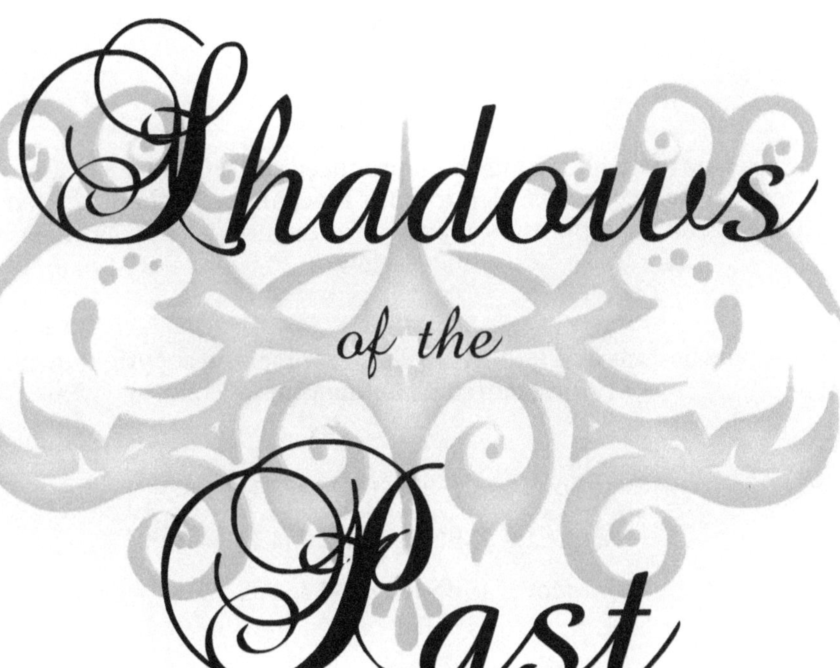

# Shadows
*of the*
# Past

# AMNIE ◆ YOUNG

eBook ISBN: 978-1-7 364 351-3-7

Paperback ISBN: 978-1-7 364 351-4-4

Hardcover ISBN: 978-1-7 364 351-5-1

First edition: February 2025

To all the people who've touched my life
and left too early along the way.

# CONTENTS

CONTENT WARNING:

This book contains descriptions of sexual content, abuse, violence, and physical injuries.

Her sea-green eyes stared up at the small window above, through which countless stars danced beyond the shimmer of the ship's shields. She closed her eyes as her mind harkened back to the moment she felt his hand slip to the back of her neck. Then, gently cradling her head, he slowly pulled her in and pressed his lips against hers. Surrendering to the memory, she let herself drift wistfully into the waiting arms of night.

Chapter 1

# Good Intentions

*"The worst consequences can linger long after the best
motivations have faded."*
~ *Doctor Wynn Tyronis*

The blackened abyss stretched in all directions around her. A stark silence filled the empty space with an uneasy ambiance. The heels of her patent leather boots clacked against a hard and unfamiliar surface as Kensy slowly began to evaluate her surroundings. Without warning, the ground began to shift and tilt with a horrendous guttural moan. She stumbled against it, clamoring for a footing on the slick surface.

Red lightning violently erupted in front of her causing her to cower from the blast. She glanced up toward a shadowy female figure among the blazing light. It began to reach for her. Echoing all around her, a familiar voice cried out in desperation, "Run. You have to run!" The words continued to resound through the emptiness over and over again, "Run. Run. Run!" She scrambled out of the shadow's grasp and staggered into a sprint. In the distance a furious red glow rose from the darkness below, illuminating the structure on which she stood.

Immediately she recognized the haunting silhouette as it loomed around her. The Vagabond's warship seemed impossibly massive under her feet. "Elle! Elle?" Kensy screamed at the top of her lungs as if it would bring her

1

answers or escape. She climbed over a ridge in the hull plating and staggered a few meters away. An ominous hum rose from the bowels of the ship. She turned around just in time to see a thunderous wave of energy as it traveled up the ridge with tremendous force.

Her gaze followed the path up the spines of the ship to where all the pulses gathered together and spiraled up into a single devastating beam. Her eyes widened, and she screamed. She watched it sail toward the graceful visage of her own ship, the DeCadejra. The beam ripped through the ship with no resistance, disintegrating it before Kensy's eyes.

She covered her mouth and sobbed. After a few faltering steps backward, she slipped on the smooth hull plating. She felt herself cascade into an uncontrollable slide. The curve of the ship dropped out from underneath her. Despite desperately grabbing for any semblance of a handhold, she fell helplessly into the darkness.

Kensy gasped, snapping upright in bed. Her labored breaths slowed as she took in her surroundings. The room was still and quiet. In a huff, she threw back the covers and snatched a heavy dressing robe from beside the bed. Holding one shoulder, she wrapped it around her body as she stood up. The left side seam closed together upon contact. Gossamer flowing sleeves draped from the velvety bodice of the robe. It had been a gift that she found great comfort in, especially on cold sleepless nights like this one.

She folded her arms across her body and stormed onto the captain's balcony beyond the foyer outside her quarters. The vast virtual windows looked out onto the starry expanse through which they sailed. She leaned on the forward railing and took a deep breath. The foyer elevator doors slid open and hurried steps shuffled toward her door before changing course to the balcony. His pace slowed as he drew closer.

"I'm sorry," she uttered without looking, "I suppose you felt that."

He stopped short, evaluating her body language. "The effects of the link are still fading. But... yeah, I sensed when you woke up." He stuffed his hands in his pockets, "I came to see if everything was okay."

She sighed, "I guess we're still suffering the side effects of my good intentions." Shaking her head, she muttered to herself, "It's never over, is it?"

Gently, he placed a hand on her shoulder. There was a warmth and comfort in his touch. She turned her head toward his hand as he leaned in to kiss her forehead. Very carefully, he lifted a finger to brush a stray hair from her face. "Another nightmare?" Jackson's bright blue eyes peered out from under his messy charcoal hair and met with hers. She nodded, *yes*. He opened his hand and slid it to the nape of her neck. Thoughtfully he rubbed her back little by little working down past her shoulder blades. She breathed deeply, gradually melting into his touch, "What was this one about?"

She cast her eyes away, her voice barely above a mumble, "Failure." Gracefully she stepped past him and slouched onto a nearby ottoman. Cradling her head in her hands, she tried to force herself to relax.

He pivoted toward her. Tenderly, he began to comb through her hair with his fingers, making sure not to pull on any errant tangles. "I know that look. What's bothering you?" he asked softly.

Exasperated, she pulled her hands down and folded them together, "I feel like we're spinning out, chasing our own tail. No matter what we do, we can't seem to get ahead. We're interrupting Vagabond's moves but we can't stop them. People are dying because I can't figure this out." She shook her head in frustration.

He clutched her shoulders firmly and bowed his head down toward her, "Kensy, you can't look at it like that. Every time we interrupt an attack that's at least one more person he doesn't get to kill. Every one is a victory, and there are thousands of them." He knelt down beside her and pulled her around to face him, "We may not have figured out this whole mess yet but we will, together. We'll stop him." He placed his palm against her cheek, "And then when this is all over, we'll take a month of shore leave. Just you and me."

She smiled slightly, "I'll hold you to that, Commander."

"Now," he stood back up and held one hand out toward her. She wrapped her fingers around his, letting him lift her to her feet. "...think you can try getting a little more sleep?" Reluctantly she acquiesced with a nod. He brushed her hair from her face again and slipped his hand toward the back of her head. As he pulled her in for a kiss, she ran her free hand up the side of his dashing olive green and black trimmed uniform jacket.

The moment broke as a cynical voice rang out from behind them, "Enough with the kissy crap. I need a word with Princess." Jackson raised his head to glare at the intruder. Kensy turned around, confused by the interruption. As her eyes darted between them, she could feel the tension building. The two of them were at odds more often than not and tonight was clearly no exception. Jackson stepped toward the window, the muscles in his jaw tightening in frustration. He crossed his arms and ankles as he leaned back on the railing, staring down the mercenary across the room.

The woman stood tall in a defiant pose; the amber colored bodice of her outfit highlighting her singular similarly colored eye. Tattoos ran down the left side of her face, interrupted only by her ornate cybernetic eye patch. Her dark lined makeup gave her a sharpness to match the spiky reddish-purple layers of her chin length hair and hard edges of her armor's plates. Leathery webs of material tied into a circular buckle in the center of her chest while two crisscrossed belts hung low on her hips.

Kensy graciously smiled at her old friend and folded her hands together in front of her, "What can I do for you, Neira?"

With little more than a glance she could see the echoes of some unknown agitation in Neira's movements. Moving closer, Neira shifted her stance as she flicked her wrist forward, nearly tossing a datapad from her fingers. Kensy reached for the datapad held before her. She furrowed her brow upon reading the contents to herself. Looking away in contemplation, she absentmindedly passed it to Jackson. Under her breath she asked, "Why now?"

He drew it from her hand, confused by the shift in her manner, and slowly began to read the memo, "Notification that Psilyria Kensington Frost is to be awarded the Nova Crescent for valor in the defense of the colony Bhelnir Prime. The aforementioned is ordered to appear in person at the Terra Ascension Core Citadel on Aepexia for presentation and ceremony." Jackson scowled, his mind turning back to the battlefield where he had first found her broken and alone.

Kensy shook her head, to push back the memory, "It's been more than a year. Why now?" Screams and explosions rang through her thoughts. She could smell the sweat and burnt flesh in her nose again. She felt the sting of loss as she recalled the faces of her adepts dying around her, and the sense of helplessness that followed.

Jackson shook his head, "Leave it to the brass, always slow to the punch... unless someone creates an intergalactic incident." He shot a sharp look toward Neira as the bitterness between them became palpable.

She returned his glare, "Well, excuse me for getting you in command of a profoundly advanced alien warship that pretty much no one knew about." She gestured to the ship around them then crossed her arms with a sneer, "Maybe next time I'll let you negotiate your own way out of the political witch-hunt."

"Enough, both of you. We'll go," Kensy turned back to them, blinking her eyes clear, "It'll be good. The crew's been hard at work for too long without reprieve. We'll take some time. Resupply. Give everyone a few days downtime, then come back with fresh eyes."

Jackson studied her seemingly mercurial shift for a moment. Despite their posturing he saw the unease in Neira's swagger and the apprehension in Kensy's masked composure. He glanced between them, "Alright," he conceded pushing off the railing, "I'll go tell Threaux to lay in a course." He paused as he passed Kensy, leaning in for a whisper, "Get some rest." Promptly he departed for the lower decks, leaving the two women in the calm of the balcony.

Quiet filled the room around them as they waited to hear the lobby elevator close before either spoke. Neira hooked her thumbs on her belts and glanced out at the starscape, "So, you and Soldier-Boy figured things out yet? Or are you still just dancing around each other like lovesick puppies?" An unmistakable twinge of disdain resonated through her voice.

Kensy ran her fingers across her forehead, "I don't know. Fraternizing isn't exactly...."

"Hey!" Neira interjected, "As much as I hate him... I know he makes you happy. Don't go getting caught up in someone else's regulations. They mean nothing out here," she gestured toward the window, "For once in your life screw the rules."

Kensy gave her a pained glance, "I've done that before... and I lost everything."

"I didn't mean...," Neira sighed, "...foot, mouth, got it. I just meant... sometimes the rules are *worth* breaking." She fidgeted in frustration, "Let yourself be happy. You deserve it."

Kensy sighed and set her head on her friend's shoulder, "Yeah, but for how long...." She glanced down to the bracer that covered her left arm, knowing what lurked beneath it.

Neira leaned her head against Kensy's, "Forever."

Kensy chuckled and straightened her posture, "You and I both know, I don't have that long. It's just not in my stars." Sorrow filled her face, "I'm not even sure how I've made it this far," her voice trailed off.

An awkward silence filled the room around them. Neira drew an uneasy breath over her teeth, "So..., Aepexia. You really okay going back there? I'm not gonna lie, this kinda feels like it has *him* written all over it."

"I signed up for this," Kensy fussed with her fingertips, pushing the knot in her stomach aside. "I can't very well avoid the main hub of the Ascension just because there is a slight chance that I *might* run into one man. Aepexia is a big place. Not to mention, a lot has changed in the last couple years. And I'll hardly be by myself. I'll have you and Jack with me. We'll deal with any chance encounters, *if* they happen, *when* they happen." Kensy turned away as her brave face faltered ever so subtly. "Good night, Neira," she said over her shoulder as she sauntered out of the room toward her quarters.

Neira watched Kensy disappear from sight, her expression hardening at the thought, "It's not a *chance* encounter I'm worried about...." The lines within her eye patch slowly churned as she crossed her arms. "At least one of us will have to be prepared."

Chapter 2

# Aepexia

*"Few sights inspire and inform us of the resilience of
organic life quite like the Pillar of Civilization."*
~ *Aepexian Historian J. Zeratech*

There was a subtle shift in vibration as the ship disengaged the faster-than-light drive core. On the outer hull a large number of rune-like openings began to seal closed, leaving a seamless silhouette and slowing the vessel to shorter range, sub-light speeds. Kensy floated weightlessly in the psionic submersion interface beam that extended from floor to ceiling of the nearly two story bridgehead. Her vision transferred into the ship's perspective, shifting both the scale and scope of her sight.

She felt the deceleration and looked around as she sailed smoothly through the black void before her. Gracefully the ship danced around asteroids and nebulous clouds of dust that collected along the inner rim of the star system. The DeCadejra's pilot, Flight Lieutenant Morgan Threaux, guided the ship around a massive mining station, bringing their destination into view.

Aepexia drifted effortlessly among the brilliantly colored gas clouds left over from her parent star's collapse. From across a great distance, the glittering core beckoned them onward through the dust and debris. Her unusual contours set Aepexia apart. The long dead planet sat broken and hollow against the curtain of space. Even so, she teamed with light

8

and life. A central pillar spanned the axis of the planet, surrounded by millions of small platforms interlinked and ever-changing.

Kensy glanced to her side as information streamed into her field of view, "Looks like we're cleared to dock." She swiped her hand aside, casting the information down to Morgan's display. "Bring us in. Looks like they want us coming into a platform in the civilian sector."

He smirked, "That's just fine with me, fewer stuffed shirts telling me how many guidelines I've broken in the last five minutes."

Kensy changed her focus to Morgan. Jackson thumped the back of his chair, "Don't get too excited yet. We have a meeting in the Ascension Citadel before you skitter off to whatever shenanigans you'll be up to for shore leave."

Morgan raised an eyebrow, "Do you always have to ruin my fun?"

Jackson smirked, "Oh, that's not ruining it yet. If I really wanted to put a damper on things I might say something like: behave yourself. If you get detained, we'll just leave you here and I'll have Bryden drive."

Morgan's expression soured, "I swear, you just can't help it, can you?"

"It's my job. I'm your boss, remember?" Jackson quietly paced behind Morgan's chair.

Morgan made a mocking face before speaking again, "Hey, she's my boss too," he thumbed toward Kensy, "and she doesn't feel compelled to dash my hopes and dreams at every turn."

Jackson shot a quick glance up to Kensy before leaning over Morgan's shoulder, "That's because she's nicer than I am." Kensy smiled politely at the exchange and shook her head. Behind her the gradually rising sound of footsteps in the corridor drew her attention. She turned to inspect as Neira and another pilot crewman approached the bridgehead. The crewman jogged down the left side stair toward Morgan, "I'm here to relieve you, sir."

"The approached is locked. Kick back and enjoy the ride," Morgan remarked as he swiveled around and rose from the chair. The crewman nodded to him in acknowledgment. Morgan looked back to his commander, "So, what's the game plan boss?"

"I'll need a word with the two of you," Neira interjected glancing between Jackson and Kensy from the landing at the beam entrance.

"Head down to the hangar bay. We'll be right behind in a minute," Jackson dismissed him with a pat on the back of his shoulder as he passed. Morgan jogged up the stairs and disappeared down the corridor. Slowly Jackson ascended the stairs. "What is it now, Cross?" He reached the top, holding out a hand for Kensy to grab as she stepped out of the beam.

In a hushed tone she stepped toward them, "We have an appointment before you go gallivanting off to the Ascension Citadel, a little Graven business to attend to. It shouldn't take long."

Kensy and Jackson looked to each other, then back to Neira. Jackson furrowed his brow, "What kind of business are we talking?"

"We're just making contact, then you'll be free to go about your day," Neira replied.

"You haven't told us anything about the Graven so far," Kensy looked at her friend with a similarly concerned gaze. "Is there something we should know going into this?"

Neira shook her head, "I didn't exactly play things by the book when I conscripted you two. So far the powers-that-be have let that slide, but I imagine that leniency will be wearing thin if we don't take some initiative." Neira began to walk as she explained the situation, "So, we go say hi, make some friends, and figure out what comes next."

Jackson leaned down to whisper in Kensy's ear, "I thought you were her only friend." Subtly, she elbowed him in the side. He smirked for a moment and straightened his posture. Together, the trio passed through the Strategic Operations Center and entered the waiting lift. As the doors closed, he cleared his throat, "So, Cross, is there an actual rule book for the Graven? Somehow, I don't picture you handing out manuals."

Neira gave an indignant grunt, "There are *guidelines...*," she gave him a sideways glare, "but there's nothing to keep me from kicking your ass."

Kensy sighed, "Can we skip the posturing for one day? Please." Neira and Jackson eyed each other before nodding in acquiescence. The elevator doors slid open and Kensy strode out first, the others flanking closely behind. They made their way to the largest of the hangar bays through the ever churning sea of crew. Scanning the massive room, Kensy spotted Morgan engaging in lighthearted banter with the DeCadejra's first officer, Lieutenant Commander Daniel Bryden.

"Nah, I'll bet two maintenance shifts you're wrong," Daniel smiled warmly as he watched his captains' approach. His deep brown eyes met theirs with respect.

"You wouldn't be conspiring to shirk your responsibilities, now would you?" Jackson scrutinizingly stared down the two officers.

Morgan shifted toward his fellow pilot's side as he turned to face the approaching group. Fidgeting slightly, he hesitated momentarily before responding. As he opened his mouth to speak, Daniel elbowed him, not so subtly, in the ribs, "Just a playful wager. Nothing to concern yourselves with."

A soft smile curved around Kensy's lips as she watched the exchange, "Just so long as you can keep your focus for a little while longer. I promise you'll get downtime before we leave port."

Daniel tipped his head toward her politely, "Of course! Whatever you need, just say the word." The ship shuddered beneath their feet as the docking clamps engaged. The mechanisms of the hangar bay shifted with a boom and began cranking the doors open, revealing the bustling port before them. Together, the officers of the DeCadejra descended down the massive ramp. A flurry of crew men and women hustled past in a rush to secure the area and begin the resupply process. An air of anticipation filled the dock as they anxiously worked toward the pending shore leave.

At the edge of the platform, a grumpy dock worker impatiently waited alongside his cargo hauler. He barked gruffly at a nearby crew member, "Where's your captain?!" Kensy glanced over as the young woman pointed him in the direction of the clustered officers.

Gently she brushed the back of Jackson's elbow with her fingertips, "I'll get this." He shot a quick look over his shoulder and nodded. The heels of her black patent leather boots clacked against the platform as she confidently strode toward the dock worker. Her mat charcoal slacks drew graceful lines from the cuff of her boots up to and under the bodice of her uniform jacket. The rich plum of her double-breasted top was unmistakably bold in the glittering lights that flooded the docking area. The cityscape reflected dazzling colors across the armored bracer that covered her left forearm and the ornate metallic bands and wires of the psionic control clasp on her right.

The dock worker sneered at her as she approached, "Go fetch me the captain, or get out of my way!"

Gently, Kensy spoke, placing her hand on her chest, "I am captain of this ship. One of them, at least. What is it that I can help you with, sir?"

He narrowed his glare as he looked her and the ship over disdainfully, "Got some crates for ya." He begrudgingly handed her his holographic tablet, "Just sign."

Quickly, she reviewed the invoice and cargo. "Oh, very good. Psicorp finally approved our requisition request." Her fingertip gracefully danced across the document, "Although the shipment will need to remain under guard until the quartermaster can take custody of it." She handed the tablet back to the rather unpleasant man. Turning away slightly, she grabbed her own datapad from the side of her gun holster belt to message the quartermaster.

The worker grunted loudly and muttered, "Yeah, of course. Always special fucking treatment for the glitter-bitch in charge...."

Jackson spun around, hearing the boorish slur. He saw the emotional sting of the words in Kensy's eyes, yet her composure did not falter. Furious, he paced toward the man. Raising her eyes from her datapad, Kensy glimpsed the fire in Jackson's eyes. Swiftly she interceded, placing a hand on his chest to stop him. He tightened his jaw, "I won't stand for him disrespecting you like that."

Speaking in a hushed tone, she replied, "Your harsh words will fall on deaf ears. The only way to make a difference with people like him is to be a better person than he believes I can be, to show through example." She feigned a smile for him, "You can't save me from this." Her eyes pleaded with him until his posture began to relax. Turning back to the worker, she clipped her datapad back into place, "I only expect that protocol be followed. Please keep the crates under guard. The quartermaster will be along shortly." Graciously, she nodded to him, "Thank you."

Before he could reply, she pivoted on her heel and began to usher Jackson back toward the rest of the waiting officers. Daniel shook his head as they approached, "You are a far better person than I. Don't know that I could have held my tongue in that circumstance."

Kensy gave a lighthearted laugh, "Oh, I don't believe that for a second."

"With all of our advances, it's crazy to believe people still cling to hate. You'd think we would've outgrown that," the first officer looked at her with concern, "Do you get a lot of that?"

Kensy thought on it for a moment, "Not among our own crew. Outside of the ship... more than I'd like, less than a lot of other people deal with." She shrugged, "I learned a long time ago that anger only makes it worse on all sides, so this is one war I fight with a smile." Looking around at the somber faces surrounding her, "Now, if I'm not mistaken, I believe we have some places to be." She skipped ahead a few steps and spun on her toes, "Coming?" Leaving the dock and the confrontation behind, they headed in toward the shining heart of the city.

Chapter 3

# Detour

*"Watch your step. The shifting of platforms can catch you off guard if you're not careful."*
~ *Crewman B. Benson*

Kensy watched gleefully as Morgan, Daniel, and even Jackson marveled at the dazzling cityscape before them. The glittering Pillar of Civilization, as it had come to be called, was a mosaic of architecture and creatures from all across the know galaxy. Each platform housed hundreds of buildings of varying sizes and styles. Periodically, a far off siren would announce an impending shift in a platform's position.

Kensy smiled, "I take it this is your first time here?"

Jackson raised an eyebrow at her, "And I take it this is not your first time here."

She laughed, "No, no it's not." Her eyes settled on one of the highest tiered platform, "I studied here." She placed one hand on his side and pointed upward, directing him where to look. He leaned in to follow the line of her finger. Softly she continued, "That is the main Psicorp Academy campus. It's where Elle and I lived after we were rescued." Jackson shifted his gaze back to her. Their faces hovered only inches apart for a moment.

"So...," Morgan feigned a cough. Kensy and Jackson pulled away from each other suddenly. A mischievous grin crept cross Morgan's face, "are, uh... you two...." Daniel interrupted him with a swift elbow. Immediately, Kensy turned her face away as it flushed red, and Jackson glared at Morgan in annoyance.

Rolling her one good eye and sighing deeply, Neira walked forward. She sauntering toward their destination, forcefully shouldering her way through the flight lieutenant along the way, "The bridge we need is over here." Kensy shot her a grateful glance and mouthed a silent *thank you.*

Daniel stepped around Morgan with a warm expression, "Kensy, I was wondering how they determine the docking order on the platforms. Everything here seems to be in constant motion." Slowly, he began meandering in the same direction as Neira.

Recomposed, Kensy twirled around to face him, "It's not as chaotic as you might think." She skipped ahead, "Each platform has a set range of places it can dock. Then, depending on the time of day, they also have a priority for the docking spaces. The highest priority at any point in time gets the spot. Special events and holidays change priorities of certain platforms." Kensy pranced her way to the edge of the platform and paused, "Hmm, this is unusual." Jackson looked at her quizzically. She pointed to the paths connecting this platform to the next, "Only the footbridges are active. They must be restricting commercial access in the next sector."

Jackson furrowed his brow, "Is that something to be concerned about?"

"There could be any number of reasons to close it down," she glanced around, "but I don't see anything that could warrant it right off."

Neira circled back to survey the area. "Well, be careful all the same," Daniel commented, stepping up beside Jackson, "I'd rather not cause problems by walking into a construction zone or the like."

"Good idea," Kensy affirmed, walking over the footbridge first. As she crossed the far edge onto the next platform, a blaring horn signaled the activation of the safety barrier behind her. She spun on her toes. The sudden buzz of the energy shield caused her to totter a few steps back without looking. Jackson leapt backward as the wall on his side pulsed into being. "Kensy!" he called out in concern. Escaping all notice, a silent figure predatorily stalked up behind Kensy from the shadowy recesses of an adjacent building.

"Jack?" She staggered back another step, "I'm okay. It just--." As she turned, a strong hand seized the side of her neck. She felt the slightest prick at his touch, but her attention was wrenched away as the man before her forcefully kissed her. In the shock of the moment, Kensy froze. Jackson, Daniel, and Morgan looked on in stunned silence.

As Kensy's awareness refocused, she began to struggle against his grip, but the man held too tightly to her. With his free hand, he grasped the psionic clasp embedded into her right forearm. The energy she fought to summon around her arm sputtered to no effect. Seeing her rising panic, Jackson slammed a fist against the humming barrier between them, "Kensy! Get your hands off of her!" The stranger shot him a snide smirk, tightening his grip and pressing further into the violating kiss. Kensy whimpered as his fingers crushed her neck.

Vaulting off a nearby crate, Neira caught a holographic sign mast and hoisted herself up. Without hesitation, she leapt for the next highest one and swung over the gap that separated them as smoothly as a seasoned gymnast. She flipped and came down in a thunderous barefisted strike at the man. Deftly, he sidestepped the blow, releasing Kensy. Neira tumbled to break her fall and lifted lithely back on to her feet to square off with the man.

Kensy's vision blurred. She waiver in place slightly as an unfamiliar heat coursed through her veins. Jackson's eyes darted between Neira's detour and Kensy. He had some agility, but not enough for a maneuver like that. Along with his fellow officers, he watched helplessly from the sidelines, a rage simmering within his gut. Daniel turned his gaze to Morgan and spoke in a low tone, "Go get Rauk." Morgan nodded, skipping backward he bolted toward the ship.

Very deliberately, Neira cracked each of her knuckles as she stared the assailant down, "I believe I made myself perfectly clear last time regarding the consequences of coming near her."

The man wore a sleek suit and kept an all too tidy appearance. He raised an eyebrow at Neira. A conniving grin crossed his thieving lips. "I don't believe I hear any protests," he sneered. "Not that this isn't amusing, but I have more important things to attend to than a washed up cyclopes," he waved one hand at her dismissively and strode confidently away.

The blaring horn ceased as he faded from sight among the shapes of the cityscape. Upon seeing the barriers drop, Jackson and Daniel darted across the platform gap. The lieutenant commander walked up beside Neira, "What was that about?" Neira said nothing but furrowed her brow as she analyzed the series of events in her mind, unsettled by it all.

Jackson rushed to Kensy's side, "Kensy, are you...?" His fingertips touched her shoulder gently. In a blur of instinct, she turned away from the point of contact and released a pulse of energy accompanied by a shriek. Jackson reeled from the blast, holding his arm. Daniel and Neira turned their heads toward the commotion. Kensy covered her mouth and tears began to pour from her eyes. She staggered away from the group in horror. "Kensy?" Jackson spoke up in pained curiosity.

She shook her tear-stained face, "I'm so sorry!" Her vision became more hazy as she stared down at her hands, "No, no, no!" In a fit, she bolted away from them and leapt from the platform.
"Kensy!" Jackson and Daniel attempted to run after her. Catching sight of the drop-off before them, they both skidded to a stop and teetered at the edge. Like a glittering purple

comet, Kensy arced to a lower platform. The residuals of her power dissipated into a chaotic cloud as she sprinted into the busy city streets.

Neira looked back to where her adversary had vanished. Jackson grunted in pain, clenching his fist to shake to feeling of the blast. "We have to go after her. Something's wrong."

At long last, Neira spoke up, "It won't do you any good." The two men approached her, apprehension clearly visible on their faces. "If she doesn't want to be found, you won't find her. And if she's as emotionally turbulent as she seems, she won't want to be found. Not to mention, depending on her state of mind, she could be dangerous to anyone she runs across."

Daniel looked to his captain, "Then we have to tell the authorities."

"And do what?! Endanger them? Get her in trouble so that she never sees the light of day again?" Neira huffed at him, "What good will that do? Listen, she's running because she hurt you. She blindly reacted." Her gaze shifted to Jackson. "If she suspects she could lose control, what do you think will happen if she hurts someone trying to bring her in?"

Jackson straightened his posture, "Cross, who was that?" They looked at her in anticipation.

"Vesok Mordwell, one of Kensy's ex's," she sighed, "and he's what I'm really worried about. He surrendered that fight far too quickly. He never gives up so easy. I know he's up to something, I just don't know what... yet." Neira shook her head in disgust, "Kensy's known her share of bad relationships, but Vesok is a special kind of worthless. He's arrogant, idiotic, and ridiculously wealthy. He is a dangerous slimeball with enough money and influence on this rock to make that *everyone else's* problem." She crossed her arms over her chest.

"Why has she had such bad luck with relationships?" Daniel inquired with concern.

The mercenary looked away in sorrowful contemplation. "She has some shadows from her past that are not easily revealed, or left behind." Her expression shifted. Determination flashed in her amber eye, "Let's keep this under wraps for now. Gabel, you and I have a meeting to keep. It's probably still our best course of action." Jackson and Daniel nodded.

"I should be able to stall the Ascension meeting for a while, but I'll need to head back to the ship. Keep in contact. Encrypted comms only. I'll wait for your call." Daniel tapped on his nahdvi, "Threaux, ...found Rauk and Kigh? Good. Stay put. I'm on my way back to the ship. I'll need your help with something," he darted away.

Jackson looked back to Neira, "Alright, Cross, we'll play this your way." His cobalt eyes held back a simmering fury. "How are we going to stop this guy and help Kensy?"

Neira nodded, "Follow me. I know some place we can get the help we need." Together, they slipped between buildings and off the main roads.

A leering smile stared down on the empty path below, "Tell your master the ambush worked and the serum is in play. Once I have the Psilyria in my custody, she will no longer be a problem." Vesok stepped from the shadow in which he loomed. "Then, and only then, we can discuss further dealings."

A female figure remained cloaked in darkness, a hood obscuring her face. As she spoke, her voice came out coarse and mechanical, "Make sure you move swiftly, before her allies can intercede. You have been given every advantage to remove this threat. The Vagabond does not abide failure."

He glared at her with a slippery smile, "Neither do I."

Chapter 4

# Prey

*"You've never seen an unhinged psionic? I don't doubt it.*
*After all, you're still breathing."*
*~ Aepexian citizen from platform D-23,520*

Sickly yellow and green lights flickered in kaleidoscopic patterns across the shantylike structures of the platform through which Kensy blindly wandered. A myriad of different rodents and insects skirted around the equally as diverse assortment of denizens mingling at the edge of her perception. The voices that filled the air were a gibbering fog of incomprehensible mutterings as they fell upon her ears.

Her sight distorted. Her eyes burned, making every shape and silhouette press toward her chaotically. She shuffled through the streets aimlessly, each step jarring her erratically. Kensy ripped the tie from her hair and clutched her head in a vain attempt to exert some external control over the haze that filled her mind, but it only grew worse with each passing moment.

Thoughts of the earlier confrontation flooded her awareness. The sensations of pain from Vesok's grip and the invasion of his kiss festered on her skin. She clawed at herself, trying to erase the feelings encroaching on her mind. A drizzle of simulated rain began to mat her tousled locks and mingle with reddened streaks of her tear-stained face.

In a blur, her memory zeroed in on another person looming at the edge of her peripheral vision. She could feel the shock in Jackson's voice as he called out to her. "I'm so sorry," she uttered just above a whisper, "I should have told you. I should have warned you." A knot formed in her stomach as she envisioned Jackson watching Vesok overpower her so easily, "I'm sorry! I should have been stronger." She stumbled to a stop, choked with tears of grief.

The shadow of Jackson's presence pushed toward her, his voice echoing through her mind as he grew closer. She wrapped her arms tightly around herself as she fought to control her rising powers. In the breadth of a heartbeat, a pulse of power emanated from her body, sending a tremor through the immediate area. As quickly as it had risen, it began to fade, washing away from her like a dying ripple.

That moment replayed over and over in her mind. Aghast, she watched Jackson recoil in pain from the blast. For the briefest instant, there was fear in his eyes. He was afraid... of *her*, and for good reason. Those few seconds lingered. He had never been afraid *of* her before. He had been afraid *for* her, been concerned, been apprehensive, even been coldly cautious of her and her abilities, but never before had the terror of what she was crossed his expression.

The psionic wings that sprouted from the mark of the void on her back flickered into tenuous being as a delicate violet fog of energy poured off her body. Overwhelmed by her rampant emotions, Kensy let out a gut-wrenching scream and slowly sunk to her knees on the wet pavement. Wearily she hung her head and wept as the precipitation soaked through her clothes.

Bleary-eyed and numbed by the flood of emotions, her attention was drawn by the echo of footsteps encroaching upon her. Without raising her head, she rose unsteadily to her feet. She closed her eyes and fought to focus in on the sound. *Heavy steps. Bipedal, Humanoid. More than one of them. Coming from one direction? No, circling.* She pressed a hand over her eyes, rubbing them to alleviate some of the ache. *Focus. They are closing in... slowly. Wait. One is approaching. No sudden moves. Assess, then act,* she coached herself. Apprehension and curiosity calmed her dolor.

A low grumble passed between the strangers. Very casually, one stepped toward Kensy's solitary form. Quietly, he studied her as he sauntered around her. Kensy remained still, her sopping hair falling around her down-turned face. *If he was going to offer aid, he would have already. No, he's gauging me, looking to take advantage of my obvious distress.* The last vestiges of her sorrow melted into simmering anger, *I will not be your prey.* She took a subtle breath but still did not move.

Drawing in close beside her, he lifted a strand of her hair and smelled it. He looked her over, "You're a long way from the academy. What terrible thing could have driven you into our little corner of the pillar?" Even without looking, she could feel his conniving smile oozing through his words. She stared at the ground in silence. "You're right, this isn't really the best place to talk," he gradually shifted behind her, "I mean with the rain and all. Why don't we find someplace warmer and we can get you out of those wet clothes?" The surrounding figures snickered.

Her fist clenched. "...not your prey," she whispered.

He leaned over her shoulder, "What was that?"

Just as his hand grabbed her shoulder, she blinked, and her demeanor shifted. Thunder and lightning cracked across the atmosphere above them. Tilting her head toward him, her furious gaze lit up with a blazing violet fire. Calculatingly, she seized his hand and slowly pried his fingers from her shoulder. "I will not be your prey!" The grin dropped from his face.

A pained cry escaped his lips as she wrenched his wrist backwards. He snapped his hand from her grip and stepped back with a disgusted snort. "Yeah, well, we'll see—," he sneered, "—about that." His balled up fist swung wide as she swept to the side under his outstretched arm. She cupped her hand as it rose up behind his head. Using the momentum of his swing, she pulled him down across her rising knee.

Shouts erupted around her as the leader doubled over and fell to the ground. She straightened her stature. The psionic energy oozing off her body began to coalesce into glass like shards like her crystallizing rage. Behind her, the sound of metal scraping across the ground drew her attention. The assailant lifted a pipe from its resting place and rushed toward her.

In the blink of an eye, his downward swing was abruptly stopped by a jagged blade, analogous to her psiblade, formed from her raised fist. She locked the pipe against her blade and forced it in a wide circle, ultimately flinging it from the man's hands. The leader scrambled away frantically, "Well, don't just stand there! Kill her!"

Her blazing eyes turned back toward him. She raised her blade, pointing it straight at him, "Your villainy ends here." The sword in her hand flashed into a bolt and sailed toward the leader. He turned aside as it grazed past him and struck the nearby ground. A purple fire erupted in front of him, spreading around the plaza in both directions. The psionic wings flared brilliantly from her shoulder blades. The gang's lecherous greed melted into desperation as they took up arms against their would be victim.

The psionic energy shards collected around Kensy as she walked with purpose toward the one who had started it all. Gun shots rang out through the stormy air. The churning shards caught the projectiles and discarded them harmlessly onto the ground around her. Weapons in hand, several more figures darted at her. With only the slightest twitch of her fingers, spears of light manifested and shot from her wings, cutting down all who approached, yet her gaze did not falter from her target.

She closed in, intent on her attacker. Hastily, he searched the area for some means of escape or defense. In her last step, she flew toward him with an unnatural speed and clutched him by the throat. Power coursed over her, bolstering her strength, as she lifted him off the ground. "I am not your prey!" He stared into her burning eyes and beheld the unchecked fury within her.

A single stinging shot pierced the air. Kensy shrieked. Her wings detonated, sending razor sharp slivers of energy into every corner of her surroundings. Her mind flickered back to the reality of the moment as the man in her hand coughed. Blood dripped over his lips and began to saturate the front of his shirt. Her augmented strength drained away, causing her arm to quake under his weight. She dropped him and looked down at herself. A trickle of her own blood seeped from a wound just below her right collarbone. She gasped for breath. Slowly, she turned her gaze upon the gunman lying prone behind her. The firearm slipped from his grasp as the life faded from his eyes.

She staggered, taking in the carnage that surrounded her. Horrified and stunned by the sight, her tears began to flow once more. She covered her mouth with a bloody hand as she stifled a wail. Fatigue soaked into every muscle in her body. Mustering the last of her strength, she placed a hand over the wound and used a burst of power to cauterize the bleeding. The rush of pain gave her another much needed moment of drive. Sluggishly she hobbled away, tattered and soaked, into the stormy haze of the pillar's lower platforms.

Chapter 5

# The Hub

*"I'm not sure which is trippier: the architecture of the Hub
or the fact that everything in the galaxy passes through
that one room in one way or another."*
~ *Communications Officer P. Sagan*

Neira deftly navigated the ever-shifting maze of streets and alleyways, with Jackson following close on her heels. A hushed word from the Graven mercenary to the right denizen opened doors and made back passageways available as they pushed further into the bustling pillar. Every platform brought new sights and sounds, which would have been of more interest to the commander if his thoughts were not otherwise occupied. Instead of seeing the marvels of civilization around him, he quickly assessed his surroundings for any and all points of strategic interest.

At long last, they emerged in a grand plaza surrounded by an assortment of towering structures, majestic in both scale and scope of detail. Confidently, Neira quickened her steps as she strode toward some unknown destination. Jackson scanned the surrounding, "Cross, where exactly are we going?"

Without so much as a glance toward him, she replied, "You'll see soon enough. We're almost there." Jackson rolled his eyes and muffled a frustrated sigh, *This had better be good. We've lost valuable ground by not following Kensy.* Neira's boots clacked against the glossy stone steps before her as she ascended toward a massive pavilion-like building. Dozens of figures passed in and out of the various tiers of stonework, some flying, some walking, and some aided by unfamiliar technologies. Neira glanced back over her shoulder at him, "Pick up the pace, soldier-boy. We're burning starlight."

Quietly, he grumbled as he jogged up the stair behind her. Looking up at the arches and pillars surrounding the entrance, he furrowed his brow, "What is this place?"

"The Hub. It's the primary communications and control center for the entire pillar, and the base of operations for our contact—," she began.

Suddenly, Jackson let out a pained cry. Neira spun around as he clutched at the fabric of his uniform just to the right of his sternum, below the collarbone. With a few stumbling steps, he slammed backward into the nearest pillar and tried to catch his breath. A flood of searing pain flashed through his body beneath his hand. A moment passed and with it went the sensation. Jackson's piercing blue eyes met Neira's gaze, "Something's wrong."

Neira stepped up close to him, "The link?" He nodded, *yeah*. She tucked her hand around the inside of his arm as if to help him back to standing and spoke in a low tone, "What did you feel?"

Jackson mimicked the gesture, wrapping his hand around the inside of her arm. He pushed off the pillar as she pulled, "If I didn't know better, I'd say she's been shot. Then probably cauterized the wound with her powers. It was reminiscent of the patch job she did on me when we were launched through the portal on Galliane Prime... only less controlled." He clenched his jaw, "You sure this contact of yours can actually help us?"

Neira glanced up at him with a determined ferocity, "Just try to keep up."

As Neira tried to turn away, Jackson tugged at her arm briefly, "I haven't felt anything that... intense since we tried to sever the link. If that's any indication, she's in bad shape. We need to find her... now."

"Then I *suggest* you let go of me," she scowled at him. Jackson released his grip on her arm and straightened his posture. Neira pivoted on the heels of her boots and stormed toward the Hub's main entrance.

Jackson glanced around briefly. Few of the passersby gave him more than a fleeting glance as they bustled about their day. In fact, he had garnered the attention of only one silent observer. She waited patiently in the shadow of the stone column listening for his footsteps to begin fading away. As they did, she cautiously rolled around the side of the column, her crystalline eyes falling on him as he slipped into the building and out of her sight.

Inside the Hub displays, holograms, and walls of control panels mixed harmoniously with fascinatingly detailed sculptures of influential figures from Aepexia's founding race, the olhreleth. Each effigy reached upward, their hands supporting the scaffolding of the upper walkways. Grand wings stretched from their backs, forming the dome of the central chamber. Light emanated from the chiseled eyes, illuminating the room with a soft blue light. The figures were adorned in flowing robes that subtly shifted, and their lattice-like hair formed into stunning geometric patterns. The colors and textures of the statues would have made them seem almost lifelike had it not been for their massive scale.

In the very center of the room, a holographic representation of Aepexia relayed real-time information to the personnel buzzing about. Jackson stared at the wireframe rendering of the hollow planet with only its axis pillar remaining. His eyes searched the flurry tiny platform symbols that surrounded the heart of the planet for some clue as to where Kensy might have fled. The overflowing volume of information before him, however, proved too great for his hurried assessment.

Neira dodged her way toward an olhreleth figure pacing in front of the display. At the tip of her neatly folded wings, she stood a little over ten feet tall. Her blank, glowing eyes shifted between yellow and orange tones, signaling her agitation. The light of the room danced across the navy-colored metal of her sleek armor and her xeik'quael, an imposing pendulum shaped axe that lay slung over her back.

Her figure may have passed for a likeness to ancient angelic renderings were it not for the heavy armor and sour expression. Grimacing she turned to a small clockwork butterfly that hovered beside her, "This is absolutely infuriating! I should be out there, hunting with...." Her rant dropped off as she spied Neira's approach, "It's about time you appeared. I swear, it's almost like you can smell trouble."

Neira waved her off, "Where's Nevan?"

The olhreleth woman grunted, "Don't you dare give me the same damn line about your little secret club that he did. I've had about enough of this standing around. If there is something to hit, I want to be there!"

A light pulsed within the clockwork butterfly's crystalline core as it fluttered toward Neira, "Please, don't mind her, Miss Cross. Nevan left her behind when he went to investigate a disturbance on the lower platforms. Her temperament has soured in the interim." The construct approached and circled Jackson as it scanned him, "I see we have a new guest. Welcome, Terra Ascension Core Navy Commander Jackson Dean Gabel."

Jackson took a step away from the butterfly as he stared it down incredulously, "...thanks... I think."

Neira sighed and rolled her amber colored eye. She gave the butterfly an aggressive tap, "What have I told you about scanning people without permission in social situations?!" She huffed, "Gabel, this is Whitakat, a xyak sage *who knows better*," she waved her hand aside, "and Marieke Ara Kivanisma, *former* Aepexian Guard Sentinel."

Marieke sneered, "Still a sentinel just not with the guard. And you are the last person who can give me crap for not playing well with others."

"We don't have time for this!" Neira snapped, "Now that introductions are done can we get on with figuring out what to do next?"

Whitakat turned back toward the Graven mercenary. "Perhaps if you filled us in on the situation as you perceive it, we can formulate a new course of action."

Neira crossed her arms and tapped the toe of her boot as she pondered how to discreetly inform her allies of the situation. She shot a glance toward Marieke, "Shit went sideways after we docked. It's Mordwell. He made his move."

A smile curled across the warrior's almost hauntingly beautiful face, "Good. I can pummel him."

"No!" Neira emphatically replied, "We don't know his game yet. That's why I needed Nevan. Mordwell got the drop on Princess before I could pound his face in. We have to figure out what he's planning before he can do any more damage than he already has."

Suddenly Marieke's posture changed as she looked around the room with concern. Her eyes shifted to a dull gray, "What happened? Where is she?"

"I'm not completely sure—," Neira began.

"He attacked her, took off, then... *she* ran," Jackson interjected, being careful to not speak Kensy's name, "We don't know where she is. But chances are, she's in trouble." A sneer crossed Marieke's face again as she listened to the news.

"It seems," Whitakat pondered, "we are in need of a tracker."

"Agreed," a voice chimed up from the entrance. There stood a petite female figure clad in charcoal slacks, black patent leather boots and an almost familiar plum uniform top. Loose sleeves flowed from the crest of her shoulders. The bodice of her uniform top dipped to the middle of her sternum to allow the maze of wires and nodes of her control clasp to descend from her collarbone unobstructed. She looked almost human save for her glimmering crystalline irises and the ringlets of braided wire that served as her hair. She ran her crystalline fingernails across the metal choker that encircled her neck. "Ready when you are," she stated with a cheerful smile.

All faces turned toward the voice. Jackson furrowed his brow, "And you are...?"

She spoke with a bubbly enthusiasm, "Oh, right, right, right!" She popped to attention, placing a hand on her chest she bowed slightly, "Psimehna Gabrianna Ciphar. But you can just call me Gabby. Now if I'm not mistaken time is of the essence. We should really get going." She looked around at the staring faces for a moment and took a deep breath, "Okay let me just summarize this. A certain princess, who shall remain nameless, encountered a certain jerk, who all of you would like to beat down, but you can't because you don't know what he's planning, but it has to do with said nameless princess, who you lost earlier when things went sideways, and you need a tracker to find her because she's in trouble and probably injured, which you figured out from some sort of connection that you have to her." She looked to Jackson with a smile as she concluded her rapid-fire assessment of the situation, "Did I miss anything?"

Jackson put his hands up and blinked at her, "Assuming I actually caught any of that, I'm still a little hazy on how you fit into all this."

Gabby giggled, "Oh, right...." She closed her eyes for a moment and inhaled deeply. A bright emerald energy began to gather around her, seeming to seep into her body through her clasp. She exhaled and opened her eyes. They glittered with a vibrant emerald energy. "I can see things...," she approached Jackson with a new curiosity, "that other people can't. Fascinating." she reached out and touched some invisible thread. His eyes widened as Jackson felt the slightest tug at his chest. She smiled up at him. "There's not much of a connection left but I can work with this!" She bounded toward the entrance, "So are we going, or do you want to stand there arguing all day?"

Jackson shot a glance toward Neira, "Looks like we have a tracker."

Chapter 6

# Hunted

*"In the darkest shadows, the line between hunted and*
*hunter can disappear entirely."*
*~ Nevan Nahlen, Graven Adjudicator*

Heavy shadows hung over a gray and dismal landscape. Long discarded mining equipment filled the open spaces with treacherous silhouettes while faintly flickering emergency lights fought against the darkness. Trembling, Kensy's left hand grasped the latticed bars of the containment fence. Her knuckles blanched as her fingers struggled to keep hold. Fatigue permeated every fiber of her body. She pressed her forehead against the cold alloy of the bars and drew an unsteady breath. "One... more... step...," she quietly mumbled to herself.

Wobbling her head against the metal, she glimpsed the glistening wound below her collarbone. The shoulder of her uniform jacket blackened as blood slowly seeped into the deep plum colored material. "Damn," she coughed. Pain surged through her chest causing her to let out an agonized but abbreviated shriek. Succumbing to the tide of weakness, she wavered and collapsed. She rolled to the side, letting her back rest against the barrier. Her head lulled despite her valiant efforts to stay alert.

A flash of dark violet and indigo light erupted beside her. The sharp feline form of the Nexus crackled with energy as he looked up into her weary expression. The brilliantly glowing slits of his eyes scrutinizingly surveyed the damage inflicted upon her, "Hm." With the tilt of his head he quickly scoped out the surrounding environment, "It seems there is much to attend to, but this is certainly not the place. What do you say we get you back on your feet?" He snaked around her ankles, passing energy off his psionic form to revitalize her.

Kensy closed her eyes for a moment as she drew on his power. With a quaking breath she nodded, "Thank you." She opened her eyes and shifted to the left. To keep from exacerbating the wound below her collarbone, she clutched her right arm firmly. Only a few meters away the path opened up. Numerous placards framed the gateway with warnings in a myriad of languages, but she stared past all of them. "I need to keep moving. If I can get into the heart... I won't be a danger to anyone else. I won't hurt anyone else."

Nexus moved into her line of sight, "What lies beyond that gate may not be the solitude you desire. The last remnants of this dead world still stir within. It will be dangerous and your physical being is already taxed by toxins and blood loss." His tail circled lazily around his feet.

"I know—." she paused as her mind processed his words. "Wait, what?" she glanced to him questioningly, "Toxins?"

"Indeed," he affirmed, "It seems the encounter that launched you on this trajectory was more than a simple attack. A very disruptive substance is circulating through your system."

Her mind replayed the moment when Vesok seized her and forced his kiss upon her, "The sting I felt," she reached up to her neck, "He drugged me."

"Yes, it seems humans have a high propensity for insidiousness," he noted with a quick sideways glance.

Kensy shook her head, "He's the exception, not the rule. Trust me. I'm just really good at finding the awful ones." As she pushed aside the thought of her ex, her mind turned to Jackson.

Nexus gave her a subtle approving nod, "Well, I am encouraged that you have managed to keep such dubious characters out of your present inner circle." He butted his head into her side and rubbed the length of his flickering form against her as he released another small charge of power, "Now, let's proceed."

"Yeah," Kensy laced her fingers through the bars once again and pulled. She staggered for a moment as she fought to gain a balanced footing. Steeling herself, she trudged toward the gateway. She paused at the threshold examining it. Her eyes closed for a moment as she whispered, "Stars guide me." Drawing in a deep breath, she stepped across on to the jagged rocks. With Nexus beside her Kensy trudged into the hostile landscape.

Unscrupulous eyes watched as she moved away. He pulled a small device from his side and clicked it on. "Status?" a steady, masculine voice on the other end of the connection prompted.

"You're right. Looks like she's tryin' to slip away from the riffraff. She just dropped through the dump zone, headed for the heart." He narrowed his stare, "She been a bit roughed up along the way by the look of it. Maybe even trippin' a bit, keeps talkin' like some'ums there."

A long silence listed over the communications channel, "How damaged is the prize?"

"Hard to tell. Bleedin' but still on the move," the watcher replied.

"Everything is falling into place. Continue to track. I'll be along shortly to claim my prize," the voice responded with vicious glee.

The watcher glared at his communicator for a moment, "The heart'll cost you more, Mordwell."

With a coldness Vesok snapped back, "You think I gave a damn about the pittance it costs to hire you or any other thug on this rock? Either you complete the task or we will renegotiate your contract in blood." After a moment a cold composure returned to Vesok's voice, "Now, proceed."

The watcher tightened his grip on the small device as the line disconnected. With a sneer he emerged from his hiding place and looked around. The entire area was ghostly still. Cautiously, he shuffled toward the gate, grimacing at the placards. Gruffly, he snorted and rubbed his face in contemplation.

A flit of metallic sheen caught his eye as a strange Y-shaped bug landed on his shoulder. He lurched, throwing the creature from his sleeve. With a sickening crunch, he stomped it into the ground in disgust. "Humph, damn bugs." He cast his gaze back toward the rugged path ahead. In a low menacing voice, he whispered, "Here girly, girly...," as he pulled his sidearm. From behind, another small bug-like creature latched onto the edge of his jacket and subtly skittered up his back unnoticed. Menacingly, the watcher stalked into the jagged terrain after his mark.

An eerie stillness claimed the area once more. Breaking the calm, a subtle growl rolled out of the darkness, followed by a lithe, towering humanoid. Even heavily armored he crept noiselessly toward the blood stained fence. He knelt down and scraped a clawed finger through several droplets as he examined the freshness of the sanguine fluid. The corners of his reptilian-like lips curled upward into a smirk. He stood to his full height and rolled his shoulders back into a very deliberate stretch. He drew from his sheaths two beautiful ornate daggers and the armored scales of his majestic mane and tail quaked with excitement. With a raptor-like speed and agility he darted forward through the gate after his prey.

Chapter 7

# Bleed

*"Sometimes expecting the worst isn't bad enough."*
*~ Neira Cross, Graven Mercenary*

The air was thick with humidity as Jackson drew in a cautious breath. His eyes traced the lines of the ramshackle structures that lined the streets. At every corner the building eaves dripped with the last vestiges of synthetic rain, soaking everything in sickly echoes. He apprehensively glanced toward his lead. Her control clasp subtly hummed with the continual pull of energy. There was a lightness to her steps even as she intently followed the trail.

"So," Jackson broke the quiet, "what exactly is of interest to you in this whole mess?"

Gabby giggled, "You want to know what I get out of helping you." She skipped in a circle as she moved forward, "I have a question for her, when we find her. And I can't very well ask her anything if she is killed or captured. It just doesn't work very well that way. So I help you, I get to ask my question." Gabby began to walk backward as she enthusiastically explained her desires, "And really, I've always wanted to meet her! She's kinda a big deal in Psicorp. I heard that even as a kid she could control her abilities before they ever gave her a clasp. And she was like, way so good too!" Gabby giggled again and spun around, suddenly stopping in her tracks, "Oh, shit—."

37

Jackson furrowed his brow, "What is it?" Neira, Marieke and Whitakat closed in behind them, keen to hear.

Gabby looked at a violet fog that filled her vision as it hung in the air before her, "That's no thread...." She took one hesitant step toward the slowly dissipating mist. She reached out collecting a mote of emerald power at the tips of her crystalline nails. As the two disparate energies met a spark flashed in everyone's vision. For a brief moment the cascading reaction illuminated the haze for everyone to see, "...that's a lot of latent power." She turned to the others with her wide glittering eyes, "It's unspent. She's bleeding energy. And I've never seen this much in one place before."

Neira examined the data from the flash in her cybernetic interface as she crossed her arms sternly. "What does that mean?"

Marieke raised an eyebrow as her eyes shifted to a curious gold color, "Should make her easier to track right? It's basically like giant docking lights saying, this way!" Her wings flexed restlessly.

Whitakat darted over by Gabby's shoulder, "Perhaps. However, that is not all."

"Yeah," Gabby fidgeted nervously as she contemplated how to explain her concern. "When a psionic uses their power it alters the pattern of it, it expends it, and the remnant is unstable once it's no longer sustained. This," she gestured to the air, "looks like it filtered through her in its raw state. It's just lingering. If she's bleeding this much, she could risk tapping out or worse... burning out. Even without injury that kind of expenditure could kill her."

Jackson clenched his jaw for a moment before sharing a sideways glance with Neira. She subtly shook her head, don't. With trepidation he spoke up, "She can't tap out. She, uh... has... the Mark of the Void." Neira glared at him as all attention turned in his direction.

Gabby choked for a moment on his statement, "She actually... holy Ahdras...." Her mind churned through the ramifications of this new information, calculating the bleed and path. "This is bad. This is really bad." She waved her hands toward the cloud, parting and dispersing bits of it. She jogged ahead. To her left, the street opened up into a large square. She let her power drop as she stared at carnage before her. The others followed questioningly. "She's not just a danger to herself—."

"She's a danger to everyone around her," Neira scanned the area with her eye-patch.

"That's why she's running," Jackson walked forward into the open square. A shifting noise stirred at the edge of an adjoining alleyway. He reached for his sidearm instinctively. The haggard silhouette of a human woman shuffled toward a body and plucked a piece of jewelry from the fallen man. Jackson relaxed his gun back into the holster and rested his hand on it as he approached her, "Excuse me, ma'am. Did you see what happened here?"

The woman looked up at him with joyful tears and a renewed brightness in her eyes, "Oh yes." She shuffled toward him, her shaky hands outstretched, "It was an angel!"

"An angel?" Marieke lifted into the air and surveyed the aftermath with scrutiny before landing across the plaza, "One of my people did this?"

"No, no, no," the old woman shook her head, dismissively she waved the hand that clutched the piece of jewelry. Hobbling toward Jackson, her raspy voice filled with awe, "It was a *real* angel, with wings of pure light. She smite them wicked men for their deeds then wandered away." She shook a weathered fist in the air, "When they hurt my Lizzy, I told them they would pay for their evil ways. They wouldn't listen to me." She shuffled back toward the alley, "Called me old, called me crazy, but an angel appeared, and they paid... yes they did...." Her voice trailed off as she continued her rant into the empty street.

"Wings of pure light... that's gotta be Kensy," he turned his head to Neira.

Carefully she stepped over bodies, bullets, and casings as the data came together, "It looks like an entire gang descended on her, and she fended them off."

Gabby ran her fingers across scarring on one of the walls, "She didn't just fend them off. She boxed them in. There is scarring all the way around the plaza. Psionic fire." Gabby's expression shifted as she contemplated the scenario, "She turned on them."

Marieke lifted into the air once more using her powerful wings. She traced the patterns of movement on the battlefield. "Look there." She pointed to the edge of the plaza where the body of a man lay crumpled on the ground in front of an area devoid of projectiles.

Neira focused her analysis on the area of interest. Carefully, she stepped over the ring of crumpled and discarded plasma shards. Crouching down she examined the fatal wound and general position of the deceased. As the calculations streamed across her visor's virtual interface, she stood and waved Jackson over, "I need you to stand... right...," she guided him into position, "there." Confused by her sudden request, he complied. She leaned to the side picking out the remains of another assailant lying behind his right shoulder. A spent pistol rested on the ground just beyond the corpse's finger tips. The pieces came together in her mind. Standing straight, she sternly locked eyes with Jackson, "Pick me up by the throat."

He gazed at her incredulously, "What?"

"Pick me up by the throat," she repeated earnestly. He stared at her skeptically. With a heavy sigh she rattled on, "Oh, come on. I just need you to pick me up for a minute so I can verify a theory. It's not like I'm asking you to choke me out. I'll tap your arm when its okay to let me down."

Jackson scowled, "You know, that's not exactly a gentle lift. You could get hurt."

Neira rolled her eye, "It can't be any worse than Malek back on Rosealleon."

"Fine," he reluctantly agreed. Apprehensively he wrapped the fingers of his right hand around her neck and lifted Neira from her feet. As she raised above his shoulder, she could feel the strain in his arm as he tried to maintain a grip without causing undue harm. She collected her desired readings and tapped his forearm. Quickly but cautiously, he set her down in front of him again.

She coughed as he released his grip, "I know how she got hurt."

Jackson looked down at the bodies surrounding him, "You don't think—." He began mumbling as he tried to piece it all together.

Neira stepped off to the side and prodded him to stand upright. Pulling his arm into position as if he was holding her up again, she looked over his arm, "Point with your other hand to where you felt the link activate." He pressed two fingers into the fabric of his uniform jacket. At the same time Neira pinched the cloth on his back. His eyes grew wide.

"Oooh, what am I missing?" Gabby eagerly inquired.

Neira glanced to her, "Princess grabbed this unfortunate bastard." She kicked the corpse's mucky boot. "And while all of her attention was on him, that poor sap," she pointed to the man splayed out on the ground behind Jackson, "got a lucky shot off, probably with his last breath from the look of him."

Jackson clenched his jaw as he crouched down. His eyes examined the ground for signs of Kensy's next move. Carefully, he shifted toward the nearest alleyway. His gaze turned toward the wall where runoff smeared away the last remnants of a bloodied handprint from the masonry. Drawing a sharp breath over his teeth, "We need to pick up the pace. There's a lot that can go wrong with a wound like that." He turned back toward the others, "Even in the best of cases, if she continues to push herself, she could run the clock out before we get to her."

Gabby closed her eyes and inhaled deeply as she summoned her powers forth. Blinking she nodded to Jackson, "Try to keep up." She sprung forward into a gradually quickening run. Jackson and Neira followed her strides down the twisting path. Overhead Whitakat and Marieke trailed the others in aerial pursuit, gliding past signs and scaffolding. The air of urgency built up with every passing moment, every rapid footfall, and every powerful wing beat. Now time itself was an enemy as the minutes slipped away.

Chapter 8

# Complications

*"One more thing... of course, there's always one more thing."*
*~ Lieutenant Commander Daniel Bryden*

The glow of the war room table reflected in Daniel's deep brown eyes and illuminated his somber expression as he leaned in to examine the projections before him, "Maggie, can you amplify the psilyria's nahdvi signal? We're getting a flicker." His fingertips tapped against the interactive surface, rotating the perspective and scale of the pillar hologram.

"Maximum passive amplification already in effect. Assessing...," the mechanical voice of the ship chimed back, "Low-grade geographical interference detected. Compensating.... Neurological interference detected. Analyzing... foreign compound detected. Compound identification inconclusive. No matching substances in available databases."

"Foreign compound?" he furrowed his brow in concern, "Is that what's causing the flicker?" He glanced to his left.

"Let's see what we have, shall we?" beside him the ship's doctor, Wynn Tyronis, set her diagnostic pad down within one of the table's illuminated interface rings, "Classify–priority Medical, and transfer compound data to Chief Medical Officer Doctor Wynn Tyronis, authorization M-436-EX-9772." She pensively brushed her silver and brown streaked hair behind her ear as she watched the data compile on her pad. Upon

43

completion the spinning ring of light shifted tones. She snatched it up and began sifting through the information.

Daniel scoffed in frustration as he replayed the attack in his mind, "She was shaken but I don't recall him wounding her. Though it would explain why she ran off. How quickly could something like that take effect? How could he have administered it?" he shot a questioning glance toward Doctor Tyronis.

"I could try synthesizing the compound; however, just by looking at the structure it could take quite a while," she skimmed over the data, "Without more information, the details are best guess only. The possibilities for a transmission vector are extensive. I could—."

An incoming correspondence chirped over their communicators. Daniel's fingers danced across a holographic interface on the table, "Encrypted connection confirmed. Go ahead, Gabel."

"Bryden, the meeting was a no go, but we've enlisted the help of a tracker. We're currently following K's path through the pillar. Listen, we have reason to believe she's been injured. Severely," Jackson's voice filled the room. The sounds of his labored breath followed as he ran while he talked.

Daniel gripped the edge of the table as he shifted backward, letting his head drop with a sigh. "Seriously?!" he muttered, "Is there no end?"

Jackson spoke again, either ignoring or not noticing the commentary of his first officer, "I'm gonna need you to get Doc and put an extraction team together. We think she's heading into what the locals call the Heart. It's the central remains of the planet. There should be mining convoy access corridors you can fly into to meet up with us. But I won't sugar-coat it. We lost track of Mordwell. We could be walking right into the middle of whatever he has planned."

"Copy that, Commander," Wynn reached out and maternally patted Bryden's shoulder. "I'll begin prepping for an extraction immediately. So you know, I've been assisting Lieutenant Commander Bryden with interpreting the nahdvi data we've been collecting on Psilyria Frost."

"I haven't been able to get a bead on her. Have you been able to establish communications?!" Jackson eagerly replied.

"No, unfortunately we have not," she informed him, "We've seen a bit of interference from the surrounding area; however, the lieutenant commander and Maggie have managed to cut through enough of it to capture a reasonable amount of data. Still, the connection is very limited."

"Have you at least been able to get a read on her vitals?" Jackson inquired with concern.

Doctor Tyronis furrowed her brow as she looked again to the information processing on her holopad, "To some degree. She's alive, but I am concerned about what I'm seeing. Commander, we've also managed to decipher one more piece of the puzzle. The psilyria...," she paused, "I believe she has been exposed to something, some kind of neurological toxin. I'm still analyzing what exactly its effects are. Judging from my initial analysis, it is likely impairing her ability to reason. Be careful. She may not be in control of her actions... or abilities."

A long silence hung over the connection before Jackson sternly responded between breaths, "I understand." His tone remained steady as he continued to run, "Prep for an emergency medical extraction. Rendezvous on my location ASAP."

"Yes, sir!" Daniel acknowledged as the line cut. He turned sharply to the doctor, "Get who and what you need. Meet in the shuttle bay. I'll be right there. I have some backup to call on." With one touch Daniel shut down the war room table display, and they departed their separate ways with haste.

Daniel rushed down the bridgehead, where Morgan and Rauk waited impatiently. The pilot swiveled around in his chair but before he could rise, Daniel held out a hand to stop him, "Threaux, I need you to stay here. Keep running those mock drills we talked about. We are making an emergency extraction." The lieutenant commander turned his attention to their imposing friend, "Rauk, you're with me just in case we need the extra backup. We don't know what we are walking into."

The towering form of Rauk nodded. As a zog, his massive form was a hulk of muscles, fur, and cybernetics mixed with patchwork armor. His booming but articulate voice filled the room, "Of course, whatever you need. I'll round up Kigh and Gizmo and we'll meet you at the shuttle momentarily." He lumbered up the stairs and down the corridor away from the bridgehead.

Morgan furrowed his brow, "I thought Gabel and Cross were gonna handle things on the down-low. An emergency extraction is gonna raise some eyebrows."

"Yeah, well...," Daniel watched Rauk fade from view, "the situation has changed. Our psilyria was potentially drugged by that creep that ambushed us, and is now very possibly critically wounded, so subtly isn't really an option."

"Shit," Morgan scoffed.

Daniel turned a stern gaze toward him, "That's why I need you here. If there's anyone who can give the brass a run around, it's you. Keep them in the dark and preferably distracted without raising too much ire. We'll sort everything out after."

Morgan squinted as ideas flooded his conniving mind, "Define *too much*...."

Daniel snickered, making his way to the stairs, "Just imagine dealing with Gabel after this all settles down and let that image guide you." Morgan grunted with discontent at the thought. Daniel picked up the pace, jogging down the hall toward the elevator. As he approached it, the door slid open in anticipation, "Thank you, Maggie." He stepped in and pivoted around to check the control panel.

"Your destination has been set. Be advised, her nahdvi signal continues to transmit sporadically. Further distress on the psilyria's end could result in signal degradation," the computer chimed back.

"Understood," he unclicked his belt and jacket, shedding the outer layers of his uniform as the elevator descended. "Unlock the emergency armory in the hangar bay and ready docking clamps on Shuttle One for departure."

"Already done."

The doors swung open, and Daniel expediently hustled toward the hangar. He rounded the corner into the bay as the shuttle settled into launch position in front of the loading platform. Rauk reached forward, opening the side door for the doctor and other extraction team members. The rhythmic clacking of weapons being checked at the edge of the room drew Daniel's attention. There stood the members of the DeCadejra's primary strike team, readying themselves. Lieutenant Lindsay Rasken popped the bubble formed by her chewing gum and glanced up as Daniel approached. "Alpha, load up!" with the wave of her hand, the others finished grabbing their gear and began to head for the shuttle.

"I take it rumors reached you already," Daniel tossed his belongings into the equipment locker and snagged a combat jacket from the racks. Quickly, he slipped it over the top of his black uniform undershirt.

"I don't know the whole story, but my captains' are in trouble and I might get to shoot something, so, I'm in." She blew another bubble before turning away from the lieutenant commander.

Daniel shook his head as he fastened the last closures on his armor. He pulled a sidearm and leg holster from their resting places, then kicked the container closed, "Re-secure emergency armory," he called out to Maggie. The sound of heavy metallic locks emanated from behind him as he hustled toward the waiting transport.

Chapter 9

# Fight

*"In the darkest night, the smallest light can be a beacon."*
*~ Philosopher Chris P. Crucias*

Dirt caked to the scuffed surface of Kensy's once glossy patent leather boots as she staggered through the hollowed out tunnels of the Aepexian Heart. She planted a bloodied hand on the rough stone walls to steady herself. The world blurred and tilted between her labored, gasping breaths. Blood from her saturated uniform slowly drizzled over her clasp until, one drop at a time, it fell to the path over which she traversed. Fatigue and injury caused her head to bob slightly as her eyes tried to decipher the landscape. A shadow across the tunnel beckoned toward her silently.

Pushing away from the edge, she wobbled for a few steps before pitching forward onto her knees and armored arm. A cloud of fine dust kicked up under her and she coughed it away. In an attempt to rise, the toe of her right boot scrapped across the gravelly ground before finally catching enough to allow her to struggle back to her feet. Unsteadily, she managed to propel herself in the direction of her destination. Nearing the opposite wall, her balance surrendered. With a dull thud her good shoulder slammed into dark grayish-brown rocks.

She tilted her head around the earthen outcropping beside her, *Good. It's just a spur, not another tunnel.* She clamored into the crevasse, *I can rest in here. No one should see or bother me if I can keep out of sight. I just need a few*

48

*minutes....* Within the shadow Kensy curled into a tight ball, cradled by the cold stone. Her head lulled to the side as she slipped from consciousness.

With a gasp, Kensy snapped up into a sitting position and looked around curiously. The carefully groomed landscape of an indoor atrium filled her ears with peaceful sounds. Remembering her state only moments ago she turned her attention toward her own being. She patted her hands across her body. No pain or wounds were revealed by the inspection. She stood cautiously. Even her clothes were different. She was dressed in slouchy black boots that cut off just below her stocking covered knees. A loose white blouse tucked into the top of her plain black skirt. Over the top she tugged at her plum-colored vest. *My academy uniform? What the —?*

A door slammed behind her. She pivoted around sharply. At the side of the door a woman, dressed in similar fashion with long ebony hair in two cascading braids, frantically jammed a tool against the portcullis to slow anyone who would follow. Quickly, she darted toward Kensy, snatching her hand and dragging her behind. Together, the two women ran through familiar but empty halls. "Elle, where are we going? Where is everyone?" Kensy hollered toward her longtime friend.

"Quick, in here!" Elle shoved Kensy through a side doorway. Kensy stumbled into her old dormitory room with its bunk beds, desks, wardrobes and standing mirror lining the walls exactly as she had remembered. Swiveling toward Kensy, Ellise Neru's expression became concerned and stern, "What are you doing here?! You have to get out! Get away!"

"You shoved me in here," Kensy furrowed her brow trying to reconcile her thoughts.

Elle shook her head and paced further into the room, "Not in this room, in this dream. You have to wake up! Your mind is being changed. If you don't fight back you, me, everything will be erased." She glanced toward a darkened window at the end of the room, "He's close—." Sharply Elle shrieked as tendrils of shadow erupted from the floor-length mirror behind her and wrapped around her body. With tremendous force, they ripped her backward though the glassy surface, cutting off her scream.

Kensy lunged toward the mirror, "No!" Her fist met with the unnaturally resilient surface. Helplessly, she watched the shadows silently consume her childhood friend. Ripples emanated from her fists as she pounded on the mirror in frustration, tears welling up in the corners of her eyes. Once more the shadows sprung from the surface, coiling around Kensy's forearms. Futilely, she struggled against the oppressive grip. Slowly but steadily, it dragged her into the smothering tar-like darkness.

A loose rock shook from its resting place and skittered across the ground setting Kensy's watcher on edge. Muttering under his breath, he crept down the corridor of quarried stone. Annoyed with his task, he wrinkled his face in displeasure as he tried to decipher the blood trail she had left behind. Catching sight of the turn toward the shadows he primed his weapon and stepped into the middle of the cavern toward the far side.

Pain spiked through the back of his neck. Grunting, he arced his head backward and tried to claw at the source. His fingers slid futilely over the smooth bug-like construct that dug into his spinal column. Wires and tendrils snaked through the man's body wresting control of his form away from him. He gave out one last agonizing holler as the thrall bored his eyes from his skull. Testing and tuning its control, the creature flexed the man's empty hand.

His communicator chirped from his side. Slowly and deliberately, he pulled the small device and stared at it with his hollow eyes. With one strong squeeze, he crumpled the device to pieces and discarded them. He straightened his posture with new purpose. Closing the remaining distance to the shadowy crevasse, he raised his sidearm toward the curled figure within.

In a voice not entirely his own the enthralled watcher spoke up, "thE thREat wiLL Be NeutRALizED."

From the shadows further down the tunnel a blade sung through the air, embedding itself into the watcher's hand as he pulled the trigger. The rocks beside Kensy's head cracked at the impact. Hot plasma seeped from the fracture caused by the narrowly missed shot. The watcher hissed in dismay and turned his attention in the direction of the blade's origin. A tall, armored figure emerged from his hiding place with nary a sound. His majestic mane of scales quaked menacingly as he turned two elegant blades over in his clawed fingers.

Suddenly and swiftly the alien lunged forward, striking at the watcher. The blades sunk into the watcher's right arm and shoulder severing several key points. The watcher ripped away as articulated cables knitted his arm back together. He hissed mechanically at the alien attacker and extended his left hand toward the sidearm that had dropped from his grasp in the attack. Wires sprung from under his fingernails and shot toward the side arm. It pulled the gun toward his grasp disassembling and reconfiguring the pieces within moments. Blood poured from his flesh as the reconfigured weapon tore through and merged with his hand.

"Well, that's an interesting trick," The alien readied himself, studying his opponent carefully, "Aren't you just full of surprises?!"

The watcher sneered, "inTErruPtioNS wiLL NoT bE TollERatED!" A large burst of hot plasma sprayed forth from the construct in his hand. Deftly, the alien sprung toward the cavern wall to dodge the super-heated fluid that splashed across the gravely ground. Bounding toward the watcher, the alien sunk his blades into the man's chest and drove him backward onto the ground.

The watcher grabbed at the alien's armor as he pressed the residually hot, but now empty, plasma core into the alien assailant's side. His scales quaked as he roared from the pain.

With a grunt, the alien pulled one of his blades free and plunged it into the watcher's neck. Sharply twisting the dagger, he severed the spinal column and sundered the small metallic Y-shaped bug that had embedded itself there. Electricity arced through the wound and the watcher's arms fell limply to the ground.

Pulling his blades back and sheathing them, the alien flexed his fingers as he shook the sensation of the final jolt from his clawed fingers. He stood, snatching his throwing knife from the backside of the corpse's right hand, wiped the blade clean, and tucked it back into his armor. Directing a scrutinizing glance toward the motionless body he meandered toward Kensy's alcove.

He glanced into the alcove to assess her condition, "Well, well, what do we have here?" He noted the cracked rock beside her head from the skewed shot. Reaching forward, he pressed the back of one of his fingers into the side of her neck. Faintly her pulse thrummed under his touch. A tingle of energy passed over her skin. He recoiled as he watched crackling violet fog begin to ooze off her body.

The distant sound of machinery rumbled down the tunnels toward them. Apprehensively, he looked between the origin of the rising noise and the unconscious form of Kensy. Quickly, he pulled a small stick-like implement out of his gear and gently but swiftly inserted it into her shoulder wound. Pressing a button on the end it flashed with light for a brief moment. He pulled it out and backed away as the noises grew louder. Gathering the body of the fallen watcher, he retreated into the shadows once more to watch and wait.

Darkness imposed on Kensy from every direction. She clawed wildly at the emptiness searching for any sign of Elle. A myriad of voices echoed back upon her,

"Where is everyone?"

"Another nightmare?"

"Failure."

"What are you doing here?!"

"It's never over, is it?"

"You have to get out!"

"You have to wake up!"

"...you, me, everything will be erased."

Kensy wrapped her arms tightly around herself as her eyes scanned the darkness for some sliver of hope. Her lower lip quivered, and a chill ran through her body. Fatigue began set into every fiber of her being. Elle's voice rang softly in her ears, "You have to fight." Her eyes began to fill with tears as the darkness began to crawl up her body.

She shuddered, "Is this finally it? Is this the abyss I'm destined for?" choking on her words she curled her body inward, "I'm not ready to go anymore. I just...," tears broke free, streaming down her weary face, "...just a little bit longer."

A streak of red lightning shattered the darkness. It spiraled up around her in a furious tornado. A warmth began to build at her fingertips. She pulled her hands away from her body as a violet glow spread down her forearms. She caught her breath and blinked the tears away.

"You have to fight."

She closed her fists and her eyes, focusing on the sensation of power coursing through her body. She crossed her wrists in front of her as the lightning closed in. "Stars, guide me," she whispered. Throwing her arms wide, a tide of violet energy expanded in all directions, scattering the lightning back into the darkness. Her face turned upward; she opened her eyes. There blinking in the distance, a single star beckoned toward her faintly. She smiled weakly, "Thank you."

Chapter 10

# Found

*"Yes, boss. Whateve' you sayz, boss."*
*~ Henchman #4*

A clamor of heavy footfalls resonated through the caverns alongside the crawl of five large vehicles as Vesok Mordwell's private army snaked through the quarried tunnels in pursuit of their wounded mark. Suddenly from the head of the pack one of the advanced scouts shouted, "Hey, we got somethin' here," flagging the convoy to a halt.

The massive industrial tires of the transports ground to a stop on the calculous ground. From the center vehicle, two burly bodyguards emerged. Between them stepped the visage of Vesok, "Yes?" he inquired, straightening his suit jacket fastidiously.

The scout approached, holding out a piece of the sundered communicator, "We're just about on the last transmission coordinates and I found this. Pieces seem to be scattered about a bit, seems likely there was a scuffle here recently."

Vesok turned the shambled piece over in his hands running his insipid eyes along the sundered contours of the device. With an indignant grunt he shouted out to his hirelings, "Fan out. I want her found and detained. She couldn't have gone far." His troops began to disperse along the diverging pathways in search of any lingering trails. Pivoting back toward the scout, he the rolled remnant over in his palm. "Now, show me exactly where you found this."

The two hulking bodyguards followed a short distance behind as the scout hustled back to his position at the head of the convoy to show his boss the location of the find. Nearing the site, Vesok paused for a moment studying the ground. With the toe of his exorbitantly priced dress shoe, he nudged a piece of loose rock. It tumbled over revealing a still glistening crimson coating. He narrowed his glare, "...seems likely there was a scuffle? The area is quite literally painted red, and you only noticed this?" He held up the piece again. Before the scout could reply Vesok cast the device remnant aside, "Remove him."

One of the guards grabbed the scout with an unnaturally fast and crushing grip, dragging the shocked and whimpering man away. Vesok turned to intently study the terrain. Raising an eyebrow he commented with little interest, "...so hard to find decent help." He let out an annoyed sigh.

Meticulously, stepping between the worst of the blood-spattered areas, he gazed over to a smeared handprint along the far wall trying to piece together the visual variables. A faint buzzing reached his ears under the sound of the humming vehicles, clomping footfalls, and intermittent shouts. Slowly, Vesok craned his head in the direction of the sound, inching toward its very gradual crescendo. His lips curled into a wicked grin as the alcove and Kensy's curled form came into view.

He approached with cautious confidence. She failed to react to his approach. A soft violet fog rolled off her motionless form so faintly he paid it no heed and reached toward her cheek to caress her soft skin. The latent energy stirred and crackled. A wandering bolt leapt for his hand, surging painfully through his fingers before dissipating into the maze of gadgetry that lined his palm. He lurched back and shook his hand in disgust.

Recomposing himself, he whistled up to his underlings. A small group tromped toward him in response. He non-nonchalantly gestured toward the alcove, "Our guest will need assistance. Extract her *carefully*." The group glanced in to assess their target and exchanged dubious stares. "Quickly!" he viciously asserted with a sneer, "No further physical damage is to come to her. And remember, incompetence will be rewarded accordingly." Further up the tunnel a man's sharp cry resonated—abbreviated by an even louder concussive blast. Vesok tucked his hands into the pockets of his slacks and headed for his transport.

The most senior among them elbowed one of his compatriots, "Go get a gurney an sum insulator packs. There's no way we's dragging the boss's electric girlfriend outta here without sum gear." As the cohort turned to run back to the convoy, the ground began to rumble. The shaking intensified. An eerie chorus echoed through the tunnels. All fell still and silent once again. "Make it snappy. I don't wanna be here when those things get hungry." Nods and furtive glances passed among the underlings as they quickly set to work gathering equipment to extract Kensy's unconscious body.

Chapter 11

# Wraith

"Not even prayers can save you if you wake the<br>
Heart of Aepexia."<br>
~ ancient Aepexian proverb

Gabby squinted her power-infused, crystalline eyes as she analyzed the thread connecting Jackson and Kensy. She drew an apprehensive breath over her teeth as she tried to deduce the best path to follow. "It's getting thinner," she muttered.

Jackson stepped up beside her, "Then we need to—." the nearly imperceptible link flickered. Feeling the attachment shudder, he wavered for a moment. He placed one hand on his chest and braced himself against the cavern wall with the other. A sudden intangible tug jarred him. In that moment a spike of sharpness surged through his body as the connection was ripped from him. He paused to catch his breath, and the attention of the others eagerly settled on his expression. "It's gone.... I can't sense her anymore."

For a moment, his eyes searched the ground as he cogitated on the meaning of the lost link. His resolve hardened, "We're out of time. I'm going to find her!" He charged past Gabby toward the next jog in the rock with little heed for what might be around the bend.

Jackson's quickening footfalls reached the senses of a figure hidden in the shadows of the cavern. The reptilian-like alien slowly drew his blades and folded his mane scales tightly against his body as he silently prepared to intercept this interloper. Jackson's shadow crossed in front of the alien's hiding place. Swiftly, the alien leapt from his perch. He swept toward Jackson in a flash. Seeing the blur of movement toward him, Jackson reactively yanked the hilt of his folded tech sword from his belt, stopping the blade mere inches from his throat.

They both froze, sizing each other up, the alien with his second dagger poised to strike, and Jackson with his fingers clutching his now drawn sidearm. Neira shook her head and approached. She crossed her arms over her chest and glared at both figures, "Play nice!"

Jackson shot her an incredulous glance while keeping his focus on the alien, "You know this... assassin?"

The alien pulled back and stood tall, a smirk curling across his lips, "Ha!" He sheathed his daggers. "Good to see the company you are keeping these days has some skill."

A snarky smile crept up on Neira's face, "Good to see you aren't getting rusty while you sit in the capital and twiddle your thumbs." The alien and Neira clasped hands and pulled each other in close. Both figures wrapped their free arm around the other's back and gave an affectionate tap with the side of their fist in a display of camaraderie.

Disinterested in the reunion playing out in front of him Jackson spoke up. "Enough. We don't have time to waste, Cross."

Neira rolled her eye, "Nevan, Princess is in here somewhere and we need to find her. She's probably in pretty bad shape. You got anything?"

Nevan looked across the group, "You are going to want to be very quiet from this point on. Mordwell brought a small army down here with him. Not sure what he's up to, but I did kill one of his men." He stepped back to reveal his hiding spot where the watcher's body now slumped against the rocks. "The guy had some crazy hardware going on. Took more than it should have to drop him."

Concerned, Jackson knelt down beside the body to inspect it. Nevan continued, "I did find Princess, and tried to stabilize her but she started to radiate energy. I couldn't move her."

Standing up, Jackson pivoted toward Neira and held out his fingers. A fine green dust covered the tips, "Mordwell isn't the only thing we need to worry about. The Vagabond's here."

She looked down at his hand, scanning the familiar nanite residue. A string of expletives rolled out of her lips as she muttered under her breath. She placed her hands on her hips and gazed down the tunnel deep in thought, "That explains some things." Her attention snapped back to Nevan. "Listen things are stupidly complicated right now, but our number one priority has to be securing Princess. I will fill you in on the rest after we get done navigating this shit storm."

The scales of his mane fluttered briefly as he stretched to his full height for a moment, "In that case let's use the assets Mordwell is so generously providing for her extraction." A rumble passed through the ground. The echo of discordant howls filled the passageway. Gravel skittered across the trembling ground before settling back down. "Mordwell's caravan has drawn some unwanted attention. We can take advantage of that." He turned toward the olhreleth woman at the group's flank. "Feel like wreaking some havoc, Marieke?"

She smiled mischievously and pulled the xeik'quael from the sling on her back. She tapped the haft of the weapon against her open palm, "Point me in the direction."

"Back about 100 meters there is a tunnel in the ceiling. Double back and come in from above. We'll need you to draw the guard away from princess when they start moving her," Nevan instructed. She nodded and spread her wings, lifting her armored form off the ground with ease. He turned toward Gabby, "Psicorp, specialty?"

Her eyes darted around the group, "Um... tracking, infusion, nothing very flashy."

He strummed his clawed fingertips against the scales around his clavicle for a moment as he contemplated the task at hand, "How are your accuracy and recoil compensation? Think you can handle laying down a few precision bursts to give covering fire for our CQC members to close in?"

Gabby thought on the acronym for a quick second, "Close quarter... oh, right, right!" smiled and snapped to prompt attention, "Absolutely, can do!" She pulled a compact firearm from her hip and adjusted it for burst fire.

Nevan turned toward Neira and Jackson. "I'll take up position across the path here." He snagged a long rifle from its hiding place alongside the watcher's corpse, "I should be able to snipe up into the lead vehicle and disable it. If we box them in and create a little chaos, you should be able to slip in, dispatch the escort crew and secure princess."

"We may have backup on the way, but I have no idea when to expect them," Jackson informed Nevan.

Nevan nodded in acknowledgment, "Then we *don't* expect them. If they show great, if not we have to be ready to cut and run when the opportunity presents itself." Jackson nodded. A smile curved around Nevan's reptilian lips. "Whitikat!"

Their fluttering companion darted to his side. "Ready to assist," it informed him.

"Think you can cover comms? Coordinate a telepathic net between our friends here? We'll need a little coordination, to pull this off." Nevan gestured toward Gabby and Jackson.

"Whoa there!" Jackson interrupted, "I don't need any... butterflies or voices in my head."

Nevan laughed, "He won't actually be in your head. Whit here has a very useful little trick where he can capture disparate sound vibrations from scattered targets and relay them to other very precise locations, like my words into your ears. He uses his natural physical structure like a relay. For simplicity's sake, most humans tend to think of it as a form of telepathy." Nevan nodded to Whitikat, who in return, bobbed in affirmation. Nevan flexed his scales, "Let's go rescue us a princess."

"...and hope she's not in another castle," Jackson grumbled. Nevan looked at him curiously. Jackson waved him off, "Don't mind me. It's just a little ancient human jest. Let's do this." He pulled his techblade once again and reached down to his side unfastening a heavy handle from its attachment point. His thumb slid across the controls, readying the device to activate at a moment's notice.

Jackson shuffled toward the corner of the tunnel bend and pressed his back against the rock. Ever so carefully, he peeked around the corner, getting a glimpse of the convoy up the path from them. Another chorus of baleful howls echoed through the passages. Everyone froze waiting for the moment of silence that followed.

Neira looked between Nevan and Jackson and mouthed, *They're getting closer.* They both nodded in acknowledgment. She pulled her Ausk-Chelkai, two elegant wing like blades from her back, and pressed up along the wall beside Jackson waiting for the charge.

Wide-eyed, Gabby made one final adjustment to her gun, suppression. She did not want to draw any unwanted attention with her shots. While not perfect, the sonic limiter, would at the very least ensure that Mordwell's forces would be generating far more sound than her. She nodded to the others, *ready!*

Nevan pulled his scales in close and carefully snaked across the shadows of the lower tunnel, finally taking a prone position alongside the far wall. He gazed down the scope of his rifle, sighting in the underpinnings of the lead vehicle. As he exhaled he whispered, "Go," and squeezed the trigger. The armor piercing round sailed through the air, ripping the target transport's suspension to shreds. The vehicle jarred sharply and collapsed under its own weight.

Marieke shrieked in delight as she crashed down upon the rear vehicle axe first. Her heavily armored boots landed on the roof with a heavy thud. An articulated visor closed around her face giving her already imposing figure an even more menacing appearance. She flailed her xeik'quael in wide sweeping motions as the thugs of Mordwell's private army attempted to goad her from the top of the vehicle.

One either brave or foolish man attempted to scale the grill and hood of the vehicle to face off with her. Marieke kicked forward forcefully, catching his chin with a snap and flinging him backward.

Confused by the pandemonium, Kensy's escort crew skirted around the lead vehicles, hustling for cover from the berserk olhreleth at the rear of the caravan. Gabby confidently strafed out from the tunnel, her eyes glittering with emerald energy. With a subtle *pop, pop, pop* she zeroed in on the outermost escort and his body dropped limply on to the gravel.

Jackson pivoted around the corner, activating his plasma shield from the primed handle and pushing up along the wall toward the convoy. Neira remained close on his heels. *Pop, pop, pop.* Gabby riddled a thug as he emerged from the opposite side of the transport gun raised.

As they neared the scrambling escort, Jackson pulled away from the wall. They helplessly unloaded their sidearms into the shield to no effect. Neira dashed around him and closed in on one of the men. She guided her blade in an uppercut. The length of the blade with its graceful points and curves raked through his lightly armored flesh. She continued the turn piercing the man on the opposite side of the gurney through the chest.

Jackson bashed the final escort with the searing face of the shield, sending him reeling backward screaming in agony. Swiftly, Jackson flicked his sword in a circular motion, cutting the man's screams short. Neira pulled the end of her Ausk-Chelkai free and turned toward the rest of the caravan to cover

Jackson from further attackers. Jackson deactivated his sword and shield, grabbing the hovering gurney with both hands to guide it up alongside the sundered transport. Furiously, he tapped through the readings on the gurney's interface.

"Talk to me, soldier-boy," Neira called back to him.

"Looks like they tried to stabilize her," he shook his head, "but she's not doing well."

Suddenly the door beside Jackson flew open, causing him to duck down instinctively. There was a dull, sickening sound as the protective curve in front of Neira's blade grip sunk into the would-be-assailant's chest. She wrenched him out of the vehicle and onto the ground. With a glare, she turned her attention toward the man in the driver's seat and roared with calculated fury. His eyes widened. He fumbled for the door handle, stumbling out and beginning to run away from the mercenary.

Jackson shook his head, "They have an onboard psionic suppression system. It is cranked to max, and it is barely keeping her in check. We have to get her medical attention, now." A tremor rose in the ground beneath their feet. A guttural wail crescendoed, amplified by the quaking gravel and stone. Jackson slowly let his thoughts slip from his lips. "Oh... shit."

Marieke hunkered down, smiled under her visor and pulled one of her adversaries close to whisper tauntingly into his ear, "Just wait for it...." The wall above her exploded into a hail of rock and debris as she launched the man into the air. The gargantuan piercing maw of an Aepexian core wraith opened around the hapless victim slamming its four mandibles immediately closed again. Its long body flew over her and broke back into the ground on the other side of the vehicle she had thrashed. Another massive wraith erupted beneath the second convoy transport, tearing though it and anyone unfortunate enough to be inside.

Mordwell glanced at the pandemonium around him and sneered with contempt. He snapped back to his bodyguards, "Get me to safety!"

A hired soldier backed up toward Mordwell, "Boss, what about the woman?"

He glowered at the man, "I am not dying for a trophy." He booted the man away from himself and toward the thrashing wraith. The man let out a panicked cry abbreviated by the four-pronged maw of a smaller wraith closing around him as it leapt from the ground. Its leathery wings guided it to the ground with its ensnared prey. Upon landing the wraith's powerful clawed hind legs tore at the rocks to propel it into the ground again. Its long-spiked tail thrashed about preventing anyone from approaching, or attempting to keep the creature from fleeing with its meal.

The cacophony of chaos filled the tunnels with screams and gunfire of the panicked henchmen, the baleful wails of the ravenous wraiths, and the shattering and rending of rock and metal. Jackson looked down at Kensy lying on the gurney in his hands, her violet energy flickering and faintly roiling off her skin. He reached toward her, gently brushing her strawberry blonde hair from her face even as the psionic energy stung through his armored glove. He bowed his head to whisper, "Please, come back."

## Chapter 12

# The Calvary

*"It's good to have friends."*
*~ Crewman K. Morrison*

Daniel's fingers played across the controls, making the Scythe transport shuttle dance around the twists and turns of the heart's mining tunnels. He furrowed his brow as he tried to decipher the readings on his display. "Maggie, any chance you could clean these readings up, they are bouncing off the ore in here. I'm having trouble narrowing down a route."

"Allow me," Maggie's computerized voice chimed back through the nahdvi on his ear. The navigational data shifted from a live read to a more static map with moving indicators. "Plotting optimal route.... Direct approach not recommended due to active engagement with enemy forces. Alternate route will provide a more advantageous approach vector." Two distinct lines illuminated for the pilot to assess.

"Looks like that way has a few less obstacles too, alternate route it is." Now confident in his navigation, he reached for the thruster control and slammed it forward. Without so much as a glance over his shoulder, he shouted back to the onboard crew. "I hope you have a plan. We'll be coming in hot very shortly."

"Our clever little malckiev friend is concocting something... I think." Rasken popped a bubble with her gum and intently watched Kigh furiously fiddle with some piece of tech in his long spindly fingers.

"Kigh, fiddle-fix noisy-screamy-soundy so wraithy-badness go bye-bye." Deftly, their two-foot-tall companion skittered around everyone's legs toward the front of the shuttle, his long fluffy tail trailing behind. He used his powerful marsupial-like hind feet to spring up into the co-pilot's seat and began reaching for one of the communication panels on the side wall.

"Great," Reily said flatly. She turned her head toward the rest of alpha squad, "Break out the earplugs."

Kigh chittered as he worked to attach his jury-rigged component to the transport's external communications array. "Noisy-screamy-soundy no hurt human ears. Kigh fiddle-fix so only bother wraithy-badness. Tickle scaly-hairs and make them go diggy-dig away." He finished fussing and grabbed the shoulder of the seat, looking back on the rest of the company, "Kigh want to save Kensy-lady. Kensy-lady nice to Kigh."

Rauk piped up from the rear of the shuttle, "And we will, buddy. The device will take care of the local fauna but according to the captain we could also be walking into a firefight." He glanced toward the spherical construct floating beside him. "Gizmo, think you could manage a directed flash to blind anyone who tries to fire on us?" The drone bobbed and rotated end over end in affirmation.

"And we've got the covering fire," Ensign Kyo nodded.

The sounds of the ongoing battle reached the shuttle's auditory sensors as they veered around a corner to the final approach corridor. "Get ready!" Daniel hollered. "Engaging in three, two—." He veered around the last corner, swinging the tail end of the shuttle toward the fray. Kigh triggered his device. A low tremor shook the air and the nearby wraiths squealed in their discordant tones before diving back into the rocky surfaces. The rear hatch opened, allowing Gizmo to dart into the air over the conflict. The mercenaries turned their gazes toward the battle's new participant. In that moment, Gizmo released a blinding flash.

Reeling from the burst, Mordwell and his bodyguards retreated back to the last of the functional trucks in his convoy. Plasma flew through the air as the remaining henchmen fired blindly. Alpha descended from the transport in a coordinated formation with Rauk close behind.

Neira curled around the front of the foremost vehicle to assess the shifting battle. Spying Rauk's hulking form, she waved toward him. "Over here! We need a hand," she yelled over the commotion.

"Cross!" She snapped her head around at the sound of Mordwell's voice. "This isn't over yet, Cross!" He sneered and ducked into his vehicle. The wheels ground against the gravel as it peeled out and circled away from the dying conflict.

She glared venomously in his direction. Rauk lumbered up beside her. Without averting her rancor gaze, she spoke. "Princess, is on the back side of the truck with Gabel. Get her loaded up. We don't have much time."

Rauk circled around the direction Neira had come from. There, beside the vehicle, Jackson kept a close eye on the gurney's onboard systems as he guarded Kensy from flying shrapnel and debris with his shield and his own body. One enemy mercenary rounded the rear of a nearby sundered vehicle, advancing on the commander and his charge. Rauk swung the back of his fist toward the unfortunate assailant. The force of the blow lifted the man into the air with startling ease, sending him helplessly sailing through the air toward the cavern wall.

"Time to go." Rauk brought his arm back in a sweeping motion over the commander's hunched form. Cradling the gurney, he lifted Kensy into a protective position. Jackson ducked back, turning his attention toward covering her extraction. Together, they shifted around the front of the forward vehicle, past Neira, and headed toward the transport. Neira nodded toward Jackson, "Meet you back at the ship. I have something to take care of." Her gaze shifted toward her other allies on the battlefield. Through her crystalline friend she relayed one word, "Ghost."

As the last of Alpha drew back to the shuttle, Marieke lifted into the air once more and sailed back through the tunnel from which she had descended. With a hiss, the rear hatch closed. The final few surviving mercenaries of the convoy cautiously peered out from their hiding places. The echo of the shuttle's engines faded from earshot and the battlefield fell silent as they realized they were alone.

Aboard the shuttle, Doctor Tyronis and her medical technicians worked furiously to stabilize their patient. They cut away the shoulder of her uniform to allow access to the wound site. "We've got a through-and-through with debris. Get me a pulse tube and flash bandages!" One of the techs passed over a cylindrical device and stood at the ready with several metallic pads in hand.

"She's had a couple patch jobs on the bullet wound but the tissue has seen some extensive damage and ruptures. We need to clear out what we can before closing her back up." The doctor informed Jackson as he wordlessly stood back and watched. Gradually, she worked the tube into the bullet's exit point, forcing the free-floating clots and torn tissue from the wound track. "Eyes!" she shouted to those on board. Everyone averted their gazes as a brilliant flare emanated from the device. She adjusted rings on the exposed end of the cylinder. "And extracting excess air from the chest cavity... there we go. That should help ease her breathing."

Wynn lifted Kensy's shoulder, wiping the blood and tissue from under her body. Before applying the metallic pad to the entry wound on the psilyria's back. A faint glow curled around the edges of the bandage for a brief moment before fading again. "Keep the pulse tube in place until we can get her on the table. How are those neuro readings looking?"

The other tech furrowed his brow, "Not good. We're seeing significant waveform variance and the beginning of pathway remodeling." He tapped through the readings furiously.

"Call the ship. Have them ready a neural enforcement kit for our arrival and prep for surgery." Doctor Tyronis's voice became a blur to Jackson as she launched into the more technical terms of diagnosis and procedure.

He focused past her onto his shuttle pilot. There Daniel sat intently focused on expediting their return to the ship. His hands danced over the consoles as he balanced readouts and vessel navigation. Jackson caught a moment of hesitation in his movements.

Discretely Jackson bowed his head away from the commotion between himself and his pilot. "What do you have for me?"

The other sounds of the shuttle dimmed as their nahdvi communication devices adjusted for the private conversation. Daniel's voice came through clearly, "Evidently when we didn't show up to the debrief, the debrief decided to come to us. I had Threaux running interference, but we have brass onboard now."

Jackson took a sharp breath in and cursed under his breath. He glanced toward the ceiling of the shuttle, suppressing his frustration. "It was too much to hope we could pull this off without drawing attention. Tell Threaux to keep them busy. I'll deal with them when we get back."

"Understood, sir." Daniel reached up to a control above him and made an adjustment. "Coming into aft port side hangar. Ready to disembark." The shuttle hummed as it decelerated into the docking clamp. The crew braced for the moment the clamped locked on. They swayed slightly before the bustle began again. Daniel opened the hatches for the passengers to offload from the craft as he began to run his post flight procedures.

Everyone cleared the way for the medical team to expedite their patient to the auxiliary lift. Without pause Jackson jogged out of the hangar and headed for the main elevator, "Maggie...."

"Awaiting your arrival, commander," Maggie's mechanical voice preemptively answered. He gave her a nod as he stepped into the open doors. Promptly the doors closed as the lift began to ascend. He glanced down at his dirt-caked and blood-spattered visage with a shrug. Taking a deep breath to settle his frayed nerves, he straightened the lines of his uniform.

He confidently strode from the elevator toward the bridgehead. Three dark silhouettes stood across the railing above the Morgan's station watching, waiting. His steps drew their attention. The familiar faces of Admiral Khaivol and Captain Hadarian flanked another commanding presence. Stunning black ringlets framed her stern silvery gaze. Her rich cocoa skin made her uniform almost look regal. She opened her mouth to speak as he approached.

He tilted his head in a gracious nod, "You have questions. If you would please follow me to a conference room. I will be happy to answer all. Sirs, this way." He turned on his heel and led them back down through the halls toward the conference wing where he had originally been given his role aboard this ship alongside Kensy.

His thoughts drifted to her for a moment. He wanted nothing more than to be beside her now. He pushed the thought aside. *No, I can do more for her here.* As the door before him swooshed open, he stepped back and held his arm out to invite his superiors in to the room beyond.

They circled the main table, but no one sat. Admiral Khaivol cleared his throat to cut the tension. "Thank you, commander." Gesturing toward Jackson's former captain the admiral spoke. "You of course already know Captain Hadarian," his attention shifted, "but I would like to introduce you to the Admiral of Intergalactic Affairs, Aiaka Davir. Admiral Davir this is—."

"Commander Jackson Gabel," she interrupted. "You certainly do present an interesting first impression, commander." She raised her chin.

"I believed you would not appreciate being kept waiting for any longer than necessary." Jackson took a wider stance, stuffing his restless hands in his pockets. "In the spirit of being transparent... my fellow captain, Psilyria Frost, was attacked and separated from the company shortly after our arrival. The situation escalated quickly. We enlisted local assistance, extracted her, and returned to the ship."

Concern crossed Admiral Khaivol's face, "Attacked? Explain."

Jackson's mind flashed back to the moment the barriers sprung into being between himself and Kensy. He felt the heat of his rage as he recalled her attacker, "A civilian set an ambush on one of the egress platforms. Using the emergency barriers, he separated her and assailed the Psilyria's person."

Admiral Davir strummed her fingertips against the top edge of the chair in front of her, "I received no such report upon your arrival."

Jackson shifted intermittently, "Not knowing the motivations or parties involved I opted to investigate further before reporting in."

Captain Hadarian interjected, "And what did your investigation turn up?"

Jackson locked his gaze with hers, "The Vagabond." The others exchanged furtive glances.

"The Vagabond, here?"

"How?"

"Why?"

The conference room door slid open to the presence of Nevan Nahlen's towering delrn form, "I believe I can answer a few of those questions." He held up a small vial of fine green nanite dust for the assembled humans to see. "It seems we have a great deal to discuss."

## Chapter 13

# Reflections & Realizations

*"The little moments sometimes weigh the most."*
*~ Medical Technician A. Moore*

The medical bay hummed with an intense energy as technicians and personnel scurried about with supplies and reports. The main traffic was focused around the primary operating room that branched off the left side wall. Jackson could feel the tension in the air as he wove between bustling crew. He approached the wall outside the room as it shifted into a virtual window for him. He watched Doctor Tyronis conduct the personnel around her with the efficiency only an expert ship's doctor could all the while actively tending to Kensy's wounds.

His mind harkened back to the first time he had ever seen Kensy. Her body lay before him among the corpses of her psicorp adepts and the civilians that had died in the initial attack on Bhelnir Prime. Her ruddy blonde hair was held in a disheveled ponytail, slaked in blood, and caked with rubble.

The skin of her right arm had been seared by plasma burns from her sundered control clasp. Her uniform was tattered and soiled by the viscous battle she had fought beyond the point of exhaustion. He remembered thinking her wiry voidir frame looked frail and weak as if it would break at the slightest touch. Still he reached for her neck, pressing his fingers to the side, feeling the pulse that gently beat against the pressure. Within the memory, the words that came out of his mouth melted into nothingness.

He surrendered to the pull of something unseen and unknown. He recalled carefully slipping his hands beneath her frame, letting her motionless figure fall against his chest. His memory shifted again. She smiled genuinely at him and danced lightly on her toes as she skipped ahead of him. It slowed as she lead him forward. His thoughts flashed between more of the soft moments they had shared and the broken and terrifying moments he feared losing her.

A hand brushed his sleeve, causing him to lurch in surprise. "Sorry, Commander." The young female tech waved her hand over the wall, turning it back to opaque. "Doc told me to have you checked out, make sure you didn't get wounded in the firefight."

He nodded as he collected his thoughts, "Yeah, right. Let's get this over with."

She pointed to an exam room across the main bay, "Head in and disrobe, I'll have someone come in to do your check momentarily." She took a few steps toward the office before glancing back to him. "As soon as Doc's done, we'll get you in there. It'll be okay." She forced a smile for him. Jackson tipped his head toward her for a moment, *The crew's worried too. Keep it together cap, they're looking to you.* He scoffed at himself and proceeded into the exam room.

The door whooshed closed behind him. Piece by piece he shed the layers of his uniform. His eyes lingered on the heap of lightly armored fabric on the exam table. Blood spattered the olive-green material and dulled the satiny black trim. Some of that blood was hers. It wasn't the first time her blood had gotten on his clothes, but every time he had hoped it would be the last.

Again his memory stole him away, he recalled their talk on the observation deck about the details of her file, and the loss of a friend. Then through her weakened smile, he felt for a moment as though he could see all the sadness that she had hoped to hide. She wavered before him. The flutter of her eyelashes caused his heart to leap into his throat again as he saw her collapse into his arms. He felt as helpless in that moment as he did right now.

Nevan was still in the conference room two decks above, steeped in conversation with the admirals. The Graven, the Ascension Navy, a whole galaxy of threats and all he could focus on was *her*, hoping... praying that he had been fast enough to save her. Even as the med tech entered the room, his attention was elsewhere. He answered the questioning, endured the poking and prodding at his bruises and minor scrapes with minimal effort. After the examination the tech lingered for a long moment, silently studying his expression. Nonchalantly the tech stared back down at his data pad. "...and then I told him, if you're going to have any future liaisons of that nature, you're gonna need to start buying stock in purple goo."

Jackson turned his head to glance incredulously at the man standing in the room with him. "What?"

The tech smiled, "Oh nothing, commander. Just making sure you're still with us." He finished his report before nodding at Jackson. "You're good to go. Maggie should have a clean change of clothes arriving for you any minute." He headed for the door, "You know, neither of them are gonna give up. Doc and the psilyria. Both have a habit of kicking the odds in the decimal point. I sure as hell ain't gonna bet against either one."

A slight chuckle escaped Jackson as a grin cracked across his concerned face. The door slid closed as his examiner departed, leaving him once again alone in the silence of the exam room. He allowed his mind to embrace the emptiness of the room around him.

He stared blankly at the wall until Maggie's familiar mechanical voice disturbed him, "Replacement uniform delivered. Please deposit the contaminated uniform in the delivery pod once the new uniform has been extracted." A panel formed and opened in the wall beside him. He reached for the capsule within. Twisting its ends apart he drew the clean clothes from it and replaced them with his soiled and saturated articles. He pressed the capsule back into the wall which promptly and seamlessly closed back up.

"Thank you, Maggie." He dressed quickly. With a deep breath he straightened the lines of his jacket and strolled out of the exam room. His eyes lingered on the far wall as he reluctantly left the medical bay. He stuffed his hands in his pockets then trudged down the hall toward the primary lift.

The doors slid open in anticipation of his arrival. He stepped in and glanced upward, "Deck three. If anyone needs me, I'll be in the war room."

"Right away, commander," the mechanical voice affirmed. The lights of the intervening floors flashed by, plunging him into another memory. He recalled an expeditious elevator ride through the many levels of his old ship, the Themiscyra. He recalled launching out of the doors as they opened and racing down the halls toward a maintenance tube in hopes that he could reach the exterior hatch in time. He felt every rung of the final ladder in his white knuckled grip, and the force of the hatch as the wind ripped it from his grasp.

He saw her standing there, unwavering, in the face of insurmountable odds. She was willing to place herself at risk for the chance to protect the rest of the ship from certain destruction. Moved by her determination, he stood with her. Once again, he could feel her delicate frame against him as he held her and anchored the both of them to the hull with his mag boots and tether. He felt the heat of her power envelop them. Then the blast came. The elevator dinged to announce his imminent arrival as the final floor flashed by.

He took a deep breath and curved out of the elevator doors, proceeding down the curve of the hall as it brought him to his intended destination, the war room's main entrance. The doors slid open for him and for the briefest moment he half expected to see her standing over the holotable sorting through data and evidence. He walked into the room slowly, his eyes tracing the familiar landscape.

In a daze he sat down on a nearby bench and dropped his head into his hands. He couldn't force her from his mind. Or was it that he didn't want to? The silence of the room bore down on him as he wrestled with his jumble of thoughts and feelings. The doors slid open again, causing him to straighten his posture in reflex.

The towering form of Nevan gazed at him with a scaled grin, "I do hope I'm not interrupting. I had been told I could find you here." He stepped forward and paused, "I can come back if this is a bad time."

Jackson shrugged, "Take a seat."

Nevan looked up toward the ceiling, "Maggie, my dear, consider this a conversation among Graven. We are not to be disturbed." The door latched closed behind him as he sauntered toward the bench beside Jackson.

"So, I take it you are the contact Neira intended to introduce us to."

Nevan reclined against the railing behind the bench, "Indeed. Though, seeing you in action does a great deal more for justifying why she recruited you as well as Psilyria Frost. I do wish it had been under more agreeable circumstances." He folded his clawed fingers together on his abdomen. "With our line of work that, unfortunately, is not a luxury we are likely to be granted."

"So what happens now?"

"Now," he sat up slightly, "now you and I have a modicum of small talk while I try to keep the wait from driving you mad."

Jackson raised an eyebrow toward Nevan, "I thought you had some dire Graven things to discuss with the whole...," gesturing toward the sealed door.

Nevan gave a brief chuckle, "Nah, that was just an excuse to give you a break." He studied Jackson's expression carefully, "We *can* talk about Graven stuff if you want. But that..., that is the look of a man in love and distressed."

Jackson blinked, "What?! No, I mean I like her... but...."

"A question then, can you count the number of minutes you have spent thinking about things *other than her* since the attack on one hand or two?"

"I...," Jackson looked down at his palms then pressed his face down into them, "Fuck."

Nevan patted his back, "It happens to everyone at some point... well, almost everyone. Not too sure what passes for affection with Whitakat sometimes..." his expression twisted, "correction, ever."

Letting his hands drop, Jackson sighed, "I'm going to have to get transferred."

"I wouldn't be too hasty with that." Nevan's tone shifted sternly, "From the reports I have received from our dear Miss Cross, your presence is very much needed right here alongside Psilyria Frost. This mission, as we have seen, takes its toll in unexpected ways. The two of you compliment and compensate for each other's weaknesses in a manner I would very much qualify as mission critical for ending this threat."

Jackson stood, pacing toward the central table. "Of all the stupid, idiotic... why did I have to fall in love *now*."

"Discovering feelings for another is rarely convenient but can be an excellent motivator." Nevan smirked, "I dare say though, you two are going to need a little more help along the way. I recommend expanding your crew with a wide variety of specialists and perspectives. And as a Graven commander I am uniquely qualified to provide you with the assets you need to achieve this." Jackson pivoted toward him attentively.

Nevan continued, "Marieke will go anywhere she can find a decent scrape. Whitakat has a penchant for finding his way into information he shouldn't have, not to mention, he owes me a small mountain of favors. My own skills are none too shabby and I believe the bubbly psimehna could be persuaded to sign on given her eagerness to assist the psilyria earlier. Think you can make room for a few more crew members? I could also help to make sure the heat of the Ascension's gaze falls more squarely on critical issues, and less on the interpersonal dynamics of her officers."

Jackson scowled pensively, "Seems like I'm getting more out of this arrangement than you."

"The colony attacks were a point of concern, although low priority, they seemed scattered and isolated to human jurisdiction. Which is why Miss Cross was assigned. However, the Vagabond's presence on Aepexia makes this everyone's concern, especially mine. I would like to see this threat ended before more people are put in danger."

"I get that," Jackson nodded. "Just because I'm morbidly curious, where is Cross? I half expected her to be back here berating me for some perceived failure or another."

Nevan pulled a datapad from his belt, "Right about now, she should be meeting with the squad that is going to apprehend Mordwell."

"Hmph, you must not want him alive then."

Nevan laughed, "Accounting for her tendencies is precisely why I assigned her an entire unit to corral. She won't let him get away, but they won't give her the time to put him in a body bag." His demeanor sombered, "All joking aside, she knows we need information out of him. She'll bring him in."

Jackson tilted his head and slouched back against the edge of the central table. "Either way, his day is about to get a whole lot worse."

### Chapter 14

# Elle

*"I'll always be here...."*
*~ Psionica Ellise Neru, deceased*

Kensy lifted her head as her eyes opened for the first time in what had felt like forever. She glanced at the corridor around her. The familiar smooth lines and soft floor of the deck seven hallway gently hummed with the ghostly visages of indistinguishable crewmen and woman bustling about. Kensy's heart sank. "I'm not out yet," she slouched back against the wall in defeat. Nexus curled around her ankles from behind.

"You are resting. I believed this environment would be more conducive to your recovery." His brilliant, glowing eyes gazed up at her. "Was my assessment of your memories incorrect?"

She smiled weakly, "No, I just wish I was *really* here... with the people I care about." Her voice trailed off toward the end as her thoughts drifted toward Jackson, Neira, Daniel and the other crew with whom she had grown familiar.

Nexus walked a few steps away. He turned his gaze back toward her, "Take a walk with me." Kensy pushed off the wall and fell in line behind him. Their path rounded two corners before proceeding into the medical bay. With the flick of his tail the wall separating the operating room from the main space faded away. Kensy watched as figures danced around her own motionless form. "They spent quite a few arduous hours doing their best to save you."

Kensy cast her eyes toward the ground, "So I've finally died then."

"Tsk, tsk," Nexus rebutted from the end of an adjacent medical bed. She turned her gaze and caught sight of her own form again. She was laid peacefully out across the surface, warm blankets and sheets tucked around her. Movement braces curled around her shoulders and across her forehead. A transparent hood covered her face over which a holographic graph steadily hummed along. "Such defeatism! As I said, you are resting. They have done what they can about the physical damage you had sustained, and recovery will take some time. However, the rest is up to you. Do you accept that this is the end, surrender to despair and throw all of their efforts to the cosmic winds? Or... do you reclaim yourself and come back stronger than before, forged into the instrument of your own destiny?"

Kensy thoughtfully looked at her sleeping self. "I'm sure you've seen, I have no destiny, no future. When the seers tugged at my thread of fate there was nothing but void. How am I even still here?"

Nexus gave an almost indignant shrug, "Hmph, with all you've seen of the galaxy, you still hold on to such silly superstitions." She looked at him curiously. "You cast off the shackles of your past by believing in the possibility of a future for one whom had already been condemned. Why hold now to a fatalistic belief for yourself? Discard it as you did before, and make your own destiny."

"He's right, you know," a sweet voice piped up from behind her. Kensy pivoted abruptly toward the voice, finding herself and her company among the verdant greenery and brilliant colors of a carefully sculpted atrium. Elle's silky black hair tumbled loosely beyond the shoulders of her sweeping deep blue dress.

Kensy gave her a pained look, "I'm sorry, I couldn't save you."

Elle smiled, "My fate is not your fault or responsibility." Elle reached up to smell one of the brightly colored blooms. "Hindsight being what it is, I certainly would have liked things to have turned out differently but...," her words caught in her throat, "You can't stop living your life because of me. I need you to live in *spite* of me." Elle sauntered toward her and clasped Kensy's hands, "You already saved me. I would have died alone in that capsule, adrift in space, if you hadn't been there. No matter what challenges you face moving forward, you have to remember that!"

A shadowy tinge crept up in Elle's eyes and at the edges of her face for a moment. She winced and fought back the unseen force that pulled at her. Kensy's face contorted with worry, "Elle?"

Slipping her hands away Elle smiled, "I will let you rest. No matter what lies ahead, don't let go." She smiled again and faded from Kensy's vision. Elle pulled herself back from the fringes of Kensy's consciousness. She uncurled her fingers, releasing her hold on that tenuous sliver of the outside world. The tethers that bound her exerted their oppressive weight upon her, drawing her back into her abyssal prison.

Elle opened her eyes and looked up at the encompassing cage. A harsh mechanical voice rang out, "Maekon internal asset detected. Awaiting confirmation...."

She glared toward the disembodied voice, "Yeah, I'm here you asinine bucket of bolts." She pulled her knees up and wrapped her arms tightly around them. "I'll always be here," she muttered quietly. "It's not as if there actually was any chance of escape." The whirl of electricity and grinding of gears echoed around the space, nearly drowning out her thoughts and whispers. She screamed over it all, "What do you want from me?!"

The sounds faded before the mechanical voice began again, "Target survival confirmed. Remote asset failure confirmed. Termination of remote asset authorized."

She shook her head, "Of course you want me to kill for you. You only ever want me to kill for you." Her jaw tightened, "But this one, ...this *one* I will do gladly." She stood and inhaled. Her silvery eyes closed. A nerve searing chord resonated through her senses. She opened her eyes, a sickly red-orange light glowed from between the mechanical irises.

Her head ratcheted around to face the direction of the remote asset as he entered his private abode cursing and fuming with every step. "Useless fools the whole lot of them. I almost had her!" He swung a hand at a nearby lamp, lifting from the side table on which it sat and shattering it into the opposite wall. A subtle flutter of a curtain startled him from his rage. He flicked his hand in a gesture that was intended to bring up the lights around him. No reaction. "Lights...." Nothing. Panic stirred in the back of his throat. "Hello?"

The darkly cloaked female form glided from the shadows before him. Her harsh mechanically warped voice called out, "The Vagabond does not abide failure." She drew back her hood that he might see her twisted visage.

His eyes widened. He fumbled for his words, "But... but... but. It's not possible. No, ...you're... you're dead." He stumbled backward, searching for an escape while his eyes remained locked on her scarred olive skin and tangled black hair. Chittering geometric arachnoid constructs crawled from the shadows and recesses of the room, closing off his retreat.

Heavy knocking resounded from the front door, "Vesok Mordwell, open up by order of the Aepexian Council Police!"

Her gaze slowly rocked toward the door and back to him. She narrowed her glare. Her voice came out a coarse, guttural whisper. "Scream." As he opened his mouth, she shot a hand toward him. Mechanical tendrils sprung forth from her fingertips, choking his scream. They coursed down his throat and pierced through his vital organs from within. The pounding at the door continued. His body crumpled in a pool of blood.

She cast the viscous fluid and tissue from her tendrils as she withdrew them. Turning away, she swept toward the balcony and pulled her hood down over her face. The constructs scoured the residence for any evidence of Vagabond's involvement, destroying it before dissolving into fine green dust that trickled out in curling tendrils in the wake of their master's avatar.

Outside the door, Neira nodded toward the lead officer. He gestured toward the entryway in response. Another stepped forward with a large breaching ring, affixing it to the door. Everyone in the hall bowed their heads away as it detonated with a flash and a muted concussion. The unit rushed into the main room fanning out in all directions to sweep the residence for threats. Neira and the main officer stepped over the threshold as shouts began to relay back the all clear.

The officer walked forward and crouched down, analyzing the gory mess before him. "Right," he stood again and glanced back over his shoulder, "Looks like you weren't the only person that wasn't exactly a big fan of his." He shrugged toward the heap of a man before him, "Any ideas on this?"

Neira glared at the corpse, "Visiri Analyze." Light from her eye patch traced over the environment as she slowly scanned the room. She zoomed in on traces of green around the edge of the patio access door. *Nanites*, hushed expletives rolled off her lips. She surveyed the penthouse view for the threat she knew lurked somewhere beyond. "Tell your superiors, Phantom One, escalation confirmed." The officer pulled a data pad from his belt. "Oh, and while you're at it, we're gonna need a nanite decontamination team on site immediately."

The officer pivoted back to face a number of his men. Circling his hand in the air, "Lock it down!" They immediately set to work isolating the residence.

Neira tilted her head down discretely. Her communicator subtly clicked to signal that the other end of the call had been received. The pause lingered for a long moment on both ends of the call before Neira spoke in a hushed tone. "We were too late. V's been here. The thread was cut."

Nevan's voice resonated back through her device, "Mordwell?"

She shot a brief glance back at the remains, "...is going to be hard to scrub out of the carpet."

"Hmm. Trail?"

She shook her head, "A trail of dust right off the balcony. I don't know what crap he's pulling out to disappear into thin air but I'm real sure I can't follow. Haven't quite mastered flight yet."

Nevan's voice curled into an amused smirk, "Didn't figure you for a slacker, Cross. Has the time away made you soft?"

Neira glared out the window, "You can take your 'soft' and stick it—."

"Ma'am," the voice cut her retort short. "Perimeter is set. Decontamination team eta two minutes." She waved the officer away.

She let slip a frustrated grumble, "I'm going to be here for a while. If you need me—."

"I'll get along just fine. Enjoy your quarantine!" He cheerfully disconnected. She rolled her eye, *He's enjoying being on the outside of this entirely too much.* She raised an eyebrow toward what remained of Vesok Mordwell. *Who's washed up now?* She smiled to herself and folded her arms across her chest. *Always knew you wouldn't amount to much more than a mess.*

Chapter 15

# Awake

*"With as much time as the commander's been spending in medbay this week, there has to be something going on between him and the psilyria. They're so cute together!"*
*~ Crewman T. Holloway*

Her eyelashes fluttered open as she took in the dull light of the room. The familiar sterile ceiling above felt cold but comfortable. A soft rustle a short distance away drew her attention. With a soft gaze, she watched Daniel removed a holopad from the hand of the sleeping figure in the chair beside her medical bed. He glanced toward her and smiled. Quietly, he circled the end of the bed to approach her far side. Keeping his voice low he inquired, "Feeling better?"

She nodded in affirmation. Opening her mouth to speak, she found her voice raspy and laborious to muster, "How long--?"

He put a hand up to interrupt her. "It's okay. It's been a week, and dare I say, there will be many faces happy to see you awake again," he shifted his eyes toward Jackson. "He comes down to read reports. No one bothers him when he's in here." He watched her tender expression fill with concern. "Don't worry too much. We make sure to send him food regularly." He suppressed a chuckle, "I would say this is one puppy you will have to take home with you but you kinda already did." He lifted his hands to gesture toward the ship around them.

She began to laugh, only to be seized by a coughing fit. The pressure in her chest pulsed with every hack. Jackson startled from his slumber, snapping his attention toward her, "Kensy!" He leapt to his feet. Seeing Daniel beside her, he straightened his posture and his uniform jacket as he composed himself.

Water from the pain welled up in the corners of Kensy's eyes. Daniel kept his voice calm and even, "Hey now, it wasn't that funny. Slow measured breaths." She focused on inhaling through her nose and exhaling a slow gentle breath over her trembling lips. "That's it. Nice and easy there." With a smirk his eyes darted between the pair, "I should let you two have a few minutes alone. I'll let Doc know you're awake." He bowed subtly, excusing himself from the room.

Jackson watched him go. As the door swished closed, he turned his eyes back to Kensy. He reached out, brushing a few stray strands of hair from her face, his touch lingering as he soaked in her beautiful sea-green eyes again. "You okay?"

"Yeah."

A soft smile cracked across his face, "It's good to have you back."

They basked in the moment, relishing each other's presence for several silent minutes before Kensy's mind flashed back to the instant that had started it all. Anxiety overwhelmed her as the feeling of being ripped away from him by the platform barrier echoed through her thoughts. She struggled to fight back the rampant emotions of the instant before everything went wrong; she tilted her head down. "Jack!" The tears poured from her eyes, "I'm so sorry! I—."

"Hey, hey, hey. No need for that."

"But—."

He crouched down to be in her line of sight and gazed up to into her water clouded eyes. His voice became firm and reassuring, "What happened back there, it's not your fault." He cupped her face with his hand again. "And he can't hurt you anymore. He can't hurt anyone anymore."

Her eyes searched his expression for an explanation. "But he—."

Jackson ran his hand down to her arm to lace his fingers through hers. "Let's just say he fell in with a bad crowd and they didn't take his screw up well." She relaxed back against the bed, trying to process the vague information. He squeezed her hand, "I promise, he can never hurt you again." He shifted to sit along the edge of the bed beside her, keeping his fingers laced with hers.

"I should have told you... warned you. I didn't believe he would try something so... brazen." She stared solemnly at their shared grasp.

His gaze was stern and steady. "Don't blame yourself. He might not have been so bold if he hadn't had outside help." She looked up at him questioningly. "The Vagabond." He set her hand down, covering it with his own. "You believed we've been spinning out, as you had put it, not making progress toward stopping the Vagabond but he felt threatened enough to weave his way into the shadows of Aepexia to strike at you, at *us*. We're getting closer and he knows it."

"How could he have gotten here without anyone noticing?"

Jackson folded his arms across his chest, "There were a few who noticed. We've been tracking down every whisper and trace of its infiltration. We haven't found its agent yet, but the unraveling of that thread is well under way. Let's just say, there has been no shortage of targets for Cross to direct her anger at in the last week." He sighed, "I'm pretty sure she'd dismantle this whole damn planet if Nevan let her off the leash."

"Nevan? As in Nevan of Aepexia Core Security, Neira's drinking buddy?"

"As in Nevan Nehlan, Graven Adjudicator." He watched her eyes go wide with the realization. "Have you met before?"

"Only in passing, years ago, a while after...." Her eyes darted toward the bracer covering her left forearm. "...after Alpha Bael. After she left the service." The holes in her memories of Neira's past began to fill with understanding. "He was the contact. He is the one who—." Kensy drew in a gasp only to be seized by another coughing fit.

He stood and braced himself against the side rail of the medical bed. "Easy now." She focused her breathing, fighting against the tightness in her lungs. He waited for her to relax back into a state of rest. "I have to ask," he hesitated, "how much do you remember after," he flexed his fingers, recalling the feeling of the shock he received, "...after you began running."

Her eyes darted back and forth as she tried to search for the memories, "I... it was cold, wet. I was so scared. There was this haze, it filled my thoughts. Then there was this overwhelming anger, I can't remember why. Then pain, so much pain." She lifted her eyes to catch a glimpse of Nexus' electric form sitting upright at her feet staring back at her. "And tired.... Sorry, it doesn't make any sense. It's just fragments, flashes." She looked up toward him.

He straightened his posture, "I honestly didn't expect much more." Relief swelled within him. Perhaps she would be free of any memories of the encounter in the lower platforms. "Mordwell, had drugged you. Doc mentioned that it may have clouded or even inhibited your ability to form short-term memories for the time it was in your system. Either way, you don't need to worry about that anymore. All that matters is you're safe now."

"Indeed, safe and recovering." A warm maternal voice spoke up from the doorway. Jackson pivoted backward to allow Kensy to see Doctor Tyronis standing in the doorway. "I'm sure you have lots of questions, which we will answer in time. But there's no rush. Now why don't we have a look at you?" Doc approached the foot of the bed, unaware of the spectral feline observing the room.

A realization occurred to Jackson, and he turned to inspect the area around the chair he had dozed in, "And I should go find Bryden and my datapad. I'll leave you to it." He nodded to both of them and bowed out of the room. Turning the corner as he exited the medical bay, Jackson felt the dull tap of his datapad against his chest. He glanced to the side to see the hand that held it.

Daniel pushed off the wall, "Figured you were about to come looking for this."

Jackson snatched the holopad from his first mate's hand, "Thanks." They began down the hall toward the elevator in equal stride.

Daniel raised an eyebrow toward him, "You're going to have to come up with a new excuse to linger in there now that she's awake."

Jackson cleared his throat, "I'm sure I have no idea what you are going on about. The relationship between myself and my fellow captain is strictly professional."

"Oh, of course, sir." They stepped into the waiting lift. "Strategic deck?" Jackson nodded in confirmation. The door closed, and the elevator began its ascent. A smile curled around Daniel's lips. "You should take some downtime while we're in port. Get out, see some of the sights. You've been working hard on tracking down the security leaks. I'm pretty sure the Aepexian Guard and Graven can take it from here." With a soft ding, the doors slid open once again for the men to disembark. "I heard a rumor there was a cute little wyrran analyst at the hub that was eyeing you last time you stopped in to speak with Nevan."

"Not interested," Jackson grunted. He stared down at the information streaming across the holographic screen in his hands.

They strolled into the low light of the war room. Daniel shrugged, "It was just a thought."

"Think quieter."

"Listen," Daniel leaned back on the table, crossing his ankles as he relaxed, "we're down to a skeleton crew with minimal need for oversight. Take a little shore leave for yourself. After all, we wouldn't want our illustrious captain to get burnt out before we get back on mission." He crossed his arms as he watched his captain.

Jackson quietly groaned, giving him a suspicious sidelong glance. "You're not going to let this go, are you?" Daniel grinned at him. "Fine," Jackson sighed in resignation, "I'll go sightseeing... tomorrow."

Daniel reached out tapping Jackson's shoulder with the side of his fist. "The fresh air will do you good. Now, was there anything you needed of me?"

Jackson entered his access code into the console's interface. "Solitude."

"Yes, sir." Daniel snapped to attention with a slight tip of his head, before pivoting away. Approaching the door, he slowed his steps, "One last thing... just in case it needs to be said, everyone on this ship knows and supports the partnership you've been building with the Psilyria. If you ever need someone to talk to—." Jackson shot a scowl at him. Daniel threw his hands up in surrender as he backed out the door with a smirk, leaving Jackson alone in the dimly lit room.

"Privacy mode, Maggie. I don't want to be disturbed unless the universe is imminently ending." His thoughts drifted to Kensy. A heat spread through his chest as he recalled staring into her glistening sea-green eyes again. Jackson shook his head, *I'm so screwed. Ugh. Getting all dopey over her isn't getting me anywhere. Focus, find the Vagabond's agent. That's the best thing you can do to keep her safe.* He breathed deeply to draw his attention back to the data at hand.

Chapter 16

# Negotiations

*"Getting back to 'normal' is never easy."*
*~ Ambassador L. Twing*

Kensy slowly eased herself out of her own bed. The soreness was still there, along with the tightness in her chest. She focused on the sensations. *You're fine. Doc said there would some stiffness, but everything's healed up. Measured breaths, just like we practiced....* She fought to draw a deep breath and carefully exhale. *See? We're fine. We're fine.* Kensy stood. *Ooof, lightheaded but fine.*

She glanced at the time on a nearby display, "Really? That late already? Maggie, why didn't you wake me?" Kensy began her usual morning routine.

"Doctor Wynn Tyronis placed a system order to suppress any and all notifications for you. Commander Jackson Gabel signed off on the order. Your official status is marked as light duty with a rest order attached."

"I should have known," Kensy mumbled. "Can I at least have my person alarm clock back?"

"Until rest restriction is removed, request cannot be fulfilled."

She finished readying herself in silence, calculating every movement and assessing what she felt as she moved about her quarters. Her fingers fastened the last piece of her newly repaired uniform. She turned her eyes up toward the mirror as she ran her palms down the bodice to smooth out any errant

93

wrinkles. A half chuckle escaped her lips, *...almost as if it never happened. Just like before.* She lifted her chin. *But nothing like before.*

Kensy gripped her left arm above the bracer, "Maggie, what's the status of my implant?"

"Scanning... device integrity maintained. Stasis field active. Viral entity remains in a dormant state." Her grip relaxed as she exhaled slowly. *At least there's that.* She turned away from the mirror.

The image of Mordwell's smug grin intruded on her mind for a brief moment. *He's dead. You're not.* Her mind flashed through a dizzying flurry of near-death moments. *...again.* She glanced up at nothing. *I'm not sure why you haven't taken me yet, but if you're listening...* memories of her moments with Jackson flooded her thoughts... *thank you.* She closed her eyes and whispered, "Please, just give me a little bit longer."

A crackle of violet energy drew her gaze as her eyes opened, "I do find it quite interesting that humans talk to themselves audibly, when your thoughts are already so loud."

"I was talking to the universe, if it's listening." Kensy tilted her head to the side, "Though sometimes I suppose it helps to hear a voice, even if it is just our own." She shrugged heedlessly, causing a surge of soreness to radiate from her chest muscles. She rubbed at the area of reconstructed flesh and walked toward the door. "I should probably head down and see if there's anything I can work on. I'm gonna go stir crazy if I don't do something normal."

She walked toward the elevator with a brief glance back toward Nexus. He lingered for a moment before following, "That does indeed make sense with what I've observed from your neural processing." Her private quarter's door slid closed a moment after her spectral feline companion had passed the threshold. Kensy stared at her room door suspiciously, *did it just wait for him? Can the ship sense his presence?* The elevator dinged, disrupting her thought process.

Kensy stepped in alone, shaking the ridiculous notion from her mind. "Strategic Deck." The lift descended smoothly to is destination. The doors slid open, and she strolled in the direction of the war room's main entry. "There has to be something I can work on—." A wave of dizziness slammed into Kensy, jarring her steps. She blinked, and it faded as quickly as it had arisen. She pulled her hand back from the wall where she had braced herself out of instinct. "Okay, probably still feeling some aftereffects of... everything." She furtively glanced about at the empty halls and breathed a sigh of relief. "Right."

She resumed walking into the dimly lit ambiance of the familiar planning room. Slouching into a seat at one of the peripheral consoles, she began tapping through the mundane work logs looking for anything of interest. A dull silence set in, amplifying the tedium of her task.

With a whoosh the war room door slid open and quickened steps hurried into the room. Kensy looked up in confusion. There stood an energetic figure of a wyrran woman in a psicorp uniform. Her crystalline eyes made a hurried glance about the room, searching. Kensy stood, "Hello. May I help you?"

The figure snapped around to face Kensy. She dipped her head down in a salutatory nod. As she spoke her words tumbled from her mouth like a chittering chipmunk. "Psilyria, ma'am! I have a request, ma'am, if you have a moment, ma'am."

Kensy smiled, "I have many moments available as of right now. We can have a chat, though you may need to slow down for me just a bit, Miss...?"

"Right, right, right." She cleared her throat and focused arduously on speaking more slowly. "Psimehna Gabrianna Ciphar, at your service, ma'am. Most people just call me Gabby. I...," she fidgeted nervously, "I was part of the team that found you. Well actually first, I heard that you would be coming for the awards thingy. And then I was going to try to meet you at the docks. And then stuff was weird so I couldn't get to the docks. And then I saw...," her voice sped up ask she rambled on. Kensy gave her a pained smile. Pulling back to the moment, Gabby abruptly blurted out, "I was hoping to get a chance to ask you a question."

Waving her over, Kensy sat down and patted the open bench. "Take a seat." Gabby hesitantly sat down. Kensy slouched back against the wall behind and crossed her legs at the knee. Her neatly folded hands rested in her lap. "First off, thank you. I was told there had been a member of Psicorp who had volunteered to assist in my rescue. I owe you more than simple gratitude, so what question can I answer for you?"

Gabby straightened her posture. "I would like to join your crew." She shook her head, "May I join your crew?" Before Kensy could reply, Gabby's excitement burst forth once again. "I've heard so many stories about you. You're basically a legend. And all I've ever wanted is to be like you, and to study under you, and to meet you, and not in that order. And there are all these rumors about all this big stuff going on but no one's saying anything. But now there's all this other stuff that happened, and...," she took a breath, "and I just really want to help."

Kensy smiled sorrowfully, casting her eyes down toward her hands. "I can appreciate the desire to help...."

"Please," Gabby pleaded, "Whatever is going on, ...I know it's scary stuff, but I know it won't go away by closing my eyes. After everything I saw, after what happened to you...," a look of pure determination met with Kensy's concern, "I *need* to help."

Kensy nodded, *yes*. Gabby squealed. "I'm not doing you any favors by accepting this request." Gabby stifled her excitement and nodded in understanding. Kensy acquiesced, "But it will be nice to have another psionic aboard the ship." Gabby leapt up from her seat, "I'll submit the transfer request right away. I'll take care of everything. Thank you, thank you, thank you! You won't regret this!" She bounded from the room exuberantly.

"I just hope you don't come to regret it," Kensy mumbled.

"Regret isn't the worst possible outcome," a commanding female voice rose from behind Kensy. She turned her attention toward the auxiliary war room door. There stood the dignified silhouette of a woman adorned in the trapping of a naval admiral. "One can only regret if they survive long enough to reflect on their circumstance."

Kensy gave a salutatory nod, "Admiral...?"

"Aiaka Davir, Admiral of Intergalactic Affairs. And you are Psilyria Kensington Frost." Her ebony ringlets danced around her face as she gracefully descended the few steps toward the center of the room. "Now that introductions are out of the way, let's have a chat."

"Of course. I'm not sure where he is right now, but if you would like I can summon Commander Gabel." Kensy hesitantly shifted toward the planning table.

The admiral raised a hand dismissively, "No need. I'm here to meet the woman all the fuss was about."

Kensy felt her scrutinizing stare, analyzing her every gesture. "I am sorry for that."

Folding her arms across her chest, Admiral Davir raised her chin, "Do you make it a habit of apologizing every time you are ambushed? Or were circumstances different from what I had been led to believe?"

Kensy cast her eyes toward the ground. "No, it was definitely an ambush. I just should have been more alert to the environment. I should have—."

"What's done is done." Admiral Davir approached the war room table, "Seems to me like you lived long enough to form a regret."

Kensy scoffed, "Yeah, I guess I did."

"Good, now get over it." Kensy turned a startled glance toward her. The intensity and earnestness of the admiral's stare met her gaze. "Learn from it and do better, by yourself, by your crew. You are in command of a warship of the Terra Ascension Core Navy. There is no room for you dwell on mistakes that cannot be changed."

Kensy drew in a cautious breath, then steeled her resolve and nodded, "Of course." A thought occurred to Kensy, "Admiral, if I may... what happened with the awards ceremony?"

"It went according to schedule. Your fellow captain attended and accepted your medal on your behalf while you were unfortunately detained by *negotiations* that ran longer than expected." She smirked.

Kensy looked at her questioningly, "Oh, I will have to thank him for attending in my place."

"It was as tedious, as expected." The admiral dryly sniped. "However, in light of your accomplishments with the negotiations, I would like to extend a slightly different invitation. The Aepexian Assembly diplomatic ball is being held in a few days. It will be attended by dignitaries from close to a dozen different species and more than twice as many factions. This is easily the highest profile and highest *security* function Aepexia is host to, with the Graven helping to oversee the event.

"You and your fellow officers of the DeCadejra are slated to attend. This will be paramount to maintaining your cover, having just finished diplomatic negotiations with the krith." The admiral pulled a holopad clip from her belt, "I am forwarding the negotiation notes to you for review." She paused, "This is a black-tie affair. Make sure to dress appropriately. I would perhaps even encourage you to pick out some civilian formal wear. You will seem more inconspicuous among the garrulous pageantry."

Kensy smiled to herself at the admiral's derisive commentary, "Thank you."

Clipping her holopad back on her belt, she refolded her arms across her chest, "Make my efforts worthwhile. The Vagabond infiltrated my dominion by coming to Aepexia. After all the fanfare is done, I expect you to root out this cancer so it might be excised."

Kensy straightened her posture, "Yes, ma'am!" They shared a quiet moment, soaking in the weight of what was next to come.

## Chapter 17

# A Fool's Errand

*"And guess who the fool running it is...."*
*~ Commander Jackson Gabel*

The Aepexian streets hummed with life from all across known space. Malckiev traders chittered furiously over salvage and strange baubles with a creature that appeared as a concentrated cluster of ribbon-like helices. A hulking zog lumbered alongside a well-armed delrn, both adorned in Aepexian Guard garb to denote their authority. Overhead bustling olhreleth flew about to and fro, traversing the air from dozens of different directions. The colors and sounds of the ever-churning crowds overflowed into the architecture and civic adornments.

Jackson looked past the chaos, scanning the crowds and structures for some sign of his target. He pulled back the sleeve of his armor lined jacket and glanced down at the monitor he had strapped to the inside of his wrist. The signal was still broadcasting. His target wasn't far now. He pulled his jacket sleeve back down as he navigated toward the far side of the market platform.

The closer he approached his target, the stronger the monitor's subtle vibrations grew. He pressed up close to a building and checked one more time, just to be sure. *It hasn't moved.* He glared at the monitor for a long moment. *It's definitely a trap. No way this thing lingers here in such an exposed space on accident.* His eyes scanned the crowds a short distance away. *So many civilians, and probably not one witness. Whatever it's using to navigate unseen must be somethin' else.*

He discretely pulled his pistol from the small of his back, checked it over, and tucked it back in place. Pulling his plasma shield handle from one of the large pockets in his heavy ballistic fabric cargo pants, he jostled it back and forth between his hands as he debated his next course of action.

*It's gotta be expecting someone to come looking for it. I'll go in quiet, see if I can get eyes on it. Even if I can't take it out by myself, knowing what we're looking for should make it easier to track.* He tightened his jaw. *This could go horribly wrong. You could walk in there and die and no one would be any wiser. Backup plan, you have to have a backup plan.*

His eyes fell on the edge of the monitor under his sleeve. *I could leave it on a delay burst. If I don't report back, they'll at least have a trail to follow.* He unfastened the wrist strap and began programming the broadcasting conditions. He glanced toward the nearby Aepexian Guard officers walking their rounds. *They wouldn't be properly prepared... Nevan. I'll have it broadcast to Nevan. He can coordinate a way to deal with this bullshit.* He set the timer, *five minutes. That should be plenty of time to sneak in check it out and get back if this ends up being nothing. Or... plenty of time to get yourself killed.* He scoffed at himself.

He checked the signal one last time. Glancing down the alley beside him, a shift in the shadows drew his attention. *I guess we're kicking this thing off now.* He activated the timer. Deftly sliding the monitor between conduits on the corner of the building, he slid his thumb over the handle controls to prime his shield.

Stalking cautiously into the shadows of the alleyway, he kept vigilant for any threat. He could feel the weight of his folded sword against his lower leg and the dull heat of his readied sidearm at his back. He slipped his free hand under his jacket, curling his fingers around the pistol's grip.

Crash! He snapped into a defensive stance, pistol in hand supported over his shield arm. He narrowed his eyes at the stack of ramshackle crates as they clattered to the ground along the right side of the alleyway. Silence settled back into the corridor. He exhaled a measured breath as he examined the scattered pieces. *Rotted wood, fucking boxes.* The low groan of a misaligned door further ahead redirected his attention.

One careful step at a time, he slinked toward the sound. Stale air rolled out the blackened opening of the doorway. He rolled his shoulder around the threshold, slipping into the interior shadows. He stopped. Clink. A pipe dropped further within. Echoes rippled through the air as it rolled lazily across the bare hardened floor.

His eyes adjusted to the darkness. He scrutinized every shadow for any additional shift or abnormality. Seeing no immediate signs of hostility, he crept toward the center of the room. He let out a slight huff, *probably a fool's errand. And guess who the fool running it is….*

A subtle whine rose behind him. He turned back in time to see the rickety door slam shut, sealing him in. His heart raced. He pivoted around, trying to see the entirety of his surroundings at all at once. A futile effort. It was too dark, too open. He gritted his teeth and activated his shield. A flash of light burst from the handle as the energized particles filled the titanium webbing and tiny scales which expanded into the shield face.

A painful buzz filled the air with an agonizing pressure. Jackson winced, fighting against the signal's bombardment. His grip on the shield faltered, his steps became jarring. He struggled to keep his eyes open through the disorientation. From the deepest shadows a tendril whipped out toward him, ripping the shield from his hand. He loosed a hail of shots into the darkness.

His breathing grew ragged as he fought through the intensifying signal that bore down upon him. He felt the shift of air beside him. In one quick move, he tucked backward into a roll, away from the source of movement, and faced the disturbance. From his crouched position, he reached across his body, unsheathing his folded sword with his off-hand. In one swift motion, he flicked his wrist to extend the blade.

The core shape across from him was smaller in stature than he expected, but several long tendrils extended from the cloaked figure in different directions. The signal distorted his vision causing the details of his assailant's form to elude him. She cast an arm out toward him and the tendrils shot forth.

Jackson leapt from his crouched position. The sweep of his sword redirected the attack to where he had been. He raised his pistol toward her. Another two quick shots. The impacts rung out as the projectiles struck the metallic plates that covered her central mass. She swept her extended appendages back toward him, wrapping around his left leg. From the other side, she unfurled another two tendrils to seize his right arm and thigh. Held by the coil around his left ankle, he struggled to shake her continuous bombardment of lashing blows.

She drew closer to him with an unsettling grace. Red energy crackled from the ground beneath her feet as she was lifted to his eye level by her mechanical limbs. The crimson lightning jittered up her body. She raised a hand toward him and for the briefest moment the glow illuminated her ghastly transformed visage. Hollow mechanical eyes stared back at him, and her ragged ebony hair fell over the extensively scarred flesh of her face.

As her power pooled in the palm of her hand, she reached out. Her fingers wrapped around his face. He screamed furiously as the energy coursed through him. He continued to fight against the crushing grip of her hand and tendrils.

Discordant tones erupted from her mouth at the edge of hearing. They pulsed through the whole of his body. The cascading pain wracked his mind for a moment before he felt his consciousness descend into darkness.

Jackson stumbled forward in a shapeless, blackened expanse. As he looked around, the darkness began to give way to towering pine trees, limitless blue sky, and crisp mountain air. His boots scraped across the wood of a well-worn dock. He looked out over the serene lake water with its gentle ripples. Releasing a defeated sigh, he placed his hands on the hips of his navy-colored denim pants. *Yep, fuck. Died.*

"Not quite yet," a female voice called out from behind him. He spun toward her. Her satiny black hair fell in a long tidy braid. Her silver eyes met his incredulous glance. She stood before him with a flawless olive complexion and a simple blue dress.

He narrowed his glare, "Then where are we?"

She raised an eyebrow, "I would think you would recognize your own memory." She looked back toward a humble cabin up the hill from them. "I don't know the place personally, but it is very peaceful." She turned back to him, "And it is the only place I could access that we could talk... privately."

"Elle, what are you doing in my head? Last time I saw you, you pushed Kensy and me into a nightmare where we were running for our lives."

She sauntered past him toward the far end of the pier, "Relax. If I was here to kill you, I wouldn't have armed you." She sat down with her legs dangling over the edge. The toes of her boots skimmed the lake's surface. She stared down at the darkness in her reflection, trying to drive it into the watery depths.

Jackson examined himself for the first time. Seeing his sidearm holstered on his hip and the shield handle tucked into the interior of his utility vest, he rolled up the sleeves on his flannel shirt. Crouching down adjacent to her, he eyed her with consternation. "Never mind the fact that you armed me in a *dream*, I'm going to ask again... why are you here?"

She blinked and looked away, "It's the only place we can't be found." Taking a deep breath, she shifted. Her right leg folded beneath her as she turned to face him. "I went to a lot of trouble to arrange this little talk."

"And what exactly do *we* need to talk about?" He dropped an anxious knee to the wooden slats to stabilize his stance.

Elle gave him a deadpan stare. "Kensy." He drew a sharp breath at the mention of her name. "You are going to need to keep a clear head if you want to save her. She's the only one with close to enough power to do what has to be done. But she's too emotional when she's by herself."

Jackson shook his head as he rose and began to pace away. "She's safe. I got her back. She's on the ship, recovering."

Elle hopped to her feet, shouting after him, "You think that's enough?!" He shot her a dagger like stare. "She's *still* chasing the Vagabond. Do you think he'll stop coming after her? Do you think she'll hesitate to put herself in harm's way if she thinks she can save someone?" She paused, "Do you even remember what I told you last time?"

Jackson's jaw tightened. He inhaled deeply and slowly, "Never let go. Ever."

Elle blinked away her fervor. Smiling softly, she shifted back on her heel. "Well at least you remembered that much." With an agonized gasp, she wrapped her arms tightly around herself.

"What's wrong?"

"Just slipping," she said dismissively. "Things are going to get *far* worse before the end." She cast her eyes toward the lake. "I don't even know if she *can* stop him." She gritted her teeth, "But... I *hope* she can... for all our sakes." Her silver eyes held a great sadness, similar to the weight he had glimpsed in Kensy dozens of times before.

The intensity of his gaze melted away. He pleaded, "Do you know *anything* that can actually help me? Help her?"

"Some truths along this road she's walking will hold the power to destroy her."

The image of his assailant flickered through his thoughts. The black hair, the pale olive skin, ...the eyes, those empty eyes... he shook his head to clear the sight from his mind. "She thinks you're dead."

Elle's melancholy pervaded through her smirk, "I am."

"Right...," he ran his fingers through his hair. His thoughts churned tumultuously as he tried to process everything.

She clamped a hand down on his arm. "Be her voice of reason. Be the shield that protects her, even from herself. And never—."

"Never let go. Ever." He nodded in affirmation "Yeah, I get it. But what does that even mean?" His eyes fell upon her white knuckled grip. He felt the pressure of her hold. "And...," he hesitated, "May I ask, what is happening to me... you know, out there? Right now." He gestured wildly at nothing.

She met his gaze, "Nothing you won't recover from." Elle winced as a pulse of darkness flashed across her features. She pushed back against the tethers, trying to bide just a few last moments. "It seems we'll have to cut this short." She forced her fingers to release his arm and slowly pulled her hand back. Taking a few faltering steps backward, she increased the distance between them.

"Elle?"

She staggered against some unseen force. Jackson's hand instinctively shifted to his sidearm. She gasped, "Oh, and if you ever break her heart, I *will haunt you*." Her form faded from view as she withdrew from the serenity of his lakeside memory. "Elle! Elle?" he shouted after her. Only the stillness of the memory echoed back to him. He paced around the secluded area, scanning for some sign of her. Nothing remained. A whimsical pair of sparrows flitted across the sky above him.

Feeling the weight of his solitude, his eyes traced the horizon for some way out of this strange space. With a heavy sigh he muttered to himself, "Great, fucking great. I'm having a near death experience and talking to Kensy's dead friends. I am legitimately losing my mind." He shook his head, "I am so screwed."

## Chapter 18

# To Find a Captain

*"The commander occasionally displays bouts of reasoning
free of conventional logic."*
*~ Doctor Micah Hirayama*

Nevan glanced down the hall toward a dark-haired woman waiting patiently, all the while tinkering with some small device in her hand. He gestured toward her, "I take it that is the researcher you were speaking of?"

Daniel glanced up from his datapad as they approached. "Ah, yes. Nevan Nahlen, I would like to introduce you to Doctor Micah Hirayama. She is the lead research and development scientist on board. She has actually been on the DeCadejra longer than any of the rest of us."

She smiled and reached a hand out to greet Nevan. He met her handshake with a nod. "Well, my experiences were certainly of a different quality while I was initially assigned to the ship," she shrugged. "You know, before becoming stationed aboard the ship."

Nevan gave a hearty laugh, "I can imagine. I heard about the ship's activation and all of the excitement that came along with it."

Micah tucked her device into the crook of her arm with her data pad. "Don't get me wrong, the experience has presented some unique challenges and opportunities." She began to lead the group further down the hall. "I spent the first few months just chasing down systems *we didn't even know we had,* right up until they turned on. Although I think we're pretty well settled now. Speaking of getting settled...," She pointed toward the far end of the hallway. "At Commander Gabel's request, I have arranged accommodations for you. While your room is the furthest out on the deck, it is also the most spacious."

Daniel tucked his hands in his pockets as he strolled alongside Nevan, "I have the mirror of it on the other side of the ship. And I gotta tell you, all of the exterior walls can become virtual windows, while we're traveling, you really can't beat the view."

"I look forward to seeing it for myself." The door opened in front of Nevan. "I know it's been a while since I've been on a ship for more than a passing cruise, but even still your ship certainly seems *unique*." Nevan smiled as he admired the flowing lines of the interior architecture.

"That she is," Micah assured him.

Nevan stretched to his full height effortlessly, "And the interior spaces are very accommodating for someone of taller stature."

Daniel glanced upward, "Yeah, I didn't remember the ceilings being so high, but you'll find the ship has a way of adjusting to accommodate, mostly when you're not looking."

"I do make every effort to provide a seamless transition when changes are required," a mechanical voice chimed in. "If you require any additional accommodations beyond what has been provided, please put in a request."

"And that is Maggie. She is the computer brain that handles pretty much everything we don't manually control," Daniel explained.

"Advanced complexity engine and tactical assistant, to be precise. If you need anything, Maggie can either get it or put in a requisition request." Micah explained, "Beyond that, she has also proven *invaluable* for assistance and analysis in the labs." Micah pulled her device forward again. "With the information we've been collecting on the Vagabond, Maggie here has assisted me with developing this signal detector. This should, in theory, have the capacity to detect any machine, down to a nanite, that's utilizing the vagabond's unique encryption signature. Though I haven't been able to test it in a practical situation as of yet."

Nevan raised a scaled eyebrow in her direction, "I'm sure an opportunity will arise with our current mission. Either way, it is an interesting and important first step in countering our adversary."

Micah held out the detector for Nevan to inspect. "I'm still trying to increase the potential scanning range. And I had been collaborating with one of the Aepexian engineering labs on a jammer based on this concept, but I heard last night the lab was broken into and a number of their prototypes were stolen, including the jammer." She huffed, "It is a frustrating development."

Nevan's lips pulled into a pensive expression, "I will look into it. Whether intentionally or incidentally, anyone stealing Vagabond focused prototypes has my attention." The datapad on his belt pulsed urgently.

Daniel nodded to Micah as, he watched Nevan pull the communicator forward to check his notification. "We should probably leave you to—."

"Not so fast." Nevan shot a glance to the lieutenant commander, "It seems you have a captain in need of assistance." Micah and Daniel closed in as Nevan passed over the device.

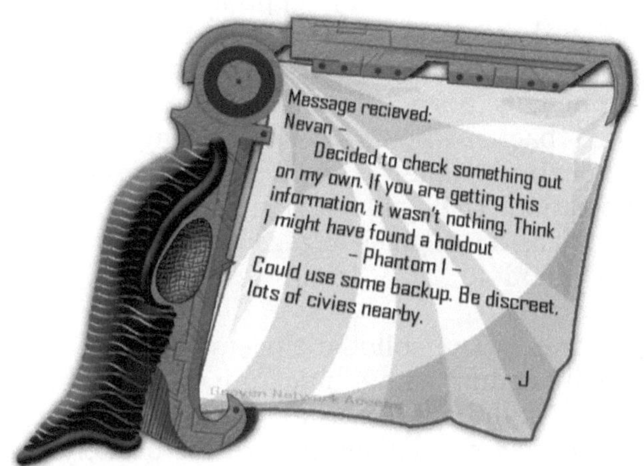


Daniel finished reading and shook his head, "Dammit, Jack!" He handed the device back and looked to Micah.

She pressed back toward the wall. "Go! I can hold down the fort here."

Nevan nodded, "I'm going to need your piloting skills." He tried to return her prototype, but she shoved his hand back, "No, take it. Go!"

Daniel pivoted with a nod of confirmation, "We'll grab Dagger One." Both men, human and delrn, broke into a run down the corridor. "It's a five-man transport, small, fast, sleek, well equipped and I can prep her for launch in less than two minutes."

Nevan smirked, "I'll get us clearance while you get us in the air."

Rushing to the elevator, they quickly descended to the eighth deck. Daniel navigated them a short distance down the hall. They turned into the upper level of the aft starboard hangar bay and Daniel slid down one of the catwalks toward a small craft hanging from the docking hooks.

The side door opened at his approach. He glided into the pilot's seat and began activating the transport's systems. Nevan ducked inside, curling his towering form to a more manageable height. "Sorry, probably a little cramped for you." Daniel called back without looking. "Hang on." The door slammed shut. Immediately, the docking clamp shifted out of its parked position. They glided toward the opening bay doors. The craft shook as the engines engaged.

"We are good to go," Nevan assured him. "Uploading coordinates and path."

"Roger that." The pilot's fingers danced across the controls, finally ending with a quick tap on a side button. The clamp released, and they were away. Dagger One danced along the specified trajectory, delving toward the densely populated market platform from which Jackson's signal had originated.

Nevan sifted through streams of data on his datapad. He zeroed in on the signal Jackson had followed. "I think whatever he found is still there."

Daniel brought up the shuttle's communications display. "Maggie? Do we have telemetry on Commander Gabel's nahdvi?"

"Signal is broadcasting; however, data being transmitted is scrambled due to local interference. Status of personnel is unknown."

Daniel began scanning for an acceptable landing point close to the destination, "I hope you can narrow things down with Gabel's data. Doesn't look like we'll be able to pinpoint him while whatever is scrambling his nahdvi is in play."

Nevan reached over Daniel's shoulder, "Set us down there. Gabel had it narrowed down to one building. His dead-man's signal is transmitting from that corner. I would suspect he's close by. Probably dropped his transmission device as close as he could to the source."

Daniel swung the transport around and lowered toward an open area street-side. "How do you figure?"

Nevan smiled, "Because it's what I would do."

"Fair enough." The vehicle jarred to a stop as the engines disengaged. "Right, let's go find a wayward captain." Together Daniel and Nevan secured the parked transport and disembarked on to the bustling thoroughfare.

As they moved toward the signal, a bystander's attention was drawn in their direction. Morgan watched the pair retrieve a small device from behind the building's pipe works. He studied the exchange of glances and noted as they discretely drew weapons. Curiosity gnawed at him, what were they up to?

A delicate hand tugged at his arm, "Come on, flyboy. We've got places to be." She giggled.

Morgan turned toward her with his ever-charming smile, "Tell you what, beautiful...," he kissed the back of her fingers. "I'm gonna step away for just a minute. You keep going, and when I catch up, I'm gonna sweep you off your feet with the most romantic night you've ever experienced." She pouted at him. He twirled her in a circle and dipped her into his arms. With a sly wink, he stood her back up, "More later, I promise."

She playfully pushed him, "Fine have it your way, but you're gonna have to make it up to me... all night long."

"Oh, you know it." He bowed away from her and slipped toward the alley Daniel and Nevan had disappeared into. He knelt down, pulling a compact sidearm from his ankle holster. Quietly, he slipped past the broken crates toward the open door into the adjacent building. Cautiously, he peered around the edge of the frame. Across the dark room he caught sight of a figure kneeling over a crumpled shape on the floor. "Bryden? Tell me that's you."

Daniel snapped around to the sound of the voice, "Threaux?! What the hell are you doing here?"

"Sacrificing my date to watch you suspiciously lurk down dark alleyways."

The warehouse lights flipped on, casting their sickly flickering light over the main space. Daniel looked up to the catwalks above, then shifted his attention back to the door. "Well then, make yourself useful and come help me." Morgan sauntered toward his XO.

"What—." The shape in front of Daniel became recognizable as Morgan closed in. "Gabel? What the hell happened?"

"Not sure yet. Keep an eye on him for a minute. I'm gonna go grab the field trauma kit from the transport. Nevan is doing a sweep. Just make sure nothing else happens to him before I get back."

"Yeah, man. I got it."

Daniel jogged out of the building. Morgan took up an uneasy stance, his head on a swivel. Every creak and groan of the building around him set his nerves on edge as he stood sentry over his captain. Nevan descended from a nearby stairwell a small crate in his arms, "Seems I've found our missing prototypes.... Ah, Lieutenant Threaux, I did not realize you would be joining us."

"Yeah, well neither did I. Bryden ran out to—."

"—grab the med kit from the transport." Daniel approached, a small hard case in hand. "Nevan, you still have Doctor Hirayama's detector thing? You should probably do a scan while I get these burns and cuts patched up."

Nevan pulled the device from a pocket. "Figure this out for me," he slapped it against Morgan's chest as he walked past. "I'm going to sort through these and see what's in here besides the jammer I just disabled."

"What is it?" he turned it over and over poking and twisting at anything on the device that might turn it on. "And what are we trying to detect?"

Daniel carefully removed Jackson's jacket and shifted him onto his back, resting the commander's head on the rolled-up jacket. Once the commander's limbs were straightened out, he did a quick medical scan over the commander's body to ascertain the extent of his injuries. "Let's see... he's got epistaxis, second degree electrical burns on the face, as well as dozens of superficial lacerations accompanied by bone bruising and hairline fractures in extremities." He read through the scanner's results. Morgan shifted a collar on the device and it activated, telescoping out into larger shape. He fussed with the now accessible buttons trying to operate the mechanism. Daniel glanced up at him, "Hmm? Oh, that. That's a Vagabond nanite detector, if it works."

"What?!"

"Fuck, you're loud." A low, raspy groan came from Jackson as his eyes began to flutter open. He tried to move but pain surged through his body.

Daniel dropped down beside him, placing a firm hand on his chest to still his movements. "Not so fast. You took a beating. Haven't had a chance to patch you up yet." Rifling through the medical kit, Daniel pulled a rolled bundle forward. He unfurled the heavy fabric to reveal a metallic lattice woven into the interior. He pressed the lattice against the skin of Jackson's right arm and wrapped the material around, sealing the sleeve closed. As the final contact connected it began to hum. A gentle tingle and soothing warmth passed though the damaged tissues and down to the bone.

Morgan fussed with the scanner nervously. "I thought this shit was getting rooted out by the locals. How... what the... why...," he struggled to collect his thoughts into a coherent question. The display on the detector shifted to the view in front of him. A line of light traced over Jackson and Daniel. "Finally, stupid...."

Jackson raised an eyebrow toward him, "Don't strain yourself, Threaux."

Daniel pulled a clean cloth and water bottle out. As he doused the fabric, he studied Jackson's weary expression. "Here. Clean your face up a little," he gestured to his nose and mouth area, "and then maybe you can tell us what the hell happened."

Jackson accepted the damp cloth with his free hand, wiping the blood from under his nose. "I wandered down the wrong alley...."

"Or the *right* one." Nevan eyed him knowingly.

The cold cloth felt good against his skin as he breathed deeply into it. Jackson acquiesced, "Yeah, not so accidentally. I was going on a hunch. Trying to find the *thing* that keeps slipping through the cracks. Thought if I could do a little recon maybe we could figure out what we're really up against. Maybe take it out. Make things a little safer—." He dropped the sentence abruptly as his thoughts turned to Kensy.

Glancing up from the kit in front of him, Daniel fished for answers, "And?"

Jackson stared at the bloodied cloth in his hand. His thoughts traced the lines of his assailant's face. "It was super dark in here. I couldn't see shit." He dropped his hand to rest on his chest. *If I tell them, they might assume I've been compromised. Hell, maybe I have been. Or nuts, probably nuts. They could just think I'm crazy. Hey yeah guys, the monster in the dark is Kensy's dead friend. Riiight. Yep, not dead yet but still screwed.* Daniel narrowed his gaze for a long moment.

"Hey, I'm not getting anything on this thing," Morgan interjected.

Daniel stood up, pulling the detector from Morgan's outstretched hand. With a few small adjustments, the display sorted the incoming data from the scan. Nothing. "Looks like you're clear. No nanites," he reported. He turned to Morgan, "Think you can handle doing an area sweep with this thing? Just to cover our bases."

"Yeah, whatever." Morgan snatched the detector back and began circling.

Nevan stepped away from the crate, re-approaching Jackson as Daniel went to work treating the burns around the edge of his face. "Could be that whoever stole this lot was trying to lure in an unsuspecting or desperate lab junkie and didn't expect you. You're sure you didn't see anything that could tell us who attacked you?"

Jackson let out a heavy breath. "I got hit from multiple different directions. Tried to fight back, but it was over pretty quickly." He tried to shift slightly with a pained grunt. "Not my finest moment. Maybe later I can recount it for you in all its horrible glory. Right now, I've got a killer headache."

Daniel gave an amused snort, "I bet. Seems like whoever it was, gave you a jolt. Luckily, you got away with very minor inflammation in your airways, according to the med scan." The contact on Jackson's arm wrap popped. "Looks like the lattice is done treating your arm fracture. Still gotta get your legs treated before we get you back on your feet. And we're gonna need to have Doctor Tyronis take a look at you when we get back to the ship."

"I'll get checked out, submit to whatever scans you want, but we don't need to cause a fuss about this." The commander pulled his arm up to unwrap the lattice. *Last thing I need is for Kensy to hear about this from anyone other than me. She'll tie herself in knots worrying. There's nothing she can do now, anyway. It's done and over with.* "Out of curiosity, did you find my shit?"

"We found your sidearm, sword and shield. They're a little worse for wear, might need some repairs. But you'll have to check your own pockets. Didn't know what all you had on you to begin with." Daniel shrugged. "We should probably at least let your co-captain—."

Jackson seized his arm and stared up at him, "No! Not one word!" Nevan, Daniel and Morgan exchanged furtive glances. Jackson's steely glare fell on each of them, *"Not one word."*

## Chapter 19

# Recall & Recovery

*"Wait, wait, wait."*
*~ Psimehna Gabrianna Ciphar*

Kensy strode toward the center of the center of the psionic lab's testing floor flexing her fingers. She closed her eyes and drew in a deep breath to calm her muddled thoughts. "I crossed the footbridge." She pushed her hands out in front of her slowly. Snapping into an about-face, "and was caught off guard by the barrier activating. I took a step back." She shifted back on one heel. Her breath caught as she tried to push past the memory of Mordwell's assault.

"Keep going. What did you try to do next?" Nexus gently coached her.

She swept her right arm in a circle and released a small burst of energy from her hand, "I tired to push him away. But," she pulled her arms in grabbing her clasp with her other hand. "...he disrupted the manifestation." Roaring with frustration, she let loose a stronger wave of energy, tossing the floor tiles into disarray. After a moment they righted themselves again. "And then everything starts becoming hazy."

Nexus tilted his head in thought, "The memories seem to cause you emotional anguish. Why does it seem so important for you to recall?"

"I feel like I'm missing something important. I know I hurt Jackson. I think I ran away, I mean I had to have. Then I remember our discussion in medbay; before I woke up." She wrapped herself in a familiar shell of energy. "The rest is flashes, images and emotions that make no sense, all jumbled together. I evidently got shot and I don't how or why." She ran her fingers over the healing exit wound just below her collarbone. "But I can still feel the pain." The wrapped energy dissolved away as she looked to Nexus. "I don't know how to deal with something I can't remember. And I can't have whatever memories are loose in there springing up in the middle of a mission where I could get someone killed by an emotional crisis on my part." She paced in a circle. "No, better to dig it up and deal with it now, while the worst thing I have to worry about is picking out a dress."

"Perhaps so. *Or* perhaps your focus should be directed more on the completion of your current recovery, rather than generating more turmoil to then recover from."

Kensy stopped and stared at him. "Doc's done all she can for my physical recovery. Time is the only thing that can help that now... unless you know something I don't." The lab doors opened on the far side of the room.

"My observations have shown me that your kind can manifest emotional stress in physical forms. It might not be advantageous to the continuation of your physical recovery to complicate the situation," Nexus reasoned.

As Jackson walked into the room he spied Kensy on the testing floor, her eyes trained on something off to the left side of the space. "I am not complicating things! Everyone is so focused on making sure I have *no* stress...." She caught sight of Jackson and sighed. "We can continue to debate this later."

He furrowed his brow trying to figure out what or who she was speaking to. The memories of his encounter with Nexus on Galliane resurfaced. "You're talking to the weird ass cat thing again, aren't you?"

"Yeah, the Nexus." She feigned a carefree smile for a moment. As they closed the distance toward each other, she noticed the reddened patches of skin on his face and the slight limp in his gait. Concern filled her expression. "Jack? What happened? Why are you limping?!"

He focused on correcting his stride for the last few steps. "Before we get into that, know that I'm fine. Doc checked me over, it's just a few bumps and scrapes. Nothing to worry over."

She scowled at him, "Prefacing your story with that just makes me worry more."

He pulled her in caressing his hands down the back of her arms. "I'm fine. I promise." He kissed her forehead. "I went sightseeing, took a bad turn and ended up stumbling into a bit of a mess. I was seemingly mugged." Alarm flooded into her eyes. As she opened her mouth to respond, he continued. "They didn't get anything. I just got knocked around a bit. I'm fine!" He brushed her bangs out of her face. "Your glittering pillar of civilization has some not so shiny spots in the mix. Next time I'll opt for the guided tour," he jested.

Kensy looked down at her hands that rested in the center of his chest. "We just can't seem to win, can we?"

"I'm more worried about that conversation I walked in on. What was that all about?"

Kensy shook her head. She turned out of his arms, shooting a fleeting glance at her ethereal companion. "I've been trying to remember what happened after I was attacked. I have bits and pieces but nothing that makes any kind of sense." A knot formed in his chest as he recalled sights of the bloody square on the lower platforms. *Some truths along this road she's walking will hold the power to destroy her.* Elle's voice echoed in his mind. "I don't think you should fight it." Kensy turned a questioning gaze toward him. He took her hand in his. "Listen, Doc said the drug might have scrambled things or even kept you from making the memories in the first place. There might not be anything there for you to remember." He hesitated, "Please don't tie yourself in knots over this. If there was anything *worth* remembering, I would tell you." He pulled her back to himself and wrapped his arms around her. *Please, just forget. Please.*

Kensy melted into his embrace. *He's hiding something.* She nuzzled her face into his shirt. *I need to trust him. He wouldn't keep secrets from me if it wasn't important. She sighed. Besides, it's not like I can give him crap for keeping secrets, not when I have so many.* She looked up into his eyes. *I promise, someday I will tell you everything.*

Jackson leaned down toward her, cupping her face in his hand. Her hands slid across the fabric of his shirt and she rose up onto her toes. Their lips came together in a soft, sweet kiss. Nexus silently slipped out of the room into the hall, leaving the pair alone in the solitude of the psionics lab.

He strode toward the center of the hallway, watching as a new crew member walked toward him, lost in her own thoughts. His energetic form caught the edge of Gabby's peripheral vision and she took a startled step backward. She looked around and back to Nexus questioningly. "Umm...."

"Very interesting," he noted in amusement. "I see we have acquired another aboard the ship that is capable of perceiving my form. I believe that makes you the third. Hmm, I suppose the commander makes four, but I don't believe that counts as that was only temporary." He curled his tail around his dagger like feet lazily.

"What... *are*... you?" She examined the strange alien creature.

He nodded his head in acknowledgment, "Of course, pardon my manners. I am the Nexus, the conduit through which all psionic energy in the universe flows. I am from the calm beyond the veil, given physical form by a bond forged by a mortal being." He looked her over, "And you are a psionic, of considerable potential. It is good to see one of your kind has developed the ability to the measure you have. There are not many who have tapped into that particular talent."

"You mean among wyrrans? No," her power flashed in her crystalline irises, "I am considered an aberration among my own people. Dangerous and unpredictable."

"That is unfortunate given your natural potential. I look forward to our future interactions." He nodded toward her respectfully.

She smiled tentatively, "Thank you?" She reviewed the conversation in her mind as she tried to process the being speaking to her.

"I would, for now, recommend you come back to the laboratory at another time." Nexus turned to look at the wall. "The captains are having a quite moment. And their conversation should not be disturbed, quite yet."

"Wait, wait, wait. You said earlier I was the third person on board to be able to see you, and the commander *didn't* count...." Gabby ran through what she had been told of the crew. "Who...?"

"It was delightful speaking with you, but I must retire for now." Nexus walked around her vanishing as he passed.

"Wait...." She realized he was gone and dropped her hands to her hips with a huff. She looked back and forth between the lab door and the hall behind her. "What the hell?" Confusion overwhelmed her, "Hi, I'm Gabby by the way. Three? What three?" She shook her head and turned away from the lab to return to her quarters.

Chapter 20

# Swept Away

*"They would be picture perfect if only the commander
could pick his jaw up off the ground."*
*~ Chief Engineer Allen Petroski*

The tips of Kensy's delicate fingers pressed against the ridges of her shooting star pendant as she ran it back and forth along its champagne color chain. Her thoughts drifted listlessly while she waited for her pending meeting. Her strawberry blond hair fell in cascading curls, pinned into place with elegant pearl and crystal accents that matched the adornments of her sea-green gown.

"Psilyria Frost," a purring voice stirred her attention. Kensy spun around to face the krith diplomat who called to her. The diplomat stood upright with a gracefully tall almost feline shaped body. Their lean form and softly furred skin was draped in elaborate layers of complex patterns and textures. Intricate jewelry chimed musically as they approached.

"Lynxirah Amasha, it is good to meet you...." Kensy smiled as she caught herself, "again."

"Of course." As Amasha bowed their head in acknowledgment, Kensy noted the beautiful feathers that made up the lynxirah's colorful mane, the tips of which seemed to bend ever so slightly upward with the gesture. "But please, no need for titles. Just Amasha will do. After all, we have been steeped in negotiations for many days."

Kensy smiled grateful for Amasha's eager disposition toward the fastidiously crafted cover scenario. "Same, please just Kensy." She indicated herself. "I do hope the joint exploration and colonization efforts born of our arrangement will be a great boon to both our peoples."

Amasha held out an arm toward Kensy. She curtsied and placed her arm over theirs. Together, the pair walked down the lavish corridor. "I have no doubt that it will be challenging, mayhap even a bit daunting, but rewarding for everyone involved. Just think, if we are capable of establishing a viable colonization process for rogue planets and other extrasolar bodies the kinds of opportunities that could present." They continued down the hall between the lines of meticulously dressed guards, as they proceeded toward the main ballroom.

"Truly." Kensy smiled. "I can't emphasize enough, thank *you*."

Amasha patted Kensy's hand gently, "I know circumstances were not ideal, but this gave me the opportunity to get my proposal pushed through, to gain the assistance I needed. So thank you."

"I must say, Amasha, you look magnificent tonight."

"And you my dear, look positively radiant." As they reached the grand doors, Amasha held up a hand toward the main room. "Now, shall we bless the other attendees with the pleasure of our company?"

Kensy chuckled and nodded, "Absolutely." Her eyes looked out over the crowd of elaborately adorned guests, searching for one very particular face.

Jackson stood rigidly among his fellow officers. Daniel leaned over to him, "You could *pretend* to be enjoying yourself."

Jackson shrugged, "What good would that do? Someone could get the idea that I might be able to hold a conversation. No. I'm perfectly good being avoided. Not socializing, not dancing, not—." His words stopped in his throat as he saw her for the first time.

Kensy stood atop the ballroom stairs, poised and glittering in the soft golden light of the venue. Swags of shimmering sea-green fabric ran up her body and around her neck, creating a plunging neckline and covering over the latest of her scars before wrapping down her right arm and terminating in a flowing sleeve that covered her control clasp. The bodice of her dress hugged the gentle curves of her lithe voidir frame. It melded into another swag of fabric that gathered at her left hip. From there it flowed down into a gently fluttering skirt that swept against the floor around her. The pearl and crystal beaded accents glimmered with the most subtle of her movements. The shimmer of her skin seemed especially ethereal in this light and her curls danced lightly around her face.

Without thinking, Jackson straightened the lines of his crisp dress uniform and began to walk in her direction. "Not finishing your sentences." Daniel turned his gaze to see what had drawn his attention and grinned knowingly. "Well, we've lost him now."

"And rightly so," Allen nodded.

Their laughter faded away as Jackson shifted through the churning crowd. He stepped clear, approaching the stairs where she descended toward him. Her brilliant sea-green eyes were made even more vibrant by her dress and delicate makeup. She bashfully dipped her head and blushed as he stared at her.

Butterflies filled her chest as her eyes traveled up his body from his impeccably shined shoes, up the lines of his crisply pressed slacks to the dapper navy colored jacket with its satin black and silver trimmings. Jackson's usually disheveled hair was immaculately combed into place. His intense blue eyes fixated on her demure expression. He studied the shine on her lips and the delicate flutter of her eyelashes.

Kensy stepped closer. Her heart pounded in her chest. Giddily she whispered, "Jack, please, you're staring."

The fabric cascading down her right arm rippled with his soft touch. "I'm sorry. You're just...." His words caught in his throat. There were no words he could find that would do her justice right now. He glanced about trying to regain his composure. "Would you care to dance?" He held a gloved hand out toward her with a bow.

She placed her fingers against his palm and looked into his eyes. "I would love to, Commander." He gave her hand a slight squeeze and led her toward the center of the dance floor. She placed a hand on his shoulder. He slipped his across the graceful curve of her waist and pressed against her lower back, bringing them closer together. One step at a time they fell into a sweeping rhythm as he guided their movements. The rest of the room and myriad of faces faded away.

The intensity of their beating hearts was amplified by the waltzing cadence. Kensy's flowing dress fluttered spectacularly with every spin. Everything slowed as she spun away from him. He pulled at her hand, drawing her back. Their bodies connected again like two magnets colliding. An unseen energy coursed through every touch and staggered breath. Starlight danced across the trimmings of their respective outfits in mesmerizing patterns, enrapturing all who gazed upon them.

As the music slowed, their movements attenuated until they were left with little more than a soft sway and close embrace. The sounds around them crept back into perception once again. Kensy let out a demure giggle, "If I didn't know better, I'd have sworn that was well practiced."

Jackson raised an eyebrow, "Would you believe me if I said I hate dancing? With you though, it feels almost natural...," He lifted a curl out of her eyes, "I dare say even enjoyable."

Kensy ran her hand down his chest, between the buttons of his double-breasted jacket. "I guess you just needed the right partner."

"Kensy, I...." For a moment he became lost in her eyes.

Raised voices across the grand hall pulled Kensy and Jackson out of their moment of quiet. She pulled away from him, weaving through the other attendees in the direction of the voices. Jackson followed closely on her heels. Through the shifting crowd she laid eyes on a young woman in a waitstaff uniform. Her furrowed brow and balled up fists seemed directed at a well-dressed human dignitary near the edge of the room.

"If you have a grievance, take it up with my office." He scowled back at her.

"I have been 'taking it up' with your office. I have called every day for the last three weeks. When are you going to do something about it?!" She screamed back at him.

Kensy turned a concerned look to Jackson before activating her nahdvi. "Maggie. I need some information on a woman. She appears to be waitstaff for the event, probably terran, dark-colored hair, brown eyes, braided band around her left wrist."

"Retrieving surveillance data... target located, identifying...." Maggie replied, "Target is one Bethany Derien. I see numerous communication requests and complaints to a Magistrate Robert Radith concerning her missing brother."

Jackson tilted his head down, "What does the magistrate have to do with her brother?"

"Nathan Derien was reported missing by Bethany Derien two months and seven days ago while working as an engineer aboard the Cor'Thrae colonial station. Station communications were restricted two months and thirteen days ago. Reason not stated. All communication requests have since been denied. Reason not stated."

"Well, that's not suspicious in the least...." Jackson sarcastically grumbled.

Kensy turned on her heel and quickly strode toward the woman. As she closed the distance, she placed a sweet smile.

"Oh, my gosh! Beth? Bethany Derien? Is that really you?" She interposed herself slightly between the arguing parties. "It's been ages! You probably don't remember me." The woman gave her a confused look. Kensy looked back over her should at the magistrate. "Oh, I'm so sorry! Was I interrupting something?"

He huffed at her, "Sell your sob story to your friend, Miss Derien. We're done!" He stormed away.

"Damn it!" She stared daggers back at Kensy. "Do you have any idea how long it took me to get into a room with that man?"

Jackson stepped up behind Kensy as she straightened her posture. "He does seem the difficult sort. Now, why don't we find some place private to catch up." Her voice became quiet and her demeanor became stern. "Then you can tell us what happened to your brother." The woman's anger dissolved into confusion. Kensy gently urged her from the main hall.

Jackson turned to his fellow officers who looked on questioningly from a distance. He motioned for them to follow with a nod. Glancing about the room he spotted Neira. They shared a long scrutinizing stare. With a quick whisper to her side, Neira triggered several key figures around the room to shift positions as they kept close watch on the guests. Jackson spun around, accompanying Kensy as they departed.

The woman opened a door a short distance away from the ballroom. Kensy walked into the spacious sitting room with her and took a seat on a plush sofa. "Please, Miss Derien, can you tell us what that exchange was about?"

Bethany paced along the far wall as Jackson, Daniel, and Allen entered the room. Daniel rechecked the hall, whispering something to a figure beyond view of the doorway, before closing it behind them. She watched them warily.

"This has something to do with your missing brother?" Kensy gently prodded. "Why don't you start from the beginning?"

Bethany wrung her hands together and took a deep breath. "My brother Nathan is a colonial engineer. He mostly works on colony stations doing retrofits, system upgrades, major maintenance, repairs, or refurbishing on infrastructure. It keeps him on the move. A job might last a few days or weeks then he moves on to the next. About three months ago he got a contract for work on the Cor'Thrae colonial station. It was only supposed to last for two weeks but he hasn't come home."

Jackson folded his arms across his chest. "What does the magistrate have to do with your brother? And what makes you think he didn't just move on to another job without telling you?"

She glared in the direction of the ballroom. "Magistrate Radith has a cousin on the Cor'Thrae administration council. There's no way a man like that doesn't know what's going on with his own family. I figured he'd know if something happened to the colony or he could get a correspondence through to them." She slumped down on the sofa beside Kensy and buried her face in her hands. "I just want to know if he's okay. We talked *every* day. If he knew he'd be out of comm range he'd leave timed messages for me. The last thing he told me was that he was going to be getting on a shuttle to come home the next day. Then *nothing*. NOTHING!"

Kensy rubbed her back to soothe her. Allen looked to Jackson, "Do we think it could be related?"

Jackson contemplated the variables. "They cut comms two months and thirteen days ago. You reported him missing two months and seven days ago. Why the delay?"

Bethany looked up to him, "It was the soonest I was allowed to report him missing. I was told: until I could confirm that he wasn't on the scheduled transport, he wasn't considered missing." Tears filled her eyes as she balled her hands into fists. "I even chartered a shuttle out to the station. But when I got there, they said the station was closed to visitors. I told them I wasn't there to visit, just to pick up my brother. Even then, they refused to let us dock!

"I *know* something's wrong. Something is *keeping* him from coming home. And I'm tired of being ignored or passed off by everyone. My brother wouldn't just stop talking to me, flake off, or whatever the hell they think he did. And I'm not stopping until I get some answers, until I find my brother."

"We'll find him." Jackson replied flatly.

"Gabel?" Daniel raised an eyebrow toward him.

"Either it's related, and we have our next lead, or it's a quick pit stop to reunite a family and we get time to *find* our next lead. Both options allow us to keep our investigation moving."

"Fair enough."

Kensy softly squeezed Bethany's shoulder, "We have our own ship. We can look into this for you."

The woman's eyes lit up. "Please, take me with you! If Nathan got into trouble, he would have left a message, and I know where to look."

The DeCadejra crew exchanged furtive looks. Allen stepped toward her with a warm smile, "Of course, my dear. While we're en route you can tell me all about your brother. I'd love to learn more about him. I am an engineer, myself." She nodded and hope filled her weary eyes.

Chapter 21

# Shadows & Starlight

*"DeCadejra, you are cleared for departure."*
*~ Aepexian Flight Control*

The lights of the passing decks flashed by as Jackson and Kensy rode up to the captains' deck alone. She leaned against his arm, her tired eyelashes fluttering against the fabric of his sleeve. The elevator doors opened, and she took a deep breath. Jackson took hold of her hand. He guided her out into the lobby. "It's been a long night. Go get some sleep." He kissed her forehead.

She looked up to him with a smile, "Yes sir, Commander." She slowly shifted backwards toward her quarters, her hand lingering in his grip until the last possible moment. "Good night, Jack."

"Good night, Kensy." He watched her drift into her room before heading for his own.

Within the confines of her space, Kensy waved a hand toward the outer wall. It shifted into virtual window mode. She walked up to it and gazed out at the shimmering silhouette of Aepexia slowly fading into the distance. For good or bad, she was leaving it behind once again.

The pressure of the room changed. It oppressively bore down upon her. She rubbed at her temple. A haze of movement at the edge of her vision startled her. Before she could turn to investigate, a searing jolt of crackling red energy slammed into the back of her neck. Dizziness overwhelmed her senses.

Disoriented, she grabbed at the wall to steady herself but to no avail. She stumbled sideways, falling upon the nearby bed. The darkened figure of a woman wreathed in red lightning towered over her as she slipped from consciousness.

Kensy stumbled against the glassy stonework. Coppery colored lines traced through the geometric sculptures around the dais. This was all too familiar. Galliane Prime. The last time she stood on this spot Jackson sat curled against one of the pillars, wounded and bleeding. She stared at the portal that hummed before her, within the central archway.

Elle stepped up beside her silently.

"It would have been beautiful, if it weren't for...." Kensy's voice trailed off as she glanced down to a dried red stain on the stone beside her.

"Even here, he can still reach you." Elle looked to her with sorrowful eyes. "The Vagabond. He has ways of reaching into your mind and using it against you."

Kensy chuckled, "If he only knew, I do that to myself already."

"Kensy. You *have* to steel yourself. His reach is far...," she glanced away, "and there are other dangers, older dangers. It's all intertwined now."

"I don't remember you being this cryptic when you were alive. But I suppose that's because you're just a memory now, a figment of my imagination." Kensy pivoted to look down upon the colony ruins below.

A shadow pulsed through Elle's features as she fought back against her controller. She descended a few steps and turned her face toward Kensy, "Listen to me, or listen to yourself, however you want to think of it. You will only find the truth in dark places." Kensy watched curiously as Elle tried to shake the growing influence on her mind. Curling away from Kensy, Elle shrieked. Slowly dark tendrils crawled up and enveloped her.

Dread suffused every fiber of Kensy's being. *Not again, please. Not again,* she begged within the confines of her thoughts.

The twisted visage of her friend rotated to face her and screamed, emitting a harsh mechanical chord. The concussion of the sound knocked Kensy from her feet. It forced the air from her lungs. Scrambling in desperation, Kensy backed away from the looming figure. Her heart raced and frigid sweat beaded up against her skin.

Pushing to her feet, Kensy lunged toward the portal. It swallowed her whole. She found herself falling into an abyssal darkness. From within her chest, Kensy felt a heavy chain emerge. Her eyes followed it up to the silhouette of a man. He reached out as she plunged further and further away from him. The chain pulled taught between them for a brief moment. Then... *snap.* Broken links scattered in all directions.

Kensy bolted upright from her bed, gasping for breath. She took a few faltering steps toward the door. It whooshed open. Jackson bolted to catch her as she collapsed in front of him.

He felt the cold clamminess of her skin in his hands and the heat of her labored breath against his dress shirt. Attempting to provide some comfort, he wrapped his arms around and held her. "When will the nightmares be over?" Her whole body shook as she sobbed uncontrollably into his chest.

He slumped against the side of her bed on the floor. Cradling her tightly against himself, he steadied and slowed his own breathing. He rested his head on hers. There they sat in silence as seconds became minutes and minutes headed toward hours.

Curled against him, she listened to the steady cadence of his heartbeat. The soft rise and fall of his chest eased away her anxiety like a gently ebbing tide. Little by little she calmed in the warmth of his embrace. She looked up to him with her bloodshot eyes and tousled curls. Without a word he wiped a tear from her reddened cheek. She smiled weakly at him, "I'm sorry."

"Now, what do you think you need to be sorry about?" He carefully brushed her bangs from her face.

She tilted her head down, "I've made a mess of your dress shirt. I—."

He lifted her chin with one hand, "None of that. Maggie will clean it... or replace it. Sometimes I'm not sure which." He shrugged. She gave a slight chuckle. Her fingers found his skin at the base of his collarbone and slid down between the lapels of his shirt where he had begun to unbutton it before rushing to her aid.

She furrowed her brow, "I can't sense you anymore, but right now I can't stand to lose your touch." She gazed at him with pleading eyes. "Stay the night with me?"

He grabbed a hold of her hand and kissed the back of her fingers. "Is this what you *really* want? Are you sure?" He stared into her eyes, trying to steady the quickening pounding in his chest. "I'm here for you, any way you need me. But I will go if you have even a shred of doubt."

Without hesitation Kensy pulled him into a passionate kiss. He wove his fingers through her curls as he lost himself in the kiss for a moment. They breathlessly pulled apart. He looked up at the jewels and baubles still woven through her hair. He pushed up onto the bed, "Sit with me and let me help you with these."

She looked at him longingly, then sat on the bed with her back toward him. He caressed her shoulders and placed a soft kiss at the base of her neck. She gasped, closing her eyes to focus on the sensation of his breath against her skin. He swept her hair back toward him and began to unravel her updo. One by one he unfastened the pins and adornments. Her curls relaxed as he played with her hair and ran his fingers lightly across her skin.

Gradually she melted into his touch, and began to slump back against him. He gathered the pieces he had removed from her strawberry blonde locks and set them on the stand beside her bed. She twisted into his embrace so she could face him. Her fingers traced across his forehead then down the side of his face. He turned his head and kissed her palm as he laid her down in the bed beside him.

"Jack, I...."

He brushed a hair from her face, "No need to say anything. I know you're tired. It's okay. I'm not going anywhere." She smiled and nuzzled into his chest. He watched as she drifted off to sleep. "Sweet dreams," he whispered.

The lights dimmed, letting starlight twinkle across the virtual walls and ceiling. Jackson stared at her peacefully slumbering expression until the weight of the day caught up with him. He kept an arm wrapped around her. The warmth of her body against him and the steady rhythm of her breathing lulled him into deep and tranquil sleep.

Chapter 22

# Interruptions

*"I apologize; however, your query as to the location of*
*Commander Jackson Gabel cannot be fulfilled at this time.*
*Please try again later."*
*~ a.c.e.t.a. designation "Maggie"*

Kensy's eyes fluttered open and her breath caught. She looked up at the chiseled features of the sleeping man beside her. She felt the weight of his arm still curled around her petite figure. Her heart pounded as she realized he had spent the entire night at her side. She ran her fingers across the material of his dress shirt and smiled giddily. He grunted and furrowed his brow as he stirred. Upon opening his eyes slightly, she gave an embarrassed wince. "Sorry, didn't mean to wake you."

He chuckled, "I don't mind. Can't think of anything I'd rather wake up to right at this moment." He stared adoringly at her. "Did you sleep alright?"

"Yeah." She sighed, "I kinda wish we could stay like this all day."

"Probably should at least get changed." He pulled at the shoulder seam of his dress shirt. Kensy glanced down, realizing she was still wearing her ballgown from the previous night. He shrugged, "And then there is that whole 'work' thing we should probably get around to at some point." He lifted his arm off her.

She sat up and turned away. *You're grinning like an idiot. Get a hold of yourself. He just spent the night sleeping beside*

136

*you. Nothing else happened. She tilted her head thoughtfully. Despite your best efforts.... Way to go, sleeping beauty. Beauty, right, I probably look like a mess right now.* Kensy took a deep breath, stood up from the bed, and moved toward her closet. She paused to watch him shift and sit up. She coyly turned her back toward him. "I, uh... might need help with my dress."

He swallowed hard as he gazed at the gentle curves of her body. "Yeah? I might be able to help with that." He stood and slowly moved toward her. His jaw tightened. He ran his hands up her arms and down her back. His fingertips found the closures that held the bodice in place. One by one he gingerly released them and pulled the material apart, working his way down her spine. After the final one released, he pressed the back of his fingers to her bare skin and began to caress upward.

"Pardon the interruption," Maggie's voice shattered the tension of the moment.

Kensy bit at her lip, "Yes, Maggie?"

"Psimehna Gabrianna Ciphar has requested your presence in the psionic laboratory at your earliest convenience."

Jackson cleared his throat, "I should... make sure everything's running smoothly since we left in a bit of a hurry." He glanced at his attire again. "You know, after I get... cleaned up... and changed."

Kensy nodded, "Yeah, we should—." Awkwardly they parted. Jackson slipped from the room in the direction of his quarters. Kensy planted her head against the mirrored door in front of her with a heavy sigh. "Yep, that happened."

She shook her head and pulled the pieces of her uniform from the closet. She shrugged out of her gown. Heading to her private bathroom to clean up, she readied herself for the day ahead.

Kensy emerged from her quarters. Awaiting the elevator Neira stood quietly observing as Kensy approach with slightly more exuberance in her steps. She raised an eyebrow, "Someone's in a good mood."

The elevator arrived, and the two women promptly stepped inside. Kensy tried to suppress her giddiness. "Just because you're always in a sour mood, doesn't mean there aren't things to be happy about."

"Did you get laid?" Neira flatly inquired.

Kensy's face flushed red. "What? No! I.... Why would you--? I'm just having a good morning."

"Mmmhm." Neira dubiously grunted in reply. "I'm sure that whatever caused your good mood had *nothing* to do with our good Commander Gabel not being in his own room at o-dark-thirty this morning. And isn't why Maggie spent the entire morning giving 'unable to comply' notices when she was asked to ping or contact him by members of the crew." Neira waved a dismissive hand as she stepped out at her destination, "Whatever delusion you are indulging in, I'm going to go get to work before you infect me with your sunny disposition."

Kensy rolled her eyes as the doors closed again. She leaned toward the back wall. Her thoughts drifted back to the moment she had first opened her eyes, feeling his comforting presence and a sense of peace amid the chaos that was her life. A mirthful smile spread across her face again.

She absent-mindedly rubbed at her left arm above the bracer as she stepped through the lift doors and headed toward the psionics laboratory. Approaching from the hall, Kensy could hear the telltale signs of practiced psionic drills and the clatter of the self-correcting test floor tiles. Kensy paused as a bittersweet smile crossed her lips. She hadn't heard such sounds since her days training adepts on Bhelnir. Their faces flashed through her thoughts briefly.

She shook her head and breathed deeply to clear the memory as she strolled into the lab. Immediately Gabby straightened her posture and gave her a salutatory nod.

"Psilyria! I was just getting a feel for the space. The labs on this ship are amazing, there's just so much—."

Kensy held up a hand to stop her rambling. "You needed to see me?"

"Oh, right, right, right!" Gabby skipped off the testing floor toward the middle of the room. "I get most of this, clasp maintenance, practice floor, and stuff, but...," she pointed to the simulation beam on the left side of the room. "How do we use that? And what is it? Although, flip that and then—."

Kensy laughed. "This ship is special. On the bridge, and the auxiliary bridge, there are beams just like that. They are called psionic submersion interfaces. If you activate your powers and step into it, you can control many of the ship's systems. We use it to coordinate with the crew across the ship. You can even use your powers in there and they are magnified to the ship's scale and perspective." Kensy watched her awestruck expression. "Want to give it a try?"

Gabby's eyes widened, "You mean I can...?" She shook her head, "Yes, yes, yes! Of course!"

Kensy walked with her up the small staging steps, "Now, I'm going to have you activate your psionics. I want you to try focusing on collecting your power on the undersides of your arm, feet, legs. Once you feel like you have established that, you'll just step into the beam."

Kensy studied the apprehension as Gabby looked down at the drop off into the beam. "The actual beams have a bigger drop off but this one, thankfully, was made to ease you into it. Don't worry, you won't fall. It'll lift you as soon as it senses your power. Let me show you." Kensy whispered, "Ivanigis." Her psionic armor covered her body, but something felt amiss. She focused past it and stepped into the beam. It lifted her gently as though she was inside the bridgehead beam. Sharp pain pierced through her left arm. She reflexively clenched her fist and pulled back to the staging steps. "Go ahead, try it." She forced a grin to mask the pain.

Gabby nodded, "Yeah, I can do this...." Kensy watched her collect bright green tendrils of energy and infuse herself with the gathered energy. Gabby apprehensively stepped into the beam and bobbed for a moment before gaining a sense of equilibrium. "Oh, my gosh! This is amazing!" Gabby enthusiastically squealed.

"Good. I was hoping you'd help me share this... duty." Kensy started down the steps, teetering slightly on the last one. Her knuckles blanched as she grabbed at her arm.

Gabby looked down at the psilyria's clutched arm with her augmented vision. Flecks of a pulsing red color peeked from beyond the edge of the armored bracer she wore. Gabby dropped her infusion and landed at the beam's base. She rushed to Kensy's side, "Psilyria?"

Kensy smiled weakly, "I apologize, I'm afraid I'm not quite feeling my best at the moment."

Gabby pointed to the sliver of strange color, "What is that? Is it supposed to be doing that?"

Kensy's anxiety mounted quickly, "Gabby, I'm going to need help." Kensy glanced toward the ceiling as water collected in her eyes. Choking back her fear, she called out. "Code Chimera."

"Understood, Psilyria." Maggie promptly replied. "All parties have been notified."

Another vertigo spell overwhelmed Kensy, she staggered. "Not again," she breathlessly whispered. She glanced in the direction of the calibration chairs. "Help me. Feeling a little dizzy." Gabby guided Kensy to the crown of chairs and helped her into the nearest one. Kensy laid her left arm on one of the extended arm rests and began unlocking her armored bracer. "Thanks." She grunted in pain. "I'm going to ask something else, maybe a little weird."

"Anything. Anything you need." Gabby anxiously shook her hands. "I'll go get someone. I can find help—."

"I need you to see if you can use your infusion skills...." The bracer opened as she released the final latch. The spidery glowing web of colors from the Chimera pulsed angrily. Kensy writhed in the chair. Fighting through the piercing sensation shooting up her arm, she looked to her fellow psionic. "I need you to see if you can stop it from spreading up my arm."

Gabby stood dumbstruck, "I... I don't know... if I can."

"Psimehna, I need you to try. Don't worry about hurting me." She looked to Gabby with pleading eyes, "Please, I can't do this on my own."

The psimehna looked at her idol and the strange sight before her. She rubbed her fingers against her palms as she contemplated her options. "Yeah. No problem." She laughed nervously. Her fingers wrapped around Kensy's upper arm. Gabby closed her eyes as she envisioned a sieve of energy forming between her hands. Fine threads of bright green energy wove together through Kensy's flesh until a mesh of energy had stitched itself into being. Gabby opened her eyes and cautiously began sliding it down Kensy's arm toward her elbow.

As Gabby's construct contacted the Chimera, pain seared through Kensy's body. She gritted her teeth as she visibly struggled. "It's working," she managed, "Keep it up."

The lab door swished open and several familiar faces burst into the room. At the head of the group, Chief Engineer Allen Petroski barreled in with a toolbox and a cradled bundle in his arm. Doctor Tyronis followed at his heels, kit in hand. The pair approached either side of Kensy to inspect the situation. Jackson rushed through the door and stopped in his tracks. He finger-combed damp, rumpled hair from his face as his eyes fell on Kensy's vibrantly colored arm. *Shit. But it was dormant! Did I miss something?* He scoured his thoughts as he stared on in dread.

Allen examined the device implanted into Kensy's left forearm. "We've got some searing around the core. Looks like the whole thing was fried." He glanced toward Doctor Tyronis as she laid out her supplies.

"She was showing me how the beam worked and then I saw this glowy stuff and then she wasn't doing well. And I don't know what happened." Gabby rambled.

"Thank you for your efforts," Doctor Tyronis spoke in a steady motherly tone. "Everything will be fine. Just stay with us." She smiled at Gabby before turning to Kensy.

"Yep. Good kid." Kensy nodded. Neira darted into the lab, zigzagging around Jackson without pause. Allen waved her over to remove the device. He shifted toward the adjacent chair, rolling out the bundle he had brought with him.

"What'd you do this time?" Neira deftly extracted the malfunctioning stasis generator from its holdings.

"Nothing that I can think of...." Kensy's mind flashed to the moments before her nightmare the previous night. Her eyes snapped toward Jackson. "Except... last night... in my room, I felt a jolt." She shook her head. "I think it knocked me out, caused me to have another nightmare."

*Jolt? Could it have been...?* Jackson took a deep breath and turned toward the door. In a whisper he spoke to Maggie through his nahdvi, "Send me surveillance of Psilyria Frost's Quarters from last night. Time period: our arrival at the captain's deck to ten minutes after. My eyes only, Maggie."

The ship's mechanical voice replied through his communicator, "Understood, Commander." He faced back toward Kensy, watching from a distance, helpless to assist.
Neira stepped back out of the way, dropping the extracted device onto a tray as she withdrew. Doctor Tyronis ran a sterilizing beam over Kensy's exposed arm. Allen stepped back into Kensy's view with a melancholy grin, "I was hoping to put my prototype through a bit more rigorous testing before trying it on you, but it seems we don't have the luxury of time or choice." He glanced to doctor Tyronis, "We may have to sedate her." He turned back toward Kensy. "If you're good, we're

gonna see if Miss Ciphar can push the chimera further down into your forearm before we activate the system." He paused. "It will likely be very painful at first."

Kensy gritted her teeth, "Do it."

Daniel leaned in through the doorway. He gave the situation a quick survey before drawing attention, "Captain, sir, I'm going to need to borrow you." Jackson nodded and pivoted to follow Daniel. A short distance down the hall, as they walked, Daniel finally spoke again. "There's nothing you can help with back there, Gabel. But you might be able to help someone else right now. It'll give you something constructive to focus on while they work."

Jackson rubbed his eyes, "Yeah, thanks. What did you have in mind?"

"Our new guest, Miss Derien." Daniel guided them toward the elevator. "Rasken's got her chatting right now, but I think she could use a little more assurance and a little less bubblegum." Jackson shook his head with a knowing sigh.

Chapter 23

# Much Needed Discourse

*"We need to talk...."*

*~ several people*

The ascent to the officer's deck was far too brief. Jackson stared at the beginning of the footage he had requested from Maggie. The view on the datapad revealed a quiet, undisturbed room. Light from the door illuminated her quarters as Kensy's shadow shifted toward the open space. Nothing out of the norm drew his attention. *Maybe I'm jumping to conclusions. Elle has psiwalked to Kensy before without physically harming her.* Jackson shook his head and closed the datapad.

He stepped out of the elevator and strode toward the diplomatic lounge. *No use stressing about it until I know for sure. Focus on the problem in front of you.* He entered the room.

On the far side, Lindsay Rasken leaned against the observation railing as she related a story in an overly dramatic fashion, complete with the occasional pop of her bubblegum. "I flipped that bitch up on one wheel. Spun around almost all the way around when — WHAM! My tire hit the shale and shot out from under me."

Bethany looked on, mouth agape. "Oh, ouch. You must have hit the ground so hard."

Rasken pulled up the sleeve on her muscular arm, revealing an old-mottled scar. "Heh. It certainly bit back. The bike took the worst of it. My dad just shook his head. *You're*

144

*gonna be fixin' that one."* She mimicked shaking her finger in a scolding manner, *"And no teaching your brother that nonsense."* She popped another bubble with a smile. "Rough landing but that was a hell of a rush. And I'm totally teaching my brother when he's old enough to ride." She laughed.

Jackson stuffed his hands in his pockets as he approached, "Your poor dad has at least a few more years of peace before that."

Bethany's attention snapped around at the sound of the new voice. "Commander!"

He gestured for her to remain seated and took up a casual stance beside the grand virtual window. "I came by to check on things. I know our departure from Aepexia was quite abrupt. How are you getting settled?"

Bethany wrung her hands in her lap. "I was set up in one of these close rooms. It is quite comfortable. Thank you." She looked down, "If I'm being perfectly honest though. It's a little hard to relax right now. I'm more worried about my brother."

Rasken called her out, "What did I tell you?! We're gonna do everything in our power to find your brother and bring him back." Hensley popped his head into the room and beckoned for Rasken's attention. "And don't forget it! We're gonna get this shit squared away." Rasken pushed off the railing and headed for the door. "I'll be right back and when I return, we're gonna grab some chow, starting with dessert!"

Bethany watched her disappear beyond the door before turning her attention back to Jackson. "I was hoping to get a moment to ask you something." She stood and paced toward the starscape in front of her. "You were the first to jump at helping me once I explained the situation. You seemed to have a lot less trepidation than the rest of your company. Why?"

Jackson drew in a deep breath and gazed at the glittering specks in the vast ebony canopy. "I had an older brother. I *have* a little sister." He paused, "I don't talk to her as much as I should."

Bethany glanced toward him, "Then you should know better than anyone, you never know when they'll be gone. And it's always too soon."

Jackson looked back to her somber expression. "If your brother is as dedicated and resourceful as you say, I'm sure he's not gone yet. We'll find him." She nodded in acknowledgment. "We should be there in about another two to three days. Try to take it easy until then. There will plenty of work to do when we get there."

"Thank you, Commander." She weakly smiled.

"Yo! You ready to dive into some good eats? We've got the best galley in the entire Ascension fleet." Rasken called from the doorway.

"I could probably use something in my stomach." Bethany shrugged and moved to meet with Rasken. Left alone in the silence of the lounge, Jackson's thoughts lingered on his sister. *You never know when, they'll be gone.* Bethany's words echoed in his mind. *Maybe it is time I gave you a call. Then maybe I can crawl off the terrible brother list.* He shook his head in dismay. Quietly, he trudged up to his private quarters on the deck above.

Sitting in front of the blank screen he hesitated for a moment. He pulled the badge from his belt and stared down at it. He ran his thumb across the black band that crossed the center. The etching of his family name peaked out from the edges of the emblem. He traced the contours and ridges with his eyes. *Miss you. Evidently, I'm not doing this whole brother thing very well without you. Hopefully, I'll get it figured out before... well,* he shook his head to dismiss the thought.

He turned on the console and scrolled though his options. Her name came up across the screen: Heather Belle Gabel. He pressed a finger to it and the call started up. Within moments, a smiling face beamed back at him with similar charcoal black hair and soft blue eyes. "Hey, you!" Her hair fell loosely around her face. "About time you checked in. I was beginning to wonder if they stationed you in a black hole." Her laugh was effervescent. "Now, how's my big heroic brother doing?"

He glowered at the screen, "I can't talk about specifics. But I wanted to call, had something come up that... well it reminded me...." He struggled against his thoughts.

She feigned a solemn tone, "Oof, sounds serious." She laughed again. "You don't have to tell me about job stuff. I just want to know my big brother is, you know, alive, healthy, not missing appendages...." She waved her hands in a generally self-indicating gesture.

He raised an eyebrow at her. "Well, I'm clearly alive. I'm calling you."

She cocked her head to one side with a grin. "Been shot lately? Missing any pieces?"

"Not lately. And no," he said flatly. His gaze narrowed and he leaned back in his chair.

"Good. I keep hoping someday you'll find a nice girl to woo. It will be a big help to have all the bits still attached and functional." She chuckled.

Sitting up abruptly, he scowled at her. He pointed a finger at the screen. "That is out of bounds for you, giggles."

She shrugged, "Well Gaveth isn't here to help you out, so I figure it's my sisterly duty to push you in the right direction." Jackson buried his face in his hands and shook his head. "Are you *blushing?*" Her grin widened. She curled her hands together under her chin and leaned in toward the screen. "What's her name? How did you meet?"

He sighed in resignation. "There's a Psilyria I've been working with.... Nothings come of it yet," he quickly added.

Heather shook her head, "See, this is why you need help!" She pitched her hands toward the screen accompanied by an interrogative stare. "You like her?"

He cast his eyes toward the desktop. He remembered the softness of her skin in his hands and the light that danced in her eyes when she looked his way. "Yeah, yeah I do."

"Then you need to tell her." She shifted in her seat and gave him a teasing look, "You gotta put on some moves for her. Let her know you're *interested*." She winked and watched her brother uncomfortably fidget.

Waving her away, he turned his face from the screen. "I am not talking about this with *you*."

"Aww, are we getting embarrassed?" She prodded at him. She flopped her hands down upon one another on her lap in exasperation. "At least tell me you've kissed her."

He glared at her, "Yes."

She squealed in delight. "Knew you had it in you. And maybe after she gets *it in her,* I can meet the future Mrs. Gabel." Laughter filled the air from her end of the call.

"That's it, we're done—." He reached for the disconnect icon.

She threw a hand forward to stop him. "Wait! Jack." She gave him an earnest grin, "I'm happy for you. Good luck."

Jackson bobbed his head. "Thanks. Love you, sis."

She relaxed her posture. "Love you too." She brushed a few stray strands of hair from her face as the transmission cut.

He stared at the blank screen lost in his thoughts. *She seems to be well. Still too nosy for her own good. Ugh. I didn't even ask how she was doing.* He scoffed at himself. *Yep, screwing up the whole big brother thing. Damn it, I should have—.*

His eyes shifted to his datapad.  His hand slowly closed around the device. He stared at the blank screen again. He activated the handheld device and transferred the paused footage to his main screen.

His eyes traced the lines of Kensy's graceful form in her flowing formal wear. The glittering light from the ballroom memory entranced him for a moment. He slid his hand forward and pressed play.

Kensy approached the exterior wall, and it shifted to a virtual display. He squinted as a shadow flickered at the edge of the frame. A figure burst forth from the darkness wreathed in red lightning. His eyes widened. He held his breath as she struck her victim at the base of the neck. Kensy tried to turn, clawing at the wall and air as she collapsed backward on to her bed. Jackson stood abruptly, his chair flung backward. He watched in horror as the warped visage of Elle released a torrent of energy into Kensy's helpless form. Her power surged through her friend's body, and she dissolved away to nothingness.

He counted the seconds, staring at Kensy's unmoving figure. *Move. Call for help.* He pleaded. Her body convulsed and he released his breath. She staggered toward the door. He watched her crumble into his arms as he dove forward. He backed away from the monitor.

He combed both of his hands back into his hair and began to pace. *Elle did this? How did I miss it? Does she even know what she's doing to Kensy? They're more than nightmares! How did I not put this together? If she can physically harm Kensy without....* He looked back to the screen. Kensy sobbed into his chest. He felt every heave of her heart wrenching cries again.

A knot formed in his gut. *Fuck. I spent the entire night in there with her. Was Elle still in there? Was she watching us? She could have compromised us. What if—?* He searched the surveillance footage for answers but none came. *Some truths along this road she's walking will hold the power to destroy her.* Elle's voice echoed in the dark reaches of his mind. He shook his head to clear the words clouding his thoughts. He dropped his hands to his hips. His fingers grazed the badge where it rested. He tilted it upward and stared at the engraving one more time.

*I have to tell her. She needs to know. There's nothing worse than walking in blind.* His jaw tightened. *I might not have been able to save you, but I sure as hell am not going to fail her.* He tapped the badge thoughtfully. *I'm going to get it right this time, Gaveth.* He snatched the datapad from his desk and darted from the room with renewed purpose.

Chapter 24

# Confirmation

**frustrated growl* "...weird psionic magicy bullshit."*
*~ Commander Jackson Gabel*

The alarm had been called. Jackson stood over the war room table, scanning over the faces of his attending officers. "The possibility of a security breach has come to my attention. I want a thorough search of the entire ship. Stem to stern. Bulkhead to bulkhead. Identify ANY foreign technology, possible infiltrators, or out of place personnel. I expect a full accounting for every mote of matter on this ship. You have your assignments and orders. Dismissed."

The officers broke ranks and scattered to their designated areas. Nevan lingered at the back of the room as Jackson pulled up a diagram of the ship's layout. He watched the sensor information flow through the display. "Doctor Hirayama, please advise if you need assistance linking your prototype into the sensor array."

"Shouldn't be a problem, Commander. Maggie is assisting," she replied.

Nevan quietly approached the center of the room, his tail snaking back and forth slowly. He watched the commander curiously. "This seems rather abrupt, Commander. Mind filling me in on the situation?"

Jackson tapped on the console in front of himself to tune the display. "The situation is that we may have been infiltrated."

151

Nevan tilted his head questioningly, "When?"

Jackson's hands hesitated on the controls. "At Aepexia."

Nevan nodded sedately. "And this came to your attention how?"

Jackson pressed his palms to the table and rocked backward, his head dropping as he tried to structure his thoughts. He took several measured breaths before answering. He straightened his posture, looking squarely at Nevan. "Elle was on Aepexia, and last night she was also on this ship."

Nevan began to circle the table, "Elle? As in Ellise Neru, psicorp psionica, classified deceased five years ago? Elle?"

"Yeah. *That* Elle." Jackson clenched his jaw. "Kensy's been having nightmares about her since Bhelnir. Neira thought she was psi-walking somehow. I didn't know what to think of any of this but...." He stared back at the display. "In that warehouse, back on Aepexia, what I found... was Elle. Or some warped copy of her. Crazy Vagabond tech automated thing maybe. She bested me, forced me into some weird vision thing so we could 'talk' about Kensy." Jackson turned his gaze downward. "I didn't know what to make of it. And when the scan for nanites came back negative... I just," he paused. "I lied. But last night she attacked Kensy, destroyed the Chimera stasis system in her arm and then somehow *just vanished.*"

"Hmm," Nevan's mane of scales flexed ever so subtly. "Alright. Walk me through it. What do you know, from the beginning."

"The beginning, huh?" He turned, slouching back on to the edge of the table. "Bhelnir then. The colony was attacked. I was on the Themiscyra as XO. We received a broken distress call on our way to investigate another colony. Found only one survivor outside the colony's central bunker, Kensy. Later found out during her last stand there she had 'touched the veil' yadda yadda weird psionic magicy bullshit."

Nevan cracked a brief smile as he listened. "Then we moved on to Morwhex, our original destination. The same enemy had wiped them out completely. Kensy pulled some crazy voodoo to save the ship but reopened wounds from Bhelnir because...." Jackson pointed to his left forearm. Nevan nodded in understanding.

"Neira told us what was up with the whole bracer thing. And while she was out cold in medbay, she evidently had a nightmare... about Elle. Didn't know at the time though." He shook his head. "Then there was a ton of bullshit. Blah, blah, blah. You probably already know, we ended up with a ship." Jackson threw his hands wide before crossing them over his chest.

Nevan dipped his head in acknowledgment, "Yep. Sounds about right."

"But then, three days later, Kensy has another nightmare. Manifests in her sleep. Out of control. Chaos. All of it. Nearly rips the captain's deck wide open. Managed to wake her up and get her down to medbay. When everything died down, she starts talking to me about these nightmares she's been having of her dead friend. Talks about how weird they are because in the dream they start talking then something snaps, and Elle goes all psycho-scary on her."

Nevan's gaze narrowed, "Strange. Definitely doesn't fit with what I know of the woman."

Jackson shrugged. "Next day, Neira orchestrates some cloak and dagger BS to talk to me in secret. She decides to *enlighten* me on their dead friend and Kensy's ability to psi-walk. Then she pulls up some footage of Kensy's room from before the storm. A ghostly doppelganger of Elle pops in and does some voodoo of her own, then gone.

"At this point, I'm so far out of my depth, we yell at each other. I tell her to go talk to her own damn friend and chalk it up to weird psionic—." He inhaled deeply.

"...magicy bullshit," Nevan cut in. They both chuckled.

"Then we go to Rosealleon. The Vagabond's very own little pit of horrors. In all of the craziness Kensy made a comment. I didn't think much of it at the time. Something there was touched psionically but clouded. I still don't know what that *actually* means. But the Vagabond's ship ripped its way out of the planet, and we ran.

"We get out in the middle of nowhere, as far as we can get from the system in short order. Found out later Kensy was still having nightmares about Elle. We get back to tracing the origins of this damned homicidal machine and putting pieces together one at a time.

"Then we hit Galliane Prime. After a little recon, things start going south real fast. I get shot." Jackson subconsciously rubbed at the scar. "Kensy activates some old ass portal and shoots us through space to an uncharted moon. Pretty sure it has some ridiculous alpha-number-soup designation now, but whatever. I was in bad shape evidently, so Kensy linked us together somehow with her...." He wiggled his fingers dramatically.

Nevan smiled, "You must have become quite close for the bonding process to work. I understand it is rather difficult otherwise."

Jackson paused to soak in the implication. *Even back then?* He turned his attention back to the retelling. "Anyway, after a few days we finally get picked up and are back on the ship recovering, when the weird just gets magnified. Kensy's dropped into another one of her nightmares and I get pulled along for the ride because of the link.

"And there, among some floaty ruins Kensy is just taking in the scenery. I asked her what the hell was going on and Elle pops up. Her dead friend is standing in front of me, having a conversation." Jackson shook his head as if to disbelieve his own experience.

Nevan stroked his chin thoughtfully, "Did she say anything to make you believe she was anything other than a memory?"

Jackson strode over to one of the benches. He sat resting his elbows on his thighs. "She said I was cute and gave us crap about... not being together, I guess." He shrugged. "Then I saw the change. Her whole demeanor shifted. She hit Kensy, blinked her into another part of the dream. Kept rambling on about there not being enough time. Said I had to promise her to 'never let go, ever' then sent me into the dream where Kensy was." He ran his hands through his hair. "I remember, running. *Something* was following us through the dream... nightmare... bullshit."

"Interesting. Neira never mentioned that." Nevan sat down beside Jackson.

Jackson turned his head to look at him, "Because we never talked about it. Kensy tried to sever the link after that, to keep me from getting pulled into another one." He glanced back to his hands. "After that she'd tell me when a nightmare cropped up, but I only *felt* it when things were really bad, like just before we got the summons to Aepexia. That one scared her awake."

Jackson drew an uneasy breath, "You know pretty much everything else. Mordwell's attack. My encounter with Elle in that warehouse. And last night this." Jackson passed over his data pad with the footage. Nevan watched the events transpire silently on the small screen, before handing it back.

"Well, this seems to come down to two possibilities. She could be on the ship in hiding, in which case the search and scans are prudent. *Or....*" He pointed to the image of Elle in the commander's hand. "She could still be psi-walking like we know she's done before. In which case your hunt will turn up nothing. Probably still not a bad idea."

Jackson scowled at the image, "But she's never managed to *physically* hurt Kensy before."

Nevan nodded, "True. But let's talk about psi-walking for a minute. As Neira no doubt informed you, it is a very difficult feat for even the most powerful psionic practitioners to pull off. Those that have achieved this can only observe but not interact and only over short distances. The variable that makes this exceptionally interesting is Kensy's connection to Elle, or rather her *link*."

"Link? She...?"

"I'm sure you've seen the news articles about their rescue. Two young girls gifted with psionics found adrift in a small capsule in space. As children they formed a psionic link. It helped them survive long enough to be found and continued until Elle's supposed death aboard the Icarus. It stands as the longest documented link between two psionics in history. If the being behind this is really Elle, the residual power of the link could be affording her more manifestation power."

"But why would *this time* be different?" He tapped the datapad against his palm.

"Likely? Proximity." Nevan drew on the bench between them with his finger. "If she is managing to manifest a psi-walk from the distances you've described, whole systems apart, the amount of power that's getting pumped into that ability is significant. If the power doesn't change but the distance does...." He brought his finger together. "What do you think happens to all the extra energy?"

Jackson rubbed at his temples, "So let me get this right, Elle gets killed and the link is broken. Somehow the Vagabond gets his wires into her and makes an Elle shaped puppet. He runs across Kensy at Bhelnir and starts using Elle to fuck with her head, to what... keep her off balance? Whatever is left of Elle reconnects with Kensy for old time's sake. She passes along a host of excessively cryptic warnings through some super-juiced psi-walks. Then accidentally fries the safety measure keeping her best friend alive?"

"Yeah, pretty much." Nevan looked upward. "It does confirm that the Vagabond managed to slip more than just a few small machines onto Aepexia. But more importantly it gives us another piece of the grander picture."

"If she can psi-walk to Kensy no matter where we are...." Jackson stared at the ground between his feet. "...what's to stop her from affecting the ship? The crew?"

Nevan shook his head. "The link will be the facilitating factor, but it would likely be the limiting factor as well. It is going to make it even more imperative that you are vigilant in protecting our dear psilyria." Jackson drew in a sharp breath and straightened his posture.

Nevan laughed heartily. Jackson glanced questioningly to him. A conniving smile curved over Nevan's lips, "You know, you're going to have to tell Neira."

Jackson winced, "Nope. Not touching that one." He stood and paced toward the holotable. "Feel free to inform her but I'm not about to tell her she was right. I will never hear the end of it." He sighed. "And, besides, I have my hands full. I'm gonna have to figure out how to tell Kensy. I can't let her fly blind." The realization hit him. "Shit. How am I going to tell Kensy? I don't even—."

Nevan firmly patted him on the back with a smirk, "I have confidence, you'll figure it out." Jackson's shoulders slumped. He hung his head as the drone of search reports began to fill the air around him. At least he would have some time to think it over... maybe... hopefully. Fuck.

Chapter 25

# Weightless

*"There is nothing quiet like the comfort of being weightlessly cradled by starlight."*
*~ Psilyria Kensy Frost*

Slow measured breaths. The gradual rotation of her weightless body. The gentle undulation of her flowing hair at the most subtle of her movements. Kensy soaked in every bit of it with her eyes closed. It was familiar but new all at the same time. She looked up toward her left arm. The bandages still covered much of it below her elbow.

She marveled at the new stasis harness. In its naked state, she could see the gradually writhing indigo mass of the Chimera woven through her flesh. Rings and wires formed multiple layers of safeguards against her waiting doom.

She snatched one of the sheathing plates from the air around her and snapped it into place. Another. Her mind analyzed and recorded each sensation. They pulled tightly together as if the gravity within her own arm was multiplying. One by one, she reattached the pieces until her new bracer was complete. *One more rotation. Focus. Remember. Recognize the new feelings. Discard the old ones. Understand the difference.* She inhaled deeply and exhaled slowly.

There were few things as comforting as zero gravity to her. Jackson. Jackson was comfortable. She smiled to herself. Now, if only she could gather the courage to tell him....

The training room airlock hissed as it opened from the hall side. "Bring training room gravity to one quarter of ship standard."

"Adjusting gravity generation to specifications, please stand by." Maggie replied. "Decent to training room floor is advised."

Kensy smiled to herself, "Of course, Maggie. Thank you." She felt the pull as the gravity systems kicked in. Her body glided downward until the soft tap of her boots echoed from the point of contact.

The chamber door slid open and Jackson lightly stepped in. "I hope I'm not interrupting."

Kensy smiled, "I, uh... I don't mind the interruption." She took a leaping step forward, overestimating the force need to land in front of him. He reflexively reached out to catch her. As she collided with his chest, her excessive momentum caused them spin in a circle. She airily twirled around him, until at last the residual movement was arrested. "Heh, oops." He gave her a hesitant smile. The airlock's interior door closed behind him with a dull clunk. Carefully, he nudged her hair from her face and leaned in for a tender kiss.

She closed her eyes and soaked in his touch. He lifted her effortlessly into a tight embrace and she responded by wrapping her arms around his neck. They held the moment for several long seconds before he set her down on the training room floor. He drew a sharp breath in, glancing around to avoid direct eye contact. His demeanor confused her. She placed a gentle hand on his cheek to guide his focus, "Hey. Is everything okay?"

"Yeah, yeah." He tried to wave away his nervous energy. "Everything's fine. I just wanted to talk." He lifted his head to look past her for a moment. "Um, Maggie. Can you give us a few minutes, no interruptions?"

"As long as you need, Commander." The lights in the room dimmed slightly and the security bolts on the airlock doors snapped into place. "Privacy mode engaged. Speak command to end privacy mode."

Jackson ran his hands along the back of her arms with a feather soft touch. "I'm sorry, I know I hadn't gotten a chance to visit you in medbay over the last couple days. I was, uh, trying to get some things sorted." The fabric of her plum uniform top wrinkled under his fidgety fingers. "But I wanted to come by, see if I could steal a little bit of time, you know, just you and me." He reached up to brush another floating strand of hair from her face. "And I had to check, how are you doing?"

She cast her eyes toward the center of his chest where her hand rested. "Doc said I'm doing well, get to stay in my own room tonight. And the new system Allen designed is amazing. It has more fail safes. More weight than the old one too." She scoffed, "Or maybe I'm just not used to it yet. But even with the new plates, it should be easier to conceal than my old bracer."

Jackson ran one hand down the outside of her sheathed arm. "He showed me the schematics after the implantation was done. It's a marvel, ...but that's not really what I asked. How are *you* doing?"

Kensy stepped back, biting her lip and furrowing her brow. She looked away and let out a halfhearted laugh, "Would you believe me if I said I didn't know?" Her hand slipped out of his as she pushed away and drifted to the center of the room. She waved a hand at the exterior wall, causing it to shift into virtual window mode.

The stars stretched across the room. Their glittering light shifted with the movement of the ship in flight. "I haven't been sleeping very well, probably stressed. Every time I close my eyes.... I don't understand why I can't shake these nightmares. I'm tired and...," she dropped her gaze. "It's so silly. I'm beginning to dread even going to sleep."

"Kensy, I...." Even through her poise, he could see the pain she masked. The muscles of his jaw subtly flexed as he clenched his teeth in frustration.

"Yeah, I know," she sighed. "You're probably wondering when I'm gonna get over all this dream nonsense. Dead friends. Crazy impossible visions. Dizzy spells. Will it ever end?"

"Dizzy spells?" he questioned in a startled tone.

Kensy shook her head, "Only a couple, here and there. And just since you saved me on Aepexia. Doc says it's probably residual from the neurotoxin. She expects it to fade over time."

His thoughts flashed back to their arrival at Aepexia. "I'm sorry. If I hadn't let my guard down...." He chastised himself. "Familiar doesn't mean friendly and *I* know better."

She gazed upon his visible vexation with a sorrowful expression. "Hey, you told me not to blame myself. That doesn't mean you are allowed to take the blame instead. I was the one who knew there was cause for caution and I ignored it."

The weight of responsibility hung heavily between them. He broke his stare with a nod of acknowledgment. "Blame aside, that's not what I came here to talk about...."

Kensy tilted her head and smiled at him. "Oh, yeah? What's on your mind?"

Jackson pushed his fingers through his dark, unruly hair as he fought to find the words he needed. "Shit, I've spent the last two days rehearsing how to tell you about this. Even with all that, it's not any easier," he growled at himself.

She stared toward him again, eyeing him with gentle concern. "You can talk to me about anything, Jack. What are you so worried about?"

He placed his hands on his hips. "I wanted to talk to you about the nightmares." She hesitated in her approach, stepping back on to her heels as apprehension took hold. He turned his gaze to meet hers. "They're not *just* nightmares. And they're not your fault."

She gave him a defeated smirk, "It's in my head, I'm pretty sure that makes it all on me."

He pushed forward to close the remaining distance between them. "No. Not this time. Kensy... the nightmares... they're coming from Elle."

She scowled at him, holding him at arm's length. "Jack, she's dead."

"Not entirely," he blurted out. "I don't know how or why yet, but... I *know* it's Elle. Kensy, she's been psiwalking to you before *every* nightmare. And the other night, the jolt you felt, the one that knocked you out... it was real. And *it* is what fried your chimera stasis system."

She held a scared smile on her face even as water welled up in her eyes. "And how do you know I wasn't just manifesting in my sleep again?" She choked back the urge to cry as her thoughts sifted through his words.

He drew a sharp, deep breath, "Because, ...back on Aepexia, she attacked me."

Pretense dropped from her expression and her eyes widened, "Your mugging, your 'bad turn' was...."

"Yeah," he nodded. "She cornered me. And I lost."

Kensy shook her head in disbelief, "No. No. She would have no reason to hurt you. And... I felt her die. If she had survived, she would have come to me. She couldn't.... She wouldn't...."

"She's not the one in control. Kensy... the Vagabond is. He brought her back. He's the one in the pilot's seat." Jackson could see the cracks forming in her otherwise composed veneer.

"So you're telling me, I get my best friend back, only to find out I've *already* lost her again?"

He grabbed her and pulled her into a tight embrace. She broke. Her sobs shook his chest as he held her. Softly he whispered to her, "For what it's worth, I don't think she means to hurt you." He desperately contemplated how to comfort her. "There must be something left of her. I lost my fight, but she didn't kill or compromise me. I was at her mercy and... she wanted to talk." He gave a trepidatious chuckle, "She gave me *the* talk. You know, the — *hurt my friend and I will haunt you* — one." He smoothed her hair with his hand, "I think whatever is left of her is trying to warn you, to help you." He kissed the top of her head.

"I thought she died! I didn't go to save her!" She balled her fists up against his chest. "I left her all alone out there! I should have saved her." Her voiced cracked with anger and grief.

His arms tensed around her. "None of that. You had no way of knowing." He rested his cheek against her head. "But now we can figure this out together."

She buried her face further into his chest. Her arms curled around him and her voice came out muffled but audible. "Maggie, zero-g." The artificial gravity generators cut out. Kensy held tightly to Jackson as weightlessness overcame them.

Jackson looked up at the starscape around them. "I'm sorry I didn't tell you sooner. I had a million and one excuses not to. I didn't have all the pieces. You were still recovering. But really, I just couldn't bring myself to cause you more pain. I know that doesn't make it any better. But whatever we face ahead, I couldn't let you go in blindly, not if I could help it." He pulled her to face him. "No matter what, I'll be right here with you."

"Thank you, Jack." She wiped at the tears collecting on her eyelashes, casting tiny beads of water into the air around them. "Please, just drift with me a while." She pulled herself up to his lips.

A breath apart, he nodded, "As long as you want." They held each other tightly. The space between them melted away. Their eyes fluttered shut as their lips met in a salty, sweet kiss.

Heat coursed through the sensual touch. Both surrendered to the moment as they became lost in one another. In the serene silence of the training room, their bodies floated weightlessly intertwined together.

## Chapter 26

# Contact

*"Every Psicorp officer is as thoroughly trained in diplomacy as they are in controlling their powers. Words are the first weapon they will wield against almost any adversary."*
*~ Research Assistant Eli Kirby*

The dim morning lighting of the foyer flooded into the darkened interior as Jackson stepped up to the threshold of the room. He reached toward the suppression control beside the entry and ran his fingers up the slider. Quietly, he moved toward her bedside, pausing for a moment to watch the gentle cadence of her breath as she peacefully slumbered. *If only she could sleep this peacefully all the time.*

He sat down beside her. "Hey," he whispered, "time to wake up." He ran a finger down the back of her arm in a soft caress. She stirred. "Rise and shine, beautiful."

Her eyes fluttered open, "Hmm? Is it morning already?"

"A little past, but I wanted to let you sleep in."

She rolled her shoulder toward him as she shifted onto her back. With a smile she placed a hand on his leg. "I like this wake-up call. Wouldn't mind it becoming a habit."

He chuckled, "I'll see what I can do about that." Pushing herself upright, the blankets on her bed gathered and bunched with the shift in position. She wrapped her arms around her knees and hung her head, attempting to stretch. "Still feeling it?" He patted the bed in front of him, "Turn around and let me see if I can help."

With groggy nod, she extricated herself from the covers and sat between his knees. The warmth of his hands penetrated her satiny nightgown and sent a tingle across her skin as he began to knead at her shoulders. Slowly, he worked past her shoulder blades and down along her spine. Her breath caught. *His hands feel so good. Can I just stay like this forever?* Relaxation began to soak through her muscles.

He felt her tension beginning to melt away under his touch. "I wanted to let you know, we're approaching the colony. Had Bryden start collecting long range scan data. I'll have to head back down to see what we've got in a minute. But I knew you'd want to be around for initial contact. And I figured I'd come wake you up far enough out that you won't need to rush." He leaned in and placed a light kiss on the crest of her shoulder.

She tilted her head to the side, "Thank you, Jack."

He gave her shoulders an affectionate squeeze before rising from her bedside. "See you down there."

She watched him depart her quarters before releasing a drawn-out sigh. "Right." With a glance toward her closet, her thoughts refocused. "Playing diplomat. We've got an engineer to find." Kensy approached the closet. She halted in front of the mirror, looking herself in the eyes. *Whatever you're feeling about Elle, about Jackson, about... yourself, tuck it away. There's no room for it here. We have a job to do.* The rest can wait. After a long moment, she opened the closet panel to retrieve the appropriate uniform from its resting place.

From the elegant swags of her plum blouse to the crisply pressed lines of her charcoal slacks, her confidence grew with each piece she donned. She twisted her hair back into a smooth but sophisticated updo. For her final touches, she slipped her patent leather boots under the legs of her slacks and pulled a long black jacket with silver trimmings up over her shoulders. One more inspection in the mirror, *remember your training.*

*You can do this! Find out what happened and bring him home.*

She left her quarters to meet up with the others. Daniel smiled at her as she entered the war room. Kensy nodded to him kindly, stepping up beside a pensive Jackson. "According to census data this colony is home to a little over seven thousand citizens, predominately human. It's orbiting the gas dwarf Threa'vieh Nine." Jackson informed her. "Can't seem to get a good structural look at it. The readings are coming back inconsistent." He looked to Daniel. "Are you getting this variance, or am I seeing things?" He pointed at a section of the holographic diagram above the central table.

"No, there is definitely something off about the scans of this place. I'll see if I can get the feedback sorted. You should head down to the bridge. We're about to hit comm range, and I don't think Morgan's the right person to knock on the door."

Jackson nodded, "Let me know if anything especially weird comes up."

"Yes, sir!"

Jackson glanced to Kensy. She held a hand up to halt his impending question, "I'll stay here with Bryden, help him get the data sorted. I should be able to jump into the call if it comes to that." Jackson acquiesced with a nod and departed alone as Daniel and Kensy dug into the ever-growing mountain of sensor data. She shook her head, "Nothing's ever simple, is it?"

Daniel shrugged, "I wouldn't know what to do with simple." A smiled curled across his lips. "Neither would you or Gabel, and you know it."

Kensy blushed, "I suppose we have made things spectacularly complicated, haven't we?"

"It's a good complicated." The war room door whooshed open. Two figures entered, Lieutenant Rasken and Bethany Derien. Kensy looked up, then to Daniel who just nodded.

Kensy rounded the table. "Miss Derien, we should be making contact shortly. Feel free to observe, but it will be imperative that no matter what you hear, that you remain quiet. If they prove as difficult with us as they were with you, negotiations will begin. I need you to place your trust in me. I promise we will find your brother."

Bethany took a deep breath. Rasken patted her hand and popped a bubble. "There's nothing my captains' can't do. It'll be fine, you'll see."

"Contact. Bringing it up now." Daniel called over to them.

Kensy jogged back to the far side of the table so she could watch both the room and the encounter on the display. Morgan's voice echoed over the channel, "This is Ascension Legacy Flagship DeCadejra, requesting docking clearance."

The colony operator replied, "Docking permissions denied. State your business."

Jackson's image appeared on the display, "I am Commander Gabel, Terra Ascension Core Navy and captain of this ship. Our business is retrieval of a missing Aepexian citizen. Allow us to dock."

"We are not accepting docking requests at this time. Identify the citizen you are searching for."

Without so much as a moment's hesitation, Jackson replied. "We have come to take custody of one Nathan Derien, colonial engineer. He is wanted for questioning. This is his last known location."

"One moment." The line hung in awkward silence for too long before the operator snapped back. "No records found. Docking clearance request denied—." Bethany tensed in her seat beside the alpha team leader. Rasken's hold on Bethany's hand tightened, and she shook her head.

Kensy ran her fingertips along the table's edge to define her broadcast range. With the rest of the room filtered out, Kensy connected her image alongside Jackson's. "If I may, Psilyria Kensy Frost, appointed Aepexian negotiator." She placed a hand on her chest. "I would have preferred to conduct talks in person. But if our docking request cannot be arranged, I will be obligated to conduct these talks over an open channel."

Audible hesitation buzzed over the communicator. With a soft click a new image appeared on screen, a woman with short silver hair and deep creases across her dark, leathery skin. "Unfortunately, Psilyria, we are not in a position to allow your ship to dock at this time."

"May I ask why, Miss...," Kensy inquired.

The woman's gaze narrowed, "Of course, where are my manners? Councilor Merris Udahnel. An accident in our substructure has caused complications in many of our colony's peripheral systems, including the docking mechanisms. We simply cannot facilitate safe docking conditions at this time. Our engineers are working to fix the issue but due to the delicate nature of the tasks at hand we request your ship clear the area around the station and come back once repairs have been completed. We wouldn't want anything to *happen* to your pretty ship, after all."

Kensy glanced to Bethany before smiling to the woman on the communicator. "I greatly appreciate your concern. However, I am unable to return without custody of the engineer in question or confirmation that he is not aboard your station. Might I propose a compromise?"

Councilor Udahnel gestured for her to continue, "By all means, how can we resolve this so that you may *leave*?"
Kensy quickly tapped a message into her console as she stared directly at the screen. "I see that your section four airlocks seem to be intact and large enough to accommodate a personal craft." Out of the field of view, Daniel nodded and darted from the room. "I will see that our ship withdraws to a safe distance if you allow me to bring a personal craft to conduct a brief investigation of my own. If the engineer is confirmed to not be

aboard your station, we will depart the system and continue our pursuit elsewhere."

The woman glared, "I will not have a host of people poking about, getting in the way of repairs. We have enough to deal with already."

Kensy waved a hand, "Of course, I will come alone." A flurry of direct messages flooded into Kensy's terminal. She quickly dismissed them without looking as she held a firm stare with the woman on the other end of the line.

"Fine, one small craft, you, and your ship withdraws."

Kensy tilted her head in respect. "Your understanding is appreciated. I will see you soon." The line disconnected. Kensy exhaled.

The door slid open as Jackson burst into the room. "What were you thinking? You can't go in there alone!"

"I can and I will." Kensy affirmed.

"We have no idea what you will be walking into!" Jackson protested. "Going in without backup is dangerous and reckless."

"I will have backup, you and the ship, sitting just outside of short-range sensor reach." Kensy walked past him. She smiled at Bethany as she headed for the door. "Be back with your brother shortly."

The two captains swiftly left the darkened interior of the war room. Jackson hovered closely behind Kensy. "At that distance, response time will be limited. If something goes wrong—."

Kensy placed a hand on his chest to stop him as he entered the lift behind her. "I can do this. I'll be okay."

Hesitantly, he placed his palms against her arms, "If anything happened to you...." The words stalled on his lips.

She smiled up at him. "You'll come save me. You always do." She ducked past him as the doors opened again. Jackson pivoted to follow as she jogged down the hall and into the hangar bay.

Daniel shouted down at them from a catwalk above. "Almost ready for departure." He shuffled some items between a crate on the catwalk and open side door on the Dagger One transport. Kensy lightly ran up the stairs toward Daniel.

"Am I the only one who thinks this is a terrible idea?" Jackson hollered.

Daniel clicked a final few pouches onto his uniform belt and kicked the crate closed. "Don't worry so much, Gabel. She's not going to be alone. She'll have an ace pilot with her."

"You're not helping."

Daniel took Kensy's hand to assist her into the small craft. He activated his nahdvi with a glance toward Jackson. "We've got this. I'll watch her back. You just keep the engines warm. We'll stay in contact." Daniel stepped aboard after Kensy, closing the door behind them.

Jackson watched from the floor of the hangar bay. Jarringly, the transport shifted from its resting position into a launch configuration. He sighed, "Be careful, head on a swivel. Come back safely." Reluctantly, he turned away, the knot in his gut twisting around his better judgment. Every instinct screamed at him to stop them. He took a deep breath and headed for the bridge again.

## Chapter 27

# A Cold Welcome

*"The psilyria talked her way onto a potentially hostile
colony, what could possibly go wrong...?"*
*~ Ensign Ashar Kyo*

Daniel handed Kensy a tightly wrapped bundle, "You asked for this."

"Thanks," She unwrapped it, revealing her old armored bracer.

"Can I ask?" He steered them toward the station, high above the golden hued clouds of the gaseous planet below.

"I need some pieces out of it." Kensy quickly worked at disassembling the thin mechanisms lining the inside of her old bracer. "Tell me you have something akin to a long, thin needle among your knickknacks in your gear."

"I have a few options I can finagle in a pinch, why? What's up?" He glanced toward her curiously.

"I'm going to disable my control clasp, make it so I can't manifest for our initial greeting. They will probably respond better if they don't think we're a threat. I just needed to know we can undo it in a pinch." She pulled the hardware from the inside and wrapped it around her clasp. "This kept my manifesting from messing with the Chimera system, dampened the effects. And if it's directly on the clasp...."

Daniel nodded, finishing her thought as she secured the device. "You dampen your ability to create fireworks in the first place, got it."

"I'm going to ask you to lock away your guns. We shouldn't appear to be armed. And I don't want to give them the opportunity to seize any of our gear."

"A step ahead of you on that one." He patted the pouches on his belt. "No guns, just tools to help us improvise."

"Thanks, Daniel." She took a deep breath. "They might get a little fussy about you being with me, given I negotiated coming alone."

"Well, you needed transportation, and I *am* a first-rate shuttle pilot."

She nodded, "Just don't be surprised if I talk you down." With a cunning smile she glanced toward him. "I need them to underestimate you."

His gaze met hers, "Yes, ma'am. I'm just here to serve you ma'am. Whatever you say."

"Thanks." She rose from her seat and approached the door as they pulled into the airlock. The shuttle jarred slightly as Daniel set it down.

"Airlock bay doors secured behind us. They appear to be pressurizing the compartment." Daniel shut down the ship, locking the control systems. "They should be able to poke around in here without gain." He rose from the pilot's chair and took up position behind Kensy's right shoulder. They listened for the interior airlock doors to open. Upon confirmation from his handheld scanner, Daniel popped the side door open.

They were greeted by the councilor and a detachment of armed guards. Their host held a narrow glare as she looked past Kensy to Daniel. "I believe we negotiated you *alone*, Miss Frost."

Kensy stepped off the shuttle. "We negotiated myself and a personal craft. I am a diplomat, not a pilot. He is essential to the operation of my shuttle. Is there a problem?" Several guards flooded past, combing through the shuttle. Daniel stepped out behind Kensy, hands raised as pairs of guards approached to search them for weapons. Neither Kensy nor Daniel showed any signs of resistance.

The pair on either side of Kensy, pushed her sleeves up to reveal her chimera shell and control clasp. "What's this?" Councilor Udahnel pointed to her arms.

Kensy looked at her forearms, "Feel free to scan me if you like. I had a pursuit a little while back, the target proved quite *illusive*. There was a shuttle crash involved, I am still recovering." Kensy turned her palms up. "I am hoping this investigation will prove less eventful. Provided we can work together, of course."

A guard nodded from the shuttle. "Hmm, very well." The councilor returned her attention to Kensy. "See that your man, does not leave your side. I am holding you personally responsible for him and his actions."

"Absolutely."

"Now, what do you need from us so this business can be concluded quickly?"

Kensy folded her hands together and stood tall. "Given that you could not find records of the engineer I am tracking, I would like to ask around through the citizenry. Perhaps he is going by a pseudonym. If I can discern the name he is going by, I can bring it to you for prompt resolution. If no one has seen a man of his likeness, then we will be done here."

The older woman crossed her arms, "We are a small colony and receive few visitors. I think you will find many of our people are... shy. Do not be surprised if they are less than eager to answer your questions." She guided them toward the interior airlock door. "And do not wander into the marked work zones. They are dangerous, and we wouldn't want anything getting in the way of finishing your investigation in a timely manner." The woman held an arm out, "Welcome to Cor'Threa."

Chapter 28

# Uneasy Ambiance

*"I've seen ghost towns with friendlier residents."*
*~ Lieutenant Commander Daniel Bryden*

One after another, Kensy and Daniel walked past bleakly barren store fronts and empty windows. The hard gray lines of the local architecture were cold and unwelcoming. Heavily shadowed figures ducked out of sight at their approach. Kensy furrowed her brow, "They really nailed the whole unsettling ambiance thing."

"I see why they don't let visitors on the station." Daniel shuffled to one of the windows and peered in. "This whole place screams creepy and wrong."

"Yeah," Kensy stepped into the center of the street. In a loud voice she called out to the shapes in the darkness. "We're not going to hurt you. We're here to help. We're looking for someone." Only uneasy silence answered her call.

Daniel rested his arms on the pockets of his utility belt. "Hmm, no takers. Seems like the locals are going to be a hard sell. Thoughts?"

"Think our nahdvi can reach the DeCadejra from here?" Kensy moved toward another desolate store front and visually scanned over the empty displays.

"One way to find out." Daniel tapped his nahdvi. "Establish encrypted link to the flagship DeCadejra. DeCadejra, come in."

175

Relief echoed through Jackson's words as he replied, "About damn time you called. Status."

"We're fine. Onboard and roaming." Kensy chimed in, "But Jack, there's definitely something wrong here. How many people are supposed to be on this station?"

"Um, seven-thousand two-hundred and eighty-six by the latest census data. Why? What are you seeing?"

"This place is a ghost town. The few we are assuming are locals are lurking in shadows. Haven't laid eyes on anybody outside of the welcoming party, which by the way were armed to the teeth." Daniel recounted. Kensy glanced to him questioningly. He whispered to her, "Not too hard to spot if you know what to look for." Daniel surveyed the area around them as they spoke, "Hey Gabel, these guys were easily packing more hardware than even you do."

The pause was drawn out, "I don't like this. Any chance you could make it back to the shuttle?"

Kensy shook her head, "We're not leaving. We haven't found Nathan Derien yet." The nahdvi picked up the commander's low, frustrated grumble.

Daniel smiled knowingly. "I'm with her on this. We came to retrieve one guy, but whatever is going on here is a bigger problem. We need to get to the root of this."

"You guys don't have the gear to take on a whole station."

"Don't worry, we'll let you know when to send the cavalry in. Just be ready." Daniel tapped his nahdvi again to suspend the connection. He began sifting through his belt's contents, "Now let's get that—," a shift of movement snared his attention. He glimpsed a dirt-smudged face peering at them from down the row of shops. "Hey!" Daniel pushed past Kensy and ran after the figure as they ducked out of sight. He skidded to a stop at a gap between the structures. He called into the shadow. "We just want to talk...."

Kensy took a wide berth behind him, hoping to catch sight of the evasive figure with her wider perspective. Daniel took a cautious step toward the darkened gap. Arms shot out of the shadows. They wrapped tightly around Kensy, smothering her startled scream. She was pulled out of the light of the street in an instant. Daniel took another slow step forward. He opened his mouth to speak. An inky blackness descended over him, and unseen pressure stifled his alarmed outcry. As the shadows swallowed them whole, an aberrant stillness settled back into the desolate street.

Jackson stared at the readouts over Morgan's shoulder. "Bryden, if the information we managed to gather on sensors is correct, we are going to need a whole lot more than two of you over there to clear this place." An unusual silence filled the bridge. Only the periodic beeps of the sensor feedback disturbed the stale air. The moments crawled by laboriously. Finally, the commander broke the stillness. "Bryden? Kensy? Are you still with us? Report." Nothing.

Morgan shrugged, "It sounded like they were gonna call back later. Maybe we should just wait—."

"Tell alpha and our newest entourage of friends to gear up." Jackson folded his arms across his chest rigidly and began to pace.

"Um boss, we've got no way to get them *on* that station," Morgan hesitantly pointed out. He swiveled around to face his commander, "Not without Bryden and Frost. Unless you want to create a major incident—."

Jackson shot a piercing glare toward him, "Tell them to gear up."

Morgan threw his hands up and swiveled back around to face his control panels. His hands slammed down on the interface as he sent the alert to their most seasoned ground forces. Morgan quietly muttered under his breath. "Don't say I didn't warn you."

Jackson ignored him, "Maggie, get me a direct line to engineering."

"Direct line to Chief Engineer Allen Petroski established."

"Commander?" Allen's voice called back, "What can I do for you?"

Jackson ascended the stairs of the bridgehead. "I need schematics for this station. Someone's gotta have records of this place. Dig into the databases and get me something, anything."

"We'll get right on that. Any idea what we're looking for once we get the schematics?" In the background, Allen began doling out instructions to his crew.

"Alternative points of egress. Bryden and Frost went in through the section four airlocks. I need another, less conspicuous, way to get boots on that station." Jackson activated the strategic command console to rise from the bridge walkway as he approached. He called to the faces looking up at him from either side of the command center. "Get me every scrap of data we can on that colony." He pointed to one crewman on the far-left side. "Prep secure comm buoy. I want encrypted full stream communication with our team on station. Call down to the hangar bays, I want all shuttle pilots on standby. Tell them to be ready for *either* deployment or extraction."

The hum of the command center built into a crescendo as everyone set to their assigned tasks. Jackson let out a measured breath as he filtered through the information that flooded his console. A call rang through to his nahdvi, "Commander, I've got something for you. Meet me in the war room?"

Jackson nodded, "Let me get this sensor data relayed and I will meet you up there in a minute, Chief." He turned his attention to the crewmen and women around him. "Forward all findings to the war room feeds. I want a status update on that comm buoy and readiness check-ins for all teams currently on standby." He pivoted and headed for the main lift.

"Comm buoy ready and awaiting deployment, sir!" the crewman shouted over the bustle.

Jackson pointed to him, "You are go for launch." He pulled his hand back to cover his ear. His nahdvi called up to Morgan on the bridgehead. "Threaux, pull us back a little after the comm buoy is deployed. I want us in position to launch shuttles toward that colony at a moment's notice."

"Whatever you say, boss."

Jackson stepped into the elevator. The doors closed behind him. The knot is his gut nagged at him. *They cut comms intentionally. There is no reason to expect that they are in trouble... yet.* Jackson growled at himself. *One step at a time, just like always. We'll get through this.* With a heavy sigh, he emerged from the lift at his destination and headed for the war room.

The typically dark room was aglow with diagrams and data streams. Allen and two of his techs busily sifted through and correlated the information as it came in. "Good you're here." Allen pushed his glasses back up his nose. "We've generated a model of the station based on original design files filed with the Ascension Building Commission and Aepexian Trade Guild. We're working on noting discrepancies between that and the sensor data we've collected to try forming a more up-to-date view of the station after remodels and repairs."

"Good."

"There is some new shielding on the lower levels that is making it a muddy mess. Sensors fed back some muddled information, like they were getting bounced around... here... and here." Allen pointed out the problem spots "There are clear visuals of alteration we saw on approach, but I'm having some difficulty figuring out exactly what they did or *why.*"

Jackson approached, "Hmm, maybe they encountered something unexpected with their proximity to the dwarf that required compensation?"

Allen crossed his arms and curled a hand up toward his mouth. He shook his head. "The lines are all wrong. The design is actually more vulnerable now than it was originally, unless there is something behind it all that—."

The auxiliary doors opened abruptly. "What the fuck, Gabel?" Neira stepped into the room, hands on her hips. She glared at him intently.

Jackson ran his fingers across his forehead in exasperation. "This is not the time, Cross. Whatever your issue is, it can wait." He turned his attention back to the projections. Neira stomped down the steps toward him. "Unless you are finding a way to get me on that station, *no* it can't. You sent her in *alone!* What the hell were you thinking?"

He snapped around to face her as she approached. "First, yes, we are in the middle of an in-depth analysis of the station. So, if you want on that station, I *suggest* you let us work. Second, I didn't send her in. She arranged her own terms of entry *despite* my opinions on the matter. *And* she didn't go in alone. So save your bluster for the ass-hats on the station that wouldn't let us dock, because I have work to do."

The few seconds of silence that passed between them were thick and awkward. Neira narrowed her gaze again, "Who?"

"Who, what?" he sniped back.

She tilted her head back slightly and tightened her jaw. "Who is with her? On the station."

His posture stiffened. "Bryden."

The lines of her cybernetic eye patch shifted slowly. *"Just Bryden?"*

Another bout of painfully still moments passed, neither of them flinching. The engineering techs shared an apprehensive glance. Allen cleared his throat to shatter the tension of the moment. "Miss Cross, I do believe you have experience with a broader range of environments with your line of work. Perhaps you could aid us in our analysis."

Both turned questioning gazes toward the chief engineer. He pointed to the diagram. "Problem at hand."

Neira skirted around the table away from Jackson. "Yeah, whatever."

Allen looked down at his console as he pulled up additional information from the long-range sensors. Casually he remarked, "Don't worry. I'm sure we'll find plenty of time for you to scream at each other once we no longer have people in potentially hostile territory." He overlaid the latest data. "Now, let's see what we can learn about Cor'Threa." Heads bowed as everyone uneasily set to the task at hand.

Chapter 29

# Beneath the Surface

*"The true character of a colony can be seen in the care of its substructure."*

*~ Kyle Brenevargas*
*Colonial Engineer, deceased*

Muffled voices roused Kensy. Her vision hazed in and out of focus as she began to stir. Daniel turned his head in her direction. "Hang on. She's coming around." He jogged to her side. Crouching down, he placed a hand on her shoulder.

"Daniel?" She sat up, still trying to shake the fog from her mind.

"Yeah, you okay?" He brushed her hair from her eyes. His face came into focus with a few blinks. "It took a bit for my head to clear too. Just give it a second."

Kensy groaned, "What happened?" She rubbed at her temples. "Last thing I remember was that deserted street with all the empty buildings."

A second figure became discernible over Daniel's shoulder. He glanced backward for a moment. "Yeah, about that...,"
The figure stepped forward, his features vaguely familiar but new to Kensy. "Nathan Derien, colonial engineer." He held out a hand toward her. She noted the thoroughly calloused texture of his skin and layered scars from years of hard work. Shaking his hand, she sorted through the confusion that swirled her thoughts. "Sorry about the rough introductions. Things have been, um, ...*difficult* here. It's not safe to be in the open anymore."

As she pulled her hand back, she noted the dampening harness had been removed from her clasp during her comatose state. Kensy took a moment to examine her surroundings for the first time. Utility pipes traversed the walls and ceiling of the corridor they were in. A large grate covered the end only a few meters away. Down the opposite direction two more civilian figures stood sentry, wielding improvised weapons. "Where are we?"

Nathan stood back and waved her toward the grate. "Colony substructure D-73." Kensy stood up from the crates she had been laid across in her unconscious state. Daniel followed closely behind her. Stepping beside Nathan she looked out into an open industrial area. The machinery below churned noisily in its task of distributing vital resources across the station.

Kensy shook her head, "I don't understand. Why are we in the substructure? What's going on here?"

"I'll show you. Follow me." He headed down the hallway. "We kept you away from everyone else until we could verify that you hadn't been... compromised." He nodded to the sentries. "I don't know when things started here. But a few months ago, I got a contract to come do some repairs. Came with a partner, Kyle Brenevargas. As we worked, things just became stranger and stranger." Nathan led them through a tangle of maintenance tunnels. "Station police stopped patrolling. People would disappear overnight. Shops would get closed and raided, seemingly at random.

"Then, the day before we wrapped up the repairs. Bren comes back, rambling about something he ran across running lines to an old sector. Couldn't make sense of what he was saying so, I told him to show me but when we went back the access corridor wasn't there. He swore up and down that the place was changing itself. I didn't believe him." Nathan paused. "I should have believed him."

Kensy looked to him with concern as they walked. "What happened?"

"Bren had been my partner for nearly five years." Nathan drew in a sharp breath. "We were working on a patch on the inner hull... out of nowhere, the outer sheathing buckled. The rupture pulled Bren out so fast I didn't have time to react before his safety line snapped. I watched him get shot out of the station, straight toward the planet."

"I'm sorry, man. That's rough." Daniel ducked past a bundle of wires.

"That wasn't even the worst part," Nathan shook his head. "When I went to repair the rupture, they told me some of their own had done a makeshift patch. They just wanted me to ensure it was structurally sound."

"Is that unusual?' Daniel inquired.

"Well, I was here in the first place because they didn't have all the equipment they needed for the modifications we were asked to do." Nathan opened a hatch for them to crouch through. "When I got up close to inspect the patch, I noticed something... off." Kensy knelt down in the small crawl way tunnel. "I could still see some of the damage at the rupture site." He furrowed his brow. "There were no stress marks or material fatigue. It looked like it had been *eaten* away."

"Eaten?" Kensy glanced to Daniel questioningly.

Nathan continued. "And I couldn't figure out *how* they made the patch without the proper tools. No way a human being gets into a breached section like that without the right gear." He opened a hatch in the crawl space floor. "Got a little jump down here." He dropped through the opening. "Come on down. It's not much further."

Kensy inched toward the opening, gauging the drop distance. *Just a couple meters, maybe slightly more. Shouldn't be too bad.* She hopped into the opening, bouncing back up to her feet as she hit the floor. "And you think something other than a person fixed the hole?"

Daniel jumped down behind her. Nathan snapped the hatch closed behind them. "More than that, I think some*thing* created the breach intentionally. And then repaired it to cover their tracks." Nathan placed his hands on his hips. "It probably would have escaped a layman's inspection. Fortunately, or unfortunately, I'm exceptionally good at what I do. I would bet whatever it was, also compromised Bren's safety line. I know for a fact he kept his gear in immaculate condition. Shouldn't have failed like it did."

"I get all that but, how did you end up down here?" Daniel gestured to the structure around them. "Suspicious findings to crawling around in the ductwork is still a little bit of a leap." Nathan began to walk again, waving to them to follow. "It didn't take much to realize anyone who voiced their concerns went missing. So, I talked to those who had proven trustworthy and found I wasn't the only one with questions. Then this happened...." Nathan stepped out of the corridor, revealing a larger compartment. In the space beyond him, countless people of all ages bustled about a colorful tent city nestled among the station machinery. Laughter of small children mingled with the whine of generators. The din of adult conversations provided a steady hum alongside the thrum of water processors.

Kensy and Daniel stared wide-eyed at the unexpected scene. "How?

"A little bit at a time." Nathan stuffed his hands in his pockets. "Once I realized something was wrong, I couldn't just go home and leave these people to sort it out on their own. I started looking for a way to help. I found this section of the substructure was uniquely suited to be a sanctuary. I was able to isolate our systems, but honestly, this is a patch job at best. These people need a way off this station. I'm hoping you can help with that."

Kensy looked to Daniel, "This rescue mission just got a whole lot more complicated."

Daniel watched the assiduous commotion, "This is going to dramatically affect mission parameters. Do you have access to shuttles, transports, anything?" Nathan shook his head, *no*. "We are going to need to contact our ship and give them a rundown. Do you at least have a head count?"

Nathan pulled a datapad off his tool belt. "At last count, a total of 564 bodies. 238 of those are under the age of 15, another 59 are under the age of two." He clipped the datapad back in place. "We lost a lot before I got this place operational." Worry creased Kensy's brow, "So many kids..., we *have* to contact our ship. Will broadcasting an encrypted signal expose your sanctuary?"

"We'll have to move away from this section to get a signal out at all. It's part of the reason I picked this place. The way the shielding here was constructed wreaks havoc on any signals coming in or out. They get bounced and scattered like crazy." He pointed to the unusual angles of the visible seams and panels encompassing the area.

Daniel resolutely turned to Nathan, "Get us a safe broadcast point and any station schematics you can provide. We'll get our ship working on the exit strategy. Then the three of us will be free to figure out what the hell is happening on this station. We'll get these people outta here."

"Good." Nathan pushed off the wall he had slouched against and took to a brisk stride. He smirked over his shoulder, "Let's take the express." Daniel and Kensy swiftly followed on his heels as they doubled back into another maintenance corridor. After a couple quick zigzags they caught sight of a worker manning a conduit system control node. The system machinery hissed and churned noisily.

Daniel and Kensy's nahdvi filtered down the deafening sounds that flooded around them. She glanced toward him, "Do I have you to thank for this?" She held up her clasp arm.

Daniel nodded, "Yeah. When I woke up and got introduced to our host, I figured you might need it. And I had a fair bit of time to pass before you came to. Dismantled it and tucked the pieces away, just in case." He patted the larger of the pouches on his belt. Kensy smiled and mouthed the words, *thank you.*

Nathan approached the operator as they spoke. He leaned in toward the man. "Hey, Owen, we've got three for the express to charlie-fourteen."

"I got ya, boss." The gruff man shifted several levers and switches across his control panel. Striding toward a hatch along one of the conduits he spun the hand wheel effortlessly and wrenched the door open. He shouted over the ruckus, "The hatch at fourteen should still open, Kerso went down a bit ago to check on a disturbance."

Nathan clapped the man on the shoulder with a smile, "Thanks. Lock it up behind us." He waved Kensy and Daniel in close. "We're gonna take a ride. We need to daisy chain on the way down. I'll go first so I can pull us off the line." He looped a braided cord around his wrist. "We're gonna be moving fast so whatever happens, don't let go of your tether."

Daniel nodded. He looped the other end of Nathan's tether around his own wrist before tethering to Kensy. Carefully, the trio stepped into the slick tube. Nathan illuminated a light bar sewn into the shoulder of his shirt as the hatch closed behind them. Crouched, Nathan guided them toward a steep slope. He shifted into a sideways slide as gravity took over. Daniel and Kensy mimicked the positioning, holding tightly to the tethers between them.

Residual oleaginous fluid along the cylindrical walls made the traversal swift and smooth. Deftly, Nathan guided their descent through the twisting tubes with the skill of a seasoned surfer or boarder. When external light finally breached the conduit to signal their exit, there was only a moment to process the impending shift. Nathan shot out the opening, swinging by an adjacent handle and bracing to pull the others out behind him in one well practiced and fluid movement. Even against the dry floor of the new area Kensy and Daniel slipped and wavered.

Nathan smiled and tossed them a set of work towels from a stash beside the opening. "Wipe the gunk off your shoes and clothes, it'll help with the balance readjustment." Turning back toward the conduit, he reached up, gripping a pair of slide bars. He pulled the hatch down. With a strong push, he set the panel back in place and locked the handles. He spun the handwheel at the center until the dog arms were fully extended to seal the hatch. Grabbing a towel for himself, he approached his companions. "We'll head toward the auxiliary generator room. You should be able to get a signal out there and the transmission should blend in with report system noise."

"Nice. Gabel should be wearing a trench in the war room floor by now. He'll jump at any hiccup this station makes." Daniel nodded, handing his towel back to Nathan. "Just maybe, if we're real lucky we can keep our intentions masked for a bit longer. Might even get a plan in motion before we're found out."

The camera lens refocused on the trio. Its glassy eye followed the group as they disappeared between machines, beyond the visual range. The signal flowed through the surveillance system wiring, climbing higher and higher through the station's structure in a fraction of a second. The screen flipped from one video feed to another. The operator thrummed her fingertips across the desk as she impatiently hunted for the disruptive interlopers. *Lost them, dammit!* A fist slammed the desktop. She flattened her hands out and drew a slow measured breath. A harsh mechanical voice crept up behind her chair. "OpERatiONs hAVe beEN coMPRomiZEd. CorRECtiVE actION mUst be taKEn!"

The councilor shot a narrowed glared to the side. "*I* will deal with this! You're the reason they are here in the first place." She shut off the feed. "Your indelicate rush drew their attention." The shadow behind her chair ominously swelled.

She shook her head, calling up the station schematics on her console. "There are still resources on this station that can be salvaged—." A sharp pain pierced the base of her neck. Electricity seared through her body, cutting her words short.

"ReSOurCEs eXprOPriATed." Strangled screams drowned under the harsh mechanical chords that filled the isolated chamber as enthralled guards surged into the room and set to their insidious work.

Chapter 30
# Zombies

*"Shhhh...."*

The whine of the auxiliary generators covered the sounds of their approach as Nathan, Daniel, and Kensy darted from one point of cover to another. Nathan held up a closed fist. They stopped, listening for any anomalous sounds amid the cacophony. He carefully peered around the corner. His eyes scanned the shadows and structures that filled the chamber. Exhaling, he stepped cautiously toward the bank of control consoles at the heart of the room. No sign of movement except his own.

He waved his companions onward. Swinging around to the front of the console, Nathan busily dove into the workings of the system. Kensy moved to his side. She pointed to her ear then the computer questioningly. Nathan briefly held up a finger for her to wait. He sifted through the readouts isolating the report channels and data streams.

"Excellent!" He brought up the channel he was looking for. "I'll tap us into this feed. You said Bethany was on your ship?" He glanced toward Daniel.

"Yeah, she was the one who led us here to get you."
Nathan busily typed away at the console. "Good, hopefully your people are letting her help. Otherwise, I imagine she'll be driving them up a wall." He smiled.

190

Daniel grinned knowingly, "Your sister is nothing if not persistent. And Gabel's probably watching every hiccup from this station with every set of eyes he can recruit... except for maybe one." Daniel's gaze shifted toward Kensy. *Neira, ugh. She's gonna have words for me after this.* She shook her head at the thought.

"Well if my sister is anywhere close to a signal scanner, she'll see the transmission burst." Nathan sent to channel information to their communicators. "The channel should accept your login now."

Kensy tapped her nahdvi and listened for a moment. "Sounds like I have a successful connection. Begin encryption...."

Bethany anxiously sifted through the signals captured by the comm buoy. Her fingernails strummed rhythmically against the war room table as the raised voices in the background droned on in heated debate. The data stream she had flagged flooded with additional information. She stopped tapping and examined the transmission. Allen glanced in her direction. Frantically, she searched through the console's commands. He sidled up beside her, watching. "Ugh, how do I open the line?" She huffed in frustration.

"Here." Allen pressed on the signal line, to bring up the command options. The transmission connected.

Neira's voice boomed over the table. "Bullshit. This colony is a bunch of fuckwits. We just go blow in the airlocks and pull them out. No more of this pussyfooting around."

Jackson snapped back at her. "You do that, and you'll turn a powder keg into shrapnel bomb. I will not jeopardize them, just so you can flex on some colonial rubes."

"I'd be saving her. Which is more than I can say for you! You had the chance to stop her and you didn't."

Listening to the exchange Kensy rubbed at her temples, with a heavy sigh. "I'm not a damsel in a fairy tale that needs rescuing. But there are a whole lot of *other* people here who *do* need saving. Please put your energy toward that."

Startled by the sound of her voice, Jackson and Neira both snapped their attention toward Bethany and Allen across the table. Jackson shrugged off the argument, "Talk to me. What do we got?"

Daniel spoke up, "Roughly 560 to 570-ish civies that need evacuation. No shuttle access."

Neira drew in a sharp breath, "What are we up against?"

"Time. These people are in hiding from whatever is on this station." Kensy paced thoughtfully. "The station has been experiencing targeted faults that have seemingly repaired themselves. We have suspicions but nothing confirmed. But Jack...," she shot a look toward Nathan, "there's kids. A lot of them."

Jackson's jaw tightened as his mind rapidly churned though tactics. "Allen, start clearing cargo bays to make room. Everything is gonna have to get real cozy here for a bit. For extraction we'll send over one of the boarding shuttles with Alpha on board. We can use it to punch a hole and make a new airlock. Do you have a location we can use?" Nathan furiously ran through the station schematics on his datapad.

Daniel piped up, "Working on getting that. One sec."

"Once we have a secure point of egress, we'll start chaining transport shuttles in for evac. If we're real lucky and do this fast enough, they might not have time to respond."

Neira examined his plan. "Those transports will be target practice for the station defenses if we don't hit them first. Give me a few fighters to strike in tandem with the boarding pod and we'll make sure the air is clear." Jackson eyed her for a brief moment before nodding in agreement. Allen and Neira hurried from the room.

Hesitantly, Bethany interjected. "Is my brother—?"

"I'm fine, runt." He spoke up. "Sending schematics over. There's a bay for container storage on D level that should work.

If you punch through between the marked points, it should be structurally sound enough to handle the breach without rupturing the entire section."

Jackson examined the forwarded schematics. "Any chance you could use those containers to pre-load your people? Then we could tow them back in bulk."

Nathan wavered on the thought. "Mmm, I don't know. They should be insulated well enough, but I would need to do a detailed inspection. The smallest gouge or puncture could break the seal, make it a death trap for anyone inside. Might be possible to rig up a short-term air recycling system inside a couple of them. But I start into work like that, and I'll have to cannibalize some of the station systems. I just don't have the resources otherwise."

Jackson nodded in acknowledgment. "See what you can manage without drawing attention. Either way, we start moving pieces into place for this evacuation and our plans won't stay secret for long."

"Will d—." Clang! The noise echoed across the room. Everyone stopped and watched. Nathan waved Kensy and Daniel back as he shifted behind a large pipe. With soft steps and careful movements, they slowly eased back toward the shadows. Their eyes darted about, searching for the source of the disturbance.

Kensy flinched as the ring of the fallen pipe echoed in her mind. A small fragment of memory nagged at her. The scraping of a pipe being picked up echoed in her ears. Rain. Glass? The clatter of the pipe against the ground. A wave of fiery rage. None of it made sense. Her hands trembled. Dizziness twisted the world around her. She clawed at her sides of her head, *Stop! Stop, stop... please.* Water welled up at the edges of her eyes but she pushed the feelings back as she drew one long, ragged breath inward. Her eyes closed, and she gradually pushed the air from her lungs. *Slow down. Be here, be now.*

She opened her eyes, searching for the figures she knew were hidden around her. Daniel had slipped out of view completely, but Nathan's silhouette pressed against the conduits between the computer banks and the source of the sounds. Something was moving.

Within the shadows of his darkened alcove, Daniel quickly typed a massage out on his datapad and sent it.

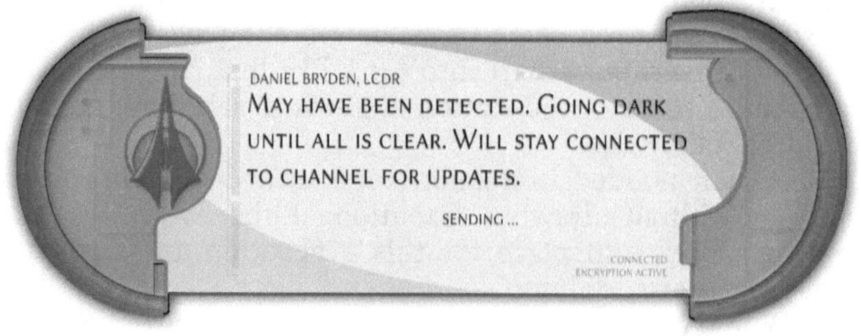


A metallic warble echoed through the air as a pipe rolled into the central light of the room. Kensy covered her ears to muffle the sound. The rigid pad of work boots against the generator room floor announced the stranger's approach. A weathered man with shaggy, warm, brown hair and facial scruff stepped toward the computer consoles and glanced about. A glint flashed over his eyes as they narrowed. He tried to focus on the deeply shaded corners without shuffling beyond reach of the light.

He pivoted to face the direction Nathan had slinked. Nathan stepped forward with a wry smile, "Kerso? Why are you lurking about down here? I thought you were checking on something."

"I was. Turned out to be another whole lot of nothin'. Why're *you* down here sneaking about all dodgy-like?" Kerso eyed him suspiciously.

"Escorting our new friends." Nathan reached past him to wave Kensy and Daniel out of hiding. "All good guys. This is one of ours." Kerso stepped back to see where these 'friends' were emerging from. He folded his arms across his chest, tucking his hands into his armpits. Daniel emerged first. Nathan gestured toward him. "This is Lieutenant Commander Daniel Bryden." Kensy rose to standing and recomposed herself. She walked into the edge of the light, eyeing the fallen pipe at the edge of her peripheral vision. "And Psilyria Kensy Frost. I am saying that right? Psilyria."

Kensy smiled. "Yep."

Nathan turned back toward Kerso, "Owen mentioned you were headed to check something out."

Kerso grunted, "Sensor trip over by the old recycling system." He shrugged. "One of the compressors started up and was just chunking away at nothing. Checked the whole mess over. Found one of those faulty power lines was conducting just enough to give it some go. I pulled the plug so it won't come back online again."

Nathan furrowed his brow, "I don't like the sound of that, but Bren and I replaced hundreds of those damned things. Suppose it's possible we missed one. You see anything else hinkey while you were out and about?"

"Nothing more than usual. Ducked a couple zombies running the main access corridor." Kerso rocked back on his heels.

"Zombies?" Daniel inquired.

Nathan bobbed his head. "It's what we call police, and anyone else who's been compromised. After the patrols stopped, we started catching them wandering around like mindless husks, attacking anyone who drew their attention. You know, like zombies."

Concern crossed Kensy's face, "Attacked?"

"Well," Nathan thought on it for a brief moment. "Not exactly like zombies. If they were armed, they'd shoot their victims, just leave them lying where they fell. Failing that, they grab something loose and bludgeon them to death. Pretty nasty either way. Now, we just avoid them whenever possible. That is one of the many reasons we need to get people off this station."

Kensy shivered with the imagined visual. "Agreed."

"Speaking of that, we should get moving." Daniel added.

"Yeah," Nathan gave a backhanded tap to Kerso's crossed arms. "We've got an evac plan. We need to get back and get things moving before we're found out."

"Sounds good." Kerso unfolded his arms, gesturing for the others to lead the way. "You can fill me in on the way." A subtle light refracted from deep within Kerso's eyes.

As they turned to leave, a dark glint caught Kensy's eye. She looked past Daniel and Nathan, in the direction of Kerso as his body jarred unnaturally. Shrrk. A flash of violet energy flashed past through the gap between the two men. Nathan looked at Kensy with her trembling outstretched hand, wide eyes, and stunned expression. He followed the line of her arm toward Kerso. Blood bubbled out from under the white-knuckled fingers gripping the base of his throat. Electricity arced off the back of his neck as the sundered thrall construct sputtered and died. He crumpled to the floor.

"What the hell?" Nathan hissed.

Daniel inched cautiously toward the fallen man, forcefully nudging the body with his boot. The body rolled over, exposing the back of his neck. "Damn it." The men looked down at the twisted black metal and wires that Kensy had destroyed. Daniel glanced to Kerso's hands. The skin puckered around a collection of sharp ridges not yet exposed. Blood pooled just under the skin from the subcutaneous rending that had begun.

Daniel waved Nathan back. "Don't touch him. He's been compromised."

Daniel looked back to Kensy. Her hand continued to tremble and water began to collect in her eyes. She gasped, "Stars. I killed him." She recoiled and looked down at her hands. "I did it again... I didn't even check. I just reacted. What if he wasn't—."

Daniel swiftly approached her in concern. "Hey, he was compromised. You were right to react."

Kensy wrestled with the sight of Kerso's lifeless body. "But what if he hadn't succumbed yet to the control? What if we could have saved him? I killed him without a second thought. He could have still had some self-control like Elle." Daniel paused questioningly. "Stars, what have I done?" She covered her mouth with her hands.

*Elle?* Daniel pushed the confusion to the back of his mind. *I'll have to ask about that later.* He leaned down to grip the sides of her arms. Her reddened eyes turned toward him, "Nathan and I didn't see the signs. He could have blindsided us, gotten the jump on us if you hadn't reacted. You probably just saved our lives." Her breath caught. He continued, "And like you said earlier, there are other lives on this station that need saving too. I'm gonna need your help with that. Can you do that for me?" She wiped her eyes and nodded, *yes.* He smiled at her, "There's the indomitable psilyria I know. Come on. Let's get moving."

He turned her around and guided her away from the source of her distress. Daniel looked back toward the body as they walked. *The Vagabond. It had to be that damned machine.* He and Nathan exchanged wary glances. "I have more questions. And maybe an answer or two. But not here. Not now. Get us back quickly and quietly."

"Yeah...," Nathan nodded.

## Chapter 31

# Evacuation

*"We have an exit strategy. Now, we just need time to execute it."*

*~ Nathan Derien*
*Colonial Engineer*

The sounds of the sanctuary were welcoming to the trio. Daniel placed a hand on Kensy's shoulder. "Why don't you start getting people packed up to move. We'll have to hustle to get all these people up to the evac point when this gets ready to kick off."

Kensy took a deep, shaky breath to still her anxiety, "Yeah, I can do that."

"We'll be behind you shortly. Just gotta work out the last few details." He waved her on and nodded silently for Nathan to draw back with him.

Nathan stuffed his hands in his pockets as he watched her go. "You sure she can handle this?"

Daniel looked him straight in the eyes. "She can handle it. If there's one thing that woman excels at, it's protecting people. She's just been through some pretty rough stuff recently. What I'm more concerned about is what we saw down there."

"Her murdering a guy in front of us?" Nathan scowled.

"She more than likely saved both our asses there." Daniel's posture became rigid. "No. I'm concerned about what was going on with him *before* she killed him." He tilted his head. "You mentioned people becoming corrupted several times.

198

Have you ever noticed if they have a little, spiky, black plate at the base of their necks?"

Nathan pondered his few encounters. "Yeah... I guess. Never really stopped to inspect them but its certainly a possibility."

"How about green dust? Ever found it in strange spaces like those oddly repaired problem spots?"

Nathan skeptically nodded. "Yeah. Figured it was something unique to this place. It's all over the place." The puzzle pieces began to fall into place in his mind. "Especially where strange shit's been happening." He huffed. "These are some oddly specific, random things to be asking about. So why? What does it mean?"

"It means, we are in over our heads." Daniel placed his hands on his hips. "We know what's behind all this, and I need to tell my captain, *now*. We have to assume the enemy knows everything about the plan, the sanctuary, all of it."

Nathan shook his head in frustration. "Son of a—. Right. If they already know about this place, we don't need to go too far to get a signal out." They jogged down the corridor away from the main space and into an adjacent chamber. Nathan pulled down a folding stair from one of the overhead hatches. "This should lead up into an observation lab. It'll put us just outside of the scramble zone." They raced up the stairs, pushing the access hatch to the lab open with little care. A quick scan of the room revealed it to be abandoned. "Call your ship, I'll secure the doors."

Daniel tapped his nahdvi, "Bryden, calling DeCadejra!"

"DeCadejra receiving. Status." Jackson's voice rung in his ears.

"Vagabond presence confirmed. It knows." Daniel listened to the string of expletives roll off his captain's lips. "Kensy's getting the civies ready to move as we speak."

"Get those people to the containers. Load them up. We're preparing an offensive against the station defenses. We'll draw its attention." Jackson sent a message down to Neira, *ready for imminent launch.* "When you're sealed in, send the signal."

Daniel cocked his head, "Going for the smash and grab?"

"Gonna have to." Jackson took a measured breath. "We go on your signal." The deafening wail of alarms blared through the communications link. "What is that?"

Nathan looked to Daniel as flashing lights flooded the room. "Station alarm. Your Vagabond is making his move." Nathan woke up a nearby console.

"We're outta time, Gabel." Daniel shifted around to look over his shoulder.

"Buy us whatever time you can. We're coming!" Jackson's knuckles blanched as he gripped the edge of the war room table.

Daniel suspended the connection. "What set off the alarm?"

"Main reactor alert. Trying to get camera feed up...." The pixelated visual filled the screen. There in front of the massive machinery stood a small female frame. "Is that...?" Nathan zoomed in. The figure came into focus. "Councilor Udahnel." She turned around and looked directly at the camera, her eye sockets empty and her appearance disheveled.

Daniel glanced into one of the upper corners of the room. He shot a small projectile toward the device hanging there. The lens shattered and sparks sputtered from the housing. "We gotta move."

Jumping down through the access door, Nathan quickly barred the hatch. They skittered down the stairs and through the rooms and back into the hallway. The cacophony of pandemonium in the main chamber rumbled under the sharp whine of the blaring alarms.

Kensy spotted them as they approached. "What's going on now?" she yelled over the chaos.

"The councilor's been compromised—," Daniel started.

Nathan interrupted, "She, it, whatever is overriding the safeties on the main reactor, shutting down cooling systems, increasing output."

Daniel shrugged, "Guess we made it mad. Now how to we get people to those containers?"

A groan of metal in the uppermost corners of the room drew their attention. Kensy's eyes widened. "It's gonna breach! Get them out of here!" She darted toward the center of the chamber and threw her hands up, projecting a barrier across the entirety of the space. "Ivani raga khiran!" The scream of her power words echoed through the space as she tried to solidify the manifestation. Metal squealed as a seam toward the top of the room began to peel apart. The air above her barrier rushed through the tiny crack in the station housing with tremendous force.

Nathan yelled at the crowd, "Everyone to D-deck emergency access! Now!" He pointed and flagged them toward the nearest exit. Worried he glanced up at the breach. He looked to Kensy amid the crowd. Numerous people stumbled into her as she fought to maintain the barrier above them. He surged toward her, Daniel on his heels. They stepped up on either side of her, waving people around. "This shouldn't be happening," he hollered to Daniel. "We're on the outer ring, but it had to have gotten through multiple layers of the station hull to be able to depressurize this space. What the hell is this thing?"

"Psychotic AI" Daniel responded. "Probably calculated our demise before we even knew it was here."

"Lovely." A young girl tripped as she was bombarded by the rushing crowd. Nathan stood her back up, "Easy there, pipsqueak." She clung to his side as the crowd surged past them. The air began to thin.

Kensy's breath became labored, "I can't seal it... we're losing...." She closed her eyes and focused on holding the air within her barrier.

Daniel scanned over the heads of people in motion. "Hang in there, Kensy. Just a little more to go."

Nathan glanced at her, then back to Daniel. "I need to grab something. Keep them moving." He crouched down to the girl at his side. "You stay with this guy; he'll get you out." He turned her toward Daniel, who managed a glancing smile to reassure her. Nathan vanished into the crowd. With the movement of bodies and the thinning of the air, the room began to spin around Kensy. Sweat beaded up on her brow. She took slow careful breaths as she fought to maintain her concentration.

She felt a figure brush up closely behind her. Nathan's voice rang in her ear. "You're gonna have to pardon me. Have to get a little friendly here. You just keep doing your... thing." He stretched a mask over her face from behind, trying to situate it and the securing strap around her head. He carefully draped a small tube over her shoulder. She heard the dull brush of a strap being adjusted as he wrapped a belt with a heavy pack around her waist. "Take a deep breath."

She inhaled. The air was crisp in her nostrils. She nodded to him. The oxygen hit her system and Kensy felt invigorated. She flexed her fingers. The glow of the barrier brightened slightly. Daniel glanced over his shoulder, to see Nathan behind Kensy adjusting the breathing system he had outfitted her with.

As the throng of colonists filtered through to the access door, a few stragglers could be identified: some with injuries from the chaos, some panic-stricken, some too young to understand. Nathan whistled for assistance. Owen and a handful of workers emerged back into the room. Nathan pointed across to the individuals tarrying about. "Need hands. Get them outta here, even if you gotta carry them!"

Owen nodded, "You heard the boss. Get moving!"

Nathan's breath became shallow. "We're almost there. Last few...."

Kensy tried to pull the barrier down a little to condense what air was left in the chamber. Her voice came out muffled by the rebreather. "I'm trying. Not sure how much longer I can hold."

Daniel scooped the little girl up in his arms. "Last few are headed out. Can you back toward the exit?" Kensy nodded, *yes*.

Nathan waved him away. "You go. I'll guide her back. We'll be right behind you." Daniel hesitated before sprinting to join Owen and the others as they made their way to the door. Nathan watched. "Alright they're out. Start back, we'll move as fast or slow as you feel comfortable." Kensy nodded again and took a step backward.

Kensy pulled the barrier back with them with each stride. Even with the blaring alarm and groaning station hull, she could hear Nathan struggling for breath right behind her. "Take the mask back. Can't have you passing out behind me."

He forced a choked laugh, "Nope. You need it more than I do right now. You drop that barrier, we both die."

"How much further?"

Nathan glanced toward the access door held closed by Owen and Daniel. "Ten meters. Less."

Kensy made a quick gesture with her left hand. Daniel watched intently, catching the subtle twist of her wrist. "Open the door!" Startled by the command, Owen yanked on the door with him. They wrenched against the air pressure sealing the portal. As the seal gave, the hiss of air reached Kensy's ears.

She dropped her hands and spun around. Her wings flared into being. She wrapped her arms around Nathan's torso. The tendrils from her back pierced into the superstructure, and like a slingshot, they launched Kensy toward the opening like a comet. A glittering purple burst blazed through the doorway.

Daniel and Owen slammed the door closed as the flash of Nathan and Kensy passed by. They tumbled against the stairs, cushioned only by the wrap of her powers. Owen sealed and locked the hatch again.

Kensy peeled the mask off her face and placed it over Nathan's nose and mouth. "Sorry for the crash landing... and the power burns. That was taking too long." He nodded and gave her a thumbs up. "Appreciate the air though. Couldn't have done it without you." She looked to Daniel. "We need to catch up with the others. Air's gonna be thin everywhere that was open, and that one rebreather can only get us so far."

A second tone joined the cadence of the emergency alarm. Nathan lurched into a sitting position and pulled the mask from his face. "Owen, get up there. We need the containers in the hangar bay emptied and people packed in for evac. Go!" Owen skipped past the group and darted up the stairs ahead of them. Nathan pulled his datapad from his side. "Shit. No signal." He handed the mask back to Kensy as he got to his feet. "That's a second stage warning. We'll have to get up to the hangar bay so I can figure out what's going on." He looked around in concern. "Where's the little one?"

Daniel pointed up the stairs, "Sent her ahead with the others."

"Thanks," Nathan looked between the two of them. "Really, thanks... however this turns out—."

Daniel slapped him on the back, "Thank us *on the ship*, after this is all over."

Chapter 32

# Out of Time

*"Seven, six, five, four... three... two... —."*

Jackson stood at the center of the bridge, his white knuckles wrapping over the top edge of the strategic operations command console. Anxiety firmly dug into his chest as he watched the readouts. "Cross, are you in position yet?"

"Attack squad, reading for strike."

"Make it surgical, we can't risk compromising a section with the people we're here to save." Jackson thumbed through the readouts before flipping over to another channel. "Allen, I need an update on the cargo bays."

Machinery whirled in the background of the open channel. The chief engineer replied, "We'll be ready to take on passengers within minutes." He shouted toward his crew. "Disassemble that and move it up to the labs on seven." Shifting his attention back to Jackson, he shoved his glasses back up his nose and spoke with confidence. "Might be a little cramped, but we're getting it done."

The commander nodded, "Good."

"Attack squad commencing strike. Take out shields and guns only people." Neira's voice drew Jackson's eyes back to the main display. "Gabel, get your boarders lined up. We're about to blaze a path."

"Roger that."

205

Detonations on the outer hull reverberated through the station's bones. The lights flickered. Kensy flinched as she felt the structure shudder around them. Beside her, Nathan looked up toward the colonists. "We're out of time! Get everyone packed in." He made eye contact with Kensy. And with a small nod, he jogged toward his charges.

Kensy reached up and tapped her nahdvi. The line connected. "Jack?" She hesitated.

"We're just about to launch the boarding shuttle. We're getting you out—."

"No." She wrung her hands together. "Jack, the Vagabond disabled the safeties on the main reactor. It's about to blow. You have to pull everyone back."

He shook his head, "I can't do that—."

"Jack!" The line was quiet for several long seconds. "Prepare for salvage operations."

Jackson brought his voice low. "You are telling me to sit back and watch that station explode with you on it?"

She smiled through her tears. "I'm asking you to save as many people as you can." Jackson's jaw tightened. "Please, Jack, ...for me."

He reached forward and opened the global comm line. "All ships disengage and fall back. Blast imminent. Begin preparations for disaster recovery." The din of the bridge grew dull and mottled in his ears.

Her voice chimed through to him clearly, "Thank you." Her breath caught. "Jack, if I don't—."

"No. Don't—." He pleaded. "Tell me when you get back."

She closed her eyes and whispered. "I love you." Kensy tapped her nahdvi again. The line disconnected. She drew in a sharp breath and blinked away the water in her eyes. Turning toward the commotion behind her, Kensy cleared her throat. "Nexus?"

With a crackle, his energetic form appeared beside her. "Quite the conundrum you have here."

"I need to save them. There has to be a way." Her eyes traced the seams in the floor. "But I couldn't make the barrier solid enough on my own. Can you help me?"

Nexus stared up at her, his glowing eyes narrowing to contemplative slits. "Hmm. I could indeed. Fusing my form to yours would provide a stronger conduit through which you could channel enough power to create an airtight manifestation. However, I do not know what long-term effects this will have on your physiology, or psychology for that matter. Your physical form is not intended to endure that level of stress."

Kensy nodded. "It's more of a chance than they have otherwise." Her mind drifted toward the looming storm from her nightmares and the blackened abyss at the edge of her mind. "If I can save them, then the price I pay will be worth it. At least I get the chance to go out fighting *for* something." She smiled hesitantly. "It would have been nice to have more time." A third tone joined the blaring alarms, echoing overhead. With a steeling breath, she headed toward the center of the clustered containers.

Nathan sidled up beside her. "Almost everyone's loaded up. This is either going to be the most daring rescue in history, or one hell of a disaster."

She pivoted to face him. "Do something for me? Get Daniel in one of those containers."

"What are you—?" He cocked his head as he stopped in his tracks.

"It's time." Taking a few steps back, she unfolded her arms and closed her eyes. Nexus levitated up in front of her. He dove toward her, his feline form dissolving into a rippling purple cascade of psionic energy.

Nathan watched as the air warped and wrapped around her. He skipped backward into a jog. "Button 'em up! Everyone in! NOW!" Daniel rounded the corner into Nathan's line of sight. Swiftly, Nathan firmly planted his palm on Daniel's chest. "You too!" Daniel's eyes shifted past the man in his path, following the flowing lines of power lifting off Kensy's form. He opened his mouth to rebut the order as Nathan leaned close. "Don't fight me on this one, man. Just get in the container."

With a nod, Daniel stepped back and up into the adjacent pod. He examined the look of consternation clear on every face within the crowd of colonists. Feigning a smile, he spoke, "We're gonna get through this."

Nathan bowed his head as he sealed the large door. He looked toward Kensy. Then one last glance around. Every container was sealed and waiting. A half dozen figures laboriously congregated, dragging a cluster of smaller capsules into the gaps between containers. Owen rushed up next to him. "Snagged a few sleeper pods from medical. They're ready to go, boss."

Nathan patted him on the shoulder. "Nice work. Tuck in." They walked toward the cluster. One by one, they crawled into the pods and engaged the containment controls. Last man in, Nathan quietly spoke in the direction of Kensy's strangely sparkling visage. "See you on the other side."

Chain explosions shook through the station's substructure. The lights cut out. A serene purple glow wrapped around each container. The artificial gravity systems shut down. As the containers drifted off the floor, she swirled them around herself, each tethered by a tendril from her radiant wings. Her eyes glowed with an otherworldly light as she opened them.

She shifted her arms in a circular motion, pulling at the air, coaxing it to gather around her. Piece by piece, fractal patterns emerged from the fog of psionic power. As their form solidified, a circular shell formed around the amalgam of drifting shapes. The floor and ceiling of the bay warped and twisted outward to accommodate the sphere.

The alarms suddenly ceased. Kensy pulled tightly on the tethers of her power. Holding the moment and her breath. Flame and force ripped through the station. She crossed her arms over her chest and curled her head down. Her muscles quaked as she fought to brace against the sundering blast.

The structure heaved and warped. Bulkheads shattered. Flames roiled outward, consuming the escaping air as it evacuated the station. Conduits shredded under the intense force of the rippling explosion. Debris scattered in all directions. Larger fragments tumbled in spiraling arcs before surrendering to the pull of the planet below. The atmosphere of the gas dwarf flickered and quaked in response, the last energies dying out in brilliant colors and lights.

Everyone aboard the DeCadejra stared wide-eyed at their displays. Stunned silence filled the choking air. *Gone. Just gone.* Jackson wavered, unblinking. *Tell me when you get back. You were supposed to come back.* He staggered back a step, his eyes following the trail of cascading debris as it crashed into the clouds. Every second inched across his skin like an eternity of unease.

A communications crackle startled Jackson. He looked down at the readout. The pilot's voice came through amid the dissipating static. "VISUAL! I have a visual!"

"Report!" he commanded.

"A purple sphere! — where the station used to be! Can't identify contents." The pilot frantically called out. "We need recovery nets. NOW! It's beginning to descend toward the atmosphere!"

Jackson exhaled. *Fuck. She did it.* Lightning coursed through his veins, sparking him into action. "Don't let it out of your sight! Recovery crews, *go, go, go!*" His fingers danced across the screens and inputs as he orchestrated deployments.

"We're gonna lose it!" The pilot called back.

"Not on my watch!" Neira and her attack squadron dove toward the debris field. "All units transfer power from armament arrays to shield capacitors. Locking in on target. Invert formation Sierra-Charlie-six. Let's build a cradle." Like well-practiced stunt fliers, the fighters closed in on the sphere, catching it carefully along the upward slopes of their wings. "Initial assessment: sphere appears solid and unbroken."

"Recovery Two and Four in position to assist."

Jackson leaned on his console. "Bring them home." *Bring her home.*

## Chapter 33

# Fused

*"Damn, I've never seen anything like it."*
*~ Sergeant Kort Shane*

The hangar bay seals locked into place. Air hissed from every corner of the compartment as the repressurization process began. A handful of engineers waited anxiously in the wings. Their environmental suits rustled as they watched for the glowing sphere before them to show some sign of release. "Aft hangar bay atmosphere reestablished." Maggie's mechanical voice echoed through the space. A hexagonal segment of the manifestation flickered before dissolving. From the newly formed opening, the psionic shell began to peel away, piece by piece.

"We've got pods!" Allen shouted. "Grab the cargo hoists! Let's set these people down gently." The team on either side of him sprung into action. Using the weightlessness of the bay, they launched toward the ceiling. One at a time, the crew pulled lines of cables and magnetic clamps toward the containers. Allen drifted toward the shape of the psilyria at the center. "Kensy, I'll need you to untether them if we are gonna get the clamps on."

Her expression remained static as she raised her head and uncurled her body. An intense, alien light poured from her eyes. The violet wrap of her power slowly waned from each container and pod as the tendrils of her wings pulled back into her form.

Swiftly, the bulk of the engineering team secured the large containers to lifts, while a select few ferried the smaller pods to the hangar's second-floor balcony. "We're going to bring up the gravity slowly." Allen informed her. He took another quick glance around, "Double check the mounts! Ready for grav-up."

"Secured!" The word repeatedly echoed from the host of voices scattered across the bay. "All clamps secured." He gave the nod.

"Initialization of gravity systems, increasing to one percent of ship standard." Maggie announced. Shapes across the bay drifted gradually toward the floor plating. With the resounding twang of metal, the cables pulled taught. The soft thuds of boots tapped the horizontal surfaces over which they had hovered. "Increasing gravity to ten percent of ship standard." The medical pods jarred against the metallic grating of the balcony walkways.

Allen landed on the hangar floor. "Level the containers." He glanced up to the gravity defying visage of his psionic captain. "Grave, we'll start with yours. Set her down, soft-like. Maggie, keep bringing the gravity up, nice and steady."

Two technicians studiously checked over the medical pods on the balcony. They nodded respectfully to Jackson as he launched himself past them and into the room. His hands clasped the railing tightly to halt his momentum. "Maggie, I want full spectrum jamming until notified. Begin complete ship nanite scan and random interval follow up sweeps. Let's make sure we don't have any unwanted AI hitchhikers."

"Routine established."

Jackson glanced back over his shoulder as the first pod hissed open. The door slid away and the man inside clamored to extricate himself from within. He waved away the tech. "I'm good. I'm good. Get the others." Placing his hands on his knees, he shook his head and took a few nerve-settling breaths.

When he lifted his gaze, he met Jackson's scrutinizing stare. With only a few bounding steps in the low gravity, he came to rest beside Jackson. "You've got quite an operation going here, commander." He nodded the bars on Jackson's uniform. "Thanks for that." As the containers descended to the floor below, the purplish glow at the center of the room radiated toward them, casting the room in light that softened the appearance of the monotone structure. Both men were drawn to the sight. "Mind if I ask, what's her deal?"

Jackson straightened his posture. "She's the reason we're all standing here."

"Nathan!" Bethany burst forward, tackling her brother.

He winced as she squeezed his ribs tightly. "Hey, runt." He patted the top of her head.

"Gabel, you might need to get down here. Somethin's off." Allen's voice relayed through Jackson's nahdvi. He glanced to the hangar bay floor as Kensy gradually drifted downward. Hurriedly, he pivoted around the reunited siblings and bolted for the stairs. Confused by the abrupt urgency, they broke the embrace and followed on his heels.

Jackson skipped the last few steps, landing at the base, and springing forward into a brisk stride. He wove between containers and personnel with battlefield efficiency. The trio arrived beside Allen as Kensy's boots softly made contact with the cold floor.

Allen whispered, "She's barely responding to us."

Jackson stepped forward. "Kensy? You can release your power. They're safe."

Her unblinking eyes slowly turned toward him. The voice that emanated from her echoed with a strange but not unfamiliar resonance. "That course of action would be unwise, commander. The psilyria's body has undergone a great deal of stress from the manifestation. Our fusion is sustaining her... temporarily. It would be prudent for your physician to attend to her stabilization before the separation is attempted."

Jackson squinted questioningly at the being before him. "Nexus?"

"What?" Allen glanced between them.

Jackson shook his head. "Never mind! Tell Doc she's got incoming!" He looked back to Nexus. "How do we get... *you* up there?"

Bethany and Nathan exchanged uncertain shrugs. Nexus tilted her head thoughtfully. "I shall proceed to walk her up to the medical bay. If you would please provide an escort. Her powers are unstable, and she does not wish undue harm to your ship, crew, or civilian charges."

"Yeah, of course." Jackson nodded. "Chief, get these people outta the containers. Tap whoever you need to for extra hands. And tell Threaux to set course for Aepexia but to keep it smooth."

"Yes, captain!" Allen acknowledged. "You heard the man, let's crack 'em open. We've got some civies in need of fresh air!"

Jackson circled around Kensy, waving his fellow crewmates away from the path to the aft hangar bay elevator. Curious glances shot their way as they moved. Backing toward his destination, his eyes followed her stride. *Why aren't her footsteps making any sound?* Intently he studied each step, then glancing past he saw it: the scarring of the hangar bay floor. *Damn. She's radiating so much power, it's buffering her from actually touching the ground.* His thoughts drifted to the pursuit on Aepexia and Gabby's words: *If she's bleeding this much, she could risk tapping out or worse... burning out.... that kind of expenditure could kill her.* His jaw tensed. *We're not out of the woods yet. Hang in there, Kensy.*

The lift doors opened behind him. He placed an arm across the opening and pressed backward to let her pass into the elevator ahead of him. A searing tingle spread across his arm as she stepped inside. He squinted at the sensation. *How is Doc going to treat her if I get burned just by being this close?* He pivoted in after her and the doors closed.

"Proceeding to deck seven, medical team on standby for arrival." Maggie informed him.

"Thank you, Maggie."

The ascent was short. The doors opened and Jackson swiftly shifted out ahead of her. He held his arm across the threshold again. He braced in anticipation of the sensation. A noise in the corridor beyond pulled his attention away. A handful of personnel approached the end of the hall. "Back! Everyone clear the hallway. Now!" He winced as the sear of her power crawled across his arm amid his distraction.

The figures in the corridor scattered in disparate directions, all save one towering presence. Nevan drew closer, his arms folded across his chest as he watched Kensy head for the medical bay. "Maggie, medical bay doors, if you would, please." He nodded to Jackson. The doors slid open and held position at his request.

Doctor Tyronis watched as her patient entered through the main doors. She studied the strange sight briefly before nodding to one of her techs. The man beside her activated the operating room doors. "Psilyria Frost, if you can...." She gestured toward the newly opened side room.

"As you request." Nexus replied promptly.

The doctor cocked her head at the unexpected tone. Jackson rushed to her side. "I can explain, well, kinda. Kensy did something, fused, I guess, to an otherworldly psionic cat thing that she occasionally sees." He waved the notion away. "Anyway, Nexus... the *thing* inside her is piloting. Says she over stressed her body. And somehow, we need to stabilize her before it can let go?" He took a deep breath. "She's radiating power. A lot of power."

Doc glanced at his seared sleeve. "I can see that." She turned over her shoulder. "Check and treat him for burns." Her attention returned to the commander. "We'll get it sorted out. Half of my staff is helping downstairs. Once you're patched up, I suggest you head down to check in on our new arrivals.

Moore, Vale, you're with me." The trio of medical personal entered the operating room with purposeful strides.

Jackson watched the doors separating the rooms shutter away the deep violet light of Kensy's power. Even out of sight, his thoughts remained locked on her. A voice jarred him from the haze of worry. "I think you're going to need a new jacket."

Jackson's eyes fell to his charred sleeve and the fiercely ruddy glow of the skin on his left hand. He grunted in resignation. "Probably." He unfastened his jacket, sliding it off with a wince as it brushed against the burnt flesh. A medic approached with supplies in hand as Jackson glanced toward Nevan.

Nevan smirked at him. "While we have a few moments here, why don't you tell me about this otherworldly psionic cat *thing?*"

Jackson cringed at the medic's touch and Nevan's inquiry. *Today's just getting better, and better.* He huffed, "Right, that...."

Chapter 34

# Heartbeats

*"All we were, all we are, all we ever will be, is here, in*
*between these heartbeats...."*
~ *ancient human song*

A blinding light filled Kensy's vision. She squinted against it, raising her arm up in front of her eyes. Voices echoed around her. They swirled around her in a dizzying haze. "Doc?" She stumbled. "Jackson?" Tightness rose through her chest into her throat. Her voice fell to a whisper. "Anyone?" She sank to her knees, then shifted her weight to the side as she slumped onto the nebulous ground. "Anyone...?"

With heavy breath, she wavered. The tension in her body bled away. The glaring light split into many, trailing the din of the voices circling and swarming about. Her form became smothering and cumbersome, as if even lifting her head was a feat of strength. She fought to catch the breath that escaped her lips. Dull pain radiated from disparate points, nearly washing her away with a flood of undiscernable sensations.

The light shifted to a dark violet. Energy crackled around her, and a familiar resonant voice reached her. "Giving up so easily?"

Kensy labored to raise her gaze to him. The energy and light coalesced into the Nexus's familiar feline form. "I'm spent. It all feels so heavy." She gasped.

He tilted his head, "Anything worth fighting for is difficult."

Hundreds of faces flashed through her mind. Colonists. Mechanics. Children. Owen. Nathan. Bethany. Daniel. Jackson... Jackson. She lingered on him, his stern gaze, his commanding presence, his subtle smile when he didn't think anyone was looking, his words....

*"This time, I'm not letting go."*

*"If you ever need me... just say the word."*

*"...we can figure this out together."*

*"I'll be right here with you."*

*"We're getting you out—"*

*"Tell me when you get back."*

Tears poured from her eyes silently. She shook her head weakly. "I couldn't even give him that." A sharp jab into her arm jarred her. A burst of cool air forced its way into her lungs. She gasped. As her lungs filled again, she yelled toward the nebulous environment. "Why! Why am lingering in this torturous space?" Her eyes fluttered wearily. "Why can't I rest?"

Nexus narrowed his gaze toward her. "Why don't you tell me?" His tail curled around his dagger-like feet. "Who *are* you, Kensington Anastasia Gennavieve Frost? Do you need a reminder?"

A musical ring reached her ears, causing her to glance down to glittering jewels and a gossamer pink gown adorning her. She staggered to her feet. Her hair fell in spiraling ringlets around her down-turned face. "Are you a jewel long lost to the endless stars?"

A sterile coldness set in around her. Tension and dread filled her chest as she glanced up to the towering gray darkness that closed in around her. "Are you a discarded promise awaiting the embrace of the enduring void?"

The nebulous environment shifted to verdant shades. She turned, feeling the brush of her academy uniform against her skin and the soft steps of her boots under her feet. "Are you a student fumbling for purpose and understanding?"

The smell of fire and dust filled her nose. She looked down at her tattered uniform. "Are you a broken warrior grasping at emptiness in desperation?"

The weight of water and blood bore down on her. "Are you a trophy, easy prey for the weak and willful?" Unseen gravel shifted under her feet. Rage, like an unfamiliar fire, burned through her veins, threatening to consume her.

The space returned to a calm violet haze and the wash of sensations subsided. "Or are you more?"

She stood before Nexus in her favorite flowing peridot shirt and charcoal slacks. She gazed into the palms of her hands. "I have been so many fragments, trying to keep hold of pieces, of dreams, that could never be." Her hands curled closed. "All I'm left with... all I am... is just me."

He gazed at her questioningly. "And who *are* you?"

All of the names given to her flooded into her mind. Princess. Psilyria. Kensy. She smiled as she heard her name in Jackson's voice echo through her mind. "I'm just Kensy."

A satisfied grin crossed Nexus's face. "And do you know to give up, Kensy?" Images flashed through her mind. Cascading memories brought her back to her last stand on Bhelnir. She felt the shift of the ship as she stood atop the Themiscyra with Jackson, fighting to keep hold of her barriers. Shadows rose to engulf her on the dais of Ghellaine Prime, where countless machines descended on the two of them. Desperation and determination filled her from the scene aboard Cor'Threa as the seams of the station peeled apart around her.

She tilted her head with an abbreviated chuckle. "No. I guess I don't." Pressure built in her chest. *Maybe I can borrow just a little more time.* She closed her hands over her heart. *Stars, please grant me a few more heartbeats to see this through.* She whispered, "I'm not ready to fade away anymore."

Vale glanced at the monitor in his peripheral vision. The steady line tracing across it jumped to life. "We've got a pulse again! BP 122 over 83."

"BP 122 over 83, copy that." Moore called back. He continued, "SpO2 92, heart rate 68 bpm."

"SpO2 92, heart rate 68 bpm. Copy."

"Peep isolator reading ETO$_2$ at 41."

"ETO$_2$ at 41, copy." Each statistic and order echoed through the room. Keeping the team on task and informed.

"Adjust oxygen intake." Doctor Tyronis nodded to her technicians as she listened to the readouts. "Moore, rerun the neural scan. Let's see if her pattern is holding. Vale, I'm still reading slightly elevated lactate levels. Please confirm."

Vale shifted to another console and furiously tapped across the interface. A full body scan of Kensy lifted from her form. Hovering just above her, its colors shifted and flowed to show the circulation of elements through her system. "Confirmation of slightly elevated lactate levels. Looks like we'll need to maybe run a metabolic booster to help out kidney and liver processing."

Doc watched her medical nanites studiously reinforce a hairline fracture and begin to stitch together a frayed muscle in Kensy's upper arm. "We'll begin with .5 ml Noitaxaler. Prep for full body tissue regen. Run two passes of minimum stimulation, administer booster after first pass. Let's see if we can jumpstart her body's natural repair processes." Her nanites finished their work and retreated to the insertion needle as commanded. Upon retrieval confirmation she withdrew the needle, and pressed a small pulse patch over the puncture. The edges flashed with light. Her thumb ran across the patch, checking its adhesion. Perfect.

"Neural pattern stable... and clean." Moore spoke up in a semi-surprised tone. "Looks like the energy bleed is nearly gone."

Doc glanced to Kensy's serene expression under the inhibitor halo. *Nice to have you back with us, Miss Frost.* She looked to her medical technicians, "Prep for first pass." Vale and Moore secured the regeneration frame to the head of the operating table and stepped back. Moore nodded to the doctor. "Beginning first pass, full body tissue restoration. Stand by."

"Standing by," Moore echoed. The frame gradually crawled down the length of the table. It traced over their patient with a nearly invisible wall of light, save for the white line that cascaded over the contours of her body. Collectively, they glued their eyes to the holographic scan, looming over her motionless figure. At the foot of the table, the tone of the light shifted. With a soft mechanical whine, the frame began to crawl back to its original position.

Vale pulled some reading from the hologram. "Kidney and liver efficiency holding steady." He turned toward the wall and drew out a sliding shelf. Snatching the bottle from its resting place, he double checked the label. He pulled a sterile syringe from another storage compartment, and breaking the seal on both, he drew the ruby colored fluid from the vial. "Pulling .5 ml Noitaxaler. Administering metabolic booster." With measured precision, he injected the substance into her iv line.

"BP maintaining 122 over 83," Moore called out.

Vale checked his monitor to confirm. "BP 122 over 83, copy."

"SpO2 95, heart rate 68 bpm."

"SpO2 95, heart rate 68 bpm. Copy."

"Lactate levels decreasing."

"Lactate levels decreasing. Copy."

Doctor Tyronis fine-tuned her display to isolate the disparate psionic energy signatures coursing through Kensy's body. "Foreign energy signature fading throughout. Still seeing excess energy around the heart and control clasp. Get the suppression sleeve on that right arm and pass me the X." Vale grabbed a heavily weighted drape from a nearby shelf and handed it across to his boss. With a few quick moves, she opened it across her patient's chest, draping one leaf over each shoulder and down past lower ribs on either side.

Vale pulled a similarly weighted sleeve up to Kensy's elbow. It fully encompassed her arm and the support beneath it. His fingers found the connectors at the underside of the table lip and fastened them together. With a thumbs up, he signaled the go ahead.

"Raising suppression levels to dissipate psionic flow...." Doc's fingers gradually slid up the screen in front of her.

"Heartbeat irregularity!" Vale called out.

Moore watched the interface of the inhibitor halo intently. "Autonomic neural activity increasing."

"Heartbeat stabilizing."

Doctor Tyronis glanced between them, "Trying again, increasing suppression...." The cloud of energy around the heart and clasp finally began to decay on the screen.

With rapt attention Vale stared at his readings. "BP holding. Pulse... steady."

"Autonomic neural activity returning to normal levels," Moore affirmed.

Doc watched the lasts wisps of intense violet light fade from the screen. Only faint trails of color illuminated the psionic's natural energy pathways, like a pale echo of her nervous system. "Energy dispersal confirmed. Releasing suppression." Kensy's vitals held steady, and the static psionic energy remained at its normal levels. A collective sigh passed between them. "All right, stow the X and the sleeve. Then prep for second pass regen." She stepped back as they busily hustled around the medical bed. She studied the holographic scan, every color, every shifting pattern, for any sign of anomaly.

"Ready when you are, Doc."

She tipped her head slightly in response. "Start second pass." Her stare was steady and unrelenting as the procedure progressed. The various hair line fractures lit up as activity around them was stimulated to reinforce the damage. Kensy's internal temperature fluctuated within expected parameters. The wilted natural sheathing around her psionics system surged back to a healthier coating as it recovered from the manifestation's overexposure.

The frame reached the end of the table again. Its light shifted and the mechanical whine echoed through the room. "Lactate levels within acceptable threshold and still falling. All other vitals holding steady."

Doc blinked and stepped back up to the table. "Get her into an observation room, get a repeat on labs. I want full stats on the hour every hour until she regains consciousness. Reduce inhibitor influence by one step at the beginning of each check. Watch for that little hiccup we saw. We'll let the regeneration continue at its own pace. Her natural healing should be able to take it from here. Good work."

Chapter 35

# Reconnecting

*"Looks like we'll be getting down right cozy here for a while."*
*~ Ensign Kaitlyn "Kait" Reily*

Hundreds of weary figures huddled together through the port side hangar and cargo bays. Daniel looked over the sea of new faces as the crew wove through the improvised walkways with care and supplies. An engineer approached him with an armload of fabric. "Maggie manufactured some more blankets. Where do we need them?"

Daniel pointed to one of the medical technicians, "Ask, Grantham. He'll know who needs them most."

"Yes, sir!" The crewman nodded and darted toward his intended target.

Daniel gazed down at his holopad. "Hey Maggie, any chance you could make us a few more breather units? We've still got people struggling."

"Manufacturing request added to queue. Pending authorization for utilization of weapons lab processors," she chimed back.

Daniel nodded. "Authorization granted. We're not using the prototyping lab right now, anyway." He scrolled through the list of requests. His mind churned through a haze of information, trying to find the best strategy for tackling the mounting concerns. The din of chattering voices filled the space around him. Small children provided exuberant laughter

224

and benign chaos as they raced around and under the tired gazes of the older civilians.

Jackson staggered in his approach as a trio of little ones cut through his path. Daniel caught the movement in the corner of his vision. "I thought you'd be glued to the medbay." He examined the bandage descending down his captain's arm. It extended from under the short sleeve of Jackson's plain black uniform undershirt.

Jackson grunted and stuffed his hands in his pockets. "I got patched up and kicked out. How are things down here?"

Daniel gave a knowing smirk. With the subtle tilt of his head, he brought up a summary screen. "We've got all of Maggie's manufacturing facilities tasked to capacity, making breathers, blankets, bandages.... You name it, and we're short on it. We got everyone out of containers and spread through the three port side bays, but it's still cramped. The deck eight storage spaces on either side of the elevator have been transformed into sanitation facilities. And Allen has a team of engineers trying to rig sleeping quarters into the rafters from the empty pods." He pointed up to the swarm of engineers on the second-story catwalks. Daniel sighed, "We are making do, but we don't exactly have a lot of room to move."

Jackson raised an eyebrow at the readout. "Well, its going to have to be enough." He reached forward and tapped on the consumables' projections. He grunted at the numbers in front of him. "Half rations for everyone until we get back to port. We've got about four days back. And then we *hope* that Admiral Davir doesn't keep us in quarantine too much past that." His grumble melded into the ambiance of the room.

Bethany slouched back against the wall of the hangar bay catwalk. She traced her eyes over the figures beyond the floor grating, captain, crew and colonists. "I can't quite wrap my head around all of this. You saved all these people on the station?"

Nathan chuckled. "You know me, runt. I've always had a knack for making things more complicated." He shook his head. "But in all seriousness, I just managed a really elaborate delaying action. These people are the ones doing all the heavy lifting. I couldn't have gotten anyone off the station by myself." He pointed to Jackson and Daniel as they made the rounds on the lower floor.

Bethany nodded and stared down at her hands. "Yeah. No one else believed me. But I guess I made enough of a fuss at the Aepexian Assembly diplomatic ball, that I got the captains' attention."

Nathan turned an incredulous glance her way. "You didn't!"

"I did. Screamed at one of the magistrates that had been ducking me, right there in the ballroom." She shot a wincing glance his way.

Nathan laughed, "My sister, *master* of tact."

She shrugged. "Well, it worked, sorta. The magistrate still blew me off. But out of nowhere these two captains approach, one acting like I'm the best friend she hasn't seen in years. We duck into a side room with a few of their officers, and I spilled everything I knew. Of course, it wasn't much. But instead of an interrogation they just said 'yeah, we'll help' just like that. The chick that's the leader of their main ground team spent most of the trip trying to take my mind off things."

"The one with the crazy psionics?"

Bethany shook her head, *no*. "That's one of their captains. The one that hung out with me is… there." Her eyes searched the sea of faces, directing his attention to the woman. "Lieutenant Lindsay Rasken. She told me loads of funny stories about her family, her dad and little brother. I'll introduce you maybe after things settle down. Maybe. If there's time."

Nathan raised an eyebrow in his sister's direction. "Oh, she made a good enough impression on you, that you actually *want* to introduce us?" He leaned back and glared at her suspiciously.

Glancing to him she paused. "What? Oh, geeze. Not like that! I just think you might get along. She seems pretty cool, and she likes bikes and mechanic shit. You can talk shop or... something."

He threw his hands up. "Just checking. I thought I'd need a new identity after the last hookup you tried to send me on." She slugged him in the shoulder. "Violence! Aahh! I'm under attack!"

She rolled her eyes and shook her head. "I don't hit *that* hard." Bethany crossed her arms, huffing loudly as she slouched back against the wall again. "Maybe I *should* set you up with Lindsay. She could give you something to cry about."

"I heard my name! Hope it wasn't taken in vain. Or *maybe* I should hope it was?" Rasken's gruff voice carried over from the stairs. Smiling and popping a bubble from her gum, she approached the duo. With a graceful crossing of her ankles she folded into a sitting position in front of Bethany and Nathan. Holding a hand out to shake, she smirked. "You must be the brother I've heard so much about."

Nathan grasped her hand. "Nathan Derien. I was just hearing about you, Lieutenant Lindsay Rasken."

"Guilty as charged." She shrugged. "Yo, sorry we couldn't bust down the door and just swoop in to get ya. There was some pretty janky stuff goin' on with that station." Tapping Bethany's shin with her fist Rasken knuckle pointed at her. "And what did I tell you? We're getting this shit squared away! *And* we found your brother, so, score!"

Bethany nodded. "Yep, just like you said. Thanks, Lindsay."

Rasken leaned in close to the pair. "Hey, I know they are keeping things kind buttoned down to these lower decks, but do you two want to blow this lemonade stand and see the rest of the ship?"

Bethany laughed. "I've seen my share, and it's been an exhausting day. I might just head back to my room, if you don't mind."

Nathan nodded to her. "Go get some rest, runt. There will be plenty more time to talk later." He watched his sister push off the wall to stand and disappear around the adjacent door frame. "I, on the other hand, would *love* a tour of the ship." He hopped to his feet almost as quickly as Rasken did.

She glanced upward, "Maggie, you don't see anything." She waved Nathan out of the room in her wake.

"My sensors see a great many things, lieutenant. But if this is a request for discretion, your request will be transferred to the bottom of the request queue."

Rasken chuckled. "Close enough."

Nathan watched her intently. "You really like your bubblegum, don't you?"

She blew a bubble in his direction. With a resounding pop, she glanced to him questioningly. "Yeah. What of it?"

Nathan smiled mischievously. "Oh, no reason." His hand slipped into one of the pouches on his tool belt. "Just didn't realize the woman entertaining and watching over my kid sister was the same one I keep hearing murmurs about." He pulled his hand out with a small package in his grasp. He tilted it toward her. "Care for a piece?"

Rasken stopped and gaped at the pack of gum in his hand. "You carry gum in your tool belt?"

"Of course!" He confidently shrugged. "It's incredibly useful stuff. Never know where it might come in handy."

Her finger slid down the package between his fingers. Slowly, she pulled her finger back, dragging a piece from the wrapper. She chuckled, "Oh, this is going to be a *fun* tour."

Chapter 36

# Fractured Memory

*"The mind plays tricks. It is up to you which voice you choose to listen to."*

*~ Psionica Ellise Neru*

Kensy's boots slipped across the wet pavement as she stumbled into the flickering light of a dying streetlamp. She glanced around, jumping at every shadow, squinting at every unfamiliar shape. Her breath escaped her lips in ragged gasps. Solemn rain drizzled off the sagging eves. Whispers and mechanical skitterings bombarded her hearing. Her heartbeat pounded through her veins.

She had never been here before and yet it was familiar. Or was that wrong? Her mind battled against itself, unable to reconcile the fractured memories just beyond her grasp. A plaza lay just ahead. Perhaps from there she would be able to see more.

Dread filled her every step. Yet need relentlessly pushed her forward. The sky opened up over the rooftops. The shapes were a distorted haze of shadow, synthetic clouds, and tear-blurred images. She stopped in the center of the plaza, staring up into the rain. Closing her eyes, she drew in a deep breath.

An intense pulse seized her chest. With a gasp, she pushed back against it. The pulse swept out from her into the surrounding cityscape with bone rattling force. As it washed over crates and around corners, a single pipe clattered to the ground. Its metallic ring warbled and warped the space around

229

her. Memories chaotically bombarded her with disorienting images and emotions. The ring of the pipe grew louder and louder in her ears until the scraping sound was lifted from the pavement behind her.

She threw her hands defensively as she spun. Her powers manifested into a sphere around her. In a flash of memory, the pipe swung downward. The sphere shattered into countless faceted pieces. Each reflective shard filled her visions.

Again, she felt the anxiety and grief of blasting Jackson after Mordwell's attack. Then she was running, flying as fast as her feet could carry her. She felt the heartbeat in her ears, pounding the nails of distress into every fiber of her being. Then lecherous and jeering laughter swelled. A fury rose through her like a burning tide, threatening to drown her.

Kensy clutched her fists so tightly her nails dug into the flesh of her palms, and she released a scream that cascaded from every nerve. The shards rippled outward, fading as the environment shifted around her. Blood. Bodies. In that moment, everything was still, even the rain.

Her eyes traced the carnage, and she knew. This. This is what she couldn't remember. This was the memory that tormented her from behind the walls her mind had made. Her breath was ragged as the horror of what she had done seeped into her awareness.

Countless small metallic shapes flooded in from the shadows, piling in on each other as they took form. The battered and beaten form of three young psicorp adepts stood before her. Blood poured from Kean's neck, a gory hole was splayed through Lena's lean frame and shattered bones protruded from Aaron's mangled body. Beside them, the warped and sundered silhouette of Malek stood defiant. A man unfamiliar to Kensy stepped into being. His smile made her skin crawl even as she noticed the bloody mark of her fingernails on his neck. A deep red stain poured from his lips and chest. She spun to run away, but another figure faced her down. A weathered man with shaggy, warm, brown hair and facial scruff stared accusingly at her. Kerso's eyes flashed, and his skin puckered and stretched around unrevealed plates and blades.

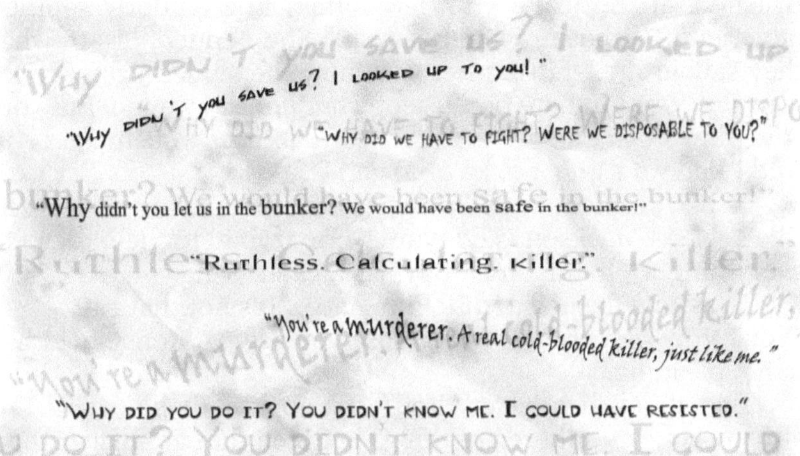


One after another, their words cut into her. The taunts tore at her, leveraging themselves in among her doubts and fears. Tears streamed down her reddened face. Kensy collapsed to her knees, buried by the weight of slander and self-doubt. She sunk to the ground. The rain became heavy, drilling into her skin with every drop.

A deep and distant voice carried under the rest. "The fateless and forgotten." Her father had never uttered those words, but she heard it all the same. His voice rung through her ears as though he stood before her, with that all too familiar gaze of disappointment staring down at her broken spirit.

A pale hand reached for her, outstretched and open in front of her face. Kensy looked up into the silvery eyes of her best friend. "He's lying, you know." Elle smiled weakly.

Kensy fought back a sob and tenderly placed her hand in Elle's. "I couldn't save them. I couldn't save you."

Elle lifted Kensy to her feet and pushed a few stray hairs from her face. "Now, what did I tell you? I'm not your fault." Brushing at the tears with her thumb, Elle tenderly soothed her friend. "I met my fate head on." She nodded. "I am what they saw in me." Lifting Kensy's chin, she smiled again, more warmly. "But I'm here because of what *you* saw in me. But you, your fate wasn't written. It can be *whatever* you make of it. And I know it's going to be *amazing*."

Kensy sniffled. "But I want to save you." Sorrow creased Elle's face. "Jackson said you were trying to help despite everything. Help me find a way. How can I bring you back?"

Darkness flashed across Elle's face. "It's not that easy." "You're my *best* friend, I can't lose you again." Kensy held her hand, pleading.

Elle shook her head. "You can't look at it like that. I'm already gone and there are things between that are bigger than you and I." With a heavy sigh, she ran a hand down the side of Kensy's cheek. "What you can do, right now... take the small moments you still have. Laugh at Neira's lack of humor, fall in love with that silly boy of yours, and live with reckless abandon for once in your life. But most of all, just be happy *now*. Because now is all any of us have.

"The hardest fights are still ahead. If you wait, like I did, you'll miss everything." Elle straightened her posture. "And after you've had time to catch your breath, go to where fate found me."

Kensy's hands trembled. "I don't know if I'm ready for any of that."

"You have to be ready. You know big, bad, and ugly will be waiting, hoping to crush everything that stands in his way. You *cannot* waiver, no matter what you see... no matter *who* you see." Elle's gaze was stern. "I have faith that you can stop this nightmare before it consumes all. Can you do that for me?"

Kensy filled her lungs with a sense of purpose and resolution. "I will do everything in my power."

Elle smiled at her wryly. "Well, we know you have that in spades." They both chuckled. "Now, break free of this dream. You have somewhere else to be." Elle pushed back from Kensy as the shadows crawled up her body. Breathlessly, she whispered, "Go...."

Kensy nodded and pivoted into a run. Her boots pounded against the ground as she ran. Purpose coursed through her veins. She skidded to a stop at the edge of the platform. Glancing back, she watched the shadows curl around the edges of the buildings, encroaching ever closer. "I'll find you." Her wings flared into being, and Kensy rocketed into the sky toward the looming visage of the DeCadejra above.

With a sharp gasp, Kensy sat up in bed. A hand caught firmly at her collarbone, halting her momentum. "Easy now." Doctor Tyronis eased her back down. "Take a moment. Can you tell me who you are?"

Kensy smiled, "Kensy Frost, psilyria first class and a co-captain of the DeCadejra."

"Ooh, I get the full introduction. Someone's feeling better. Can you feel this?" Doctor Tyronis lightly tapped each of the fingers on her patient's hand.

"Yep."

"Wiggle toes?" Kensy did as she was asked for each step of the doctor's requests. "Good, now squeeze my hand. Excellent, still have a fair grip, I see. Any numbness, tingling, vision issues?"

"Nope, across the board." Kensy shifted. "Can I sit up though? Feeling a little restless."

Doctor Tyronis elevated the head of the bed as she entered her last few data points into the computer. "Well, welcome back. You've missed a little bit of chaos, but I think you'll be pleased with the results." She slid the screen away to address Kensy directly. "But I will *insist* that you take it easy for now.

You had a few heart issues while you were out, and I want to make sure you don't have a repeat. Otherwise, you might just give a few other members of this crew heart issues and I have my hands full already." She smiled warmly. "Get some more rest, I'll open the room to visitors in the morning."

"Thank you, Doc, for everything."

"Of course, dear."

## Chapter 37

# The Awkward After

*"Oh, the joys of life after deathbed confessions...."*
*~ Psilyria Kensy Frost*

Kensy carefully coaxed the last knot from her long hair with a brush, smoothing the strands into order with consecutive strokes before setting the brush on the tray table beside her. "Thank you, Maggie. My hair was driving me mental." She continued to play with her hair, using her fingers to comb it into a gentle twist that cascaded over her shoulder.

The room door slid open. Jackson looked up, his eyes meeting hers as he lowered the hand he had raised to knock at the conspicuously open door. "I... uh, was told you were accepting visitors."

Kensy tilted her head down to conceal her grin. "Doc finally let you in?"

"Uh, yeah." He shifted through the threshold awkwardly. "How are you?" He winced at the question. "Sorry, that's a stupid—."

"I'm good!" Kensy gleefully snapped. "I mean, it's nice to see you."

"Yeah, there's been a lot going on with the colonists and everything and...." He approached the side of the bed, staring down into folds of the blinding white sheet. "I'm really glad you made it back... with so many—." His words caught in his throat as he met her gaze again.

"I'm glad too... to be back." She wrung the edge of the sheet between her fingers.

Jackson took a deep breath. "Listen, I know that things were—."

"Crazy."

"Yeah, and tensions and emotions were high. I just wanted to let you know, about what you said—."

"I meant it!" Kensy blurted out. She turned her eyes toward the knot in her hands. Her voice came out softer and slower. "I meant it. Every word. If you don't—."

"I love you too." He stared tenderly at her. Sitting down beside her, he placed a hand on hers. "I'm not really great with this kinda crap. But I love you too. I shoulda told you sooner, but I made it way more complicated than it needed to be and.... I am still trying to figure this out."

A nervous laugh escaped Kensy's stifled smile. "Sorry, it took getting blown up for me to get enough nerve to say something."

He tilted his head. "Yeah. Maybe don't do that again."

She giggled. "We are a picture of communication prowess."

He shrugged and settled into a more relaxed slouch. Tenderly, he brushed her bangs from her face. "I really thought I was going to lose you this time."

She pressed her cheek against his warm palm. "I figured out, I wasn't ready to go yet. And you know me, once I get an idea—."

"Then it's time to brace for another gray hair... or losing my hair. Not sure which at this point." He pointed to the hair at his temple.

"Hey!" She playfully shoved him.

"And I wouldn't have it any other way." He smirked. "Well, I could use a few less moments of panic, but I'm gonna die young anyway. It's the job, you know."

She waved a finger in his direction. "You're not allowed. If I have to stick around, so do you."

He threw his hands up in surrender and faced toward her. "I give! You're the boss!" As she laughed, he planted a hand on either side of her and whispered sweetly. "I love you, Kensington Frost, every stubborn atom."

She pressed her lips to his as he hovered closely. Holding the moment, she savored the taste of his kiss, then leaned her forehead against his. "And I love you, Jackson Gabel, gray hair and all."

A knock at the threshold startled them apart. Doc stood tall, her arms folded neatly across her chest. "If you give her heart palpitations, I'm kicking you out again."

Jackson stood up, shifting back from the bedside. "Yes, ma'am. I'll keep it strictly professional." She smirked and turned away from the door. "You see that? You're gonna get me in trouble."

Kensy tilted her head, "I think she's more worried, you'll get me in trouble." She patted over top of her heart.

Jackson slouched down into a chair beside the bed. "Yeah, there's that."

Kensy slapped the sheet on her lap. "So, tell me. What did I miss? How long was I out?"

Jackson took a deep breath. "Uh, well, I should probably start at the beginning. We got you and the colonists into the ship. Started getting people pulled out of pods before I realized Nexus was piloting your body.... That was incredibly hard to explain."

"He what?" Kensy looked at him with shock and confusion. "You were...." He wove his finger together. "...kinda one at the time. You were radiating power something fierce. So, he *walked* you up to medbay for Doc to take a look at."

"Radiating power? Did I hurt anyone?" She furrowed her brow.

Jackson shifted uncomfortably and pulled his uniform jacket sleeve down just a little further. "No, of course not. We were very careful." She glared at him suspiciously. Waving it away, he continued. "The colonists are taking pretty much all of the port-side deck nine bays... and part of eight. Allen actually rigged up some of the containers to the catwalks and ceiling to serve as extra housing slash sleeping space. Maggie's been in super ship mode, making shit as we can finagle resources, doing nanite watch, and just generally keeping me from pulling out any more of my hair."

"Follicle health does fall under the designation of captain and crew well-being, which remains near the top of my priorities queue." Maggie chimed in.

"Yeah, what she said." Jackson rolled his eyes. "Anyway, the entire crew has been onboard with helping out our guests as they are able. A few of the colonists have stepped up as organizers, liaisons, and general help. Bethany reconnected with her brother." Jackson tapped his index finger against his lip as a thought occurred to him. "Speaking of Nathan... I'm pretty sure he's become Rasken's new partner in crime. When she's not on duty, she's been almost impossible to nail down. And there are some random problems that have been getting spontaneously fixed, to which Maggie claims to have no knowledge...."

"To view maintenance logs, please submit a request."

"Mmhm," he grunted.

Kensy muttered. "Well, if Rasken made a new friend who happens to be an accomplished engineer, I'm sure *something's* getting nailed down." She bit her lip to stifle a snicker.

Jackson groaned. "I don't need to know. I don't want to know. I have enough to deal with already."

"Sorry, couldn't help it. The way you worded that...."

"Right," He shot her a sideways glance. "As I was saying, all in all, I think you were out for 36ish hours. That gave us enough time to get things settled, a little. Other than that, I've just been sending mission briefs to Admiral Davir as we figure shit out." He rested his elbows on his knees. "We're still several days out from Aepexia. And we haven't gotten word yet on how long we'll be stuck waiting in quarantine before we get to off load passengers."

Kensy tucked her hair behind her ear. "I'll try not to sleep in so much."

"Meh, you can sleep in as much as you want. Doctor's orders. Captain's orders too." He stood up and leaned in to gently place a kiss on her forehead. "I better get going before I get kicked out again. Get some more rest. You've earned it."

Kensy sighed at him in defeat. "Fine. But I'm calling the minute the boredom becomes too much."

He paused at the door and winked back in her direction. Kensy giggled again. Her thoughts danced lightly through fanciful daydreams as she slouched back into the medical bed to rest.

## Chapter 38

# Gabby's Angst

*"But, who is the OTHER one?"*
*~ Psimehna Gabrianna Ciphar*

Gabby stared intently at her quarry. Her arms held tightly around her knees as she balanced in a crouched position. Her eyes narrowed as his did. Sparks jittered around her braided wire ringlets to compensate for her current physical stillness. Abruptly, the door to the training room slid open. Gabby toppled backward in surprise. With a huff, she watched as the towering and lanky form of Nevan ducked through the door.

He raised the scaled ridge over his eye at her. "Am I interrupting?"

Gabby side-eyed her otherworldly company. "Nope." She clamored to her feet and straightened her uniform.

Nevan's eyes darted about suspiciously. "Really? You wouldn't happen to have been engrossed in conversation with a 'weird, otherworldly cat thing' by any chance?"

Gabby looked at him with stunned realization. "Are you the *other* one who can see him?" She exuberantly bounded toward him.

Nevan laughed. "Other one?"

Gabby pointed an accusatory finger in Nexus' direction. "The first time I ran into him in the hallway. He stopped me and mentioned that I was the third person on this ship to be able to see him. But the commander didn't count, because that was only temporary. And if Psilyria Frost is one, and I am one, that only makes two. But if I'm the third, that means there's another! But there are no other psionics on the ship, so that might not be the prerequisite, but nothing else makes any sense." She finally took and deep breath. "And *he* won't tell me who the other one is!" She stomped in frustration.

Nexus smirked as his tail lazed around his dagger-like feet.

With a chuckle, Nevan pushed into the room to find a place to sit down. "I am sorry, but your search for the illusive other will continue, my dear." He approached the crown of chairs at the center dais. He sat down on the outstretched leg rest, his clawed hands draped across each other on his knee. "Our psionic feline friend was actually what I was coming to ask you about. So perhaps we can have a conversation, if you don't mind being the intermediary."

"Yeah, yeah, yeah. No problem. I can do that!" Eagerly she agreed before her thoughts caught up. "Wait, wait, wait! If you can't see him, then how did you know? Did Psilyria Frost tell you? Does she know who the other is?"

Nevan raised a hand to slow her down. "Commander Gabel and I had a little chat."

Gabby excitedly fanned herself. "Ohmygosh! I didn't even think of asking him. Of course, he's been really, really, really, busy. But I totally could have asked him about him, because of course he did see him, but only temporarily. But still—."

"Psimehna Ciphar, breathe." Nevan interrupted.

Gabby paused with visible intention and took a deep breath. "I'm sorry. I will try... to... slow down."

A wide smile curled over Nevan's reptilian lips. "Thank you."

"And please, call me Gabby. Everyone calls me Gabby. Well, *almost* everyone calls me Gabby." Her thoughts derailed as she contemplated her own name.

He nodded in a paced acknowledgment, "Of course, Gabby."

Quickly, she spun around to face Nexus. "You! Nexus! Is there some way you can appear to people... you know, without psionics, or links, or weird energy scanners? Wait, do you show up on scanners? Is that how the *other* one sees you? What if someone is an evil robot puppet in the crew? But you *would* tell us if they were, right?"

"Gabby!" Nevan hollered toward her.

"Sorry. Yes. Right, right, right. Focus." She straightened her posture in a vain attempt to quell her animated chattering. "I'm *focused* now."

Nevan tilted his head. "When would you say, was the first time you saw our strange feline friend?"

Gabby's head bobbed as she counted back her interactions. "Oh! Right, right, right. That was the day Commander Gabel came back from sightseeing early, because he had gotten mugged. But I don't think I am supposed to repeat that rumor about it. But he was in the psionics lab talking to Psilyria Frost when Nexus stopped me. And confused me. And told me to come back later." She traced the pattern of her recollection through the air with each additional detail that sprung to mind. "Also, he can disappear. Just fade out as he's walking down the hall right around you. And it's super confusing."

"Is he still here with us now?" Nevan glanced about again. Gabby nodded energetically, "Oh, yeah. He's right—." Gabby glanced to where Nexus had been sitting. Then spun in a circle to find the foreign feline. "Over there." She pointed in the direction of the psionic submersion interface training beam. She cocked her head at him. "What are you doing?"

He smoothed an electric whisker into place as he stared up into the beam. "You inquired if there was any way for me to engage with other beings not naturally adept at perceiving my form. I figured we might as well find out, an experiment if you will."

Nevan studied her one-sided interaction. "Could you perhaps ask him when the first time our beloved psilyria perceived him?"

Gabby shrugged. "Evidently, he's trying to see if there's a way you can ask him directly." She tottered back and forth on the statement. "Well, I'm pretty sure he can hear you already. But he's trying to make it so he can answer, and you can see, and something or another." Her hands twisted through the air as she pantomimed the intent of her rewording. "I don't really know."

Nexus leapt into the beam, prancing through the space with a supernatural ease. Nevan squinted as the air within the beam parted around the unseen shape. He rose to his feet, slowly stalking closer as the small shape became more and more defined with shimmering light. "Hmm, I see. But can I also hear...?"

Gabby bit at her lip in contemplation. "That's a good question. I can't say as he actually talks. Not like we do, but I hear him, like in my head."

The resonant voice echoed through both of their minds. "I can be heard by those I wish to hear me. Though you, good sir, may have a headache later. Those unaccustomed to telepathy or energy manipulation can find the experience wears quickly on their awareness."

Gabby pointed to Nexus. "Yeah, like that."

Nevan nodded. "I understand. I have, on occasion, conversed with a number of helix kolomi, who are prolific practitioners of telepathy. I am aware of the mental fortitude required for such interactions."

"As for an answer to your question, it was the psilyria who first engaged with me in the calm beyond the veil." Nexus nodded toward him.

Nevan stroked his chin scales contemplatively. "So, it was you with which the psilyria first entreated, the one who granted her the mark of the void." Nexus bobbed in affirmation, his small feline form floating weightlessly in the beam's glow. "Makes sense. And the commander was only able to perceive you while the link they shared remained active?"

"As you say."

Nevan nodded. "I've gotten bit and pieces of the story from several sources. I'm just trying to paint a complete picture, figure out what we're against and what we have on our side."

"Of course. A tactical appraisal is quite prudent."

"Perhaps you can aid me on another matter. Ellise Neru. More specifically, her connection to our psilyria *and* her connection to the Vagabond." Nevan folded his arms across his chest, shifting his weight back onto his supporting foot. Gabby watched wide-eyed as they conversed casually.

Energy glowed brightly from the narrow slits of Nexus' eyes. "The bond between the psilyria and Ellise Neru is strong. A conduit exists between them like a groove worn into stone by a steady stream. For years they tended its path, keeping it flowing. Now it only needs a small drizzle to connect from one to another.

"Now, Ellise Neru's connection to the Vagabond is much more difficult to define. It has laid claim to the path between them, as well as her connection to the beyond. But it is a construct. While it mimics the emotion and intuition that psionics utilize to shape their powers, it is unable to fully connect or comprehend the tool at its disposal. When Ellise Neru bridges the gap to the void or to the psilyria, the Vagabond attempts to exert force through his flesh bound vessel. The process is inefficient and costly to all entities involved."

Nevan's heavily armored tail brushed the ground in slow sweeping motions. "So, for now, we have an advantage. But that could shift in either direction. He could wear out his flesh bound vessel, Ellise Neru, devastating Kensy and making him even harder to track. Or his understanding of psionics could grow and we'll have an even more challenging monster to face than just a machine. Neither path seems particularly favorable."

Gabby paced anxiously. "Not good, not good, not good. What if he gets more psionics? That would mean more data points. More data points means more understanding. More understanding means it could hurt more people." She frantically waved her hands. "We have to find a way to take away his source of information, of psionics. But that still won't stop him! For that, we'd have to find him and to find him...." Gabby's eyes darted between them again. "What if we had the psilyria connect to Ellise? Then we trace back to her. And then we capture her. And we'd have to find a way to contain her. But not contain the signal that she gets from the Vagabond. So we can trace back to the Vagabond. And then we capture the Vagabond. And then we shut the bastard down! And then Ellise will no longer be controlled. And if she's not controlled, then she's not being worn out. And because we shut the Vagabond down, then no one's getting hurt by it any more! And then we can all go home!" Gabby paused as the words rolled out of her mouth. With a tone of melancholy, she repeated it. "Then we all go home."

Nevan patted her on the back. "I like the enthusiasm, kid." He winked at her. "But that's a lot of hard work and what-ifs. Could be a pretty long haul."

Gabby shook her head to clear the thought. "Of course, of course. Wouldn't expect any less. And I'm here for it! All of it! All the... whoa, that's a lot."

Nexus swiveled toward her. "I have learned from the psilyria a quaint human expression. Home is where the heart is. I see no reason this should apply any differently to wyrrans. You are the vessel for a heart-like mechanism that resides within your humanoid form. So logically, wherever you are, your home is as well."

Gabby squinted at Nexus. "You know what? I'll take it. I don't think it means it like you do, but meh." Her eyes turned questioningly up toward Nevan. "How does this help us?"

He patted her shoulder. "When I figure it out, I'll let you know." Nevan nodded toward Nexus. "A pleasure to meet you."

"Indeed. I shall retire now. This expenditure has depleted my reserves." Nexus leapt from the beam, bounding gracefully toward the floor.

"Wait! Who is the *other*?!" Gabby shouted as his form dissolved away. She pouted. "Why?"

Nevan smiled. "I'm sure it will become apparent in time. For now, consider it a mystery. A little something to keep all your coils sharp and sparky." Gabby grunted in frustration and stormed from the room in defeat. Nevan chuckled to himself. *That kid is certainly a live wire. Should keep things interesting.*

Chapter 39

# Mistaken

*"We spend our lives trying to find ourselves. But if we're
really lucky, we find somebody who knows us."*
~ ancient human proverb

"Please!" Kensy folded her fingers together as she pleaded her case. "Please, don't make me spend another day staring at the same four walls again. I'm going stir crazy. I can hand out lunches or just listen to people who need to talk. I promise, nothing crazy. I just want to get up, walk around, do something useful with myself."

Jackson stared at her, scrutinizingly. Her sea-green eyes tugged at his heartstrings. He sighed, "Fine. You can come with me on the check-in rounds." Kensy jumped to her feet, giving him a sweet, swift kiss on the cheek. He held up a finger toward her. "But the second I feel like you're doing too much, we're done. Even if I have to carry you back here myself."

She squinted at him. "Don't worry, I won't push it... until later." She shrugged, running a finger down his chest. "Not having to walk back doesn't really sound like a punishment."

He groaned. "Why am I already thinking this is a bad idea?" She pivoted around him. Her casual psicorp uniform top flowed gracefully around her torso with each twist and sway. She tugged at his hand. "I'm coming."

Together, they departed from Kensy's quarters, heading toward the lift. "So, any objectives with this round?"

Jackson pulled his holopad from his belt and checked the pending messages. "Looks like we'll be going through the port side storage bay on this one. It is the smallest of the rooms. I think the colonists have taken to calling it mid-block." He shot her an incredulous glance. "Obviously, they are getting comfortable. Maybe too comfortable since they've taken to renaming parts of the ship." He quickly typed a reply on his device before stowing it. *I lost the bet. She's coming down to help. Not. One. Word.*

After entering, Kensy leaned against the back elevator wall. "I take that to mean they are in good spirits. And *that* is a good sign. Especially, after all these people have been through."

"Yeah. I guess." He took up a strong stance between her and the door as they descended through the floors of the ship. "Bryden and Alpha were rounding up the supplies we'll need to hand out. They should be ready to go before we get there."

The doors opened before them. Kensy smiled. "If they've already got all the heavy lifting done, then you have nothing to worry about." She slipped out ahead of him, eager to converse with the others.

Jackson slowly strolled up behind her. Listening intently to her soft laughter as she greeted crew and colonists gathered by the door.

Daniel lifted a translucent acrylic basket from his stockpile. Kensy grasped the handle and looked down into the collection within. "This whole side is rationed snack packets. Only one per person, so we'll have enough. There's a few small first aid kits here, mostly for bumps and scrapes. Bigger things we'll need to flag down one of the med crew to take care of. Next, we have some flexiglass pages for people who want something to read. I think Maggie networked them into a kinda improvised community library system. It's not the easiest to use, but it's passable. And lastly, some echo crayons for the kids who need help being entertained. Maggie assures me they can't do any permanent damage with them."

Kensy leafed through the contents. "Looks good. You've thought of everything. If it's okay, I'll start down the left side."

Daniel picked up another basket, thrusting it into Jackson's hands. "You go ahead and help her with the left side. Nathan, Rasken, Reily and Shane already started down the right side. And I just sent Hensley, Kyo and Wright upstairs. Meet you in the middle." Daniel tapped Jackson with the side of his fist to urge him into the room behind Kensy.

Jackson stared at the basket in contempt. "Oh, goody. I can barely contain my excitement...."

Daniel laughed. "The sooner we get this done, the sooner you can retreat to the quiet confines of the war room."

The commander nodded and stepped through the threshold of the cargo bay. Within the confines of the expansive room, the din of conversation filled the space with a warm liveliness. The people gathered in loosely organized clusters and rows for ease of movement.

Kensy's smiles and a gentle eagerness greeted each person she crossed paths with. Skillfully, she navigated from one interaction to another. Jackson quietly followed parallel to her, marveling at the ease with which she passed through the crowd. Mindlessly, he nodded in acknowledgment of the thank yous' that followed many of the handouts. The task was tedious and simple: make sure everyone is okay, distribute goods as needed. At least it would be over soon until the next check-in, of course.

The silver-haired silhouette of an elderly man tottered toward the captains. As he approached Kensy, he reached an old, weathered hand out for her arm. She paused. He leaned on her for stability. Glancing at the elderly man, his dull brown eyes glistened in the light as he met her gaze. "Ehvae nor kie'da vey du." He gasped, "It's you. Stars be praised, you still live. I could not be sure on the station, but you've come back! A'uhe edah va noor rae."

Jackson watched a strange familiarity wash across Kensy's expression. Sadness filled her eyes, and softly she patted the man's hand. "I'm sorry. I'm not her. That girl died a long time ago." Kensy withdrew from his grasp, turning a smile toward the next person in line. His head dropped as her words took root in his mind. Solemnly, he watched Kensy shift away to distribute the last of her supplies. Nodding to himself, the elderly man turned and shuffled toward his seat.

Footsteps encroached behind Jackson. With a quick glance, he spied Daniel's approach. "Lost in thought?" he asked. "You've still got a ways to go, especially if you're going to keep up with your co-captain."

Jackson dumped the remains of his basket into Daniel's and passed off the handle. "Hey, give me a minute. I think that old guy needs a hand."

"I gotcha." Daniel nodded.

Carefully stepping over to the next row, Jackson sidled up beside the old man. "Hey, you need help getting back to your seat?"

"Yes, that would be nice." He rasped weakly toward the commander.

With small shuffling steps, they carefully worked around a few small groups. Jackson held his arm steady, and the gentleman plodded along toward a makeshift chair along the outer wall. The man grasped at the commander's arms as he lowered into his seat. "All good? Do you need help getting comfortable?" Jackson crouched beside him.

"Oh, I'm alright. These old bones ain't what they used to be."

Jackson thumbed toward Kensy. "Is it alright if I ask what that was about?"

His knobby fingers wrapped over Jackson's shoulder, patting it. A well-worn grin creased his face. "A long, long time ago, where I was from, there was a young girl. She had sun-bleached strawberry hair and the sweetest smile. She was the heart of my people."

The man's expression fell to despair. "But she was sentenced to die for the sake of a *terrible* superstition." His hands shook as he stared down into his palms. "I forged the instrument of her demise with these two hands." He slapped them down on his lap. The sagging skin of his eyelids drooped over his tired eyes. "So, after everything, I left. To find absolution, to find some worth after all that nonsense."

He waved a weary hand in front of his face. "Maybe it's just these old eyes, searching for hope. Desperate to see it in the vision of a stranger. One who saved this old, worthless bag of bones." He sighed heavily. "If she had been that girl, maybe I'd finally be free of this old ghost that haunts me every night."

Jackson picked a blanket up from beside the chair, spreading it over the old man's lap. "Well, if that girl really was the heart of your people, I'm sure she'd forgive you for whatever happened. I know it's hard, but there comes a time when we need to let go of old ghosts and get some rest."

"You're a good sort." The old man blindly patted at Jackson's shoulder again. "You take care of that one. She's special."

"Will do," Jackson nodded as he stood back up. "And you let those old ghosts rest. I'm sure they're tired too."

Taking a few steps back, Jackson stuffed his hands in his pocket. His thoughts tried to parse through the interactions. *Hmm, senile, or did he really recognize Kensy? And what was that language he was using? I don't recognize it.* Swiftly, he wove through the crowded room and back toward the door.

Ducking out of the bay, he caught sight of her at the supply table. A few lingering individuals circled around him and pushed into the cargo bay. He leaned back against the door frame. She carefully collapsed down the empty baskets and organized them into neat stacks. With the remaining supplies, she counted and shuffled like items together. Pausing for a moment, she stewed in contemplation.

He recognized the singular focus from past experience. She was burying herself in the immediate needs to avoid something, but what? What about that old man bothered her? Jackson glanced into the room. The old man sat curled against the wall with his eyes shut. People moved past him carefully as not to disrupt his rest.

Jackson shifted his attention to Kensy. The restlessness he saw in her now was different from earlier. No playful jests, no words beyond her almost imperceptible mutterings to herself. He pushed off the wall and walked up behind her. "Hey. Did you get everything handed out?" He reached an arm across her back, resting it on her hip. He tilted his head as he looked into her face.

Kensy tucked her bangs behind her ear. "I've got a few pieces left. I'm just consolidating them down with the other partial baskets for the next set of rounds. Did you have stuff left?" She glanced to him.

"Nah, I passed mine off to Bryden. He's handling it." Jackson leaned down and kissed the crest of her shoulder. "You know, we agreed you wouldn't overdo it."

Kensy smiled at him with that all too familiar masked pain in her eyes. "I'm not overdoing it! Although, I was thinking we should probably wash down the empty baskets before reloading them."

Jackson swiveled around to sit on the edge of the table and pulled her in front of him. "How about we take a moment to talk?"

She closed a little bit of the space between them. "Oh, what about?" Her voice became softer. "We are still in a very public space here."

"This place will do just fine for now." He took her hands in his. "I wanted to check-in with *you*. You went through that room like lightning. For as much as you wanted to get out and about, that seemed a bit rushed."

"We had a lot of hungry people and restless kids in there." She shrugged. "Better to get supplies in their hands and take the time after. Just like what we're doing now."

He shook his head. "So, this need to speed through and dive into compulsive organization has nothing to do with that interaction with the old man?"

Kensy swallowed hard as her smile dropped away. "You caught that?"

"I caught that he said something, and you bolted graciously away, letting that old geezer totter away without help. And you tend to compulsively help people, so call me crazy, but it seemed a little strange."

She winced at the observation. "Oh, geez. I did, didn't I? I didn't mean to, he just... caught me off guard."

Jackson ran his hands down the backs of Kensy's arms. "What did he say that rattled you so badly?"

"It's silly, really." Kensy scoffed sadly. "I'm not the girl he wanted me to be. It's not the first time I've been mistaken for someone else." She pulled away from Jackson and inhaled sharply, filling her lungs with cool air and blinking her eyes clear. "I did know someone like that, in my childhood, worlds away. But that girl is long gone." She glanced back at Jackson. "Sometimes when people think they see her in me, I wish I could be her. But that's not a lie I can live with."

"Well, whatever he thought he saw doesn't matter now. The only person you need to be is *you*. And I kinda have this whole affection thing going on for you...."

Kensy weakly smiled at him again. She ran her fingertips across her forehead. "Uh, I hadn't stopped long enough to realize I'm a bit wiped out. Do you mind if I head back and lay down for a bit?"

"Go ahead," Jackson shrugged. "I got this and whatever else Bryden digs up for me to handle. Get some rest."

She swayed in place as her eyelashes fluttered shyly. "Come by later, when you have some downtime, maybe?"

Jackson nodded, "I'll see what I can do." Gracefully, she pivoted and wandered down the corridor toward the lift. His expression became grim, and he glanced back toward the storage bay door, entrenched in thought.

Chapter 40

# Liasons

*"Great. What now?"*

*~ Nathan Derien*
*Colonial Engineer*

"Miss Derien!" A voice echoed down the corridor. Bethany stopped in her tracks, looking for the source. "Miss Derien," Doctor Micah Hirayama rapidly paced toward her, datapad in hand. "I'm glad I could catch you. I've been looking for your brother all morning. We should be back at Aepexia in about the next day or so. Before you two leave us, I *really* wanted to talk to him about a proposal he sent to my research team. If you see him, could you pass that along?"

"I haven't seen him yet today." Bethany pondered her next course of action. "This seems pretty important...?"

"Yes. It is fairly high priority." Micah affirmed.

Bethany nodded. "I'll find him. I know someone who can help me track him down."

"Thank you." Micah's datapad beeped loudly. She pulled it back to read the notification and began to turn away. "Always something more to do. Have your brother come find me as soon as you locate him." She absentmindedly waved as she strode off with purpose in the other direction again.

Bethany muttered under her breath. "All right, where are you hiding, Nathan?" She glanced down the hallway in both directions. "Okay, find Lindsay. She'll know where to look." Bethany wove through the corridors, back to the main lift, and up to the officer's deck. She glanced down at the small screen on her bracelet. *I would send him a message, but surely Doctor Hirayama already tried that. He probably turned his shit off and forgot. Can't say I blame him. He's probably getting pinged from every direction with everything that's been going on.* Bethany sighed.

A few paces ahead of her, a door slid open. Nathan stepped out, a bundle of clothes and tool belt curled into his elbow. His laugh stirred Bethany from her contemplation. He turned toward her, his chest exposed under his unbuttoned shirt. She stopped in her tracks, eyes wide. She cocked her head and closed her eyes as she attempted to push the visual of Nathan and Lindsay from her thoughts. "I suppose I should be glad you at least got your pants on before stepping out." She pivoted away, shaking her head. "Doctor Hirayama wants to talk to you. You might want to finish getting dressed first."

"Runt!" Nathan jogged to catch up to her. "Don't be like that." He fastened his shirt closed and tucked it in. Walking backward beside her, he smiled at his little sister. "It's just a casual thing, nothing to get bent out of shape about."

Bethany threw up her hands. "I don't want to know." She shook her head. "My fault, I should have seen this coming. Not sure why it didn't occur to me, given that you weren't crashing on the couch in the diplomatic suite."

"Well, *technically*, I'm supposed to be down in the hangars with everyone else from the station." He shrugged into his vest. "But Rasken offered me an actual bed to sleep in, so I took it." Bethany raised a skeptical eyebrow at him. "Oh, and the fact that she's in it too had *nothing* to do with your decision? Getting laid is what... just bonus points?"

He laughed. "It's not *that* big a deal, runt. We're two grown adults working off some stress together." He clipped his tool belt around his hips, finally freeing his hands.

"Eew!" Bethany put her hands up by her head as if to block his words. "Just go. Find Doctor Hirayama and have your little meeting. I'm going to go... find something else to do."

"Will you stop for a minute?" Nathan gave her a pleading look as his hand caught her arm. Bethany halted with a huff. "Listen, there was actually something I wanted to talk to you about."

She folded her arms across her chest and shrugged. "So...?"

Nathan straightened his posture. "I'm going to ask to stay on with the ship."

Her expression shifted to shocked disbelief. "Why would you do that? Especially now, knowing what they are going up against?"

"Because I'm resourceful and a damn good engineer." His mouth drew a stern line across his face. "I saw up close what that thing does to people. It needs to be stopped."

She shook her head and stared up into the determined eyes of her brother. "You're not a military man!"

"Neither are those colonists, but that thing still came after them." Nathan shook his head. "If this thing isn't stopped, it's gonna hurt *a lot* more innocent people." He rested his forehead against his sister's and spoke in a hushed tone. "I've heard stories from the crew, from Rasken, this thing got on to Aepexia. If it can get to people there, it can get to anyone, anywhere." He rested his forearms on her shoulders. "And there is nothing I won't do to keep my runt of a sister safe."

Bethany released a slow, defeated breath. "You know you don't have to do that shit."

Nathan pulled back and smirked at her. Shifting an arm to wrap around her shoulders. "We both have our ways of protecting each other. You cause diplomatic incidents. I sabotage galactic murder machines."

"I am never going to live that down." Bethany rolled her eyes. "Fine. It's not like I can *actually* stop you."

He gave her shoulder a squeeze. "I know. I just figured I'd give you fair warning."

A mechanical voice chimed in above them. "Doctor Hirayama, the captains and several other officers have convened in the war room, should you wish to petition for a continued service contract."

"Thanks, Maggie." Turning toward his sister, he shrugged. "Guess that's my queue. Wish me luck." Nathan skipped back from his sister toward the nearby elevator.

"Keep your pants on this time!" She yelled toward him.

"Hey, no promises. Anything for my sister," he hollered back. The elevator door cut the audible groan of her response. Nathan chuckled to himself as he tidied the lines of his outfit and finger combed his hair away from his face. The doors opened, allowing him to stride confidently toward the war room entrance.

Several familiar faces looked up from the central table as he stepped in. "Mr. Derien, is there something I can help you with?" Jackson shot a scrutinizing glance his way. "We're currently in a meeting."

"It's not about what I need. It's about what *you* need." Nathan scanned the faces in the room: Commander Gabel, Psilyria Frost, Lieutenant Commander Bryden, Doctor Hirayama, a tall delrn man he had not yet been introduced to, an extreme-looking human woman with an eye-patch, and Rasken. "From what I've seen on this ship, you have some damn fine engineers. But they're not field engineers. I've seen what we're up against and how it works."

Jackson squinted at him. "You've been an admirable ambassador for the colonists, but this is a dangerous mission, and we can't afford to employ someone who needs a babysitter."

"I have firearms training, and I'm not too bad in a scrap." Nathan argued.

Rasken piped up, "We've sparred. I can vouch for his close quarters skills personally."

Neira's eye-patch subtly shifted colors as she stared blankly at Rasken. "We all know, when you two were in the CQC sparring room and storage closet, it wasn't the ship's equipment you were testing." Kensy snickered in spite of herself. Jackson grunted in disgust.

Daniel suppressed his amusement with a smile. "We should point out, the only reason we have as many survivors from Cor'Threa as we do is Nathan. He survived on that station while it was under siege for two and a half months, without external aid."

Nevan nodded. "Yes, quite admirable and resourceful."

Micah waved her datapad at the assembly. "He was also the one to come up with a possible way to weaponize our Vagabond scanning measures. It is largely theoretical still, but I do see possibility in his proposed design."

Jackson glanced to Kensy. She confidently nodded back. With a shrug, he turned back toward Nathan. "Then it's settled. Welcome to the team."

"Great. What now?" Nathan approached the central table.

"A new nahdvi device is being manufactured at present. Once complete, it will be delivered to your temporary quarters. More permanent quarters will be assigned, pending official authorization." Maggie announced.

"Fair warning: the earpieces are creepy, but you'll get used to it... eventually." Jackson shook his head. "You and Doctor Hirayama can work on theory crafting tech later. We have other topics to discuss first."

Daniel leaned forward on the table. "Right now, we're trying to figure out our next move after we offload."
Jackson stood tall, his arms folded across his chest as he stared at the holographic display. "Up to this point, we've been chasing down the vagabond's moves *after* it makes them. I feel like it's high time we went after the source."

Nevan toyed with the display, fanning through known events and evidence. "I would be inclined to agree, but the real issue is where to look for the source."

Rasken popped a bubble. "We tracked down the colony that dug it up. They're dust. We tracked down the first station it hijacked. They're freeze-dried dust. We blew up its little horror lab planet."

"Guessing, space dust?" Nathan interjected.

Rasken pointed a finger gun his way with a wink. "All this shit happened, and somewhere along the way it snags your bestie," she glanced to Kensy, "and turns her into techy-murder-zombie. Do we know where she was *before* going all murdery?"

Kensy pulled up some information on the console. "Well, not exact coordinates, but she was stationed aboard the ESFV Icarus. It was destroyed, all hands lost." An image of the ship slowly rotated over the center of the table. Elle's voice played in her mind. *I flew too close to the sun....go to where fate found me.* "...go to where fate found me," Kensy muttered as an idea took hold. "That's it! Go to where fate found me. She was talking about the Icarus. We need to find where the Icarus was destroyed!"

Rasken popped another bubble. "That's a little bit of a leap."

"No, she's right." Neira nodded, furiously typing into the table interface. The image shifted to one side and a second diagram appeared beside it. Neira pointed to the pieces. "The Icarus was destroyed, but the only thing they ever found was a field of debris. No bodies. No pieces that could explain *how* it was reduced to rubble. And the total of the recovered material was a fraction of the ship's original mass. The assumption that the entire ship was destroyed was based on the distribution of the identified pieces."

"Is it possible the debris field was staged? By the Vagabond?" Daniel glanced to Micah as she sorted through calculations on her datapad.

She nodded. "It is *very* possible. Running through the investigator's simulation data, there is no known phenomena that would result in that array of debris in that distribution." She looked up to the hologram. "By my cursory estimates, somewhere out there, we could find as much as seventy-three percent of the ship still intact."

Jackson started to sway and pace. "The Icarus is out doing a patrol or expedition. They run across the Vagabond in space. It assaults the ship and attacks the crew."

"My link to Elle is severed by whatever it did to her, making me believe she'd died." Kensy cut in.

Jackson continued, "Then once it had laid claim to a sufficient amount of the tech and crew, it dismantles the ship enough to make a convincing decoy debris field."
Nathan shook a finger at the ship diagram. "So, where was it *actually* destroyed?"

"And how do we find it now? It's been years. The wreck, if it is intact, could have been shifted by the gravity of anything and everything in its galactic neighborhood." Daniel posited.

Neira smirked. "The logs. Every Ascension ship sends logs on a regular report interval. The path of communication gets embedded into the transmission as it relays back to the citadel on Aepexia."

A grin curled around Nevan's lips. "Clever. Pull the data from the citadel and back trace it to the likely broadcast point."

Micah nodded. "If we can get a point of origin, my team can calculate the last position and any potential drift."

"Then we have a plan. I will contact the admiral, let her know we need those logs, unadulterated." Jackson shut down the table's display so he could clearly see all the faces gathered around. "We need to make sure we are absolutely ready. This is likely a dive straight into the wraith's den. Everyone has to be at their absolute best, we won't get a do over if we screw this up."

Everyone solemnly nodded. All in. All forward.

## Chapter 41

# Shifting Paradigm

*"....Just Silence."*

Anxious figures, both inside and outside of the ship, stared at the hangar doors in anticipation of impending movement. Standing by on the docking platforms, Terra Ascension Core service members, Aepexian Crisis Response agents, and independent medical teams readied to receive the Cor'Threa refugees. Within the ship, the DeCadejra's crew interspersed with the civilians to keep everyone clear of the bay door mechanisms. The seals audibly disengaged, and the light of Aepexia began to pour through the growing openings around the doors. They cranked down into position, echoing as they locked into place against the docking platform.

"All right. Slow and steady down the ramp! If you see someone who needs assistance, give a shout." Allen hollered in a booming voice from his position on the catwalk overlooking the crowd. "Everyone will get the help they need, so let's keep this orderly people!" His eyes scanned the figures below, watching, waiting for a break into panic or distress among the throngs of disembarking colonists.

Kensy leaned her shoulders against the rear wall as she watched the steady staggering of the crowd. She wrapped her arms across her midsection and idly tapped one heel against the floor. Jackson shot a glance her way. "Anxious?"

She sighed, "I don't know. Maybe a little. We got them here, but how many didn't make it this far? It's been here too. What if things aren't any safer here?"

He elbowed her gently. "Knock that shit off. Remember what I told you." He nodded to the masses. "Every one of them is a victory. Tying yourself in knots over what ifs isn't going to help anyone."

Kensy blinked slowly and tilted her head to the side. "I know. You're right. Old habits are hard to break. My mind is really good at finding things to worry about. Guess I'm going to have to find other things to occupy my thoughts." She smiled at him with a subtle warmth.

Nathan and Bethany appeared behind the shifting crowd, heading toward the captains. As they approached, Bethany stepped forward. "Hey. I just wanted to thank you both one more time. Without your intervention at the ball, I might never have seen my brother again." She fidgeted uncomfortably. "I know he's signed on to help you guys. If it's not to much to ask... could you make sure he gets back from this too?"

Kensy pushed off the wall and straightened her posture. "We'll do what we can."

Nathan tousled his sister's hair. "Hey, enough of the mopey face. We talked about this already." Bethany dipped away from his hand. With a glare back at him, she tried to fix her hair. He nodded toward the bay doors. "Come on, runt. This is your stop."

They turned away and meandered after the trail of people. Bethany furrowed her brow. "Seriously, Nathan, be careful."

He wrapped her in a quick hug. "I'll be fine. How about you try staying out of trouble this time?"

She shrugged. "No promises. I'm sure there is someone out there who deserves being annoyed. And I'll find them. Gotta have something to keep me occupied while you're off gallivanting across the galaxy."

Nathan chuckled to himself. "All right. You go get 'em, runt." With a knowing smile, he stuffed his hands in his pockets and watched her descend down the ramp. He paused for a long moment, taking in the grand Aepexian skyline, before retreating back into the ship.

The last of the civilians trickled toward the open doors. From the edge of the crowd, a familiar old man hobbled toward Kensy. A knot formed in her throat as her eyes watched him totter toward her with intention. Steeling herself, Kensy shifted past Jackson to approach the elderly man alone. Jackson stayed behind, silently observing the interaction.

Kensy gently caught the old man's free arm in her soft grip. "Did you need some help down the ramp, sir?"

He looked up to her from his hunched form. A worn smile curled across his lips, and he gently patted her hand. "You, my dear, may not be who I had hoped, but I felt the need to give this to you." He pressed a small device into the palm of Kensy's hand and closed her fingers around it. "Maybe someday it will bring you peace, just as you have done for these old bones."

Befuddled, Kensy shook her head. "I couldn't...."

"Call it a last request from a crazy old man who doesn't have much time left." He patted her hand again and began to turn away.

Her breath caught, and she held his arm just a little longer. He glanced back to her pained gaze. "She... she never blamed you. What happened... it wasn't your fault."

His eyes lit up with recognition. "Well, I'm sure whoever she is now, she is an incredible young woman." Water glistened in his eyes and tailed down the creases of his weathered features. He squeezed her hands and pulled away. A figure from the crowd moved to assist him.

Kensy stood straight, clutching the small device to her chest. Her grip tightened as she fought back the emotions bubbling up inside her. After several sharp breaths, she slipped the device into an interior pocket of her uniform jacket. She blinked her eyes clear and pivoted back toward Jackson.

"Everything good?" He turned his eyes toward the crowd, keeping her in the corner of his vision.

"Yeah, he just wanted to thank me for the station stuff." She smiled. "He's a sweet old man. Perhaps a bit easily confused, but sweet."

Jackson shot her a questioning glance, but did not push the issue. *She'll tell me when she's ready, just like with Elle and the veil.* His jaw tightened. *We both still have secrets, pains too hard to talk about.* He looked up at the Aepexian lights. *Maybe someday we'll both get brave enough to share.*

Skirting around the edge of the crowd, a small group strode up the ramp, the graceful and commanding Admiral Davir at its head. The DeCadejra's crew members snapped to attention, saluting the admiral as she passed. Respectfully, Jackson and Kensy presented a gesture of acknowledgment, and welcome to her. She reciprocated and nodded to them in turn. "Call your advisors and officers. We have much to discuss."

Jackson's stance remained rigid. "Of course. We will convene in the war room."

The admiral swiveled toward one of her attendants. "See that they are resupplied and any refits they require are completed immediately. I want her ready to sail by second star-rise."

"Yes, ma'am." The entirety of the entourage scurried away to complete the monumental task ahead.

Admiral Davir turned back to the captains. "After you." Jackson nodded. He pivoted, leading his fellow captain and the admiral through the interior doors in the direction the primary lift.

As they stepped into the car, Maggie's mechanical voice rang overhead. "All relevant parties have been notified. Individuals are en route."

"Thank you, Maggie," Kensy automatically responded. The ride was brief and silent. Tension filled the elevator in anticipation of the impending war room conference. The doors opened on the strategic deck and the trio of officers fell into step down the curving hallway. The carpet-muffled footsteps pounded like a dulled heartbeat in the captains' ears.

So many questions churned through Kensy's thoughts, it was difficult to make an orderly progression from one to another. *What did the admiral find? What actually happened to Elle? If we find it, what's waiting for us? Why would the Vagabond go to all this effort to conceal the actual wreck? What really happened to the Icarus? Is there anything left to find?* The questions continued to mount even as their destination approached only a short distance down the corridor.

Jackson glanced to Kensy's sternly contemplative expression, watching the wheels of thought churn through the legion of questions undoubtedly brimming under her tightly controlled veneer. The war room doors slid open, allowing entry from both sides. Figures of several shapes and sizes filed in. Officers, Graven, and their consultants converged around the illuminated holotable.

"You asked for data." The admiral slipped a hand into her jacket and pulled a small, dark metallic slab from an interior breast pocket. For a brief moment, she held the datablock up to show. Her hand dropped toward the table, slamming the block down on the holographic interface. Lights spun up around the device and its contents began to pour out across the table and air in front of them. Transmissions, star charts, astrogation routes, images, logs. It populated the space with a sprawling web of information. "At a glance, everything *seems* in order. However, out of an abundance of caution, I did not permit any of my analysts access to this information. It's time to figure out of if your suspicions are correct." Admiral Davir stepped back from the table and crossed her arms.

Neira, Micah, and Nathan lurched toward the table, eager to dissect the unadulterated data. Neira reached into the interface, snagging the bulk of the ship's report records. She fanned through transmission sent along during the Icarus' final tour. "Got logs. Extracting embedded relay data." Piece by piece, she pulled the embedded bits from the information packets.

Nevan glanced over Neira's head toward Doctor Hirayama. "I set up limited run access for you this morning. Just log into the Aepexian Hub Communication Servers with your Ascension creds."

"Thank you, Adjudicator Nahlen." Micah smiled. "It certainly goes faster with proper permissions. Pulling relay network traffic in all neighboring sectors. Already seeing partial matches to the Icarus signature across several fragmented transmissions." Micah combed through the data for every partial match or discarded blip.

"Send me the location data and timestamps on those pieces." Nathan waved at her as she flicked the broken pieces to his control space.

"I've got the log pathing." Neira brought up an astrogation chart. Amid the scattered stars and galactic landmarks, two lines emerged. One carefully traced the plotted path of the Icarus while the other crawled slowly from the shell of Aepexia through the relay stations back toward the cutoff point of the final complete log. Nathan entered the information from the scattered transmissions.

Gradually the trails connected, everything pointing toward a small dead zone amid the interstellar communications network and travel corridors. A sprawling nebula obscured the region, making traversal challenging and undesirable for everything except for perhaps research vessels.

Kensy tilted her head to the side as she stared at the converging paths. She stepped up, briskly typing in another set of variables. Jackson raised an eyebrow in her direction. Dates, times, confirmed presence. As each point was confirmed, a web began to form. Galliane Prime, Morwhex Four, Bhelnir, Rosealleon, the supply depot, and Cor'Threa all painted a picture. At the heart of the chaos sat a region veiled by the cloud's dust and debris. The trail of the Icarus dove straight toward the nebulous center point before vanishing. She whispered, "We found it."

Jackson unfolded his arms and looked toward the admiral. "What exactly was their mission?"

"Charting."

Jackson pointed to the ship's diagram. "You don't send a warship for charting. You send a science vessel, someone who can see into that mess." The admiral narrowed her gaze in his direction.

"You send a warship if you suspect someone is hiding in there." Nevan interjected. "Our good admiral here, cannot contradict the official mission brief. Or even perhaps allude to the idea that the Ascension suspected piracy or hijacking of ships along major trade routes in the region."

"It would be irresponsible of someone in my position to jump at shadows without proper evidence. I can, however, assure that my subordinates are intelligent and clever enough to make good use of the information they've been given." The admiral stood tall. "Seeing as this vessel has been granted operational autonomy and is engaged in a joint operation with the Graven, I will excuse myself. Once this investigation is concluded successfully, I look forward to reading the reports." Admiral Davir turned away, striding from the room with confidence.

Neira muttered, "I hate bureaucratic BS."

"She did get us the information we needed." Nathan shrugged in Neira's direction.

"I think I've got it." Micah pressed her glasses up her nose. "The last transmission, I think I've got it. It's heavily degraded, and still missing a significant amount of data. But we've got a few bits of audio and some rough images."

"Can you get it to play?" Daniel leaned toward her. "Let's see it."

A static hiss filled the room. Discordant tones flickered in and out. Pixelated images shuddered and jerked across the screen. Micah tuned the segments as they played. A voice broke through the corrupted haze. "Icarus to Ascen— .... not pirates," it squealed, "r-raiders!" Everyone stared with rapt attention on the broken image of a man in Ascension uniform. "... station here. Scans ... one massive computer." Explosions and cacophony filled the background. His head turned away, and the image froze. Micah jumped to the next fragment, "... being hacked. Oh g—, ... —net's n-nest. ... everywhere. — isn't ma—. ...surrounded. Hull breaches ... all decks! Syst— shutting down. Life support offline, weapons o-offline, main power is off—."

Tightness took hold of Kensy's neck. She fought against the dread that choked her. These were the last moments of the Icarus, the final desperate pleas that filled the air. Dizziness crept up behind her eyes. Where was Elle at this moment? Did she see it unfolding? The man's voice faded back in over the pervasive static. "... down to auxiliary systems. Caroway ... redirect everythi— engines online. We—," The crackle drowned out the words for a moment. "...ram it. ... take it out with us. ... Icarus —." The sound cut as chills crept down the skin and scales of everyone in the room.

Silence filled the room with a somber weight. The seconds clambered by. Micah lifted her hands from the holographic display. "That's it. All comm traffic in that region just cuts off. No distress beacons. No background pings. Just silence."

Kensy stared intently at the final broken image. In her mind, she drew the lines of his features, noted the soft umber of his eyes, and the name scrawled across his lapel: Aileth. She lifted her chin. "We have the all the information that *could* be gathered. We have the personnel with the *expertise* to deal with this problem. No other ship could address this crisis and it is very likely that none will follow in our wake. We go with the hopes and prayers of everyone we represent. We *will* return triumphant." Across the room, each of the assembled members stood just a little taller. Kensy's sea-green gaze passed across each face with gravitas and understanding.

The faintest curl of a smile crossed Jackson's lips as he stared at her. "Then let's go find a vagabond."

Chapter 42
# Feeling Alive

*"Breathe." ~ Psilyria Kensy Frost*

Resources restocked, routines reestablished, a sliver of normalcy regained as the DeCadejra sailed into the vast darkness of open space. Kensy stared out at the stars that slipped silently by. Between her fingers, a small medallion-like device flipped over and over. Her thoughts wandered through times past, echoing the sounds of laughter, confusion, and distress. She could hear her oldest and dearest friend's voice with unmistakable clarity.

It seemed lifetimes ago, and yet... she glanced down to the token tumbling between the curl of her knuckles. Arresting its movement for a moment, she ran her thumb over the ridges of the emblazoned symbol. This fragment had found her. Maybe the past wasn't so far away after all. Elle's voice rang through her thoughts, *Destiny... I guess we didn't run far enough.*

"Destiny," the word hung on her lips as she whispered it. *Is this what they meant? Are we just slaves to destiny?* She let a slow, deep breath escape. Brushing her bangs from her eyes, she stared back into the glittering darkness. *That's just superstitious nonsense. If it was true.... No, they were wrong about both of us. I will find you. I will save you.*

Gentle hands wrapped around her arms. She jumped at the sensation of fabric wrinkling under his touch. Glancing up at him, she smiled warmly. "Sorry, I didn't hear you come in."

272

Jackson leaned over her shoulder. "You seemed pretty focused. Anything you want to talk about?"

She leaned back into his embrace. "Nah. Just mulling over everything."

"That's a lot. Feels like we haven't really had much time to process it all." He rested his head against hers. "It's okay if it's too much. You don't need to take it all on alone."

Kensy slipped the token into a pocket and turned to face him. "I promise, I'm not trying to." Her fingers traced up the lines of his uniform jacket. "I know I'm not alone." He felt the heat of her breath against his chest, and the soft caress of her fingertips even through all the layers of his uniform's fabric. He cupped her face in his hands and kissed her softly.

Her lips pressed against his hungrily. As he pulled back, her breath caught. He brushed her hair from her face. "It's getting late."

"Is it?" Her sea-green eyes glittered in the low light of the observation deck. "Everything seems so quiet since the refugees left. It's easy to lose track of time."

He laughed, "Yeah, we're not getting pulled in a thousand directions at once."

She swayed against him, "I know it was a lot, too much at times, but there is part of me that liked it. Sometimes it's easy to forget how vibrant and resilient people can be. I think we all need a little chaos every now and then."

"Personally speaking, I could probably use a little less." His face contorted at the thought.

She giggled with an effervescence that rang through him. "Don't get me wrong, I like my quiet. But sometimes...," her face turned down as her cheeks blushed, "it's nice to feel alive." Her fingers danced across his chest.

Jackson swallowed hard, "We really should...."

She gazed up into his trepidatious blue eyes. "Walk me back?" she glanced past him for a moment and broke into laughter. "...you know, across the room."

He smiled, "I think I can manage that." They both broke into laughter as they meandered across the observation deck toward Kensy's quarters. She wove her fingers through his and curled against his arm. The door slid open for the pair. Jackson hesitated at the threshold as Kensy walked forward. She held tightly to his curled fingers. Pivoting to meet his gaze, she looked at him with pleading eyes. "Jack, will you stay the night? With me?"

He stared back with caution. "Kensy, I don't know if we should...."

"Please." She pulled at his hand gently.

"You're still recovering, and...." Worry creased the stern lines of his face.

She released his hand and turned her eyes away. "There's always going to be another crisis, another revelation or injury to recover from. If we wait for the perfect time, we could miss out on everything that makes life worth living."

Jackson stepped across the threshold into the room. "Are you sure?" His heart raced as he watched the graceful shifting of her body.

Her smile captured him. "I... want to feel alive, with you... tonight. But if you don't—."

In a flash, he closed the distance between them, wrapping his arms around her again. Trepidation melted into avid desire as he surrendered to the moment. Their lips met and a jolt of heat passed between them. This kiss, like a river of fire, coursed through every fiber of Jackson's being, threatening to consume him entirely. He had kissed her so many times before, sweetly, softly, but never this sensually. This was different. He lingered on every sensation, the weight of her body in his arms, the gentle brush of her hair across his cheek, the way her hands wrinkled the fabric of his uniform against his body.

Breathlessly, they parted, but only slightly. In that sliver of space between, Kensy could feel the whisper of his words. "There is nothing I want more... than you."

Relief cascaded through her as she allowed her smile to return. Her fingertips danced up his torso. Leaning down, he pressed his lips against the hollow of her neck. "Maggie, privacy mode," she gasped. The door latched in confirmation.

He trailed his tongue up her neck, causing her body to quake at the caress of his lips against her skin. She dug her nails into the back of his jacket. "Jack...." He pulled back and looked into her eyes. "I was so afraid you wouldn't want me after everything...." She glanced toward the bracer that sheathed her left arm.

He brushed her bangs from her face. "Not a chance. Kensy, you are an amazing, caring person. Anyone who doesn't see that in you is blind." He lifted her chin, pressing his lips to hers again. Carefully, he unfastened her ponytail clasp, letting her strawberry blonde locks fall freely. "You are worth any risk."

She slipped a hand into the seam of her uniform jacket and released its fastenings one by one until it fell open. His eyes soaked in the curves of her body under her form fitting tank top. She unclipped the buckle of his belt and cast it toward the couch behind him. Excitement cascaded through her skin as he pushed her Psicorp jacket down her arms with a light touch. It dropped to the ground around her feet. His fingers continued to travel down the back of her hands until he reached her fingertips. Wrapping her hands in his, he lifted them to his mouth and placed gentle kisses across her knuckles.

Bashfully, she grinned. Her hands dropped against his chest, searching for the same fastenings on his clothing. Trembling, her hands fumbled futilely and her cheeks flushed with a rosy shimmer. He ran his fingers through her hair. "Having a little trouble?" he asked through an amused grin.

Kensy shook her head. "Just a little nervous." She buried her face. "I'm giddy like a schoolgirl and have evidently forgotten how clothes work."

He cupped her hand in his and guided her touch. "Just another thing that's better together." Their hands worked down his chest and abdomen, unfastening his uniform jacket. He shrugged out if it, catching it on his fingertips, and tossing it aside in one smooth motion. Playfully, she tugged at his undershirt, untucking it from his pants, all the while stepping back toward the bedside. He let her peel the shirt off his body as they shuffled across the room.

Kensy bit at the edge of her lip. Preoccupied by the shifting of his muscular physique, the heel of her boot caught on the weave of the carpeted floor, sending her off balance. "Ahh!" Jackson lunged forward. His arms wrapped securely around her. She giggled. "You're still catching me when I stumble."

His deep ocean blue eyes gazed at her with adoration, "Always." Her breath caught as she gently gripped his biceps. Hungrily, his lips found hers again. The muscles of his arms flexed under her fingers. He held her tightly against his chest as her fingers glided up his arms like a rising tide.
Their lips parted. *Breathe,* she reminded herself. Her eyelashes fluttered open. "Guess I should stare a little less and focus a bit more on walking." She glanced around to get her bearings.

"I'll save you the trouble." Jackson swept her off her feet. "This is the proper protocol for a princess, right?"

Kensy laughed, wrapping her arms around his neck. "You do not need to buy into all that nonsense."

He shrugged and carried her the remaining distance. He set her down at the bedside. "*Maybe* it's not about the nonsense. Maybe I just like holding you. I'll take any excuse I can get." She blushed as Jackson knelt down. His warm fingers slipped under the hem of her tank top. Slowly, he lifted the fabric, coaxing it to reveal the smooth skin of her stomach and curves of her bra. Lifting the top free from her body, he tossed it aside.

Kensy leaned forward, kissing him as his hands fell to her hips. He pulled back. Letting his hands glide down her thighs toward her knees. "Let's get these out of the way. Wouldn't want you to trip again." Carefully, he removed her boots and socks, setting them neatly aside. Kensy placed her bare foot between his legs as he unlaced his own boot. Very slowly and deliberately, she traced up the inside of his thigh. "You are a distraction," he chuckled.

She smiled mischievously, "So are you, so we're even."

Hastily, he discarded his footwear and seized her ankles. As his fingers lightly grazed the bottom of her feet, Kensy gave a ticklish squeal. "Oh?" he smirked.

"Please don't," she pleaded.

"All right. No tickling." With a firm and intentional rhythm, he began kneading at the balls of her feet. "Better?"

She let out a slight laugh, and gasp as the sensation shifted to soothing. "I don't know how you are managing that...." Her head lulled as she closed her eyes and focused on the feel of his touch.

Before the relaxation could consume her, his hands slid up her ankles. "Hey now, no falling asleep just yet." Her eyes fluttered open, tracing the lines of his casually disheveled charcoal locks. He stared adoringly at her while his fingers caressed up her legs, past her knees, and up her thighs, toward the crest of her hips. He leaned forward, brushing his lips against the soft skin of her abdomen. One by one, his tender kisses traveled up her body.

Kensy's breath caught. "Jack...," her fingertips grazed his cheek, "I love you."

Jackson stood up, guiding her to her feet with him. "I love you too, Kensy." He lifted one hand over her head and spun her around. As he pulled her back against his chest, Jackson buried his face in the hollow of her neck. His hot breath sent a cascade of pleasurable chills through her body with every kiss. "You like that, don't you?"

Her breasts heaved, "Yes." Savoring the heat of their embrace, she subtly began to sway against him. Amid this sweet, slow dance, Kensy's fingers worked to release the closures first on her slacks, followed by his uniform pants. With only the slightest nudge, the sensual swing of her hips sent the loosened fabric tumbling from their bodies. He held her tightly as they stepped free from the tangle of trousers.

Only the slightest veils of material remained to separate them. Lustfully, her fingers wandered across what she could reach of his body. His hands gradually swept up her torso. As he reached the clip sitting between her breasts, Kensy turned her head to meet his lips. Hungrily, their kiss deepened. The fastening surrendered to his touch and he carefully peeled the fabric away from her skin exposing her chest to the cool air of the room.

He trailed stirring strokes across the curves and lines of her figure as his hands traveled down her skin. Upon reaching the last vestige of cloth clinging to her delicate form, his fingers slipped beneath. She clutched him tightly, almost desperate to be even closer together. A moan rose from her lips as she pulled back from his kiss to gather air into her lungs once more.

He felt her body waiver. Drawing his hand up to her lower abdomen, he held her firmly. He tilted his head down, whispering into her ear. "We should probably lie down before one or both of us fall down." His breath against her skin sent shivers through her again. Kensy giggled and nodded. Jackson turned her to face him. Their lips met as he cradled her body in his arms. Kensy closed her eyes, feeling the world shift and fade away as he knelt down on the bed.

The bedding billowed up around her as he released her into its textile embrace. Her eyes fluttered open. The sight of his muscular physique held above her caused her heartbeat to quicken. She traced her fingertips over the chiseled lines of his arms, up to his face. He kissed her open palm. Her words tumbled over her lips gently, "Jack, I want you."

He brought his mouth to her breasts, tracing the curves with his tongue, while his hands wandered down her body and slipped between her legs once again. The rhythmic caress sent a rising tide of heat through her body. She arched her back, gripping the sheets as the smallest flickers of psionic power danced over her skin. She reached out for him. "Jack...." The motes of energy passed from her fingers, trailing down his back with a gentle tingle. He rose to meet her lips, another kiss sweet and soft. He struggled to steady his breathing as desire surged through his skin at her touch. "Jack, I want to feel you again, wholly connected to me." She brushed her fingertips over his chest. "I want to feel your heartbeat with mine."

He brushed a strand of hair from her face. "I can't create psionic links, but I can get a little closer." They stared into each other's eyes for a long moment, drinking in the glow of each and every breath.

Kensy slipped her legs around him. "Please." He gently pushed into her. The sensation enveloped them as the lights dimmed and the stars glittered overhead.

## Chapter 43

# Icarus

*"She... died here." ~ Psilyria Kensy Frost*

Kensy tugged at the bottom hem of a snug, deep purple shirt. She smoothed it down over the top of her charcoal-colored leggings as she inspected herself in the mirror. Watching the reflection, her expression curled into a contented smile. Jackson kissed the crest of her shoulder from behind. "Captains, we have reached sensor range. Receiving a ping of something big out there."

"Thank you, Daniel. Please have the away team report to the hangar. I'll be down in a moment." Kensy leaned into Jackson's warm hands. She lifted her head, drawing in a sharp breath. "We have the resources, the plan, and the people to make this work. Time to kick the hornet's nest and see what comes out."

He rubbed her shoulders. "Whatever that bucket of bolts throws at you, just... be sure you come back in one piece. I've kinda gotten attached to you."

She spun around to face him. "I can do this."

"I know you can." He leaned his forehead against hers. "Just be careful... for me."

Rising on to the tips of her toes, she kissed him. "I need to get down there. And you'll be needed on the bridge."

He nodded and followed her out of the room to the elevator. Jackson cleared his throat and tried to put on his best stern expression as they descended through the floors. A slight grin flickered across his face as he stepped out on the command deck with a quick wink. She stared at his confidant swagger until the doors broke her line of sight. *You can do this. Save Elle. Stop a murder machine. Save the galaxy. No big deal....* She tilted her head side to side, stretching the muscles in her neck.

When the doors opened on the lower deck, she strode forward with purpose and feigned confidence. Entering the hangar bay, she surveyed the assembled crew and allies: Bryden, Alpha Team, Gabby, Nevan, Neira, Marieke, and Rauk. Daniel approached, datapad in hand. "Here's the sensor data so far. Silhouette paints it as one of ours, heavily damaged, but the bones are there. Seems like we found exactly what we were looking for."

She scrolled through the feed. "Most certainly a trap, all dressed up and ready for us."

"Into the fire?" He raised an eyebrow.

Nathan and Micah entered the hangar behind Kensy, a set of small devices cradled in their arms. Kensy looked to them with eager eyes. "Please, tell me we have new toys."

Nathan held up one of the compact devices with a wry smile. "We have new toys!"

"Then let's get to it." Daniel clapped his hands loudly over the commotion of the crew's gear checks. "Eyes up! Ears on!" All heads turned toward him.

Micah stepped forward. "We have constructed a countermeasure device for distribution to the boarding party. There are limited number so stay with someone who has a device." As she orated, Nathan began passing out the fist-sized mechanical orbs to select individuals. "The device has an activation band around the center. Twisting it to the left sets it to broadcast our disruption signal at the specified ranges." She pointed to the small hash marks across the band. "The farther you try to broadcast, the faster your battery dies. This means you are going to have to get cozy with your teammates if you want it to last." She turned her orb on its side, revealing the top of the device. "If you have to drop the device. Swing the cover off of the top like so. This will reveal a button. And we all like pushing buttons, don't we?! Pressing in the button will arm the device like a grenade. After a three second countdown, the core will overload and send out an electromagnetic pulse in a ten-meter radius. *Do not* be in that range when it goes off! It will kill your life support system, including your oxygen supply and temperature regulation, which will, in turn, kill you."

"Hey, Specs, you coming along for the ride?" Hensley blurted out across the hangar.

He lurched forward as Rasken smacked the back of his head. "That's *Doc* Specs to you." She popped a bubble in his direction with a smirk.

Micah took a deep breath, pushing her glasses up her nose. "I'll be here, crewman. Monitoring your equipment in case it fails or gets hacked by the AI, those devices are intended to protect you from."

Rasken blew a bubble. "Yeah, see? Respect the doc, so your shit keeps working."

"All right." Kensy stepped into the center of the assembled. "We have the ship on sensors. There is no telling how many, *if any,* of the systems are still intact. With the age and condition of this wreck, expect little to no internal atmosphere. The Vagabond has had control of this ship for *years*. Assume any and all tech has been compromised. We will be the first people to set foot on the Icarus since it went missing. We are here for answers. *If* you encounter any of the original crew on this ship, stay at a distance and report it immediately. Cataloging the dead is a two-man job, one for scans and one for identity confirmation. No unnecessary foreign contact. No souvenirs. And no one moves alone." A knot formed in her chest as she pictured her friend's olive skin and raven colored hair. "Suit up, then load up!"

Micah approached as Kensy slipped into her environmental suit. "You really think you'll find anyone over there?"

Kensy fastidiously checked every seam and fastening as she spoke. "Anything's possible. I just know there is something here. Some puzzle piece that will help us shut the vagabond down."

"Well, best of luck to you." Micah shrugged, "Chief Petroski will be on the schematics, feeding you instructions as you need it. And with Mister Derien in the field, you should be able to improvise adequately."

Kensy nodded, "Thank you, Doctor Hirayama." After twisting her hair up and pinning it flat against her head, she slipped her helmet on. With a click and a hiss, the final seal engaged. One after another, the boarding party reported to the scythe transport locked and loaded.

"Disengaging from docking clamp," Daniel announced. The shuttle jarred, and the passengers staggered. "Down and departing DeCadejra's aft starboard hangar."

"Safe sailing, scythe." Jackson's voice echoed over the comm.

The transport crawled through the dust cloud toward the looming silhouette of the long-lost ship. "Entering comm range, no broadcasts detected." Daniel activated the virtual windows on the craft. "Should have a visual in five, four, three, two...."

Kensy narrowed her eyes at the shape before them as it came into focus. Nathan glanced up from his seat beside Daniel. "Umm, I'm not a ship guy, but it's not supposed to look like that, is it?"

Daniel's hands danced across the control panels. "No. No, it's not." The contorted structure sat buckled and broken like a gnarled corpse. Large wires and conduits drifted listlessly among free floating debris. Sickly light flickered from somewhere within, casting grotesque shadows across and throughout the remains of the once proud warship.

"Stars." Kensy felt the knot in her chest twist in on itself. She shook the feeling aside and turned toward Daniel. "Can you find somewhere to dock us?"

"Working on it." He searched through the scan data. His hands lifted from the console and he leaned back in his chair. "There is exactly *one* intact docking point."

"That's our welcome mat." Kensy's hand tightened on the edge of his seat. "Take us in, lieutenant commander."

"Yes, ma'am." Daniel deftly navigated through the drifting ruins toward the docking access.

"Any chance we could just drift over? Avoid the whole docking trap altogether?" Rasken asked.

Daniel shook his head, "I wouldn't want to risk it. Between the debris and free floating wires, there's a good chance we could lose more people to suit failure than enemy encounter."

"Right." Rasken nodded. An uneasy quiet settled in among the passengers.

Kensy glanced up to Marieke's towering, armored olhreleth form. "When we disembark, I'll need you to protect the shuttle. It's our ride outta here and I fully expect it will be a prime target."

"Don't worry, princess. I got this!" The eagerness in her voice eased Kensy's concern only slightly.

The shuttled slowed in its approach as Daniel reached over the console to ready the docking systems. Abruptly, the craft grinded to a halt. Faint metallic tumblers skittered across the hull. "Well, we're here," Daniel pulled his hand back, "...one way or another." He took a deep breath. "Prepare for depressurization. Opening access hatch—." The scream of metal against metal filled the compartment for a moment before the shuttle air escaped into the void beyond.

Nathan caught Kensy's arm as she turned away. "Hey, I'm gonna hold back. I wanna see if I can wire this thing into the shuttle's systems." He held up his orb. "I'll catch up when I'm done. With luck, it'll help during extraction."

Kensy nodded, "All right. Keep me posted." She drifted out of the shuttle. "Engaging personal gravity field. DeCadejra, are you reading?"

"Roger that," Allen replied. "Reading you loud and clear. Processing new data. We'll be updating maps as you move."

Kensy looked to her team. "Let's begin a sweep, slow and steady." Like a well-oiled machine, the troupe brought weapons up, fanned out to cover every direction as they moved.

The low fuzz of an open line buzzed in Kensy's ears as she led the way through the vacuous corridors of the Icarus. Strange seams and mismatched metals lined the hall. The walls pressed in at uncomfortable angles. Every breath seemed suffocatingly loud within the sealed confines of her environmental suit. The silence of the warship's motionless cadaver gnawed at her.

Ahead, the first light flickered. "Approaching a light source," she glanced to the readout on her helmet's display. "It seems to be an exposed plasma conduit. Getting intermittent noise off it."

"Give it a wide berth. If one of the other broken systems is juicing it, disruption could cause catastrophic failure." At the DeCadejra's warning, she waved everyone around the open section of the ceiling. *You knew this place would be a deathtrap. Keep moving, keep focused.* Side-stepping the danger zone, she eyed the conduit warily.

"How is it that this thing still has enough power to sustain a plasma system?" Kyo muttered.

"The auxiliary core seems to still be on." Rauk scrolled through the cybernetic display on the inside of his forearm as he lumbered along. "The readings aren't great, but it's still chugging along. A warship like this is prime salvage, difficult and dangerous, but the payday is typically well worth it."

"Kigh no likey scary-ship. Kigh think findy-finds only badness." The small chittering voice echoed over the communicators.

"It's all right, buddy. We're gonna stop the badness." Rauk's voice was warm and reassuring. Kigh chirped and chattered nervously over the line in his native tongue.

The company approached the first point of divergence. "Two paths ahead." Wright stepped toward the left branch. "There's more of this weird plating to the left. Hey, big guy, feel like doin' a little trail blazing?" Rauk nodded to him, *yes*.

Gabby peered down the hall with her psionically empowered vision. "I'll come too. I'm seeing some weirdness. Maybe we can figure it out."

Wright shifted his gaze to Kensy, "We've got this. You guys head further in."

"Stay in contact."

"Yes, ma'am." Wright led Gabby and Rauk away from the main company.

Kensy adjusted her grip on her pistol as they disappeared into darkness. "Let's keep moving." With carefully measured breaths, she fought against the tightness in her chest. The wide main corridor stretched ahead an uncomfortably long distance. Small side chambers spotted the walls with pockets of darkness. Scattered blast marks scored the passage. *Elle walked these halls. She lived within these walls. She... died here.* She blinked the thought away. *No. Not dead, not yet.* Despite her best efforts, each step through the wreckage eroded her confidence.

The beam of her suit lights caught a dozen disparate edges hanging in the hallway ahead. Curiously, the light shifted with her movement, glinting and dancing across a shroud of shattered shapes. Closing on the fractured pall, she reached a hand out. Her gloved hand tapped a fragment. It twisted in the emptiness. Broken glass. "Move through carefully. It's a lot of sharp edges."

Kensy pushed forward. The silicate silvers collided against her suit in muted dissonance. With the ghostly light cast from each tumbling shard, the walls seemed to crawl and writhe. Alien shadows danced in her peripheral vision. She cleared the curtain of glass.

Trepidatiously, she watched the others follow in her wake, one by one. As the last man through, Kyo stepped quickly toward the group. Kensy glanced around. "Is everyone good? Do we have any suit leaks?"

Neira scanned each person quickly. "Looks like we're clear."

"Anyone else unnerved by the volume of broken glass just hanging out when we're nowhere near a window?" Kyo asked. Furtive glances cascaded around the group. "Okay, yep."

"Boarding party, we're getting a life-sign near your location." Allen's voice sent chills through the team. "It's pretty weak." Kyo rocked back on his heels and stared up at the ceiling, while Hensley tried to shake the feeling away.
Kensy's stomach lurched. "What?" She cleared her throat. "Repeat that, please."

With measured breath and enunciation, Allen repeated the finding. "A single life-sign detected near your location."

Neira caught Kensy's gaze. "Bearing?"

"Coming from somewhere in the munitions storage bay. It's a large chamber to your left. The closest access door should be about 100 meters ahead."

"Yeah, because that's not ominous at all." Rasken jeered.

"Roger that. Moving to assess." Kensy turned to face the darkened hall. Adjusting her grip again, she stepped toward her new destination. *100 meters. 99. 98. Stars, you're making this more painful than it needs to be. You knew this was coming. Get it together!* She advanced down the hall, ignoring the fear that swelled within her. Her skin bristled, but still she pressed onward. Arriving at the door, she found it askew in its frame. *Just enough room to squeeze by.* She glanced toward

Nevan's towering form. He nodded, and Kensy ducked through the opening.

She crept into the vast room beyond. One by one, her company joined her. "Hey chief, what kind of payload was the Icarus carrying?" Rasken sidled up beside Kensy.

"Full compliment. Why?"

Neira scanned the empty hold. "'Cause either our boys dropped the hammer on the way in or our wandering psycho murder-bot cleared her out." A shape shifted in the darkness on the far side of the chamber. Neira snapped toward the target. Kensy followed her sight line, stepping toward the undefined shape. The others closed in behind her.

As the attenuation crept up the figure's body, Kensy stowed her gun. She slipped a hand behind her back, open and waiting. Rasken caught the signal, dropping an orb into Kensy's palm. Kensy motioned for the others to hang back as she inched forward.

She studied the mechanical limbs that held the limp figure of her friend aloft. Black tangled hair fell around the down-turned face. Grotesque metal plates protruded through her scarred olive skin. "Elle? I did it. I came to where fate found you. I came to help you. You want that, don't you? That's why you told me where to find you." Kensy drew closer. "You talked to Jackson. Do you remember him? He's here too. We know the Vagabond has made you do some terrible things, but we're here now. We're going to make it stop. I just need to get a little closer. Is that all right? I'm just coming to help." Kensy fiddled with the device in her hidden hand. *If I can just get close enough....*

Elle's body began to sway and shift. Her head lulled and the metallic joints of her spidery limbs flexed. Neira narrowed her eye at the monstrosity. "Kensy, back away."

Kensy glanced in Neira's direction. "We're here to *help.*" She waved her empty hand toward Elle. "See? No gun. No powers. We're just two old friends that are going to have a nice chat." Kensy continued to close the gap.

Elle's head snapped toward Kensy. Eyeless. Mutilated. Her face contorted into a voiceless scream of searing agony. The reverberations cascaded through the structure, ripping apart the metal plating beneath Kensy's feet. Limbs, claws and tendrils sprung from every surface. The sundered ship began to fold in on itself and panicked cries filled the comm channels.

## Chapter 44

# Scattered

*"It's a big old shit-storm."*
*~ Flight Lieutenant Morgan Threaux*

A cacophony of chaos filled the air. Jackson sorted through the data feeds frantically. "Somebody clean up these transmissions!" A chorus of electronic feedback drowned out the flurry of voices. He grit his teeth against the nerve searing sound. Fighting against the noise, he slammed a fist down on the console in front of him. Silence filled the space. He breathed deeply. Straightening his posture, Jackson looked around to the faces staring up at him. "Get me status reports and vitals on all boarding party members! I want to know everything that is happening on that ship!"

"Commander, we need you in the war room *now*." Allen's voice rung through the diminishing haze to Jackson.

He pushed back from the command podium. "Forward all feeds to the war room." He shook his head as he turned toward the lift. "On my way up now. Ugh." Jackson pressed a finger to his tragus, closing off the ear canal for a moment. He tried to shake the residual tone from his senses. *My ears are going to be ringing for a week after that.*

He quickened his steps into a jog, making the traversal to the strategic deck swiftly. He descended the few stairs in the direction of the holotable. "What do you—?" His steps slowed as he watched the hologram contort.

"Commander, the ship, it has...." Micah paused, casting a glance toward the chief engineer.

"Frankly Jack, that ship is more Vagabond than vessel." Allen interjected. "We didn't realize until it *woke* up."

Jackson pointed at the diagram. "Then we need to rip that thing open and get our people out!"

Allen raised a hand. "It's not that simple." He hit a series of commands on the table interface. Fourteen green dots appeared, scattered throughout the ship. While they seemed to cluster into small groups, the dots were in constant motion. "Those are our people, as near as we can guess. We are calculating their movement as fast as we are getting information. That *thing* seems to be trying to isolate them from each other. If we start blind firing and we could space or even kill one of our own."

"Orders, sir?" Micah stared at him expectantly.

Jackson watched the mechanical monstrosity violently gnash at itself. Like a lit fuse, his nerves were set aflame with purpose. "Figure out who's who. Get me trajectories, where they're trying to go, and where it is redirecting them. I want to know any casualties they've sustained. See if we can pinpoint any strike zones that will force it to bring our people together. Consolidate them all in one area. Then punch a hole."

Aides and engineers took to their surrounding stations with renewed fervor. Jackson closed on the table, watching the flow of dots through the ever-changing schematic. His eye was drawn to one as it was driven away from the rest. "Who is this?"

Allen furiously sorted through the available data. "Psilyria Frost. What vitals we are getting from her nahdvi are strong, but her comm channel is spotty."

Jackson tapped his nahdvi. "Maggie, get me a comm link to Psilyria Frost."

"I will do my best, commander. Stand by." Her mechanical voice rang through, stable and steady.

One of the comm channels lit up with static. Rasken's rough voice barely broke through the interference. "Hey boss, this damn wreck is trying to kill us. And I hate to split hairs here, but I'm not exactly trained to take on animated warships. My aim is usually better suited to things that bleed. Any chance we've got an escape vector?"

Jackson pulled the feed to his portion of the table. "Working on that now. What is your status?"

A metallic skittering noise overwhelmed the line for a moment. "—pinned down with Hensley and Kyo. Lost visuals on everyone else. Commander, this whole damn place is crawling—. ...running low on ammo."

"Lieutenant," Allen interjected, "it looks like you're near one of the crew wings. If you keep moving past the private quarters, you should come to a bank of escape pods. Do you still have any of the signal orbs?"

"—passed mine to Frost, but Kyo still has—." A concussive boom drowned out her words. Pained cries, weapons fire, and incoherent shouting faded into static.

"Communications link established." Maggie informed Jackson.

"Chief, figure out what just happened." Jackson's attention snapped away. "Kensy! Kensy, talk to me."

"Jack? I'm a little busy at the moment." Her labored breath renewed his hope.

"What the hell happened? You need to get out of there."

Kensy skirted a corner and staggered to a stop, teetering on the edge of a hole in the deck. Her eyes darted around the sundered space. "I tried to get close to Elle. Figured if we could co-opt the control signal on her, we might have a chance to save her." A mix of irregular footsteps and mechanical stomping closed in on her from behind.

"She's not in control. She's driving you away from the others. You have to turn around."

"Get the others out while she's more focused on me." Kensy reached her right hand forward. A channel of glittering purple light grabbed a twisted beam on the other side of the deck breach. It groaned as she pulled it closer. "As soon as I've disabled her, I'll call for extraction." Taking a step back, she reduced the intensity of her personal gravity field and launched toward the beam. As she sailed through the air, the dark misshapen form of Elle emerged around the bend. Kensy's feet lightly tapped against the beam as she continued to propel herself forward to the other side of the gap. With a quick pivot, she faced down the monstrosity. "Elle, I know you're in there. Fight him!"

"Kensy, don't—." Jackson's voice cut out abruptly.

"yoUR frIEnd is GOne." The vagabond's discordant tone reverberated through the structure and flooded her communicator.

She smirked, "Then come get me, ugly." *Get them out, Jack. I can do this. I will do this.*

"Dammit!" Jackson slammed his fist on the table. "Did you get Rasken back? And where the hell are the others?"

"I think I've got the lieutenant. Rasken! Rasken, are you there?" Allen filtered away the static.

"Hey, chief. Good to hear you haven't forgotten us yet." Rasken's breath was ragged as she spoke. She grimaced at the panel before her. A loud thud carried over the open line, followed by a drawn-out hiss.

"What was that?" Allen furrowed his brow.

Rasken snickered. "Just a little aggressive engineering, nothing to worry about."

"Status report." Jackson demanded.

Rasken nodded toward a now opened portal. "We're still alive." She glanced down at the searing pain in her lower abdomen. A dark tinge spread beneath a gash in her environmental suit. She adjusted her equipment belt, tightening it around the opening. "We are trying to reach to the escape pods. Kyo got knocked around bit. He's got some suit damage and his visor's cracked. Hensley is helping him so we can keep moving. We're running low on air and ammo, sir." She ducked through an open door behind her subordinates. Turning to the control panel, she shut the passage behind them and muscled the manual door locks to engage.

"Is your position secure?" Jackson tilted his head down. Dark shapes flitted across the windows behind them, and a storm of metal scraping enveloped the passage. "Gonna say *no*." She reached up to a damaged panel on the wall and wrenched it open. "Son of a—!" Rasken placed her hands on her hips, grimacing at the char marks. "The wiring in this section's shot. It's all fried to shit. That's gonna make it a little harder to keep moving." She glanced to Hensley, "How's the shoulder?"

"I'm good, LT." He nodded to Kyo, holding him tightly on his feet. "We can keep up."

"Ensign, don't think you're getting outta this so easy." He nodded weakly. Rasken spit the gum from her mouth, inhaled deeply, and unsnapped her own helmet. Air rushed out as she opened the collar just enough to retrieve the gum before resealing her helmet. Swiftly, she worked the gum into the cracks of Kyo's damaged visor. "There, patched visor. Not gonna hold long, but it will buy us a little more time."

Kyo groaned, "Dying on a derelict ship in space, but don't worry. The lieutenant will fix it with her gum."

She smirked, searching the corridor for an exit point. "Damn right! No dying allowed on my watch." A dull snap filled the thin atmosphere of the corridor. All eyes trained on a small construct outside the window. It released a pulse into the glass like material. Cracks spidered through it. Rasken moved to Hensley's side, pulling the last of their ammo packs from his belt. "Don't mind me." She loaded her rifle and leveled it at the window. "Commander, we need an extraction." The rending of metal reverberated through the walls. She waved her squad to take cover behind her. "Sooner rather than later."

"Carve around them. See if we can open up a way out to the escape pods." Jackson glanced around. "Where the hell is our shuttle? Does anyone have tabs on Bryden?"

A voice chimed up from the dimmed exterior ring of consoles. "Sir! A vessel just jettisoned from the far side of the ship. Four life signs aboard."

"Our shuttle?"

"No sir, looks like an escape pod. Heavily damaged," the engineer's voice clarified.

"Get someone out there to capture it and find our damn shuttle!"

Micah zeroed in on a section of the ship diagram. "I've got them. One of the signal devices just lit up like a beacon. It's being boosted significantly. Comm connected."

"Commander, I really hope that's you. It's a shit show over here." Daniel slammed a plasma cartridge into his rifle.

"The entire boarding party has been scattered across the ship. I need you to start running extractions and so we can regroup." Jackson leaned over the edge of the table.

Daniel picked off a line of bots attempting to circle around the olhreleth warrior wildly swinging her pendulum shaped axe in wide, sweeping arcs. "Would love to. Just as soon as we can break free. I don't know if you've noticed, but there is currently a ship trying to assimilate my transport." He glanced over his shoulder into the shuttle. "How's it coming back there?"

"All wired in. Almost got it juiced up enough to repel these bastards." Nathan shouted.

Daniel focused back down his sights. "Finally, approaching departure time. Send us the pickup points." His datapad beeped in confirmation. He fired off a few more shots at the skittering mechanical pests. Before rising to his feet. "Marieke, time to cut loose."

She growled at him, "I was just getting warmed up."

Daniel raced to his pilot's seat. "Let's hope this works." His hands danced across the controls. The hull of the shuttle began to hum with the orb's signal. A sharp screech pierced through the shuttle's auditory emulators.

"Give it a little more gusto." Nathan scrambled through a cluster of wiring. "Come on, come on." He caught a glimpse of a light green sheathed connection. "There you are." He stripped the end of the wire and jammed it into an open space on the orb. He glanced to Daniel. "Hit the shields!"

Daniel slammed the shield control forward. A mechanical scream howled at them again. Holding a stanchion at the door, Marieke leaned out to observe the ship's reaction. Finger-like spines ripped across the shuttle's exterior as the smaller constructs scurried away. The eye slits on her armored helmet shifted to an intense red glow. She released her support bar and lifted out of the shuttle's open door. "He. Said. Hands. OFF!" Marieke drove the curved end of her axe up into the base of the spines. The grip on the shuttle loosened. Daniel gunned the engines, and the shuttle tore away from the docking port.

Nathan jumped out of his seat, stumbling against the shuttle's jarring movements as he navigated toward the open hatch. "Mari!" He watched the ship violently twist and thrash at her. In the silence of open space, she gracefully drifted around the strikes. Reluctantly, she retreated from the ship in the direction of the shuttle. Constructs piled over each other in an attempt to reach her.

"Status, Bryden!" Jackson impatiently tapped at the holotable. Moments dragged on as he stared at the projection.

"Nathan *and* Marieke on board." Daniel announced. "Hull damage sustained, tracking multiple faults through environmental, shield, and thruster systems. We're limping but free. Not sure if we can pull that off again."

Jackson cursed under his breath. Turning to one of his analysts, the commander pointed at the hologram. "Get shuttles out there for pickup. Doctor Hirayama, get down to the shuttle bay and see if you can rig your signal thing into any of our gunships, like Mr. Derien just did." She nodded and dashed from the room.

"Sir," another voice from the edge of the room chimed in. "Mister Rauk, the psimehna and Specialist Wright are pinned down in the forward maintenance access. They were trying to reach the bridge."

"Gabel," Daniel's voice drew Jackson back to his feed. "I think we can get to them, but the shuttle won't be able to get back out. Send me a boarding pod. We'll latch it onto the outside of scythe and use the shuttle as an airlock to get them out. Just like we were planning to do on Cor'Threa before it blew."

"Do it." Jackson waved to Allen. "Bryden, help is incoming. Get in position and stand by." Staring intently at the shifting dots, he mentally shuffled through the problems at hand. *Kensy's alone against Elle. Rasken's squad are wounded and trapped. Wright, Gabby and Rauk are pinned and under fire. Bryden's got the shuttle in a sad state. Nevan, Neira, Shane, and Reily are unknown. Maybe, probably, in that escaped pod, but unconfirmed. How the hell are we getting out of this one? Find the solution, it has to be here... somewhere.*

Chapter 45

# Extraction

*"Exit stage right."*
*~ Specialist Nathan Wright*

Gabby stared at the wall intently with her psionically infused vision. Light rapidly coursed through the diffusion channels of her specially designed environmental suit. The metal plating heaved even as Rauk held it in place. She glanced to Wright beside her. "Four millimeters."

He nodded in acknowledgment. "Almost there." He carefully lowered a dead wire bundle toward a spinning fan. It neared the blades, skipping and bounced with each moment of contact.

"It's not heavy enough." Gabby furrowed her brow.

"Just a little more...." He shifted to give the line a little more slack. Suddenly, the line snagged. He opened his hands, releasing the bundle, and lunged toward Gabby to cover her. The cables ripped through the wall as the fan pulled. A mechanical screech pierced the air, followed by a harsh grinding sound. The structure groaned. They waited for several long minutes for the inevitable silence.

"Is it—?" Snap! The gear housing gave way, ricocheting the internal wheel around the lower chamber. With a dull thud, the noise halted. Wright and Gabby cautiously looked over the edge. There, about two meters below, the ruined wheel jutted out of the chamber wall.

298

Wright shrugged. "Well, no more moving fan blades to dodge."

"Right, right, right." Gabby rubbed her gloved hands together and took a deep breath. The wall heaved again. "They're gonna break through soon," she fussed.

"Not without a fight," Rauk smiled at her.

Wright nodded. "It'll be fine. Remember what we talked about."

"Climb down halfway, bust the cover plate open and crawl in. The tunnel will be small. Crawl five meters and find the hatch to the bridge corridor. If it looks clear, drop down and double back to the captain's access elevator. Pull the emergency override and signal." She carefully recited.

"Exactly." Wright grinned, giving her shoulder a gentle squeeze. "You've got this, kid." Gabby nodded and began her descent. His knuckles tensed as he held the cable bundle steady for her. The cover plate sat buckled and bent, the top corner jutting out toward the center of the chamber. Gabby reached out, walking her fingers over the edge for a stronger grip. She closed her crystalline eyes and focused her power into the muscles of her outstretched arm. With one strong jerk, she wrenched the cover free. As she glanced up to Wright, he gave her a thumbs up. "See you on the other side!"

The wall heaved again. "You ready for this?" Rauk slammed the side of his massive fist against the bulging seam.

Wright pulled his rifle to the ready and nodded. "The kid's clear. Let's do this." Rauk lumbered around to face the wall he was bracing. With a roar, he dug his clawed fingers into the sides and ripped it loose. He slammed the rent panel into another wall, crushing the constructs between. He dropped the slab over the ventilation chamber entrance. Dozens of spider like bots swarmed up his back. Wright fired into the mechanical mob as Rauk violently mangled the metallic assailants.

The static of their communicators was lost among the commotion of the fight. Jackson paced in front to the war table. *Two groups of three left, and Kensy by herself. Scythe can only hit one point. They're all too spread out.* He eyed Kensy's dot. *We agreed no one goes it alone. Now what am I supposed to do?*

An explosion tore through a section adjacent to Rasken's team. Allen turned to one of his subordinates. "What did we hit?"

The engineer scrolled through the scans. "No vital systems, must have been a pocket of air. Something that trapped a portion of the ship's atmosphere prior to its destruction."

Allen sifted through the static until finally recovering Rasken's frequency. "Lieutenant Rasken, can you hear me?"

She coughed, tasting the iron in her mouth. "I read you, chief. You finally got the bugs to stop knocking. Thanks."

"We just hit the next section over from you. 'Caused a bit of damage. Check the door. See if you can open it now." He zeroed in on the area on the hologram.

She grunted and rose to her feet. Releasing the hold on her depleted rifle, Rasken began pounding at the door. "I dunno. Still looks sturdy from this side." The aperture remained blocked. "Come on, you stupid piece of—." She swung a kick into the bottom edge of the door, jarring it off the track. "Hensley, gonna need you for this."

He turned to his squad mate. "You good, man?"

"Yeah, yeah. Just go help her so we can get outta here." Cautiously, Hensley adjusted Kyo's position, allowing him lie down on the hall floor.

Hensley walked over to Rasken. "How you wanna do this, LT?" He surveyed the obscured opening.

"Think you can get your fingers over that top edge if I give it another good kick?" He nodded. "Okay. Here goes...." Rasken focus her might into another swift kick. The door shuddered and twisted. Hensley grabbed at the opening and wrenched down hard. Now wedged askew, Rasken surveyed the breached room beyond. "Damn! You guys really did a number on this place." She crawled through for a better view.

"Any chance you can either get clear of the wreck through the opening or at least across to the pods?" Allen inquired.

"Outlook's bad. A cloud of shrapnel and live wires lighting it up. Across probably. Looks like you demoed the first pod bay with that blast. Will have to get closer to see if the others are functional." She crouched down, pain searing through her midsection. She coughed again. "Get Kyo and come through."

"Raksen, you sound rough. How bad is it?" Jackson interjected.

She straightened up. "Heh, you know me, boss. I'll be popping wheelies and running circles around the squad in a week." Jackson and Allen shared a concerned glance. "Hey, you two slackers comin'?"

Kyo pulled himself through the gap. "Right behind you, LT." Rasken grabbed his hand and pulled. He suppressed an agonized cry as Hensley pushed through behind him. The ship groaned. Rasken looked up, "That's our cue!" The hull curled back, folding itself over the open compartment. A swarm of black constructs swelled around the deforming ship. "Grab him and get to the pods! Go, go, go!" Hensley slung Kyo over his shoulders and began running. Interference swelled, reducing the channel to static.

Jackson looked down at the table. "Why did we lose them?"

"A new source of interference, trying to locate it." Allen brought up scrolling pages of diagnostics. "Check for engine noise, subsystem startups, anything. Catalog and counter people." Allen grumbled. "That damned AI could have turned on any number of things. Whatever it is, we've lost comms on all of them."

Jackson zoomed out the scope of the hologram. His eyes darted from dot to dot. He squinted at the image. "Expand the scans." Allen looked to his captain questioningly. "Expand the scans! Get as much as you can of the surrounding cloud."

"You three, get on that." Allen pointed to a cluster of analysts. "The rest of you continue working on getting feeds back." He shifted over to Jackson. "What are you thinking?"

Jackson's jaw tightened. "I'm hoping I'm wrong."

Gabby poked her head into the captain's access elevator. Grabbing a bright yellow knob on the control panel, she pulled. "Override in place," she called. Her nahdvi buzzed in her ear. Nervously, her attention darted between the elevator and the currently quiet passage. With a loud crash, the hulking body of Rauk dropped through the elevator's canopy. He uncurled an arm, allowing Wright to roll out onto his feet. A crescendo of metallic skittering began in Gabby's ears. "We have to go! Now, now, now! They're coming."

Rauk lumbered into the main hall. "Go! I'll cover you."

With a nod, Gabby turned into a skip just behind Wright as he ran for the bridge door. Arriving at the door, he forced the panel cover open. "Come on, have power!" The light flickered faintly, then died. "Dammit!"

Rauk roared. The bots swarmed toward him as fast as he could crush them. Gabby thrust her hand onto the control panel and closed her eyes. With a measured exhale, she forced the psionic power coursing through her into the electronics. It sparked to life, and the door slid open easily.

Wright raised an eyebrow, "Neat trick. Now get inside." He gave her a soft shove. "We're in!" he shouted down the hall. Ducking through the door, he glanced around. "Find a console that has juice, or you know, make it yourself." They darted about the room, checking every access point. He rounded the corner on the astrometrics station. "I've got one. Toss me the drive."

Gabby lobbed the small device toward him. Cradling it in his hands as he caught it, Wright flipped it over and plugged it in. "It should only take a min or two." He tapped his gloves on the console, urging it to process his request faster. Gabby moved to his side to watch the progress bar fill. "We get this, and we can get out of this heap." He smirked, tapping on the console frame faster and faster. The moments crawled by and the sound of fighting drew closer.

The console beeped. Wright yanked the drive free and tucked it into one of his suit's pockets for safekeeping. "I saw two escape pods in the hall." Gabby pulled Wright back toward the door.

"Exit stage right!" he hailed at Rauk. Skittering descended over the exterior of the pod. He pushed Gabby in and thrust the orb into her hands. "Crank that up when we pop the pod." She nodded emphatically. "Come on, big guy!"

Rauk swung an arm backward, casting the wave of machines down the hall. He ejected his orb from a storage compartment in his chest and armed it. He thundered down the hall as the orb detonated behind. "After you." They clambered into the escape pod. Wright hit the hatch control with the side of his fist, Gabby cranked up the power on the orb, and the pod jarred violently upon release.

"Sir! Another pod just jettisoned from the wreckage," a tech announced. "Three life signs on board."

"Which group?" Jackson crosses his arms.

"Pod came from the forward bank, sir."

"Capture it." He stared at the remaining dots. *Come on Lindsay. Get outta there.* The open comm lines crackled, but no words were audible. A flash of psionic energy lit up on the back end of the wreckage. "What was that?" Jackson watched as the aft section of the ship dislodged. "Maggie, is there *anything* you can do about that interference? We *need* to be able to talk to our people."

"Interference signal is growing in strength. Attempts to identify and counter the signal have been increasingly difficult."

"Sir...," an analyst timidly called toward him.

"What is it?" he snapped.

"There's something in the dust cloud, sir. Something large and it's on the move."

"Bring it up!" Jackson watched the scan data collate on the central display. He cursed as the shape took form.

"Commander, we've got company!" Morgan called over the comm system.

"I can see that, flight lieutenant. Keep us outta their sights." Jackson turned toward his chief engineer. "I need to get back down there. Get those comm channels cleared up. Rasken and Kensy need a heads up."

"I've got it. Go. Go!" Allen waved him away.

Jackson sprinted from the room. Descending through the primary elevator, and rushing through the strategic operations center, he arrived at the bridgehead. "Maggie, give us a view." The walls shimmered and shifted into virtual window mode.

"Isn't that the ship we ran from on Rosalleon?" Morgan swiveled just far enough around to look at his commander. "I thought that bastard blew up with the planet."

Jackson jogged down the stairs. "We had enough time to get away, evidently he did too." He gripped the back of Morgan's chair. "Can we skirt into the cloud? Make it harder for us to be targeted?"

Morgan's hands danced over the console. "I mean, yeah, but we'll also lose eyes on the Icarus and everyone out there."

The hum of static rose in Jackson's ears. Daniel's voice came into focus. "Gabel, we've still got people on that ship. Scythe is standing by. Orders?"

"Rasken, Hensley, and Kyo still haven't made it to pods. And the entire aft section with Psilyria Frost is drifting toward that thing." Morgan's eye darted between readings. "Bryden only has one shot at either."

Kensy's line connected, "Jack, I see the ship. Get everyone clear. You can't risk the DeCadejra. I can hold my own."

Rasken's voice joined the chorus. "Commander, all of our guns are dry. We've got another wave coming."

The discordant scream of the Vagabond's monstrosities interrupted the communications briefly. A dozen voices resumed. Among them Rasken, Kensy, Bryden and Morgan all called for slivers of Jackson's attention. He stared up at the dark looming silhouette of the Vagabond's warship. What choice did he have? He inhaled deeply. His response came out stable and steady. "Bryden, extract the Psilyria."

A pause gripped the line. "Yes, sir."

"Flight lieutenant, withdraw into the debris cloud and signal all vessels for retreat."

Kensy switched over to a private channel. "Jack, don't do this. Lindsay needs you."

He lifted his chin. "The decision is made."

Rasken coughed, her lips pale but slicked with red. "I read you, boss." She shut the escape pod before turning to Hensley and Kyo. "Deep breath, ensign." Kyo inhaled. She unclicked both her helmet and his, swapping them within seconds. As the seal hissed, Kyo gasped for air. Her air tank sputtered, and she coughed again. She slumped onto the floor of the pod, dropped Kyo's broken helmet, and pulled a piece of gum from her suit pocket. "Woulda loved to teach Liam...." Rasken's voice faded as her eyes grew dull and clouded with blood. Her hand lazed open, the piece of gum still resting between her fingers. Hensley dropped his head and pulled the release lever on the pod, jettisoning them into darkness.

## Chapter 46

# Consequences

*"Bubblegum never weighed so much."*
*~ said in whispers and souls*

In the distance, a beam of furious red light lit up the dust cloud. Jackson watched in silence as the Icarus's lingering wreckage gracefully and violently destructed. Morgan's console beeped dully at the edge of his awareness. He reached over, acknowledging the notification. "Commander, the last of the pods and retrieval vessels have been cleared. They're in the hangar and are about to start offloading."

"The Admiral will want a report. Set course for Aepexia." Without waiting for acknowledgment, Jackson pivoted and walked away.

Decks below, engineers scrambled to open escape pods. Medical staff stood by, anxiously awaiting access to the soldiers within. With a pop and a hiss, the access hatches were released. The first out was Nevan. His lithe form slipped out, unfurling and stretching to his full height. He moved aside to provide a clear path to Reily, Shane, and Neira.

Across the floor, Daniel climbed out. He scanned the bay, taking note of each captured pod's passengers. The air was thick with a somber sense of reality. Not everyone came back alive.

The engineer at the most damaged pod leaned in for a long minute before waving to the waiting medical staff. "Need someone over here! Wha—?" He backed away from the opening and the large physique of Hensley crawled out. He turned back toward the open hatch. Everyone began to crowd around a little closer. With a gentleness uncharacteristic of the usually boisterous man, he lifted a smaller figure from inside. Her head lulled back, and her limp hand fell, dropping the unconsumed gum to the ground.

Tears reddened his eyes, and his face contorted from the pain searing through his shoulder. He stumbled to one knee. Several of the congregated rushed to his side to relieve him of his burden. He clutched her tightly. Shane moved up, cupping the back of Rasken's head with one hand and setting the other at the base of Hensley's neck. "It's okay, Joey, we've got her. You can let go." As sobs rose within him, Hensley's hands relaxed. Many hands carefully lifted her body, bearing her to an open space behind the pods. Even as they carried her out of view, his water filled eyes refused to leave her.

Kensy backed away from the others. She wrapped her arms tightly around her mid-section and fought the tide of emotion lapping at her heels. Jackson approached, stepping up beside her. They watched the bustle of the crew, tending to the wounded and fallen in somber silence. Kensy raised her chin. "I need a word."

"About?" He kept his eyes locked on the consequences before him.

"The mission," she curtly replied.

He drew in a sharp breath. "Conference room one. We can talk alone there."

She nodded. Each of them turned and proceeded toward the main elevator. A painful stillness filled the lift on the way up to the command deck. There were no words, no exchanged glances, no gesture of comfort. Just pain and silence.

Out and a short walk away, around three quick corners, they arrived. The door slid closed behind Jackson as he stopped just inside the large meeting room. Kensy continued a bit further, pushing away her tears. She whirled around to face him, her voice coming out angry and pleading. "What were you thinking?"

"I made a call, and it was the right call." Jackson's jaw tightened.

"You made the wrong call," she snapped. "I was fine. I could have held out!"

Jackson threw a hand up in the direction of the bridge. "I just watched the Vagabond disintegrate what was left of that ship. You can't hold out against that!"

She shook her head. "He clearly waited until we were clear... or at least until Elle was." She paced the far side of the room. "He values her. She is his most important pawn. And we had a chance to steal her away from him. To take her back!"

"You were cornered on a fraction of the Icarus that was drifting directly toward the Vagabond's flagship." He stared at her. "And that *thing* you were so keen on getting close to isn't the person you used to know. It was going to kill you."

"That thing has a name! ELLISE NERU! And I'm not going to give up on her." Fury and distress burned through her piercing gaze.

"You are going to get yourself killed." He leaned forward, the knuckles of his balled-up fists pressed to the tabletop.

"You don't know that." She shoved aside his concern. "She could have killed me a dozen times in there, but she didn't. She hesitated. I was getting through to her."

He stared at her incredulously. "The Vagabond is using your feelings toward the person she *used* to be to draw you into a trap."

"We already knew it was a trap!" she screamed.

"And still you put yourself on the line unnecessarily," he yelled back.

She pulled away, folding her arms across her chest. "I did what I had to. I told you to extract the others first, and now Rasken is *dead*." The word lingered between them, an intruder in the argument. Kensy turned her eyes away. "Why couldn't you just listen to me?"

Jackson straightened his posture, resting his hand on the back of a chair. "I made the only call I could."

"It was a bad call," Kensy softly chastised.

Jackson tugged at his uniform jacket. "I was the one on the bridge. It was my call to make."

"I had things under control. Why couldn't you *trust* me?" The frustration in her voice cut at him. Trust. He hadn't considered that.

His hand fell to the badge on his belt. "Because I can't lose you too," he confessed.

Tears overflowed her eyes. "Don't you get it? I don't want anyone to die for me—ever."

Jackson paused. *I... want to feel alive with you... tonight.* Her words rattled thought his thoughts amid a flurry of memories. Her last-minute confession on Cor'Threa, all those disparaging remarks she makes when she thinks no one's paying attention, all of it begged a question. He tilted his gaze toward her. "Do you *want* to die?"

"You can't control whether I live or die any more than I can." Kensy held up her left arm with its armored sheath.

*Of course, the chimera, the death sentence she carries with her. I had to fall for a woman that's already dying. Loving her is a losing proposition. And I'm all in. Fuck.* He stared at her arm blankly. "What's done is done." He bowed his head. *Sorry, Lindsay. I screwed up. And I can't say that I regret it. I hope someday you can forgive me. I hope maybe eventually I might even forgive myself.*

Jackson stuffed his hands in his pockets, turning toward the door. He hesitated at the threshold for a moment, but no words found him. A tear rolled down Kensy's cheek. She closed her eyes and fought against the knot in her chest. Silently, Jackson strode from the room, carrying the weight of his decision.

## Chapter 47

# Lying

*"Every lie is two-fold. It is the lie we tell to others and the lie we tell ourselves."*

~ ancient human proverb

Kensy absent-mindedly pushed her dinner around her plate as she stared at the scrolling text on her datapad. Neira watched intently from across the officer's lounge. Several minutes crawled by with no change in posture or activity. Neira huffed, rising from her chair. Approaching the lounge bar, she gestured for two drinks. The bartender retrieved the refreshment and passed them over the high counter.

Drinks in hand, Neira sauntered over to Kensy. The abrupt thump of the glass container against the side table startled her friend. "You stare at that datapad with that laser focus for much longer and you'll burn a hole through it."

Kensy sighed and tossed the pad onto the cushion beside her. "You have a better way of getting through reports? I'd love to hear it."

Neira leaned back in a chair across from Kensy and crossed her knees. "You weren't reading reports. You were somewhere else entirely."

Kensy chuckled. "Oh really? And where would that be? I am a captain of this ship, it seems like everything has to pass by me."

Neira raised an eyebrow. "You're a terrible liar. You've rearranged the contents of that plate at least four times without taking a bite. And I am betting you can't tell me what the last memo on that screen was about without looking." With a scowl, Kensy dropped her fork onto her plate, folded her hands together in her lap, and looked away. Neira took a drink. "Do I need to go track down Commander Broody and tell him you need to get laid?"

Kensy cast her eyes down. "Don't know that's going to ever happen again."

"What did he do? Do I need to go rearrange his face?" Neira's glare narrowed.

"No!" Kensy replied in alarm. "No. It's just... I don't know." Her eyes drifted to the starscape displayed on the virtual window adjacent to them. "We got into a fight after the Icarus. Things haven't been the same since."

Neira shook her head. "Let me guess, you were mad he came to your rescue instead of Rasken's and he was mad that you were trying to take on Elle on your own?"

"Yeah, I guess that's about the gist of it." Kensy's shoulders slumped. "He doesn't get it. I don't want people to die for me. It's a pointless waste of life."

Neira slammed back the last of her drink. Setting the glass down, she leaned forward. "Have you told him *why* you feel that way?"

Kensy shook her head. "There's nothing to tell. Between the chimera and...." She hesitated, waving the thought away.

"You're lying again." The lines of Neira's eye patch danced with a dull amber light.

"And it's irritating how you pick up on little things that are peripheral to the issue. Why do you have to so damn observant? Couldn't you just let the little stuff slip by this once?" Kensy fidgeted uncomfortably.

Neira shrugged. "It's in the job description."

"What job description? Being a graven?" Kensy waved dismissively.

Neira lazily pointed in her direction. "Being *your* best friend."

"Neira!" Kensy pouted.

"Fine. I'll bite." Neira rolled her eye and straightened her posture. "What is the issue you want me to focus on?"

"I told him I was fine. I was holding my own." Water began to well up in Kensy's eyes. "Why couldn't he trust me?"

Neira pinched the bridge of her nose. "Ugh. I can't believe I'm going to side with him on this. Kensy, you have a habit of jump first, think later. You've barely recovered from your last jump first scenario on that damned space station. Do we need to review how that went?"

"That's not—." Kensy started.

"Back on the Icarus, the Vagabond had a plan to pick us off one by one. A plan that we happily skipped right into." Neira stared intently at Kensy. "And when he decided to hit the go button on all of his little murder bots, everyone was separated, scrambling to reconnect. He immediately had us on the defensive. And in all that chaos Rasken was injured. There's no guarantee she would have made it even *if* he had chosen her. And what then? We lose her *and* you?"

"She would've at least had a better chance." Kensy wiped at her eyes.

"Yeah, well, if you had died back there, I'd have really had to kick his ass." She slouched back in her chair. "That just sounds like entirely too much work."

Kensy's voice became quiet. "We had a chance to take Elle back from the Vagabond."

Neira dwelt on the memory of their lost friend for a long moment. Her voice came out softly, a match to Kensy's tone. "Are you sure there's anything left to save?"

"I *know* there is." Kensy pushed her bangs out of her face. "And even if there's not, taking away one of the enemy's primary assets should be a priority. What if we never get another chance like this?"

"Let's be real. That wasn't some golden opportunity back there. It was a no-win scenario. The Vagabond had every advantage. We're lucky we didn't lose more."

Kensy sighed in resignation. "You're probably right."

"Of course I'm right!" A twinge of a smirk crossed Neira's expression.

Kensy's eyes shifted back toward the virtual window. She sat in quiet contemplation, watching the glittering starscape subtly shift across her field of view. "I should go talk to him."

Neira put a hand up. "Just make sure it's somewhere private, in case you end up having make-up sex. The rest of us don't need to walk in on that."

Kensy blushed and cleared her throat. "Maggie, where is he right now?"

"Commander Gabel is in his quarters at this time."

"Right." Kensy grabbed the drink Neira had brought her, downing the entirety of it in one go. "Here goes nothing. Wish me luck."

Neira grabbed Kensy's plate. "Just go. The only kind of luck you need is the kind that lands you in the sack. And I'm not the one that can help with that."

Kensy turned away as the rouge of her cheeks intensified. Quickly, she departed the lounge. Entering the lift, her mind recalled the feel of his touch, the comfort of his smile, and the hurt in his eyes at the end of their fight. *Rasken was his friend, and I didn't even pause to let him grieve her loss. Stars, no wonder he's pulled away.* She stepped out toward his door. *What if he doesn't want to see me? I wouldn't blame him. But I need to tell him. To let him know I didn't mean to hurt him.* She stepped up to his door. Her hand hovered just off the surface. She took another deep breath... and knocked.

"Come in," he called. The buckle of his belt clicked together. His hair fell in tousled, wet streaks over his face. The door slid open. Kensy stood there staring at his bare chest. Her face flushed with a bright rosy tone and the water gathering in her eyes glistened in the room's low light. Jackson glanced toward her. "Is everything okay?"

Her breath caught in her chest. "I... I'm so sorry!" She rushed toward him, pulling him into an embrace, her lips meeting his. The kiss lingered.

As they parted, Jackson brushed her hair from her face. "What's this all about? Sorry for what?"

"Sorry for how angry I was, for how I wasn't there for you. You've always been there for me, and I just railed against you when you lost someone. I know you were friends and—." The tears began to escape her eyes as she rambled.

"Hey, none of that now. You have nothing to apologize for. Emotions were high for everyone." He pulled her into a tight hug. *First you betray her trust, and get Rasken killed, now she's crying about how she hurt you. Way to go, dumbass.* He placed a warm hand on her cheek. "Losing people is never easy, but it comes with the job."

She managed a weak smile. "It doesn't make it hurt any less. And it doesn't make what I did right or justified." Wiping at the tear streaks on her face, Kensy turned her eyes away. "I don't blame you if you're upset with me. I deserve it after my little tantrum."

"Kensy." Jackson lifted her chin. "I'm not mad. And I don't want you to blame yourself for the decision I made. That responsibility lies squarely with me. I'm the one who gave the order." He squeezed her shoulders gently. "No more fretting. Think you can do that for me?"

"I'll try." She curled closer, resting her head on his bare chest. There she could feel his heartbeat. He wrapped his arms around her and swayed subtly from side to side. The warm, clean scent of his body mingled with the alcohol in her blood. Her fingertips began to dance over his exposed skin. "How long until you have to be downstairs?"

He smiled as his heartbeat quickened. "I'm sure it's negotiable. Why?"

Butterflies danced through her body. "Can we be just a little closer for a little longer?"

"I think I could probably make that work. Maggie, let Bryden know I'll be switching to the graveyard shift. I have an important captains' meeting to see to. And activate privacy mode, please." The door locks engaged.

Jackson leaned down, kissing Kensy passionately. He swept her up and spun around toward the bed. The sheets and comforter billowed up around them. She giggled. "Stars, you're...." The rosiness of her cheeks came into full bloom. The faintest flicker of psionic power licked against his skin under her caress.

Straddling her small frame, he leaned down close. "Now, that's cheating." He buried his face in the side of her neck, sending shivers cascading through her. She combed through his damp hair with her fingers. The tiniest drops of cold water sprinkled down her neck between his warm kisses.

"Jack?" she whispered.

He pulled back, looking into her sea-green eyes. "Yeah?"

"You'd confide in me if you needed to, right?" She ran her fingers down the side of his face. "I want you to trust me. Like I trust you."

He kissed at her palm. "I do trust you. I'm sorry I ever made you feel otherwise. There's no one I trust more." *Not even myself.* He smiled. He lowered himself only a hair's breadth away from her and whispered. "Now, just how close do you want to get?"

She unfastened her uniform jacket, pulling it open, and reaching for his belt. Her heart raced as she released the buckle. "As close as we can get." She kissed him hungrily. A passionate heat consumed them both as they surrendered to desire within the shadowy solitude of Jackson's private quarters.

Chapter 48

# Turmoil

*"I really miss the LT fixing everything with her bubblegum."*
*~ Private Joeseph "Joey" Hensley*

Jackson covered his mouth as he yawned. He blinked away his bleary-eyed tears forming in the corners of his eyes. Pushing away from the ready room desk, he stood and stretched. *Ugh. I'm gonna fall asleep if I don't move around.* Several of his joints crackled as he tried to relieve the stiffness of sitting for too long. *Come on. One lap through the bridge should about do it.* He took a deep breath before straightening his uniform.

He sauntered from the room. A few hushed conversations between crew in these early hours filled the operations center with a soft din. As the morning crew trickled in, the smell of coffee and various teas wafted through the space. Leisurely, he started down the hall to the bridgehead. The rapid cadence of heeled boots on the walkway closed in behind him. He glanced back as her hand reached his back. He felt the material shift under her touch. "You're up early." He yawned again.

Kensy tilted her head. "And a good thing too. You look exhausted."

"Quiet shifts seem to take twice as long." He stopped and leaned back against the side rail.

"Why don't you go and get some sleep?" She smiled softly. "I hope taking the later shift was worth the time we had together beforehand."

316

He pulled her close and kissed her forehead. "Time with you is worth so much more than the torture of a tedious shift."

Morgan strolled past the pair. "Do you mind not making out on my bridge?"

"Not your bridge, Threaux." Jackson dryly retorted. "I don't think I have the energy to deal with him right now."

Kensy chuckled. "Well, it's a good thing you don't have to." She kissed Jackson sweetly. "Now go get some rest. I have things covered up here."

Jackson nodded wearily. Pushing off the railing, he circled around Kensy and started toward the elevator. Their hands slipped apart. Another yawn nagged at him. The traversal to the captain's deck seemed a thousand times longer than usual. As the door to his quarters slid open, he smiled. *She made the bed. Of course, she made the bed.* He entered the room, shaking his head and shedding the layers of his uniform. Finally disrobed, Jackson slipped into a comfy pair of pajama pants, threw back the sheets, and flopped onto the cushioned surface. *So... fucking... tired.*

Jackson turned his head to the side. He could still faintly smell her on his sheets. Trying to clear his mind, he rolled toward the edge of the bed. *Nope. Not thinking about that. It'll just keep you up longer. Clear your mind, and just... go... to sleep....* His mind traveled to a high mountain lake. As he stood on the shore, the choppy waters grew still. He took a sharp breath in, and with its release, sleep finally claimed him.

The smell of iron subtly tainted the high mountain air. Jackson stood staring blankly at the lake in front of him. He felt a chill crawl across his skin. The pop of bubblegum echoed around him. A gruff woman's voice drew his gaze to the side. "Yo, boss, this is a wicked view. You always run away to the fake little corners in your mind when things go bad?" She laughed.

Jackson stared at Rasken. He knew this echo was her, but a strange sense of unfamiliarity surrounded her. He tried to squint past it. The smell of iron wafted off her. She turned to face him. Her eyes were blank and glazed over. As she smiled, blood dripped from her lips. The color drained from her skin, leaving her cold and gray.

"You look like you're having a hard time placing my face. Don't worry, boss. I got ya." She unzipped her biker jacket and lifted her blood-soaked shirt enough to expose her abdomen. In its place, she revealed a vacant space of twisted metal and gore. "Is that better, boss? Do you know me now?"

Jackson tried to backpedal from her. The towering trees became twisted girders, the calm lake overflowed with violently bubbling acid, and the mountainside deformed into ravenous shadows. His heart beat deafeningly in his ears. He gripped his head, trying to shake the vision.

"I'm the one you chose to die." Rasken's voice crackled through in disparate directions. "I'm the one who paid for you to get your dick wet. How's that turning out for you?" A plasma flash blinded him for a moment. He bolted upright in bed. The iron smell still filled his nose. "How's that working out for you?" Rasken hissed.

Jackson realized there was a shape in the bed beside him. In a panic, he grabbed her shoulder and rolled her back toward himself. Glowing red and orange veins spidered across her body and her dulled eyes filled with crimson. Crackling, sanguine lightning erupted from her lifeless body. Jackson fell out of bed, scrambling toward the door.

"You know she's as good as dead and still you chose her." Rasken's twisted form leaned down to his ear and whispered. "You know I had a little brother." The small form of a child emerged from the shadows, faceless. "Another little brother like *you*, only he's not old enough to understand. *You* did this. *You* made that choice."

Jackson bolted upright in bed. Sweat rolled down his unusually pallid skin. The air in the room was frigid and still. Beside him lay only the folded back covers. As his breath slowed, he swiveled around to place both of his feet on the cold floor. He cradled his head in his hands. A torrent of tears burst forth. He sobbed.

Each breath brought forth more pain, more memories. Holding his older brother, Gaveth, as he took his last breath. Kensy collapsing in his arms on the observation deck. The vision of her laid out on the operating table after Cor'Threa. Rasken's dead body cradled in Hensley's arms. The sum of all those moments and so many more previously held back threatened to consume him where he sat.

His chest tightened with grief as the tears continued. The seconds turned into minutes, maybe longer. He lost track. The salt water and agony burned across his face, leaving reddened streaks down his skin. The sound of his ragged breath filled the room.

As he fought to regain some sense of calm, Maggie's mechanical voice broke the silence. "Commander Gabel, you seem in distress. Do you wish for me to contact Psilyria Frost with an aid request?" Her words were somehow softer, more empathetic, than he expected.

He straightened his posture and wiped his face. "No, Maggie. I just need a minute." With a carefully measured breath, he stood. He wavered for a moment, lightheaded and exhausted. Taking in another deep breath, he steadied himself.

He stepped past the threshold to the bathroom. His eyes darted between the sink and the shower. With a sigh of resignation, he stripped back down and turned the shower on. The cold water flowed in rivulets down his body, soothing his tear-stained flesh. *What have I done?* He turned his face up into the spray of water for a moment. *I'm compromised. I let my emotions get the better of me. If I can't reign it back in, then I'm a danger to everything: the crew, the mission, even Kensy. How can they trust any decision I make? I couldn't even keep it together long enough to get everyone out alive.*

He scrubbed away the salt of his sweat slicked skin as if it would wash away the grief and doubt.

He stopped and stared at the wall. *I can't keep pretending to play captain. I have to go back, finish my training. I clearly wasn't ready for command. Fuck. I'll have to appeal to Captain Hadarian, see if she'll take me back.* He pushed his wet hair back from his face.

Shutting the shower off, he paused. *Shit, what is Kensy going to think?* He shook the thought away. *No point in worrying her or mentioning it until I know for sure. I need to do this for us, for her.* He blotted away the residual water. *Get your head on straight. Then you will be your best for her. You owe her that much.* He breathed deeply.

Entering back into the main room, he paused, glancing warily at his bed. *Probably not getting any more sleep after that.* A chill ran down his spine. He shook his head. *Just get dressed. You've got transfer papers to write up and a call to make.*

A strange numbness filled him as he dressed. It wasn't a completely unknown sensation to Jackson, though it had been years since that goodbye. He recalled the deathly calm as he stood beside his brother's casket. He reckoned his sister had cried hard enough for both of them that day. The emotions were too much. So he stood there, a rock against a torrent of bottomless feelings. No more crying, no more devastating grief, no more directionless anger. He just needed to push it all away....

Then came her smile once more. Her glittering eyes filled with concern. *You'd confide in me if you needed to, right?* Her voice resonated through his thoughts. He closed his eyes and sighed. *I just need to figure this out first. Give me a little time.*

He sat down at his desk, setting to work on the necessary transfer paperwork. It didn't take long. He had both sent and received such requests numerous times in the past. He scrolled through the contacts on his console. There it was, the entry for

Captain Hadarian of the ESFV Themiscyra. His hand hovered over the send command on his screen. "This is it. The point of no return." He muttered. *You can't protect her if you can't get your head on straight.* He exhaled and pressed the command.

He immediately called through to her. After a few rings, she answered. Her piercing eyes drilled through the screen to him. "I have the most peculiar request in my hand. Transfer request for one Commander Jackson Gabel."

"Yes, ma'am." Jackson folded his hands in front of him on the desk. "Recent events have illuminated a deficiency in my command education. With your permission, I would like to finish out my officer's training under your guidance as was originally planned."

She glared at him. "You are willing to give up your current command?"

"I am aware it is a highly unusual request. But the DeCadejra will be in good hands with the Psilyria and her current crew. I believe I can best serve the mission and the Ascension by furthering my training. Once that is complete, I will accept reassignment wherever I am needed."

Captain Hadarian stared at him for an uncomfortably long time. Jackson remained firm and unwavering. "Duty first? Humph. Well," she tapped her datapad on the desk. "I do not have an XO position available at this time. But perhaps we can arrange something."

"Whatever you think is best, I will defer to your judgment."

"Right." She dropped the datapad. "Once I begin processing your request, there is no second guessing. And there will be no guarantee you will be transferred back to the DeCadejra once your training is complete."

"I am aware. I truly believe this is the best course of action." His jaw tightened, and a knot formed in his stomach as he spoke.

She scrolled through the information on the form. "You are expecting to be back at Aepexia within a few days to report to the admiral? We will be about two days out at that point. When we arrive, you will be transferred back to the Themiscyra. See you then, commander." The line disconnected.

Jackson slouched backward in his chair. "Commander, would you like me to inform the command staff of your imminent departure?" Maggie asked.

"No, Maggie. Keep things business as usual. I will tell them myself." He closed his eyes as an errant tear escaped.

"Commander, Lieutenant Commander Bryden is inquiring as to your current status. How would you have me respond?" Maggie's voice returned to its normal synthetic tone and cadence.

Jackson glanced upward questioningly. "I'm awake. Put him through." He heard the subtle tone shift as line connected. "Hey Bryden, what did you need?"

"I didn't mean to disturb you, but we have the data that Wright, Gabby, and Rauk retrieved from the Icarus. It's been scrubbed for any non-standard programming, but we're still keeping it on an isolated system just in case. Thought you might want to know."

"Yeah, gather people up in the war room for analysis. I'll be down in a minute." Jackson straightened his posture.

"On it. See you when you get down here." Daniel disconnected the call.

Jackson dipped back into the bathroom to wash his face one more time before leaving his quarters. *Come on. You just need to keep it together for a couple days.* He took a deep breath and straightened the lines of his uniform. With renewed composure, he headed for the war room.

He stepped out of the elevator onto the strategic deck. A pair of voices down the hall drew his attention. "Go ahead without me. I've got a few things I need to deal with down on the bridge. Since he's on his way down, Jack can oversee everything for now, and I'll catch up on stuff later." Kensy's words stung Jackson as he approached behind her. He placed a hand gently at the small of her back to let her know he was there. She turned a smile toward him. "Hey." She gazed into his weary eyes, and he thought for a moment she might see right through him. "Thanks for coming down. I know you couldn't have gotten much sleep."

Jackson shrugged. "Honestly, I appreciate the distraction. You know how it is, tired until your head hits the pillow." She gave him a worried look. He quickly waved it away. "I'm just a little restless. It's fine. I'll get some sleep later...." He leaned down to whisper in her ear. "...when I have a little company." He gave her a quick kiss.

Kensy blushed and pivoted away, waving goodbye to Daniel as she withdrew. Daniel studied Jackson carefully. The elevator doors closed before he spoke up. "Now, that was a feint if I ever did see one."

Jackson stuffed his hands in his pockets. "We're all under a lot of stress. I haven't been sleeping well. No need to worry her about it."

Daniel raised an eyebrow. "If you're not going to talk about it with me, that's fine. But you should at least *consider* talking to her about it. You know she's going to worry, whether you tell her or not."

Jackson furrowed his brow. "I'm dealing with it." Daniel threw his hands up in surrender. "Now, there was something we got from the Icarus?"

"After you, commander." Daniel bowed back from the doorway. "I've already got some people working on it."

"Additional firewalls have been put in place for the war table presentation." Maggie informed him.

"Good." Jackson led the way into the dimly lit room.

A handful of figures crowded around the central table, chattering amongst themselves as they worked. Wright looked up past the others. "Hey, commander! We got started already, so we'd have something ready for you."

Jackson glanced to Daniel. "This is your show and tell. Go right ahead."

Daniel flicked an incredulous glance his commander's way before addressing the group. "Let's see it. Give me the rundown."

"Psimehna Ciphar and I found a semi-functional console on the bridge. We pulled the station's local data. As well as what I could snag off of what remained of the ship's internal network." Wright started. "As luck would have it, the console was their sensor station."

One of the techs beside him spoke up. "Most of the info is just raw data from the ship's sensor arrays. We have basic charting telemetry for their entrance into the dust cloud, a catalog of the Icarus's own systems, but the real gold mine is this." The technician constructed a three-dimensional image of a space station. "We have detailed scans of what we theorize is the Vagabond's base of operations."

Daniel crossed his arms over his chest. "Do we know if we can trust any of this? Why wouldn't it alter or just delete the data?"

"If I had to venture a guess...," Wright leaned forward on the table. "It is entirely possible the Vagabond didn't calculate a scenario where any of us survived the boarding venture. Why waste the resources to doctor information if you don't plan on anyone living?" Wright directed his gaze at Jackson. "We went in with variables he couldn't have anticipated. If I didn't have Gabby *and* Rauk, I wouldn't have made it to the bridge, let alone off the ship."

Jackson wordlessly nodded. *Good. Maybe it's enough to keep this damned AI off balance for Kensy.* He gestured for them to continue.

A young analyst across the table jumped into the discussion. "During my analysis, I did manage to retrieve some of their communications data. Most of it is the usual status reports. But there is one that shares multiple data points with the transmission fragments Doctor Hirayama recovered."

Daniel turned toward her. "Let's hear it."

She tapped the table, casting the transmission into the center. A man in an ascension uniform appeared on screen. Jackson glanced toward his lapel: Aileth, captain. His voice echoed through the room as the recording began. "Icarus to Ascension Command. It's not pirates or raiders! There's a station here. Scans say it's just one massive computer. What?!" he snapped around to one of his bridge crew. "We're being hacked. Oh g—." The captain's face contorted as a discordant mechanical tone overwhelmed the recording and the feed hazed into static.

The captain's image came back into focus. The bridge around him was drastically dimmed. Sparks from ruptured systems lit up the area from behind him. "It's like a hornet's nest. They're everywhere." He glanced across his command console. "Point defense isn't making a dent. We're surrounded. Hull breaches on all decks! Systems are shutting down. Life support offline, weapons offline, main power is offline. Down to auxiliary systems. Caroway is trying to redirect everything to keep our engines online. We'll try to ram it. If we're lucky, we'll take it out with us. ESFV Icarus out—."

After a long minute, Jackson glanced around. "So, what do you make of this? How can we make use of the new data?"

The tech beside Wright hesitantly spoke up. "We could correlate the ship's sensor data into a formula for the Vagabond's attack protocols?"

Jackson nodded. "Possibly. Anyone else? Any other ideas?" At his urging, the chattering began again. He stepped back a little, watching the process as their ideas took form through discussion. Daniel glanced his way, trying to gaze past the deviant reservation of his long-time friend.

## Chapter 49

# Scuttlebutt

*"Say the things you mean to say before they are said for you."*
*~ unknown*

Kensy tucked her bangs behind her ear as she inspected herself in the mirror. Almost everything was in place. "Thank you for mending my diplomatic uniform, Maggie. Lindsay's send-off deserves a little more ceremony than my everyday one."

"Damage sustained during the Cor'Threa mission was easily repaired."

Kensy fastened the clasp on her shooting star necklace from Jackson. Carefully, she smoothed the chain down and pressed the pendant against the skin just below her collarbone. She took a deep breath. "Almost time to go check in on Gabby. How far are we from docking?"

"We are passing the mining station and are cleared for final approach. Psimehna Ciphar, is experiencing elevated heart rate and respiration. This could be indicative of anxiety or excitement."

"Or both," Kensy smiled. "I'm going to swing by Rasken's old quarters on the way down. Just want to make sure we didn't miss anything that needs to go back to her family."

"I can run an area scan if you would like." Maggie offered. "Thank you, but... this is something I should do myself." Kensy confidently strode toward the elevator. After a brief descent, she emerged on the officer's deck. Personnel scurried about, making final preparations for their Aepexian arrival.

The door to Rasken's room was open. Nathan turned toward her as she entered. "Sorry, just taking a moment."

Kensy waved, "No, that's fine. Take the time you need. I know you two became... close." Kensy's eyes darted around. "I just wanted to make sure everything was good here."

Nathan chuckled. "Make sure you check the corners for hidden stashes of gum." Glistening emotion welled up at the edges of his eyes. He coughed and inhaled sharply. His hand dropped to his belt pouch. He ran a single finger down the length of a carefully wrapped strip, nestled among his other small knickknacks. Glancing around the room, he sighed and shrugged. "Guess I'll leave you to it. See you downstairs." He cleared his throat uncomfortably and dropped his head, lost in thought, as he turned away.

"Yeah." Kensy respectfully waited until he was out the door before she started her search. Piece by piece, she ran her fingers through the drawers and over the shelves. A rough patch on the side of one drawer caught her attention. Kensy knelt down to inspect it. Lightly carved into the side was a tiny stick figure with an enormous bubble and the words: Ha! Made you look. She traced over it with her fingers. *You wouldn't even know it was here if you weren't careful. Nicely done, Lindsay.* Kensy smiled and pulled up her datapad to take a picture.

The voices of two junior officers in the hall drew Kensy's attention. "Did you hear the commander is transferring out?" She stiffened, frozen by the words.

"What? No way. He and the psilyria are a thing. He wouldn't just leave." Kensy pressed out of sight from the doorway as she listened.

"You sure about that? Quaylah said she saw a transfer request *from him* come through the Themiscyra's priority comms line the morning *right after* we left that derelict ship behind." The voices continued to move down the hall.

The speaker gasped. "Oh! Do you think it had something to do with that big fight they had?"

"I wasn't on shift for that, but I heard about it." Kensy's control clasp sparked erratically. She clamped her opposite hand down on the clasp, trying to push the words and nervous energy away.

"It was bad. We couldn't make out the specifics of it through the walls, but we could hear them yelling at each other from halfway down the hall." She bit at her lip. *Stars, they could hear us!* Her eyes became glossy with gradually forming tears.

"So, maybe they're not such a thing after all...." The voices faded away.

Kensy grabbed at her chest as she tried to process the gossip. *Maybe it's not what they think. It's just hearsay. He would have said something.* She shoved the drawer shut and closed her eyes. *He would have said something.* "Maggie, did Jackson correspond with the Themiscyra after the Icarus incident?" Silence filled the room. "Maggie?"

With a slow and measured response, Maggie spoke. "I cannot respond to your request at this time."

Kensy nodded. "Yeah, okay... I'll have to ask again later when you're not so busy... with docking and whatnot." Her eyes darted about, searching for some bearing. *He could be requesting more aid for us. Or looking for a consultation. It could be a million things. It doesn't mean he's leaving.* She took a deep breath and exhaled slowly, trying to release the tension forming into a knot beneath her hand. Another breath. She closed her eyes. *Don't jump to conclusions. You need more information. One step at a time.*

She shook her head and opened her eyes. "Right, need to check on Gabby. One step, one step...." She muttered to herself as she exited the room. *Down the hall, down three floors, then down the bridge walkway*, Kensy coached herself. Masking her anxiety, she settled into an all too familiar soft smile. The click of her heeled boots on the catwalk announced her arrival.

Daniel acknowledged her with a nod. The ship jarred as the docking clamp engaged. "Very good, Psimehna. Seems like we are set." Daniel held a helping hand toward her.

She grabbed a hold of his fingers, descending from the beam. The moment her toes touched the walkway, she excitedly bounced. "That is so crazy, and cool, and scary!"

Kensy smiled at her. "You're getting the hang of things quite quickly. We'll see about adding a few more fun things to the beam training." Gabby squealed in delight. "Now, go ahead. Take care of anything you need to and meet everyone down in the hangar bay for the send-off."

Gabby straightened up for a moment. "Yes, ma'am!" She twirled around and bounded down the walkway.

Daniel stepped closer to the center of the walkway to watch her leave. "That kid has bottomless energy and enthusiasm. I feel tired just being around her." He glanced to Kensy. "But not as tired as you? I know that look. Something's bothering you."

Kensy tilted her head down. "Nothing slips past you. I'm not so much tired as preoccupied." They began to walk together toward the operations center. Halfway, Kensy slowed to a stop. "I don't suppose Jack's talked to you lately? Confided in you about any… personal matters?"

"Any subject in particular? Or are we trying to figure out what the weather's going to look like?" He kicked back against the side rail.

"Oh, it's probably nothing." She let out a half laugh. "We had a bit of a spat following that whole mess with the Icarus. After things settled down, we cleared the air." She took another deep breath. "I'm probably just worrying over nothing."

Daniel peered questioningly in her direction. "He hasn't said anything to you?"

"No." Her gaze turned to worry. "Guess I'm just concerned about what he hasn't said. Now that I've said it out loud, it sounds ridiculous." Her smile returned. "We should get downstairs. Surely, they have everything prepped by now."

"Yeah, after you." Daniel let her pass toward the main lift, then fell in step behind her.

The ride down was quiet and uneasy. The doors opened. Jackson looked up from a moment of contemplation. "Hey, I was just about to come looking for you." Kensy reached out a hand as she moved toward him. He tugged her close and kissed her forehead.

Daniel stepped out around the pair. "Everything ready?" Jackson released Kensy's hand, shifting to walk alongside Daniel. "It's just about good to go, but...." Jackson hesitated. "Bryden, could you do the speech?" Stunned, they both stopped and stared at him. "I know it's typically a captain thing," he glanced to Kensy briefly. "You knew her almost as well as I did, Bryden. I just feel like it would be better coming from you." *Better coming from a person the crew can still look up to. Better the person that always had her back than the one that got her killed.* Jackson's jaw tightened.

Daniel glanced between them. "Yeah, sure. Just give me a few minutes to collect my thoughts."

"Of course. We'll start when you're ready." Jackson nodded to Kensy. "We should get in there." She wrapped her fingers around the back of his arm and gave it a gentle squeeze. Jackson headed to the hangar bay. He took up a position away from the centrally stationed podium at the head of the assembly. Kensy gave a quick glance to Daniel. Then, following in his wake, she took her place beside her co-captain. Her eyes were drawn to the discreet nods and whispers among the crew. Jackson's posture remained rigid and unfazed.

A hush fell over the assembly as Daniel entered the hangar bay and stepped up to the podium. The crew stood in carefully ordered columns. He gazed thoughtfully at the meticulously draped coffin in front of him. "Today we say goodbye to one of our own. Lieutenant Lindsay Rasken, lost in the line of duty to an unfeeling enemy. That's what sets us apart, and above. Everyone on this crew feels this loss. We know the pain of losing and we still fight. We persevere. We take on this challenge to stop a tireless foe.

"No one knew this better than Lieutenant Rasken. She never shied away from her duty to protect. More than once she jumped straight into the middle of a firefight to pull someone out. She repelled down cliffs to reach team members that'd been separated from the rest. And after she'd pulled your boots out of the fire, she'd be the first to joke about it. You were especially in for a hard time if she somehow managed to use her gum to save your ass." A snicker passed through the crowd.

Daniel gave it a moment before continuing. "Today we say goodbye to a fellow soldier, a leader, a sparring partner, a friend, a bubblegum addict," another chuckle cascaded through the room. "But she was more than that. She was more than the uniform and the bubblegum. Lindsay was also a doting sister to her baby brother Liam and a loving daughter to her father, Lucas. More than comedy or crazy stunts, her family was her favorite subject of conversation. When she talked about them, you *knew* that they were one of the few things she loved more than bubblegum."

He bowed his head. "So today, we say goodbye and send her home to find rest with the family she loved so much." Daniel turned his gaze toward Reily. "Alpha, please see to her escort."

Reily stepped forward, placing Rasken's last piece of gum on the top center of the casket among the flowers. She saluted her fallen lieutenant with a moment of silence. Lifting her chin, she barked orders to her remaining team members. "Alpha, Fall In!" Nathan and Kyo stepped up into formation behind Reily as Shane, Hensley, and Wright mirrored them. "Center Face!" Each of them took hold of a handle. "Ready Lift!"

Together they raised the casket up onto their shoulders. "Ready Step!"

On her command, they began the slow procession through the columns of crew. As they passed, every last person, civilian and soldier alike, held a salute for the former Alpha Team leader. The pallbearers carried her down the loading ramp. Solemn silence followed. With great care, they loaded Rasken's casket into a waiting shuttle. Reily took a deep breath as the shuttle door closed. "Detail, Present Arms!" They snapped into position.

Water blurred Kyo's vision. Tears rolled down Hensley's cheeks despite his stern expression. The shuttle lifted off the ground in front of them and gently glided away. Reily watched it disappear in the distance. "Detail, Order Arms, About Face!" Together they pivoted. "Forward March." The company of six marched back up the ramp, through the columns, finally returning to Daniel. "Detail, Halt." Reily stepped forward. "Detail Complete, Sir!"

Daniel looked over the crew, glancing toward his captains. Jackson gave a nod. "Company Dismissed." The crowd began to break and scatter toward their duty stations.

Jackson remained rigid. Surreptitiously, he grabbed Kensy's hand, wrapping his warm fingers around hers. She looked up at him with growing concern. "Jack—?" A chorus of notifications rang out, startling them both.

Jackson pulled the buzzing device from his belt and grimaced at the message. "It seems the admiral will be expecting us at another damned ball tomorrow night." He rubbed his tired eyes. "There's always one more thing."

Flustered, Kensy shifted into her well-practiced mask. "Well, I should go make sure everything's in order. I'm sure there's something that needs my attention." She pulled her hand away from Jackson and headed for the upper decks.

Daniel stepped up beside Jackson and glowered at him. "So, why are you acting super shifty, and what aren't you telling her?"

Jackson furtively glanced between Kensy's path and Daniel. He let out a haggard sigh, "Fuck."

## Chapter 50

# The Last Dance

*"No mask lasts forever."*
*~ Lynxirah Amasha, Krith Diplomat*

Lowly lit chandeliers cast a soft golden glow across the shifting and swaying congregation of diplomats, officers, and influential civilians. Idle conversation filled the air with a measure of affability between the musical movements that echoed around the grand chamber. Neira intently watched the patronage from a balcony. She set her scanner and eye on a pair of figures working their separate ways through the crowd.

Jackson trudged through the pageantry with the enthusiasm of a lump of coal. His eyes remained fixed on a single radiant silhouette among the masses. Expertly, he ignored the attempts of any would-be conversationalists with his steady, solitary strolling.

In sharp contrast, Kensy navigated through debates and discussions with relative ease. Politely, she redirected dance requests to other nearby patrons when the opportunities arose. For the persistent few, she voiced her desire to remain steeped in whatever discourse was currently at hand. Her soft ringlets played lightly across her skin as her focus constantly shifted. Occasionally Jackson's stern gaze would catch her attention. Then she would lose herself amid the sway and swagger of the crowd.

Exasperated, Neira slammed the remainder of the drink in her hand and descended down the closest staircase. With quick steps and purposeful haste, she navigated to Kensy's side. "A word."

"Of course. If you please excuse me. It seems I am needed elsewhere." Kensy feigned a smile and bowed away from another tedious discussion. Together, they headed for an open set of elegant double doors along one of the exterior walls. Neira snatched two flutes of shimmering wine off a passing tray. As they stepped out into the crisp evening air, Neira thrust one of the glasses into Kensy's hands. "Thanks." Kensy took a drink.

Neira moved to the patio railing and slumped against it. "So, spill."

"Spill?" Kensy looked at her with a dubious shrug. "I don't know what you're talking about." She thrummed her fingernails against the glass in her hands.

"Cut the bullshit. In the last two weeks you've gone from starry-eyed, to angry, to listlessly pouty, back to starry-eyed, and now to anxiously pouty. What gives? And do I need to rearrange his face?" Neira crossed her arms and her ankles.

Kensy's shoulders dropped as she walked up beside the railing. "You don't need to rearrange anyone's face." Staring out at the glimmering nightscape, she sighed. Her eyes fell, and she stared into the bottom of her glass, swirling its contents around. "I have taken notice of a few things that just don't add up. I'm trying to piece it all together." She took a sip. "Maybe figure out where to go from here."

Neira grumbled. "You're being intentionally vague. You know I hate it when you do that shit." Neira chugged her drink. "It just means more work for me. I *will* find out, then we'll have to have this conversation twice."

Kensy let out a halfhearted laugh. "I don't think you can help me with this."

Neira rolled her eye. "If you don't want to talk about it, whatever. At least stop trying so hard to avoid him. You walk around with that damned fake-ass smile, it's like you've got a glowing 'fuck off' sign looming over you."

Kensy smiled at her. "We both know you're the only one that can see through it. The rest of them missed the memo." Kensy thumbed over her shoulder toward the ballroom. *Well, you and Daniel. I must be slipping. It's never been this hard to hide before.* She took another sip.

Neira whispered loudly toward Kensy's shoulder. "Stop avoiding him. I'm sick of seeing the sad puppy-dog look from across the room." She pushed off the railing. "Now, since you don't seem to want to talk to me. I'm going to try to find something harder, maybe make this night bearable." She waved her empty glass and sauntered back toward the open door.

"Love you too," Kensy called after her. Neira lifted her glass up in acknowledgment and disappeared back into the ballroom. *It's supposed to be just that easy, huh? Just stop avoiding him?* She closed her eyes and drew in a deep breath of cool evening air. *Stars, please let me be wrong about this.* Kensy sipped down the rest of her drink, prepared her facade, and resigned herself to rejoin the soiree. She paused at the door, watching the people within. *Into... what did the admiral call it?...the garrulous pageantry.* She chuckled to herself.

The night dragged on as she drifted around the room, engaging in more banal conversation. Jackson studied her exchanges of bromidic pleasantries and delicately rebuffed advances. His gaze followed the light, dancing off the elegant pearl and crystal accents woven into her hair and adorning her gown. His mind drifted to the last time she had worn that dress. He recalled holding her through the night after another torturous nightmare, then waking beside her. Her playful movement lingered in his mind as he remembered unfastening the clasps one by one and feeling the softness of her skin under his fingers.

Just as Maggie had interrupted them that morning, he was startled out of his recollection. A hand pulled his untouched drink from his hand. Daniel sullenly nodded toward Kensy. "Go."

Jackson tried to still his nerves as he willed his legs to move. *You're running out of time. You have to tell her. Let her know why you're running away.* He winced at the thought and took a step forward. Never had the room felt so vast and daunting. Each step brought him closer, and still she felt a million light-years away. The knot in his gut twisted and tortured every nerve in his body. There was no avoiding this dread, this pitfall of his own making. *She's gotta hear it from you.*

He finally approached her. With the warmest smile he could manage, he spoke up over her shoulder. "Sorry gents, I have need of the psilyria's attention." She pivoted around to face him. "May I have this dance?" He bowed.

Her heartbeat fluttered in betrayal. "Yes, you may." She held her hand out.

He grasped her soft fingers and led her toward the dance floor. He wrapped an arm around her, his palm gently pressing against her lower back to draw her closer. She straightened her posture in his hold. Despite her anxiousness, she found his familiar scent comforting. His warm touch against the curve of her lower back begged her to surrender to the moment. She looked past his shoulder as she fought against becoming lost in the embrace.

He led her through a dozen meandering steps before mustering the courage to speak. "You look amazing tonight. Well, you look amazing all the time but...." He fumbled. "Well, it's no wonder everyone's been wanting to dance with you."

"You were watching?" Her cheeks flushed. *Of-course, he was watching. Watching as you scurried away like a scared field mouse.* She cleared her throat. "I guess none of them were the right dance partner."

"You were holding out for someone in particular?" *Yes, you moron. She was waiting for you. Y. O. U. It spells idiot.* His jaw tightened as he internally chastised himself. An awkward silence settled in between them.

He studied the terse lines of her benign expression. The edges of her mouth curled only slightly upward, and the smile didn't quite reach her eyes. She held her chin high but cast her gaze down and away. Everything about her posture screamed at him, she was pretending. *You did this. She finally let her walls down with you and now she's thrown them back up out of uncertainty. She's putting up the brave face, trying to protect herself. Tell her. Tell her before you lose her.* He whispered to her, "Kensy."

"Mmhm," she softly responded.

He tilted his head her toward her sight line. "Kensy, look at me." She forced a wider smile but did not raise her gaze. "Kensy, there's something I need to tell—."

"You're leaving." She blurted out in a curt whisper. She blinked back the water gathering at her eyelashes and shook her head. "Sorry, you were saying...."

He exhaled his disappointment. *She already knows, you idiot.* "Yeah." He searched the static wall sconces and decorations for assistance that did not exist. "I'm transferring back to the Themiscyra, a tactical coordinator position."

He felt her breath become ragged as she struggled to withhold her emotions. When she finally found her composure again, he could hear the strain in her voice. "When?"

Sorrow echoed through his words. "Tomorrow, when the Themiscyra makes port."

"No. When did you decide to leave me?" She turned her pained gaze to meet his.

Like a thousand knives, her words cut through him. The accusation filled him with a desperate eagerness to clarify his intentions. He furrowed his brow. "I'm not leaving *you.* I'm leaving the ship." His breath caught. "I'm doing this for us. So,

I can be better for you. So, we don't have to tiptoe around regulations and steal kisses in secluded corners."

"That's a load of crap." She winced at the bluntness of her own rebuttal. Suppressing a strangling sob, her voice quaked and cracked. "You said you trusted me. You said you'd talk to me if something was bothering you. You said it was fine." She inhaled sharply. "You said *you* were fine."

He pulled her tightly against his body as they waltzed. "Kensy!" She pulled back in his arm. He bowed his head and whispered to her. "Nothing matters more to me than you. But I am only a danger until I can get my head on straight. I want to be the man you deserve."

Relentlessly, water filled her eyes. "I don't care about what you think I *deserve*. I want you. I can't do this without you."

He could feel her body trembling in his hands. *You knew this was coming. Somewhere in that thick skull of yours, you knew she would doubt her capacity to carry on alone. That's the whole reason you withheld it in the first place.* He gently rubbed her back with his thumb as they dance. "You have repeatedly proven that you are a stronger and wiser leader than I will ever be.

"When you were on that ship, separated from everyone else, I couldn't think straight. I endangered the whole mission out of a desperation to protect you." He let out a pained huff as he soaked in the reality of his next admission. "I screwed up. I made a decision that led to a friend getting killed." He averted his gaze, trying to hide the cracks in his confidence. "I can't live with the idea that my decisions might eventually endanger you."

Like a cascade of starlight, a tear ran down her subtly shimmering skin. "Why didn't you talk to me?" He spun her out and away. They held the distance for an eternity in the middle of the ballroom as he answered her with silence. He felt a biting emptiness within as he contemplated her question. Why didn't he talk to her? There was nothing to answer her with, no good reason or excuse. All of his assurances of togetherness, all the promises he had whispered to her, all of it suddenly felt empty.

She pulled her hand away, nodding to the silence. The tears began to flow unrestrained. The cascading swags of airy material that comprised her ballgown rippled like water around her lithe form as she turned away with hurried steps. She disappeared into the crowd, desperate to be anywhere else.

Daniel stepped up beside Jackson. He handed the stolen drink back, taking a sip of his own. Jackson took a big swig of wine. "I suppose now you're going to lecture me on how I fucked this whole thing up."

"Nope." Daniel took another sip. "You already know this is a huge mistake, and nothing I say is going to change what you've already done." Jackson took another swig of the sickly-sweet wine as his best friend patted him on the back and walked in the opposite direction.

## Chapter 51

# Departures

*"The most difficult goodbyes are the ones we fail to speak."*
*~ the Nexus*

Jackson double checked his duffel. All of his possessions lay in tightly packed rows within the black canvas bag. He looked around the stripped-down room. *One more check. Make sure you have everything, there's no coming back after this.* Bathroom, empty. Vanity drawers, empty. Closet, empty. Desk....

He stared at a plain black box sitting silently at the back of the top drawer. His mind drifted to the champagne-colored chain and glittering pendant set against Kensy's shimmering porcelain skin, almost as beautiful as her smile. The black box sat there glaring at him, empty, just like all of the promises he never wanted to break. He closed the drawer and took a deep breath.

"Your equipment locker has been delivered to the forward starboard hangar, pending your departure." The cold, mechanical voice informed him.

"Thanks, Maggie." He turned back toward his bag. *Right, you have to leave that too.* He willed his nahdvi to disconnect. The device drew back into itself and dropped from behind his ear. He caught it as it bounced off his shoulder. Staring down at the strange little device, his train of thought meandered. *Never thought I'd get used to this thing, let alone miss it.*

*Hmph.* He set it on the nightstand. "Bye, Maggie. Take good care of them for me, especially her."

He zipped his bag closed and lugged it over his shoulder. Pausing at the door, he took one last look over the room. The click of the door-side switch felt as though it would kill more than just the lights. Stepping out into the lobby, his eyes traced the lines of the floor. A knot formed in his gut as he glanced toward her door. *Just keep walking. You're about the last person she probably wants to see right now.* He sighed and stepped into the waiting elevator, dropping his bag at his feet. "Deck nine." The doors silently closed.

Deck after deck, the lights flashed by. With each one came another memory: Noticing Kensy's cold, bare feet as he escorted her from medbay to her quarters on the Themiscyra that first time. Getting tossed around in the colony elevator as it teetered on collapse. Racing through the ship as it hovered vulnerably in the Morwhexian sky, needing to reach Kensy by any means. Riding up to medbay with her, trying to tend to him after the attempted mugging on Hades Station. Quietly leaving the bridge alongside her after their first space battle above Rosealleon. Seeing how the light danced off her skin and dress after the Aepexian Assembly diplomatic ball. Nervously heading to the gravity training room to tell her about Elle. Feeling the searing power radiating off her body as he escorted her and Nexus to the medical bay after they had fused together.

The doors opened on the lowest level of the ship. He grabbed his bag and headed for the forward starboard hangar. The crew grew silent as he approached, shifting out of his path. All eyes watched his somber shuffle toward the departure ramp. He stopped beside his waiting equipment locker and dropped his duffel again. Deep in his tumultuous thoughts, he stared blankly out at the Aepexian skyline.

Daniel strolled up beside him, taking in the view. "All ready?"

Jackson lowered his head. "Yeah, guess so." Jackson stuffed his hands in his pockets.

"You gonna be okay?" Daniel tilted his head toward Jackson with concern.

Jackson took a deep breath. "Not sure I'm the one you should be worried about right now."

Daniel gave a chuckle. "She is heartbroken and probably more than a little angry, but *she* is going to be fine. She's tough as nails. You, my friend, are a burnt marshmallow: crispy on the outside and a gooey mess on the inside." Jackson gave his best friend a wounded glance. "Ha! Just like that." Daniel pointed at the look of consternation, then slapped him on the back with a significant degree of force.

"With friends like you... I swear." Jackson shook his head.

"Friends like me are the only reason you are still around to make bonehead mistakes." Daniel crossed his arms and smiled.

Jackson groaned. "Yeah. Not sure there's any coming back from this one. Promise me you'll watch out for her?" He fussed with the strap on his bag.

"Yeah, man. I got ya." Daniel's expression softened. "But who's gonna look out for you?"

Jackson shrugged. "I'll figure it out."

"Yeah, because you've done such a bang-up job so far." Daniel grabbed Jackson's shoulder and gave it a firm squeeze. "Seriously, take care of yourself. This isn't the end of the road, for either of you. Remember that and make sure you're there when it counts."

Jackson nodded. His holopad chimed. "That's my cue."

"Get over here, idiot." Daniel pulled him into a goodbye hug.

The holopad chimed again. Jackson reached for his things. He slung the duffel over his shoulder and activated the handle and wheels on the locker. Slowly, he trudged down the ramp. Upon reaching the end, he paused for one last moment and looked up at the graceful lines of the DeCadejra. A small section of the uppermost deck became translucent. A tiny strawberry blonde figure clad in a plum uniform watched. He blew her a kiss and turned away.

Tears collected on her eyelashes as she watched the distant figure disappear into the bustle of the Aepexian docks. Kensy stepped backward, holding her arms tightly across her midsection. "Maggie, deactivate balcony virtual transparency mode." She stared blankly at the wall as it faded to its usual dull, opaque tone.

She wiped her tears with the handkerchief wound tightly around her hand. Fixating on the simple cloth, she recalled his touch as he wiped her blood streaked hands with it. A small smile crept across her face as she remembered him tying it around her elbow. Her fingers toyed with a small discoloration in the fabric from her tending to him in the Hades Station park. She reached up to her necklace as she thought of the note he had wrapped in, and the secretive manner in which he had passed the neatly folded bundle to her.

*Stars, keep him safe.* She exhaled. *And give me the strength to keep going.* She tapped on her nahdvi. "Flight Lieutenant Threaux, all necessary personnel have disembarked. Begin preparations for departure."

"Yes, ma'am." Morgan responded.

Neira tapped the heel of her boot on the rear wall she slouched against. "You good?"

Kensy recomposed herself with a deep breath. "I'm devastated, heartbroken, furious, but I'm also the lone captain of the most advanced warship in the galaxy. I don't have time to be anything other than good." Her eyelashes fluttered nervously as she smiled. With a confident stride, she headed toward the lift.

"I still think you could have let me make him a little less of a pretty boy before he left. Would have served him right." Neira grumbled.

"And what would that accomplish?" Kensy shot her an incredulous look.

"I would have enjoyed myself." Neira shrugged.

Kensy rolled her eyes as they stepped into the elevator. "Bridge please, Maggie."

They stopped briefly at the officer's deck. The doors opened.

"Psilyria, Mercenary Cross." Nathan Derien nodded to Kensy and Neira as he and two of the junior officers stepped in.

The two officers quietly quibbled as they looked toward Kensy. Nathan smiled. Kensy politely bowed her head toward the officers. "Something I can help with?"

With a sharp elbow jab from his friend, one of the young men spoke up. "Psilyria, ma'am, we were wondering if maybe...." He cleared his throat nervously. "Since things are a little less weird now, is it alright if we call you captain instead?"

Surprise washed across her soft expression. *I guess that's right; they don't have to worry about confusion with Jack gone.* Kensy nodded, "Yes. If you prefer that, I would be honored for you to call me captain."

The doors opened on the command deck and the two officers raced out of the lift. A flurry of whispers preceded them as Kensy, Nathan and Neira stepped on to the main walkway. The crew scrambled to attention, saluting their captain as she walked forward.

Nathan and Neira held back, watching the spectacle. "I think it's safe to say that was exactly what they wanted to hear," Nathan mumbled. Neira raised an eyebrow in his direction.

Kensy stopped at the entrance to the bridgehead hallway. She looked at each attentive face and smiled. "Let's go stop a Vagabond."

"Yes, Captain!" They shouted in chorus. As the crew set to work with renewed vigor, Neira nodded approvingly. Beside her, Nathan shrugged and flashed a low-key thumbs up in Kensy's direction. Behind her lonely eyes, she silently prayed. *Stars, guide us safely through the storms ahead and steel my shattered heart for the trials I have yet to endure.*

# The Starchaser Lexicon

## <u>POWER WORDS</u>

**Heiga (he-gah)** – a sensory wavy intended to assess general shape and integrity of a space it is cast into

**Heiras Heiga (hear-ass he-gah)** – a radar-like sensory wave meant to allow a psionic to determine the details of their environment by creating varied resonance when it encounters obstacles

**Ivani raga khiran (ih-van-ee rag-a key-ran)** – an ability to bolster the strength of a manifestation such as a barrier

**Ivanigis (ih-van-eh-giss)** – a manifestation held close to the body, creating an armor-like covering for the psionic

**Ivanigis ahri (ih-van-eh-giss are-ee)** – extension of the basic personal armor barrier to encompass another individual within extremely close proximity

**Raga ami velgihr (rag-a-am-ee-vel-gear)** – the growing expansion of a manifestation, often used in conjunction with barriers for the purposes of casting hostiles away from the point of origin (like a tidal wave)

**Volgihr (vol-gear)** – a pulse released into a thundering shock wave to push back hostile creatures and constructs

**Yhir Nu'hai (year new-high)** – an attack manifestation in which arcs of energy bombard a target repeatedly

## <u>TECHNOLOGY</u>

**Comm screen** – a console that focuses on the processing of communications and data

**Daecellyon (day-cell-ee-on) ore** – a power-rich, naturally occurring, metallic compound that when properly refined generates vast sums of energy ideal for applications such as space flight

**Diklodemir (die-clow-dem-meer)** – a medicinal substance most commonly used to treat internal burns caused by implant ruptures, other uses still under investigation

**Evo-suits** – a heavily engineered suit of armor focused on providing the wearer with protection from extreme environmental hazards such as, volcanic heat, arctic cold, radiation, or the vacuum of space

**Flexiglass** – a clear and flexible 2 dimensional material which can be used to display data like a note or image, often used as a more transferable medium between disparate parties

**GC-L48 container** – a commonly used containment device used in a variety of industries for its incredible durability, superior performance, and portability

**Hard boards** – the physical, unchanging control panels for starship flight, often augmented by an additional set of holographic overlays and virtual control devices

**Holo– (technology)** – devices that manipulate light and matter to construct 3 dimensional holographic representations of data, such as a holopad (handheld) or a holotable (immovable display center)

**Nahdvi (nod-vee)** – a compact communication device that can maintain long range up-links; capable of monitoring and transmitting wearer's vital statistics as well as limited environmental telemetry, can also provide limited emergency assistance in the form of distress signals, synaptic pain control and black box transcription; the device creates a synthetic bio-fusion with the wearer and is telepathically responsive. Biologically fuses to the wearer in order to retain an extremely complex biometric encryption matrix, making the device utterly unaccessible to anyone other than the intended user

**Nanite** – a nearly microscopic machine, often used in the medical field for tasks such as tissue reconstruction, shrapnel removal and infection neutralization

**Neural inhibitor** – an external device that attaches to a patient in order to regulate brain activity and prevent damage from energy fluctuations as with psionic burnout and stroke-like events

**Stellar Industries CS675 Gravinine (gra-vin-nene) Ultra Bike** – widely considered the ultimate for single person, multi-environment transportation, this bike is stylish, fast, and harder to come by than most would prefer, can carry one passenger *if* you feel like sharing; the premier model was equipped with such luxuries as GSX Microflex-plate tires and a self-sustaining clash core power module

**Suspension chamber** – a vertical tube filled with specialized fluids to aid in medical procedures, a harness system to keep the occupant in a weightless state, and numerous tubes and conduits through which necessary substances are delivered to the occupant during the procedure. Often used for assisting in the injection of plasma-like substances for weaponized implants to prevent damage to the subject

## ARSENAL

**Ausk-Chelkai (osk shell-kai)** – a large paired set of wing-like blades originally created by an alien race, known to be extremely difficult to learn how to wield and even harder to master

**Chimera** – an experimental biological weapon intended to be able to identify friend from foe and adapt accordingly

**Combat exosuit** – a heavily engineered suit of armor designed to protect the wearer while providing external assistance to aspects such as perception, reflexes, strength or endurance

**Control clasp** – a complex maze of nodes and wires that are implanted directly into a psionic's body in order to protect the user, regulate the biological impact of their power draw, and to refine and amplify their latent abilities

**Nordux Crystals** – a highly volitile crystalline substance, initially designed for demolitions work but widely outlawed after it was determined to be too dangerous to handle and too unpredictable for common use

**Psiblade** – a manifestation created by a psionic that resembles a blade such as a sword or dagger for the purposes of combat

**Psionic (sigh-on-ick)** – an individual with a natural ability to filter the background energies of the universe into various different forms according to their will and training, often characterized by a redundant nervous system that seems to be used exclusively for conducting these ambient energies, often feared and dangerous if not properly trained; also referring to things of a psionic nature i.e. abilities, equipment, or an organization

**Psi-walk** – (master level manifestation) the psionic projects a representation of themselves, most of the time it can be only be used to observe things within a limited range from another perspective

**Xeik'quael (z-eye-k'quail)** — an imposing pendulum shaped axe, the traditional weapon of the elite olhreleth warrior class, when wielded it is swung in sweeping arcs to utilize the momentum of the heavy head piece to deadly effect

## PEOPLE & ORGANIZATIONS

**ESFV Themiscyra (them-ess-key-rah)** – a ship of the Terra Ascension Core Navy commanded by Captain Alex Hadarian

**Delrn (del-urn)** – the second oldest race in Aepexian space, the delrn are a very tall reptilian race with regal, articulates manes of scales, clawed fingers, and long sweeping tails; the delrn are a highly ordered and respected among the Aepexian races

**Kraydian (cray-dee-an)** – a mysterious isolationist race, their clergy are often joked about as the universe's most sober denizens as they cannot tolerate fermented liquids exposed to air in their presence without adverse physical reaction

**Krith** – a towering, lithe race of people with feline facial features and feet; colorful feathers drape down their head like hair, the ends of which drift and flex as a the krith express themselves

**Legacy Flagship DeCadejra (dee-kade-drah)** – a strange and beautiful alien warship at the heart of the Legacy Fleet, from which a great deal of humanity's interstellar ships were reverse engineered

**Magthaeleon (mag-thay-lee-on) a.k.a. Maggie** – the DeCadejra's advanced complexity engine and tactical assistant

**Malckiev (mal-key-v)** – a diminutive race of marsupial-esque creatures with a knack for tinkering, often overlooked for their size and broken common speech, they make fiercely loyal friends of those willing to spare the time; from somewhere past Rasktir (rask-tier)

**Olhreleth (ol-h-reh-leth)** – the oldest civilization of the Aepexian races, members of which tower among most other species, their eyes emit a soft glow often shifting colors in accordance with their emotions, massive and power wings sprout from an olhreleth's upper-middle back

**Psilyria (sigh-leer-ee-ah)** – (f) or psilyrian (m) a high ranking officer in the Psionic Security Investigation Corp; considered masters of their core power set, they are usually in command of small field tactical or training units

**Psionic Security Investigation Corp** – a specialized intergalactic military for the training of psionics; the go-to place for individuals who need assistance controlling their abilities; a.k.a. Psicorp

**Sol System Defense Force** – a branch of the Terra Ascension Core focused on protecting and maintaining the human home star system of Sol

**Terra Ascension Core** – the cooperative force of the human military between the Sol system and the colonies, often joined by those who wish to venture out to see the wider galaxy or simply to escape their home world or station

**The Divergence** – the common term for a period of about 100 years of rapid genetic change within the human race that gave rise the subraces of Terran, Solson, and Voidir

> **Solson (sol-sin)** – the heartiest of the human subraces, they developed in harsh higher gravity and high hazard environments; characterized by shorter, stockier physical builds, very thick leathery like skin and darker, ruddier tones in their skin and hair

> **Terran** – humans that tend to originate on Earth or earth-like environments, they have extremely varied body types, skin tones, and other physical features

> **Voidir (void-ear)** – often revered as the most elegant of the human subraces, they tend to originate in low or zero-gravity environments; their bodies have developed with a

lighter and leaner physical structure, their skin has a faint shimmer to it that aids in reflecting of low-grade cosmic radiation; the subrace with the highest instance of psionics

**The Graven (grey-ven)** – a secretive society of elite intergalactic peacekeepers who enforce a "for the greater good" policy across the expanse of civilized space

**The Illusive** – a renowned smuggling ship that was in service from June of 547 CS to June 647 CS when it mysteriously vanished, placing its legacy firmly in the realm of urban legends and spacer ghost stories

**The Nexus** – the living embodiment of psionic energy and the conduit through which all the such power flows, often appears as strange cat-like creature with glowing eyes and a sharp looking body from which energy constantly flows

**Wyrran (weer-an)** – a race of biological machine humanoids recognizable by their wire hair, mineral-based irises, and the fine seams that trace subtle patterns across their skin; wirehead is a common derogatory term for a wyrran

**Xyak (zigh-ack)** – a sentient race of highly psionic crystals, most often seen with technological harnesses and elaborate wings built for mobility and personal aethetic expression; due to their crystalline nature they often have difficulty understanding the spontinaity of the 'softer' races

**Zog** – a hulking race of ape-like humanoids that specialize in cybernetics and begin augmenting shortly after birth; originally from the planet Kedag (ke-dag)

## MISCELLANEOUS

**Psilic (sigh-lick) Crest** – the emblem of Psicorp

**The Veil** – the theoretical limit for all psionics, a barrier which if broken could potentially kill the psionic by flooding them with too much energy and thus frying their nervous system

## LEGACY FLAGSHIP DECADEJRA

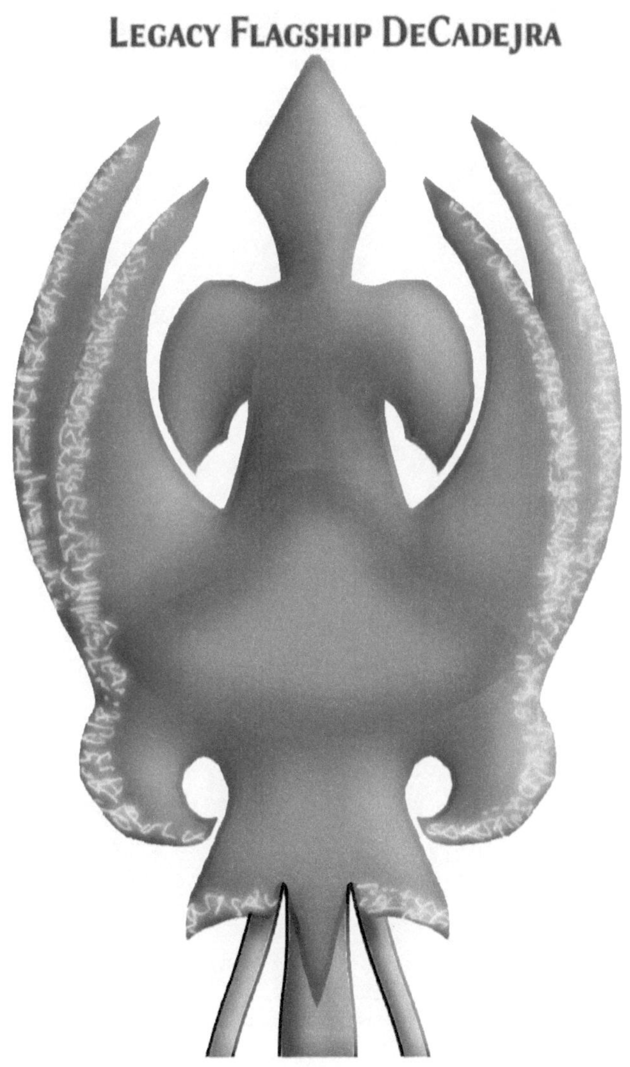

# LEGACY FLAGSHIP DECADEJRA

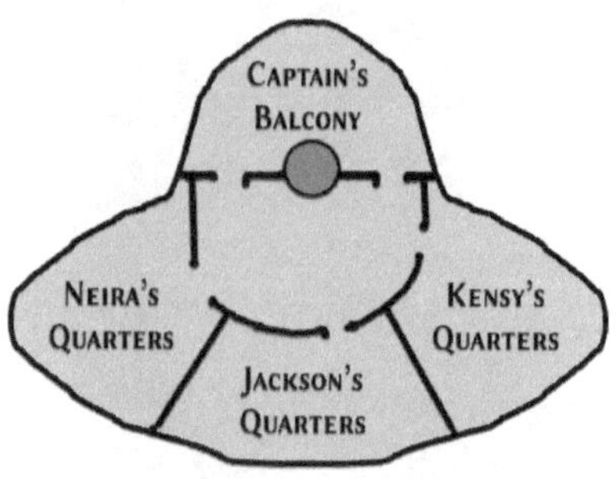


## DECK 1

# Legacy Flagship DeCadejra

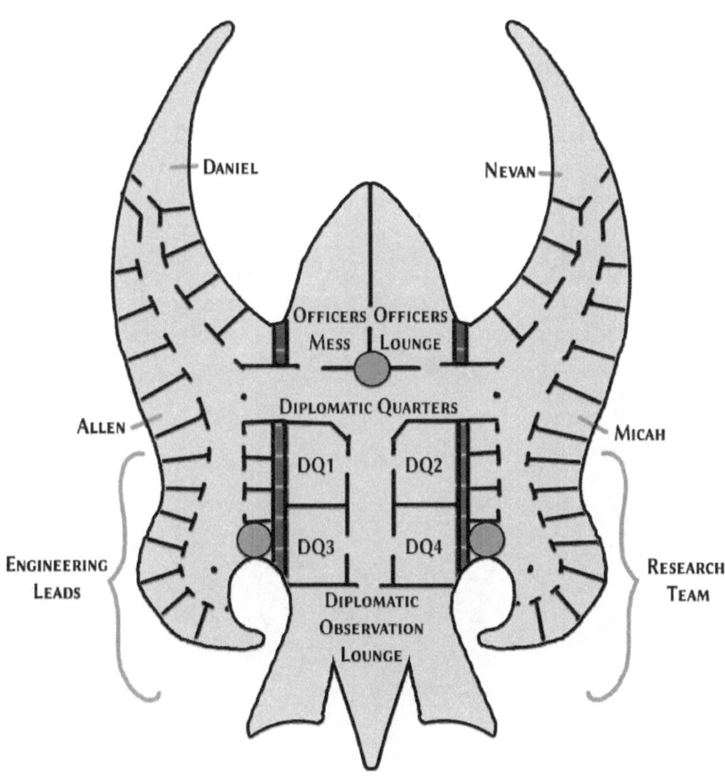


## Deck 2

# LEGACY FLAGSHIP DeCADEJRA

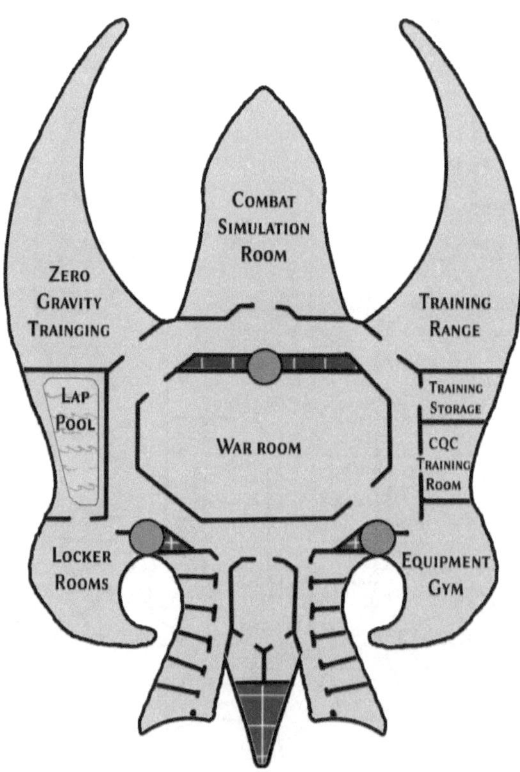


## DECK 3

# Legacy Flagship DeCadejra

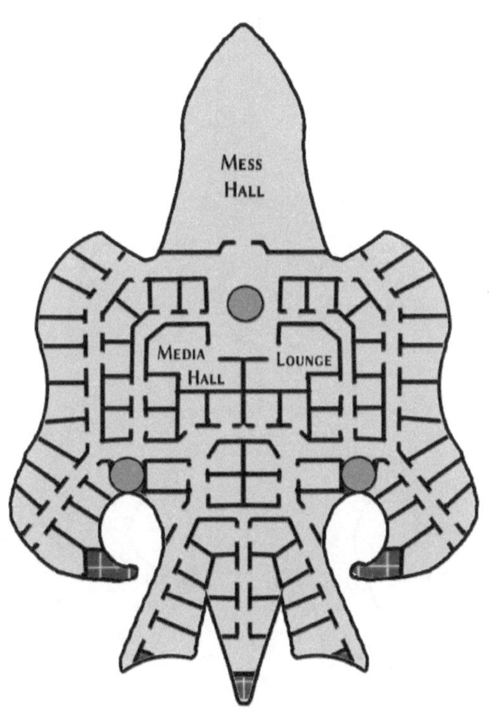


## Deck 4

# LEGACY FLAGSHIP DeCADEJRA

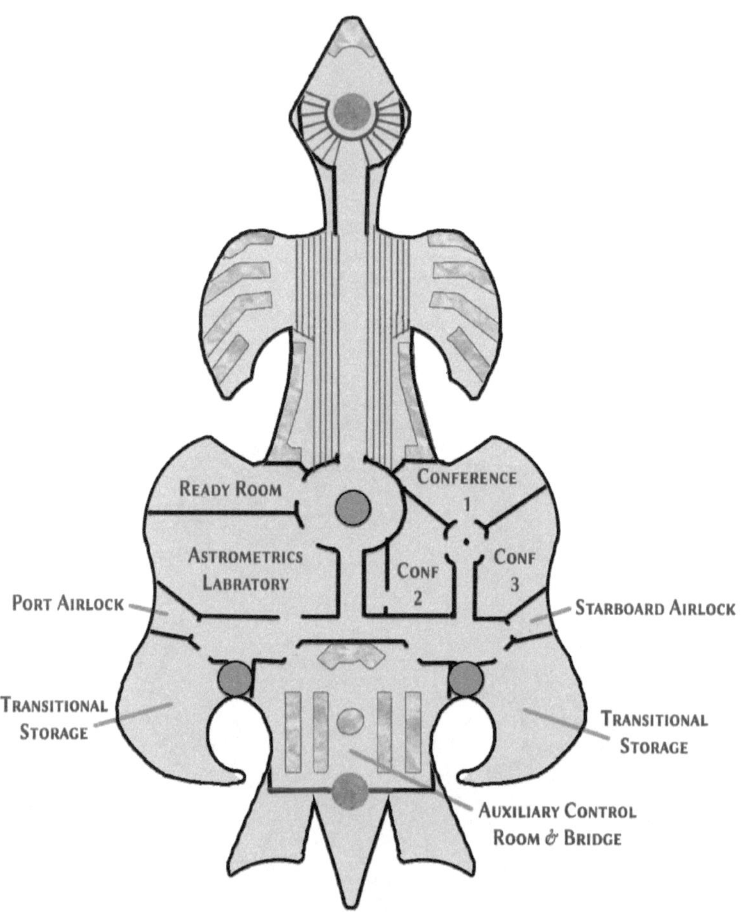


# DECK 5

# Legacy Flagship DeCadejra

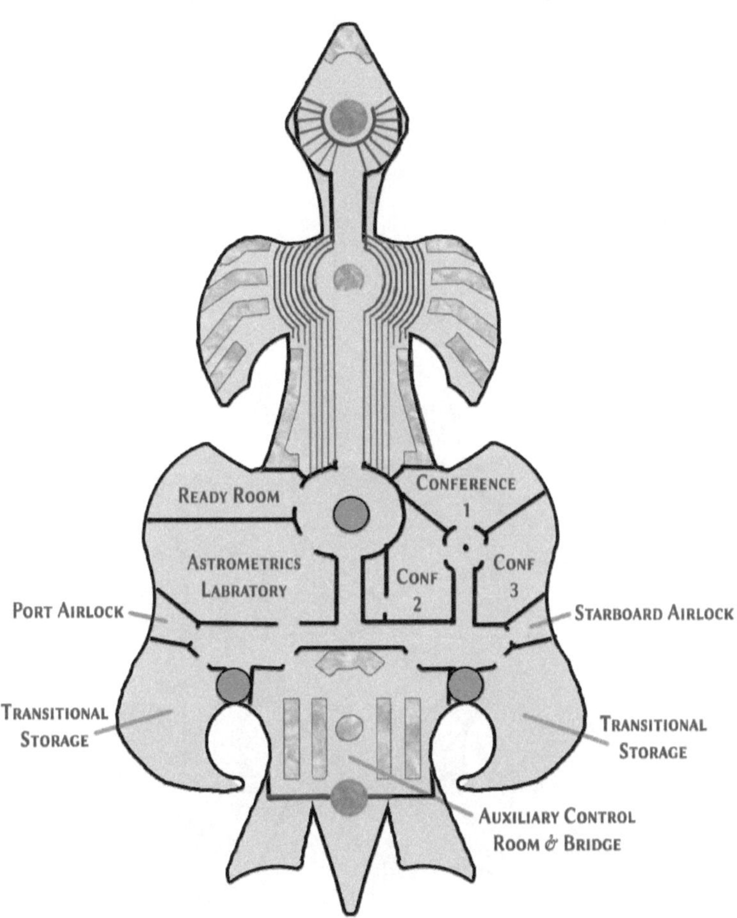


**Deck 5** — Strategic Operations Command Console Deployed

# LEGACY FLAGSHIP DECADEJRA

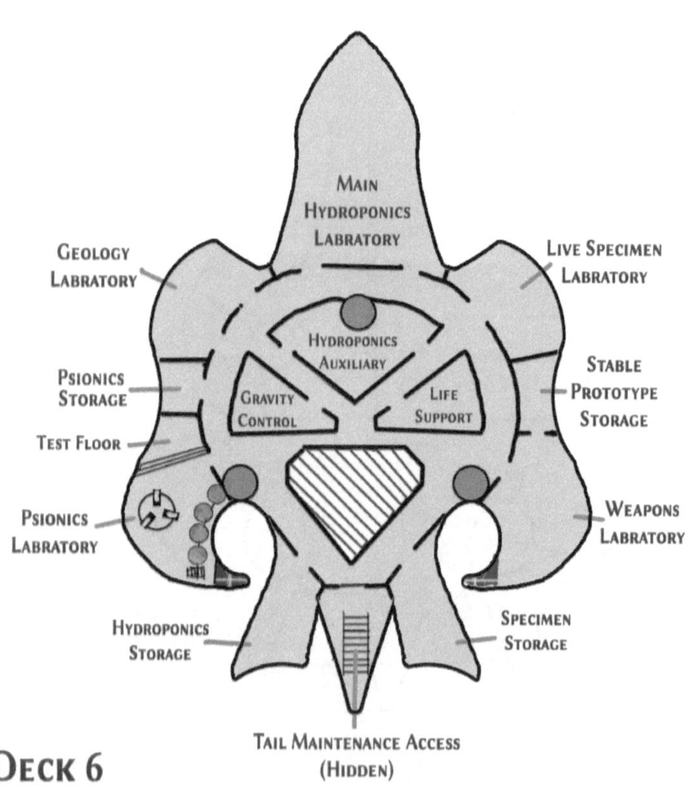


**DECK 6**

# LEGACY FLAGSHIP DeCADEJRA

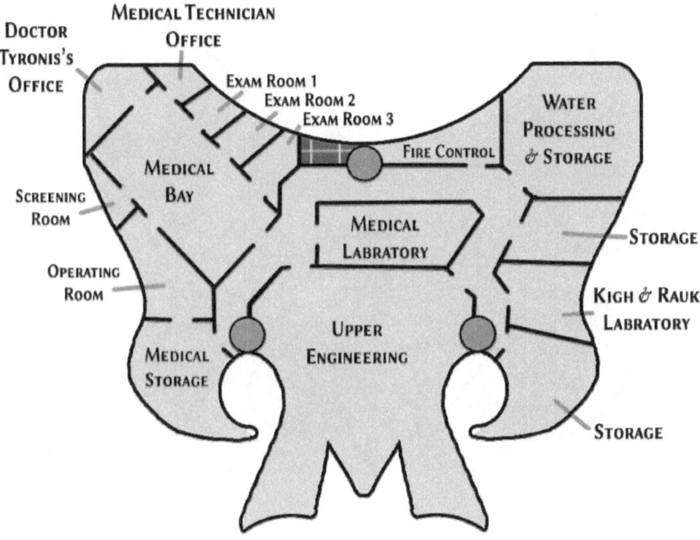


## DECK 7

# Legacy Flagship DeCadejra

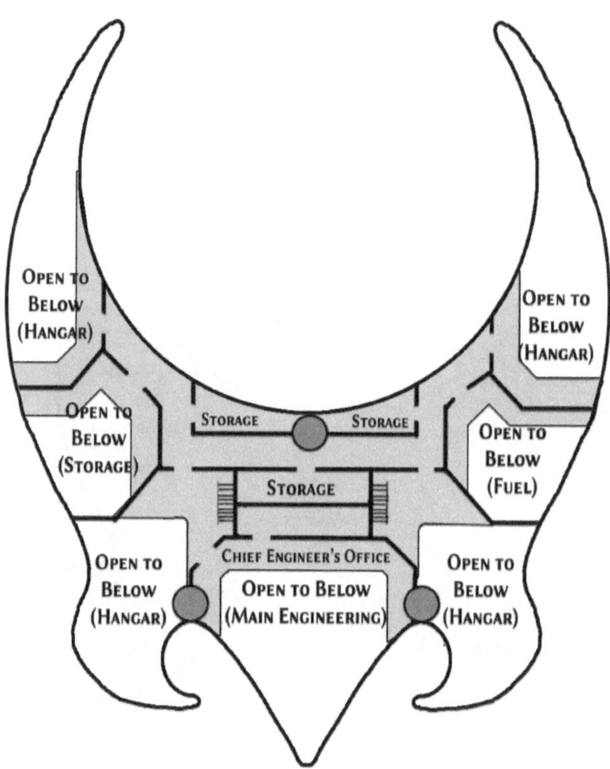


## Deck 8

# Legacy Flagship DeCadejra

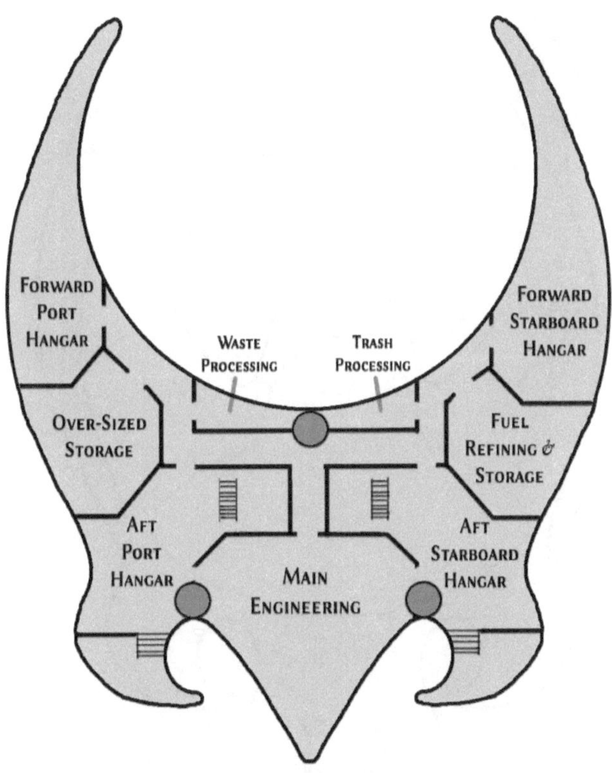


## Deck 9

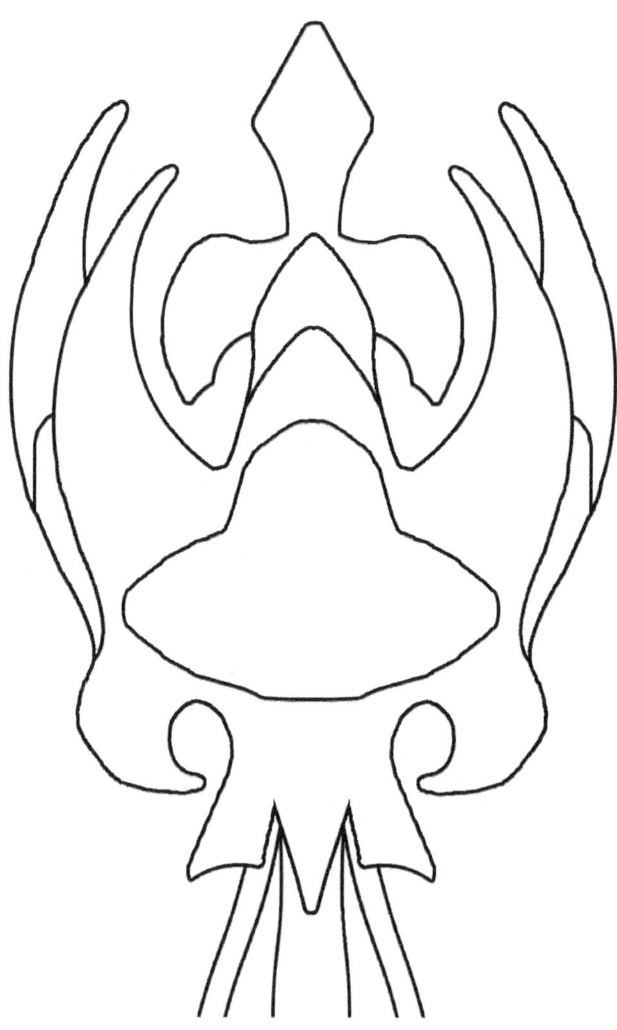

# A PASSION FOR STORIES

Since childhood Amanda "Amnie" Young has had a passion for storytelling, coming home from those first days of school with boundless excitement at learning she could make her own sentences. She grew up immersed in tales from books, movies, and eventually video games. With all of these different outlets for creativity and story expression, she often found herself torn between paths. Trying her hand at college majors, including creative writing, theatre, screenwriting, and information technology for multimedia, she tried to find what path would best suit her style of storytelling.

As a teen, and again later as an adult, she was introduced to tabletop role-playing games where she could join in collaborative story telling with friends. Empowered by faith, family, and friends, she began to bring her stories and dreams into being. You can check out more of her creative endeavors at:

Deviant Art  www.deviantart.com/stories-n-dreams

Twitch  www.twitch.tv/stories_ndreams

Patreon  www.patreon.com/Stories_nDreams

Bluesky  @stories-n-dreams.bsky.social

Kensy's journey will continue in …

THE STARCHASER CHRONICLES
Volume 3

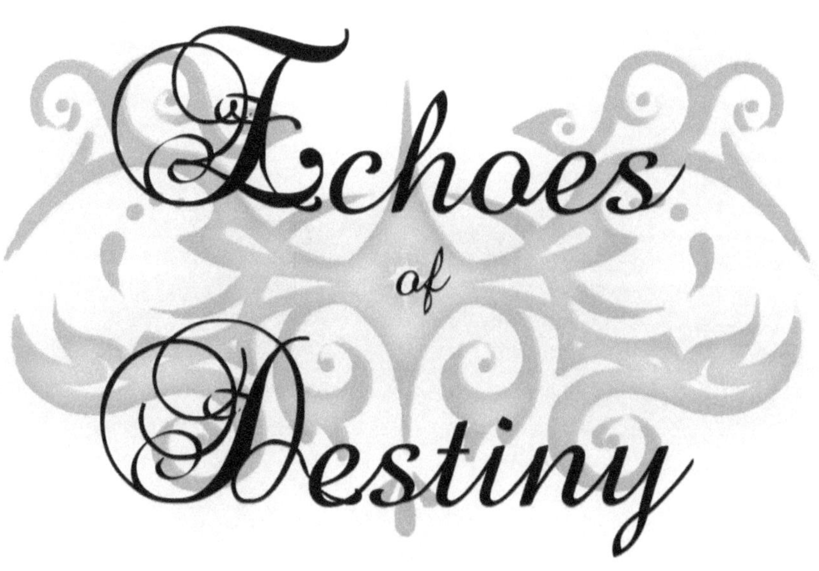

# Echoes of Destiny

## AMNIE ◆ YOUNG

9 781736 435144